LOVE STORIES FOR THE TIME BEING

LOVE STORIES FOR THE TIME BEING

EDITED BY
GENIE D. CHIPPS
&
BILL HENDERSON

PUSHCART PRESS
WAINSCOTT, NEW YORK

For information address
Pushcart Press,
P.O. Box 380,
Wainscott, NY 11975

ISBN: 0-916366-53-7

Grateful acknowledgement is given to the authors
of these stories for permission to reprint them
in this anthology.

Sara Cole: A Type of Love Story from *Success Stories* by Russell Banks © 1984, 1986 by Russell Banks.
Reprinted by permission of Harper & Row Publishers Inc.

This book is for
Lily

The editors would like to thank the following journals for first publishing these stories:

Ontario Review, Antaeus, Ascent, Virginia Quarterly Review, Southern Review, Iowa Review, Ploughshares, Shenandoah, Agni Review, Quarry West, Paris Review, Crescent Review, David Godine Publisher, *Massachusetts Review, Kansas Quarterly, Sun & Moon, TriQuarterly,* Word Beat Press, *Crazyhorse, Michigan Quarterly, Missouri Review.*

CONTENTS

INTRODUCTION

"Love is, then, not a fact in nature of which we become aware, but
rather a creation of the human imagination."

JOSEPH WOOD KRUTCH

"In expressing love we belong among the underdeveloped countries."

SAUL BELLOW

We're a culture bombarded and numbed by love stories. We watch
them glassy-eyed in installments on television. Love songs pour from
the radio at a steady beat. The women's magazines promise us love's answer. Romance fiction sells at a clip. It would seem we are fascinated by
little else than sexual lament, intrigue and the occasional happy ending.

Is that love in our time? Is the media's message what Twentieth Century love has come to? Does anyone else have a better answer? We, the
editors, think so. The twenty-six stories collected in this anthology are
written by some of our best fiction writers and each one writes about
love. They write about people passing through one another's lives,
searching for each other, finding each other, finding themselves, often
losing themselves. And in the effort, surprising discoveries are made.

Love Stories For The Time Being presents the state of love today.
And it comes to you with no commercial breaks, no bottom-line edito-
rial policy, no pat formula for sales. These writers tell their stories in un-
sentimental often unsparing ways. Some write with wit and irony, others
are perplexed, still others are even grim. But whatever the tone, they

prod and pick at the truth, telling us more about real love through their invention than we might ever gather from our own lives.

All of these fictions were originally published in noncommercial literary magazines around the country. Each of these stories was then selected and published in the annual *Pushcart Prize* anthology over a ten year period. Now they have been selected once again for their memorable treatments on the elusive subject of love.

How to sum up these love stories? Our writers witness love everywhere—between the young and the old, the young and the young, heterosexuals, homosexuals, man and wife, and lovers of all description. Lynne Sharon Schwartz sees love in the struggle and joy of having a first child; Raymond Carver gives us a dialogue in which two couples try hopelessly to determine just what this thing called love is. In "Graveyard Day" by Bobbie Ann Mason there is a bittersweet account of a family picnic; Ellen Wilbur's "Faith" details the quiet life of a woman after the loss of love; and Joyce Carol Oates carries the confrontations of love to an international arena in "Détente."

The first love of the very young is remembered in Ellen Gilchrist's "Summer, An Elegy" while Janet Desaulniers' "Age" develops affection between an old man and a girl. Anne Tyler describes the end of an unusual marriage in "The Artificial Family"; Barbara Thompson's "Tattoo" explores love in another culture; Mary Morris journeys to the local copy shop for a view of love behind the Xerox machines in "Copies"; and Stephen Dixon's "Milk is Very Good For You" shoves love in a corner and lust on a mattress.

Blissful love turns to madness in Susan Welch's "The Time, The Place, The Loved One"; pastoral love in the Appalachian hills is lyrically recalled in Bo Ball's "Heart Leaves"; and weight is the subject in Andre Dubus' "The Fat Girl." Gina Berriault's "The Infinite Passion of Expectation" combines the elderly and the young and a passion for the future; "Lost Time Accident" by Gayle Whittier evokes the first glimmerings of love in a young girl longing to cure a badly injured man; H.E. Francis' "A Chronicle of Love" is about dancing—and death; and Stephanie Vaughn's "Sweet Talk" guides us on a cross country tour of romantic questioning.

Jeff Weinstein writes of homosexual longing and the consolation of cooking in "A Jean-Marie Cookbook"; "Now I Am Married" by Mary Gordon ponders the many forms of marriage; David Krane's "Cordials" is the hilarious antithesis of the usual love story; and Jayne Anne Phillips chronicles the impact of war on young lovers in "Home." "The Cigarette Boat" by Barbara Milton casts a cold eye on an ambitious girl and her Sugar Daddy; W.P. Kinsella's "Pretend Dinners" is a devastating portrait of marriage in American Indian society; and Charles Baxter's "Harmony of the World" concerns itself with an affair, music and merit. The book closes with the unusual and unforgettable "Sarah Cole: A Type of Love Story" by Russell Banks.

The editors of this anthology can't promise you instant insight into the true heart of modern love. We may be giving you more questions than answers. But we can and do promise you a rich collection of extraordinary talent, each writer weaving his or her tale into the grand tapestry of love.

Love Stories For The Time Being is indeed for our time and perhaps for all time.

GENIE D. CHIPPS
BILL HENDERSON

ROUGH STRIFE

LYNNE SHARON SCHWARTZ

Now let us sport us while we may;
And now, like am'rous birds of prey
. . . tear our pleasure with rough strife
Through the iron gates of life.
—*Andrew Marvell*

CAROLINE AND IVAN finally had a child. Conception stunned them; they didn't think, by now, that it could happen. For years they had tried and failed, till it seemed that a special barren destiny was preordained. Meanwhile, in the wide spaces of childlessness, they had created activity: their work flourished. Ivan, happy and moderately powerful in a large foundation, helped decide how to distribute money for artistic and social projects. Caroline taught mathematics at a small suburban university. Being a mathematician, she found, conferred a painful private wisdom on her efforts to conceive. In her brain, as Ivan exploded within her, she would involuntarily calculate probabilities; millions of blind sperm and one reluctant egg clustered before her eyes in swiftly transmuting geometric patterns. She lost her grasp of pleasure, forgot what it could feel like without a goal. She had no idea what Ivan might be thinking about, scattered seed money, maybe. Their passion became courteous and automatic until, by attrition, for months they didn't make love—it was too awkward.

One September Sunday morning she was in the shower, watching, through a crack in the curtain, Ivan naked at the washstand. He was shaving, his jaw tilted at an innocently self-satisfied angle. He wasn't aware of being watched, so that a secret quality, an essence of Ivan, exuded in great waves. Caroline could almost see it, a cloudy aura. He stroked his jaw vainly with intense concentration, a self-absorption so contagious that she needed, suddenly, to possess it with him. She stepped out of the shower.

"Ivan."

He turned abruptly, surprised, perhaps even annoyed at the interruption.

"Let's not have a baby any more. Let's just . . . come on." When she placed her wet hand on his back he lifted her easily off her feet with his right arm, the razor still poised in his other, outstretched hand.

"Come on," she insisted. She opened the door and a draft blew into the small steamy room. She pulled him by the hand toward the bedroom.

Ivan grinned. "You're soaking wet."

"Wet, dry, what's the difference?" It was hard to speak. She began to run, to tease him; he caught her and tossed her onto their disheveled bed and dug his teeth so deep into her shoulder that she thought she would bleed.

Then with disinterest, taken up only in this fresh rushing need for him, weeks later Caroline conceived. Afterwards she liked to say that she had known the moment it happened. It felt different, she told him, like a pin pricking a balloon, but without the shattering noise, without the quick collapse. "Oh, come on," said Ivan. "That's impossible."

But she was a mathematician, after all, and dealt with infinitesimal precise abstractions, and she did know how it had happened. The baby was conceived in strife, one early October night, Indian summer. All day the sun glowed hot and low in the sky, settling an amber torpor on people and things, and the night was the same, only now a dark hot heaviness sunk slowly down. The scent of the still-blooming honeysuckle rose to their bedroom window. Just as she was bending over to kiss him, heavy and quivering with heat like the night, he teased her about something, about a mole on her leg, and in reply she punched him lightly on the shoulder. He grabbed her wrists, and when she began kicking, pinned her feet down with his own. In an instant Ivan lay stretched out on her back like a blanket, smothering her, while she struggled beneath, writhing to escape. It was a silent, sweaty struggle, interrupted with outbursts of wild laughter, shrieks and gasping breaths. She tried biting but, laughing loudly, he evaded her, and she tried scratching the fists that held her down, but she couldn't reach. All her desire was transformed into physical effort, but he was too strong for her. He wanted her to say she gave up, but she refused, and since he wouldn't loosen his grip they lay locked and panting in their static embrace for some time.

"You win," she said at last, but as he rolled off she sneakily jabbed him in the ribs with her elbow.

"Aha!" Ivan shouted, and was ready to begin again, but she quickly distracted him. Once the wrestling was at an end, though, Caroline found her passion dissipated, and her pleasure tinged with resentment. After they made love forcefully, when they were covered with sweat, dripping on each other, she said, "Still, you don't play fair."

"I don't play fair! Look who's talking. Do you want me to give you a handicap?"

"No."

"So?"

"It's not fair, that's all."

Ivan laughed gloatingly and curled up in her arms. She smiled in the dark.

That was the night the baby was conceived, not in high passion but rough strife.

She lay on the table in the doctor's office weeks later. The doctor, whom she had known for a long time, habitually kept up a running conversation while he probed. Today, fretting over his weight problem, he outlined his plans for a new diet. Tensely she watched him, framed and centered by her raised knees, which were still bronzed from summer sun. His other hand was pressing on her stomach. Caroline was nauseated with fear and trembling, afraid of the verdict. It was taking so long, perhaps it was a tumor.

"I'm cutting out all starches," he said. "I've really let myself go lately."

"Good idea." Then she gasped in pain. A final, sickening thrust, and he was out. Relief, and a sore gap where he had been. In a moment, she knew, she would be retching violently.

"Well?"

"Well, Caroline, you hit the jackpot this time."

She felt a smile, a stupid, puppet smile, spread over her face. In the tiny bathroom where she threw up, she saw in the mirror the silly smile looming over her ashen face like a dancer's glowing grimace of labored joy. She smiled through the rest of the visit, through his advice about milk, weight, travel and rest, smiled at herself in the window of the bus, and at her moving image in the fenders of parked cars as she walked home.

Ivan, incredulous over the telephone, came home beaming stupidly just like Caroline, and brought a bottle of champagne. After dinner they drank it and made love.

"Do you think it's all right to do this?" he asked.

"Oh, Ivan, honestly. It's microscopic."

He was in one of his whimsical moods and made terrible jokes that she laughed at with easy indulgence. He said he was going to pay the baby a visit and asked if she had any messages she wanted delivered. He unlocked from her embrace, moved down her body and said he was going to have a look for himself. Clowning, he put his ear between her legs to listen. Whatever amusement she felt soon ebbed away into irritation. She had never thought Ivan would be a doting parent—he was so preoccupied with himself. Finally he stopped his antics as she clasped her arms around him and whispered, "Ivan, you are really too much." He became unusually gentle. Tamed, and she didn't like it, hoped he wouldn't continue that way for months. Pleasure lapped over her with a mild, lackadaisical bitterness, and then when she could be articulate once more she explained patiently, "Ivan, you know, it really is all right. I mean, it's a natural process."

"Well I didn't want to hurt you."

"I'm not sick."

Then, as though her body were admonishing that cool confidence, she did get sick. There were mornings when she awoke with such paralyzing nausea that she had to ask Ivan to bring her a hard roll from the kitchen before she could stir from bed. To move from her awakening position seemed a tremendous risk, as if she might spill out. She rarely threw up—the nausea resembled violent hunger. Something wanted to be filled, not expelled, a perilous vacuum occupying her insides. The crucial act was getting the first few mouthfuls down. Then the solidity and denseness of the hard unbuttered roll stabilized her, like a heavy weight thrown down to anchor a tottering ship. Her head ached. On the mornings when she had no classes she would wander around the house till almost noon clutching the partly-eaten roll in her hand like a talisman. Finishing one roll, she quickly went to the breadbox for another; she bought them regularly at the bakery a half-dozen at a time. With enough roll inside her she could sometimes manage a half-cup of tea, but liquids were risky. They sloshed around inside and made her envision the baby sloshing around too, in its cloudy fluid. By early afternoon she would feel fine. The baby, she imagined, claimed her for the night and was reluctant to give up its hold in the morning: they vied till she conquered. She was willing to yield her sleeping hours to the baby, her dreams even, if necessary, but she wanted the daylight for herself.

The mornings that she taught were agony. Ivan would wake her up early, bring her a roll, and gently prod her out of bed.

"I simply cannot do it," she would say, placing her legs cautiously over the side of the bed.

"Sure you can. Now get up."

"I'll die if I get up."

"You have no choice. You have a job." He was freshly showered and dressed, and his neatness irritated her. He had nothing more to do—the discomfort was all hers. She rose to her feet and swayed.

Ivan looked alarmed. "Do you want me to call and tell them you can't make it?"

"No, no." That frightened her. She needed to hold on to the job, to defend herself against the growing baby. Once she walked into the classroom she would be fine. A Mondrian print hung on the back wall—she could look at that, and it would steady her. With waves of nausea roiling in her chest, she stumbled into the bathroom.

She liked him to wait until she was out of the shower before he left for work, because she anticipated fainting under the impact of the water. Often at the end she forced herself to stand under an ice cold flow, leaning her head way back and letting her short fair hair drip down behind her. Though it was torture, when she emerged she felt more alive.

After the shower had been off a while Ivan would come and open the bathroom door. "Are you O.K. now, Caroline? I've got to go." It made her feel like a child. She would be wrapped in a towel with her hair dripping on the mat, brushing her teeth or rubbing cream into her face. "Yes, thanks for waiting, I guess this'll end soon. They say it's only the first few months."

He kissed her lips, her bare damp shoulder, gave a parting squeeze to her toweled behind, and was gone. She watched him walk down the hall. Ivan was very large. She had always been drawn and aroused by his largeness, by the huge bones and the taut legs that felt as though he had steel rods inside. But now she watched with some trepidation, hoping Ivan wouldn't have a large, inflexible baby.

Very slowly she would put on clothes. Selecting each article seemed a much more demanding task than ever before. Seeing how slow she had become, she allowed herself over an hour, keeping her hard roll nearby as she dressed and prepared her face. All the while, through the stages of dressing, she evaluated her body closely in the full-length mirror, first naked, then in bra and underpants, then with shoes added, and finally with a dress. She was looking for signs, but the baby was invisible. Nothing had changed yet. She was still as she had always been, not quite slim yet somehow appearing small, almost delicate. She used to pride herself on strength. When they moved in she had worked as hard as Ivan, lugging furniture and lifting heavy cartons. He was impressed. Now, of course, she could no longer do that—it took all her strength to move her own weight.

With the profound sensuous narcissism of women past first youth, she admired her still-narrow waist and full breasts. She was especially fond of her shoulders and prominent collarbone, which had a fragile, inviting look. That would all be gone soon, of course, gone soft. Curious about how she would alter, she scanned her face for the pregnant look she knew well from the faces of friends. It was far less a tangible change than a look of transparent vulnerability that took over the face: nearly a pleading look, a beg for help like a message from a powerless invaded country to the rest of the world. Caroline did not see it on her face yet.

From the tenth to the fourteenth week of her pregnancy she slept, with brief intervals of lucidity when she taught her classes. It was a strange dreamy time. The passionate nausea faded, but the lure of the bed was irresistible. In the middle of the day, even, she could pass by the bedroom, glimpse the waiting bed and be overcome by the soft heavy desire to lie down. She fell into a stupor immediately and did not dream. She forgot what it was like to awaken with energy and move through an entire day without lying down once. She forgot the feeling of eyes opened wide without effort. She would have liked to hide this strange, shameful perversity from Ivan, but that was impossible. Ivan kept wanting to go to the movies. Clearly, he was bored with her. Maybe, she imagined, staring up at the bedroom ceiling through slitted eyes, he would become so bored he would abandon her and the baby and she would not be able to support the house alone and she and the baby would end up on the streets in rags, begging. She smiled. That was highly unlikely. Ivan would not be the same Ivan without her.

"You go on, Ivan. I just can't."

Once he said, "I thought I might ask Ruth Forbes to go with me to see the Charlie Chaplin in town. I know she likes him. Would that bother you?"

She was half-asleep, slowly eating a large apple in bed and watching *Medical Center* on television, but she roused herself to answer. "No, of course not." Ruth Forbes was a divorced woman who lived down the block, a casual friend and not Ivan's type at all, too large, loud and depressed. Caroline didn't care if he wanted her company. She didn't care if he held her hand on his knee in the movies as he liked to do, or even if, improbably, he made love to her afterwards in her sloppy house crawling with children. She didn't care about anything except staying nestled in bed.

She made love with him sometimes, in a slow way. She felt no specific desire but didn't want to deny him, she loved him so. Or had, she thought vaguely, when she was alive and strong. Besides, she knew she could sleep right after. Usually there would be a moment when she came alive despite herself, when the reality of his body would strike her all at once with a wistful throb of lust, but mostly she was too tired to see it through, to leap towards it, so she let it subside, merely nodding at it gratefully as a sign of dormant life. She felt sorry for Ivan, but helpless.

Once to her great shame, she fell asleep while he was inside her. He woke her with a pat on her cheek, actually, she realized from the faint sting, a gesture more like a slap than a pat. "Caroline, for Christ's sake, you're sleeping."

"No, no, I'm sorry. I wasn't really sleeping. Oh, Ivan, it's nothing. This will end." She wondered, though.

Moments later she felt his hands on her thighs. His lips were brooding on her stomach, edging, with expertise, lower and lower down. He was murmuring something she couldn't catch. She felt an ache, an irritation. Of course he meant well, Ivan always did. Wryly, she appreciated his intentions. But she couldn't bear that excitement now.

"Please," she said. "Please don't do that."

He was terribly hurt. He said nothing, but leaped away violently and pulled all the blankets around him. She was contrite, shed a few private tears and fell instantly into a dreamless dark.

He wanted to go to a New Year's Eve party some close friends were giving, and naturally he wanted her to come with him. Caroline vowed to herself she would do this for him because she had been giving so little for so long. She planned to get dressed and look very beautiful, as she could still look when she took plenty of time and tried hard enough; she would not drink very much—it was sleep-inducing—and she would not be the one to suggest going home. After sleeping through the day in preparation, she washed her hair, using something she found in the drugstore to heighten the blonde flecks. Then she put on a long green velvet dress with gold embroidery, and inserted the gold hoop earrings Ivan bought her some years ago for her twenty-fifth birthday. Before they set out she drank a cup of black coffee. She would have taken No-Doze but she was afraid of drugs, afraid of giving birth to an armless or legless baby who would be a burden and a heartache to them for the rest of their days.

At the party of mostly university people, she chatted with everyone equally, those she knew well and those she had never met. Sociably, she held a filled glass in her hand, taking tiny sips. She and Ivan were not together very much—it was crowded, smoky and loud; people kept moving and encounters were brief—but she knew he was aware of her, could feel his awareness through the milling bodies. He was aware and he was pleased. He deserved more than the somnambulist she had become, and she was pleased to please him. But after a while her legs would not support her for another instant. The skin tingled: soft warning bells rang from every pore.

She allowed herself a moment to sit down alone in a small alcove off the living room, where she smoked a cigarette and stared down at her lap, holding her eyes open very wide. Examining the gold and rose-colored embroidery on her dress, Caroline traced the coiled pattern, mathematical and hypnotic, with her index finger. Just as she was happily merging into its intricacies, a man, a stranger, came in, breaking her trance. He was a very young man, twenty-three, maybe, of no apparent interest.

"Hi. I hear you're expecting a baby," he began, and sat down with a distinct air of settling in.

"Yes. That's quite an opening line. How did you know?"

"I know because Linda told me. You know Linda, don't you? I'm her brother."

He began asking about her symptoms. Sleepiness? Apathy? He knew, he had worked in a clinic. Unresponsive, she retorted by inquiring about his taste in music. He sat on a leather hassock opposite Caroline on the couch, and with every inquisitive sentence drew his seat closer till their knees were almost touching. She shifted her weight to avoid him, tucked her feet under her and lit another cigarette, feeling she could lie down and fall into a stupor quite easily. Still, words were coming out of her mouth, she heard them; she hoped they were not encouraging words but she seemed to have very little control over what they were.

"I—" he said. "You see—" He reached out and put his hand over hers. "Pregnant women, like, they really turn me on. I mean, there's a special aura. You're sensational."

She pulled her hand away. "God almighty."

"What's the matter? Honestly, I didn't mean to offend you."

"I really must go." She stood up and stepped around him.

"Could I see you some time?"

"You're seeing me now. Enjoy it."

He ran his eyes over her from head to toe, appraising. "It doesn't show yet."

Gazing down at her body, Caroline stretched the loose velvet dress taut over her stomach. "No, you're right, it doesn't." Then, over her shoulder, as she left their little corner, she tossed, "Fuck you, you pig."

With a surge of energy she downed a quick Scotch, found Ivan and tugged at his arm. "Let's dance."

Ivan's blue eyes lightened with shock. At home she could barely walk.

"Yes, let's." He took her in his arms and she buried her face against his shoulder. But she held her tears back, she would not let him know.

Later she told him about it. It was three-thirty in the morning, they had just made love drunkenly, and Ivan was in high spirits. She knew why—he felt he had her back again. She had held him close and uttered her old sounds, familiar moans and cries like a poignant, nearly-forgotten tune, and Ivan was miraculously restored, his impact once again sensible to eye and ear. He was making her laugh hysterically now, imitating the eccentric professor of art history at the party, an owlish émigré from Bavaria who expounded on the dilemmas of today's youth, all the while pronouncing "youth" as if it rhymed with "mouth." Ivan had also discovered that he pronounced "unique" as if it were "eunuch." Then, sitting up in bed cross-legged, they competed in making up pretentious scholarly sentences that included both "unique" and "youth" mispronounced.

"Speaking of 'yowth,'" Caroline said, "I met a weird one tonight, Linda's brother. A very eunuch yowth, I must say." And giggling, she recounted their conversation. Suddenly at the end she unexpectedly found herself in tears. Shuddering, she flopped over and sobbed into her pillow.

"Caroline," he said tenderly, "please. For heaven's sake, it was just some nut. It was nothing. Don't get all upset over it." He stroked her bare back.

"I can't help it." she wailed. "It made me feel so disgusting."

"You're much too sensitive. Come on." He ran his hand slowly through her hair, over and over.

She pulled the blanket around her. "Enough. I'm going to sleep."

A few days later, when classes were beginning again for the new semester, she woke early and went immediately to the shower, going through the ritual motions briskly and automatically. She was finished and brushing her teeth when she realized what had happened. There she was on her feet, sturdy, before eight in the morning, planning how she would introduce the topic of the differential calculus to her new students. She stared at her face in the mirror with unaccustomed recognition, her mouth dripping white foam, her dark eyes startled. She was alive. She didn't know how the miracle had happened, nor did she care to explore it. Back in the bedroom she dressed quickly, zipping up a pair of slim rust-colored woolen slacks with satisfaction. It didn't show yet, but soon.

"Ivan, time to get up."

He grunted and opened his eyes. When at last they focused on Caroline leaning over him they burned blue and wide with astonishment. He rubbed a fist across his forehead. "Are you dressed already?"

"Yes. I'm cured."

"What do you mean?"

"I'm not tired any more. I'm slept out. I've come back to life."

"Oh." He moaned and rolled over in one piece like a seal.

"Aren't you getting up?"

"In a little while. I'm so tired. I must sleep for a while." The words were thick and slurred.

"Well!" She was strangely annoyed. Ivan always got up with vigor. "Are you sick?"

"Uh-uh."

After a quick cup of coffee she called out, "Ivan, I'm leaving now. Don't forget to get up." The January air was crisp and exhilarating, and she walked the half-mile to the university at a nimble clip, going over her introductory remarks in her head.

Ivan was tired for a week. Caroline wanted to go out to dinner every evening—she had her appetite back. She had broken through dense earth to fresh air. It was a new year and soon they would have a new baby. But all Ivan wanted to do was stay home and lie on the bed and watch television. It was repellent. Sloth, she pointed out to him more than once, was one of the seven deadly sins. The fifth night she said in exasperation, "What the hell is the matter with you? If you're sick go to a doctor."

"I'm not sick. I'm tired. Can't I be tired too? Leave me alone. I left you alone, didn't I?"

"That was different."

"How?"

"I'm pregnant and you're not, in case you've forgotten."

"How could I forget?"

She said nothing, only cast him an evil look.

One evening soon after Ivan's symptoms disappeared, they sat together on the living-room sofa sharing sections of the newspaper.

Ivan had his feet up on the coffee table and Caroline sat diagonally, resting her legs on his. She paused in her reading and touched her stomach.

"Ivan."

"What?"

"It's no use. I'm going to have to buy some maternity clothes."

He put down the paper and stared. "Really?" He seemed distressed.

"Yes."

"Well, don't buy any of those ugly things they wear. Can't you get some of those, you know, sort of Indian things?"

"Yes. That's a good idea. I will."

He picked up the paper again.

"It moves."

"What?"

"I said it moves. The baby."

"It moves?"

She laughed. "Remember Galileo? *Eppure, si muove.*" They had spent years together in Italy in their first youth, in mad love, and visited the birthplace of Galileo. He was a hero to both of them, because his mind remained free and strong though his body succumbed to tyranny.

Ivan laughed too. "*Eppure, si muove.* Let me see." He bent his head down to feel it, then looked up at her, his face full of longing, marvel and envy. In a moment he was scrambling at her clothes in a young eager rush. He wanted to be there, he said. Caroline, taken by surprise, was suspended between laughter and tears. He had her on the floor in silence, and for each it was swift and consuming.

Ivan lay spent in her arms. Caroline, still gasping and clutching him, said, "I could never love it as much as I love you." She wondered, then, hearing her words fall in the still air, whether this would always be true.

Shortly after she began wearing the Indian shirts and dresses, she noticed that Ivan was acting oddly. He stayed late at the office more than ever before, and often brought work home with him. He appeared to have lost interest in the baby, rarely asking how she felt, and when she moaned in bed sometimes, "Oh, I can't get to sleep, it keeps moving around," he responded with a grunt or not at all. He asked her, one warm Sunday in March, if she wanted to go bicycle riding.

"Ivan, I can't go bicycle riding. I mean, look at me."

"Oh, right. Of course."

He seemed to avoid looking at her, and she did look terrible, she had to admit. Even she looked at herself in the mirror as infrequently as possible. She dreaded what she had heard about hair falling out and teeth rotting, but she drank her milk diligently and so far neither of those things had happened. But besides the grotesque belly, her ankles swelled up so that the shape of her own legs was alien. She took diuretics and woke every hour at night to go to the bathroom. Sometimes it was impossible to get back to sleep so she sat up in bed reading. Ivan said, "Can't you turn the light out? You know I can't sleep with the light on."

"But what should I do? I can't sleep at all."

"Read in the living room."

"It's so cold in there at night."

He would turn away irritably. Once he took the blanket and went to sleep in the living room himself.

They liked to go for drives in the country on warm weekends. It seemed to Caroline that he chose the bumpiest, most untended roads and drove them as rashly as possible. Then when they stopped to picnic and he lay back to bask in the sharp April sunlight, she would always need to go and look for a bathroom, or even a clump of trees. At first this amused him, but soon his amusement became sardonic. He pulled in wearily at gas stations where he didn't need gas and waited in the car with folded arms and a sullen expression that made her apologetic about her ludicrous needs. They were growing apart. She could feel the distance between them like a patch of fog, dimming and distorting the relations of objects in space. The baby that lay between them in the dark was pushing them apart.

Sometimes as she lay awake in bed at night, not wanting to read in the cold living room but reluctant to turn on the light (and it was only a small light, she thought bitterly, a small bedside light), Caroline brooded over the horrible deformities the baby might be born with. She was thirty-one years old, not the best age to bear a first child. It could have cerebral palsy, cleft palate, two heads, club foot. She wondered if she could love a baby with a gross defect. She wondered if Ivan would want to put it in an institution, and if there were any decent institutions in their area, and if they would be spending every Sunday afternoon for the rest of their lives visiting the baby and driving home heartbroken in silence. She lived through these visits to the institution in vivid detail till she knew the doctors' and nurses' faces well. And there would come a point when Ivan would refuse to go any more—she knew what he was like, selfish with his time and impatient with futility—and she would have to go alone. She wondered if Ivan ever thought about these things, but with that cold mood of his she was afraid to ask.

One night she was desolate. She couldn't bear the loneliness and the heaviness any more, so she woke him.

"Ivan, please. Talk to me. I'm so lonely."

He sat up abruptly. "What?" He was still asleep. With the dark straight hair hanging down over his lean face he looked boyish and vulnerable. Without knowing why, she felt sorry for him.

"I'm sorry. I know you were sleeping but I—" Here she began to weep. "I just lie here forever in the dark and think awful things and you're so far away, and I just—"

"Oh, Caroline. Oh, God." Now he was wide awake, and took her in his arms.

"You're so far away," she wept. "I don't know what's the matter with you."

"I'm sorry. I know it's hard for you. You're so—everything's so different, that's all."

"But it's still me."

"I know. I know it's stupid of me. I can't—"

She knew what it was. It would never be the same. They sat up all night holding each other, and they talked. Ivan talked more than he had in weeks. He said of course the baby would be perfectly all right, and it would be born at just the right time, too, late June, so she could finish up the term, and they would start their natural childbirth group in two weeks so he could be with her and help her, though of course she would do it easily because she was so competent at everything, and then they would have the summer for the early difficult months, and she would be feeling fine and be ready to go back to work in the fall, and they would find a good person, someone like a grandmother, to come in, and he would try to stagger his schedule so she would not feel overburdened and trapped, and in short everything would be just fine, and they would make love again like they used to and be close again. He said exactly what she needed to hear, while she huddled against him, wrenched with pain to realize that he had known all along the right words to say but hadn't thought to say them till she woke him in desperation. Still, in the dawn she slept contented. She loved him. Every now and then she perceived this like a fact of life, an ancient tropism.

Two weeks later they had one of their horrible quarrels. It happened at a gallery, at the opening of a show by a group of young local artists Ivan had discovered. He had encouraged them to apply to his foundation for money and smoothed the way to their success. Now at their triumphant hour he was to be publicly thanked at a formal dinner. There were too many paintings to look at, too many people to greet, and too many glasses of champagne thrust at Caroline, who was near the end of her eighth month now. She walked around for an hour, then whispered to Ivan, "Listen, I'm sorry but I've got to go. Give me the car keys, will you? I don't feel well."

"What's the matter?"

"I can't stop having to go to the bathroom and my feet are killing me and my head aches, and the kid is rolling around like a basketball. You stay and enjoy it. You can get a ride with someone. I'll see you later"

"I'll drive you home," he said grimly. "We'll leave."

An awful knot gripped her stomach. The knot was the image of his perverse resistance, the immense trouble coming, all the trouble congealed and solidified and tied up in one moment. Meanwhile they smiled at the passers-by as they whispered ferociously to each other.

"Ivan, I do not want you to take me home. This is your event. Stay. I am leaving. We are separate people."

"If you're as sick as you say you can't drive home alone. You're my wife and I'll take you home."

"Suit yourself," she said sweetly, because the director of the gallery was approaching. "We all know you're much bigger and stronger than I am." And she smiled maliciously.

Ivan waved vaguely at the director, turned and ushered her to the door. Outside he exploded.

"Shit, Caroline! We can't do a fucking thing anymore, can we?"

"You can do anything you like. Just give me the keys. I left mine home."

"I will not give you the keys. Get in the car. You're supposed to be sick."

"You big resentful selfish idiot. Jealous of an embryo." She was screaming now. He started the car with a rush that jolted her forward against the dashboard. "I'd be better off driving myself. You'll kill me this way."

"Shut up," he shouted. "I don't want to hear any more."

"I don't care what you want to hear or not hear."

"Shut the hell up or I swear I'll go into a tree. I don't give a shit anymore."

It was starting to rain, a soft silent rain that glittered in the drab dusk outside. At exactly the same moment they rolled up their windows. They were sealed in together. Caroline thought, like restless beasts in a cage. The air in the car was dank and stuffy.

When they got home he slammed the door so hard the house shook. Caroline had calmed herself. She sank down in a chair, kicked off her shoes and rubbed her ankles. "Ivan, why don't you go back? It's not too late. These dinners are always late anyway. I'll be O.K."

"I don't want to go anymore," he yelled. "The whole thing is spoiled. Our whole lives are spoiled from now on. We were better off before. I thought you had gotten over wanting it. I thought it was a dead issue." He stared at her bulging stomach with such loathing that she was shocked into horrid, lucid perception.

"You disgust me," she said quietly. "Frankly, you always have and probably always will." She didn't know why she said that. It was quite untrue. It was only true that he disgusted her at this moment, yet the rest had rolled out like string from a hidden ball of twine.

"So why did we ever start this in the first place?" he screamed.

She didn't know whether he meant the marriage or the baby, and for an instant she was afraid he might hit her, there was such compressed force in his huge shoulders.

"Get the hell out of here. I don't want to have to look at you."

"I will. I'll go back. I'll take your advice. Call your fucking obstetrician if you need anything. I'm sure he's always glad of an extra feel."

"You ignorant pig. Go on. And don't hurry back. Find yourself a skinny little art student and give her a big treat."

"I just might." He slammed the door and the house shook again.

He would be back. This was not the first time. Only now she felt no secret excitement, no tremor, no passion that could reshape into lust; she was too heavy and burdened. It would not be easy to make it up—she was in no condition. It would lie between them silently like a dead weight till weeks after the baby was born, till Ivan felt he could reclaim his rightful territory. She knew him too well. Caroline took two aspirins. When she woke at three he was in bed beside her, gripping the blanket in his sleep and breathing heavily. For days afterward they spoke with strained, subdued courtesy.

They worked diligently in the natural childbirth classes once a week, while at home they giggled over how silly the exercises were, yet Ivan insisted she pant her five minutes each day as instructed. As relaxation training, Ivan was supposed to lift each of her legs and arms three times and drop them, while she remained perfectly limp and passive. From the very start Caroline was excellent at this routine, which they did in bed before going to sleep. A substitute, she thought, yawning. She could make her body so limp and passive her arms and legs bounced on the mattress when they fell. One night for diversion she tried doing it to Ivan, but he couldn't master the technique of passivity.

"Don't do anything, Ivan. I lift the leg and I drop the leg. You do nothing. Do you see? Nothing at all," she smiled.

But that was not possible for him. He tried to be limp but kept working along with her; she could see his muscles, precisely those leg muscles she found so desirable, exerting to lift and drop, lift and drop.

"You can't give yourself up. Don't you feel what you're doing? You have to let me do it to you. Let me try just your hand, from the wrist. That might be easier."

"No, forget it. Give me back my hand." He smiled and stroked her stomach gently. "What's the difference? I don't have to do it well. You do it very well."

She did it very well indeed when the time came. It was a short labor, less than an hour, very unusual for a first baby, the nurses kept muttering. She breathed intently, beginning with the long slow breaths she had been taught, feeling quite remote from the bustle around her. Then, in a flurry, they raced down the hall on a wheeled table with a train of white-coated people trotting after, and she thought, panting, No matter what I suffer, soon I will be thin again, I will be more beautiful than ever.

The room was crowded with people, far more people than she would have thought necessary, but the only faces she singled out were Ivan's and the doctor's. The doctor, with a new russet beard and his face a good deal thinner now, was once again framed by her knees, paler than before. Wildly enthusiastic about the proceedings, he yelled, "Terrific, Caroline, terrific," as though they were in a noisy public place. "O.K., start pushing."

They placed her hands on chrome rails along the table. On the left, groping, she found Ivan's hand and held it instead of the rail. She pushed. In surprise she became aware of a great cleavage, like a mountain of granite splitting apart, only it was in her, she realized, and if it kept on going it would go right up to her neck. She gripped Ivan's warm hand, and just as she opened her mouth to roar someone clapped an oxygen mask on her face so the roar reverberated inward on her own ears. She wasn't supposed to roar, the natural childbirth teacher hadn't mentioned anything about that, she was supposed to breathe and push. But as long as no one seemed to take any notice she might as well keep on roaring, it felt so satisfying and necessary. The teacher would never know. She trusted that if she split all the way up to her neck they would sew her up somehow—she was too far gone to worry about that now. Maybe that was why there were so many of them, yes, of course, to put her back together, and maybe they had simply forgotten to tell her about being bisected; or maybe it was a closely guarded secret, like an initiation rite. She gripped Ivan's hand tighter. She was not having too bad a time, she would surely survive, she told herself, captivated by the hellish bestial sounds going from her mouth to her ear; it certainly was what her students would call a peak experience, and how gratifying to hear the doctor exclaim, "Oh, this is one terrific girl! One more, Caroline, give me one more push and send it out. Sock it to me."

She always tried to be obliging, if possible. Now she raised herself on her elbows and, staring straight at him—he too, after all, had been most obliging these long months—gave him with tremendous force the final push he asked for. She had Ivan's hand tightly around the rail, could feel his knuckles bursting, and then all of a sudden the room and the faces were obliterated. A dark thick curtain swiftly wrapped around her and she was left all alone gasping, sucked violently into a windy black hold of pain so explosive she knew it must be death, she was dying fast, like a bomb detonating. It was all right, it was almost over, only she would have liked to see his blue eyes one last time.

From somewhere in the void Ivan's voice shouted in exultation, "It's coming out," and the roaring stopped and at last there was peace and quiet in her ears. The curtain fell away, the world returned. But her eyes kept on burning, as if they had seen something not meant for living eyes to see and return from alive.

"Give it to me," Caroline said, and held it. She saw that every part was in the proper place, then shut her eyes.

They wheeled her to a room and eased her onto the bed. It was past ten in the morning. She could dimly remember they had been up all night watching a James Cagney movie about prize-fighting while they timed her irregular mild contractions. James Cagney went blind from blows given by poisoned gloves in a rigged match, and she wept for him as she held her hands on her stomach and breathed. Neither she nor Ivan had slept or eaten for hours.

"Ivan, there is something I am really dying to have right now."

"Your wish is my command."

She asked for a roast beef on rye with ketchup, and iced tea. "Would you mind? It'll be hours before they serve lunch."

He brought it and stood at the window while she ate ravenously.

"Didn't you get anything for yourself?"

"No, I'm too exhausted to eat." He did, in fact, look terrible. He was sallow; his eyes, usually so radiant, were nearly drained of color, and small downward-curving lines around his mouth recalled his laborious vigil.

"You had a rough night, Ivan. You ought to get some sleep. What's it like outside?"

"What?" Ivan's movements seemed to her extremely purposeless. He was pacing the room with his hands deep in his pockets, going slowly from the foot of the bed to the window and back. Her eyes followed him from the pillow. Every now and then he would stop to peer at Caroline in an unfamiliar way, as if she were a puzzling stranger.

"Ivan, are you O.K.? I meant the weather. What's it doing outside?" It struck her, as she asked, that it was weeks since she had cared to know anything about the outside. That there was an outside, now that she was emptied out, came rushing at her with the most urgent importance, wafting her on a tide of grateful joy.

"Oh," he said vaguely, and came to sit on the edge of her bed. "Well, it's doing something very peculiar outside, as a matter of fact. It's raining but the sun is shining."

She laughed at him. "But haven't you ever seen it do that before?"

"I don't know. I guess so." He opened his mouth and closed it several times. She ate, waiting patiently. Finally he spoke. "You know, Caroline, you really have quite a grip. When you were holding my hand in there, you squeezed it so tight I thought you would break it."

"Oh, come on, that can't be."

"I'm not joking." He massaged his hand absently. Ivan never complained of pain; if anything he understated. But now he held out his right hand and showed her the raw red knuckles and palm, with raised flaming welts forming.

She took his hand. "You're serious. Did I do that? Well, how do you like that?"

"I really thought you'd break my hand. It was killing me." He kept repeating it, not resentfully but dully, as though there were something secreted in the words that he couldn't fathom.

"But why didn't you take it away if it hurt that badly?" She put down her half-eaten sandwich as she saw the pale amazement ripple over his face.

"Oh, no, I couldn't do that. I mean—if that was what you needed just then—" He looked away, embarrassed. "Listen," he shrugged, not facing her, "we're in a hospital, after all. What better place? They'd fix it for me."

Overwhelmed, Caroline lay back on the pillows. "Oh, Ivan. You would do that?"

"What are you crying for?" he asked gently. "You didn't break it, did you? Almost doesn't count. So what are you crying about. You just had a baby. Don't cry."

And she smiled and thought her heart would burst.

WHAT WE TALK ABOUT WHEN WE TALK ABOUT LOVE

RAYMOND CARVER

My FRIEND MEL MCGINNIS was talking. Mel McGinnis is a cardiologist, and sometimes that gives him the right.

The four of us were sitting around his kitchen table drinking gin. Sunlight filled the kitchen from the big window behind the sink. There were Mel and I and his second wife, Teresa—Terri, we called her—and my wife, Laura. We lived in Albuquerque then, but we were all from somewhere else.

There was an ice bucket on the table. The gin and the tonic water kept going around, and we somehow got on the subject of love. Mel thought real love was nothing less than spiritual love. He said he'd spent five years in a seminary before quitting to go to medical school. He said he still looked back on those years in the seminary as the most important in his life.

Terri said the man she lived with before she lived with Mel loved her so much he tried to kill her. Then Terri said, "He beat me up one night. He dragged me around the living room by my ankles. He kept saying, 'I love you, I love you, you bitch.' He went on dragging me around the living room. My head kept knocking on things." Terri looked around the table. "What do you do with love like that?" she said.

She was a bone-thin woman with a pretty face, dark eyes, and brown hair that hung down her back. She liked necklaces made of turquoise, and long pendant earrings.

"My God, don't be silly. That's not love, and you know it," Mel said. "I don't know what you'd call it, but I sure know you wouldn't call it love."

"Say what you want to, but I know it was," Terri said. "It may sound crazy to you, but it's true just the same. People are different, Mel. Sure, sometimes he may have acted crazy. Okay. But he loved me. In his own way, maybe, but he loved me. There was love there, Mel. Don't say there wasn't."

Mel let out his breath. He held his glass and turned to Laura and me. "The man threatened to kill me," Mel said. He finished his drink and reached for the gin bottle. "Terri's a romantic. Terri's of the kick-me-so-I'll-know-you-love-me school. Terri, hon, don't look that way." Mel reached across the table and touched Terri's cheek with his fingers. He grinned at her.

"Now he wants to make up," Terri said.

"Make up what?" Mel said. "What is there to make up? I know what I know. That's all."

"How'd we get started on this subject, anyway?" Terri said. She raised her glass and drank from it. "Mel always has love on his mind." she said. "Don't you, honey?" She smiled, and I thought that was the last of it.

"I just wouldn't call Ed's behavior love. That's all I'm saying, honey," Mel said. "What about you guys?" Mel said to Laura and me. "Does that sound like love to you?"

"I'm the wrong person to ask," I said. "I don't even know the man. I've only heard his name mentioned in passing. I wouldn't know. You'd have to know the particulars. But I think what you're saying is that love is an absolute."

Mel said, "The kind of love I'm talking about is. The kind of love I'm talking about, you don't try to kill people."

Laura said, "I don't know anything about Ed, or anything about the situation. But who can judge anyone else's situation?"

I touched the back of Laura's hand. She gave me a quick smile. I picked up Laura's hand. It was warm, the nails polished, perfectly manicured. I encircled the broad wrist with my fingers, and I held her.

"When I left, he drank rat poison." Terri said. She clasped her arms with her hands. "They took him to the hospital in Santa Fe. That's where we lived then, about ten miles out. They saved his life. But his gums went crazy from it. I mean they pulled away from his teeth. After that, his teeth stood out like fangs. My God," Terri said. She waited a minute, then let go of her arms and picked up her glass.

"What people won't do!" Laura said.

"He's out of the action now," Mel said. "He's dead."

Mel handed me the saucer of limes. I took a section of lime, squeezed it over my drink, and stirred the ice cubes with my finger.

"It gets worse," Terri said. "He shot himself in the mouth. But he bungled that too. Poor Ed," she said. Terri shook her head.

"Poor Ed nothing," Mel said. "He was dangerous."

Mel was forty-five years old. He was tall and rangy with curly gray hair. His face and arms were brown from the tennis he played. When he was sober, his gestures, all his movements, were precise, very careful.

"He did love me though. Mel. Grant me that," Terri said. "That's all I'm asking. He didn't love me the way you love me. I'm not saying that. But he loved me. You can grant me that, can't you?"

"What do you mean, he bungled it?" I said.

Laura leaned forward with her glass. She put her elbows on the table and held her glass in both hands. She glanced from Mel to Terri and waited with a look of bewilderment on her open face, as if amazed that such things happened to people you were friendly with.

"How'd he bungle it when he killed himself?" I said.

"I'll tell you what happened," Mel said. "He took this twenty-two pistol he'd bought to threaten Terri and me with. Oh, I'm serious, the man was always threatening. You should have seen the way we lived in those days. Like fugitives. I even bought a gun myself. Can you believe it? A guy like me? But I did. I bought one for self-defense and carried it in the glove compartment. Sometimes I'd have to leave the apartment in the middle of the night. To go to the hospital, you know? Terri and I weren't married then and my first wife had the house and kids, the dog, everything, and Terri and I were living in this apartment house. Sometimes, as I say, I'd get a call in the middle of the night and have to go in to the hospital at two or three in the morning. It'd be dark out there in the parking lot and I'd break into a sweat before I could even get to my car. I never knew if he was going to come up out of the shrubbery or from behind a car and start shooting. I mean, the man was crazy. He was capable of wiring a bomb, anything. He used to call my service at all hours and say he needed to talk to the doctor, and when I'd return the call, he'd say, 'Son of a bitch, your days are numbered.' Little things like that. It was scary, I'm telling you."

"I still feel sorry for him," Terri said.

"It sounds like a nightmare," Laura said. "But what exactly happened after he shot himself?"

Laura is a legal secretary. We'd met in a professional capacity. Before we knew it, it was a courtship. She's thirty-five, three years younger than I am. In addition to being in love, we like each other and enjoy one another's company. She's easy to be with.

"What happened?" Laura said.

Mel said. "He shot himself in the mouth in his room. Someone heard the shot and told the manager. They came in with a passkey, saw what had happened, and called an ambulance. I happened to be there when they brought him in, alive but past recall. The man lived for three days. His head swelled up to twice the size of a normal head. I'd never seen anything like it, and I hope I never do again. Terri wanted to go in and sit with him when she found out about it. We had a fight over it. I didn't think she should see him like that. I didn't think she should see him, and I still don't."

"Who won the fight?" Laura said.

"I was in the room with him when he died." Terri said. "He

never came up out of it. But I sat with him. He didn't have anyone else."

"He was dangerous." Mel said. "If you call that love, you can have it."

"It was love," Terri said. "Sure it's abnormal in most people's eyes. But he was willing to die for it. He did die for it."

"I sure as hell wouldn't call it love." Mel said. "I mean, no one knows what he did it for. I've seen a lot of suicides, and I couldn't say anyone ever knew what they did it for."

Mel put his hands behind his neck and tilted his chair back. "I'm not interested in that kind of love," Mel said. "If that's love, you can have it."

Terri said. "We were afraid. Mel even made a will out and wrote to his brother in California who used to be a Green Beret. Mel told him who to look for if something happened to him."

Terri drank from her glass. She said, "But Mel's right—we lived like fugitives. We were afraid. Mel was, weren't you, honey? I even called the police at one point, but they were no help. They said they couldn't do anything until Ed actually did something. Isn't that a laugh?" Terri said.

She poured the last of the gin into her glass and wagged the bottle. Mel got up from the table and went to the cupboard. He took down another bottle.

"Well, Nick and I know what love is," Laura said. "For us, I mean," Laura said. She bumped my knee with her knee. "You're supposed to say something now," Laura said, and turned her smile on me.

For an answer, I took Laura's hand and raised it to my lips. I made a big production out of kissing her hand. Everyone was amused.

"We're lucky," I said.

"You guys," Terri said. "Stop that now. You're making me sick. You're still on the honeymoon, for God's sake. You're still gaga, for crying out loud. Just wait. How long have you been together now? How long has it been? A year? Longer than a year?"

"Going on a year and a half," Laura said, flushed and smiling.

"Oh, now," Terri said. "Wait a while."

She held her drink and gazed at Laura.

"I'm only kidding," Terri said.

Mel opened the gin and went around the table with the bottle.

"Here, you guys," he said. "Let's have a toast. I want to propose a toast. A toast to love. To true love," Mel said.

We touched glasses.

"To love," we said.

Outside in the back yard, one of the dogs began to bark. The leaves of the aspen that leaned past the window ticked against the glass. The afternoon sun was like a presence in this room, the spacious light of ease and generosity. We could have been anywhere, somewhere enchanted. We raised our glasses again and grinned at each other like children who had agreed on something forbidden.

"I'll tell you what real love is," Mel said. "I mean, I'll give you a good example. And then you can draw your own conclusions." He poured more gin into his glass. He added an ice cube and a sliver of lime. We waited and sipped our drinks. Laura and I touched knees again. I put a hand on her warm thigh and left it there.

"What do any of us really know about love?" Mel said. "It seems to me we're just beginners at love. We say we love each other and we do. I don't doubt it. I love Terri and Terri loves me, and you guys love each other too. You know the kind of love I'm talking about now. Physical love, that impulse that drives you to someone special, as well as love of the other person's being, his or her essence, as it were. Carnal love and, well, call it sentimental love, the day-to-day caring about the other person. But sometimes I have a hard time accounting for the fact that I must have loved my first wife too. But I did. I know I did. So I suppose I am like Terri in that regard. Terri and Ed." He thought about it and then he went on. "There was a time when I thought I loved my first wife more than life itself. But now I hate her guts. I do. How do you explain that? What happened to that love? What happened to it, is what I'd like to know. I wish someone could tell me. Then there's Ed. Okay, we're back to Ed. He loves Terri so much he tries to kill her and he winds up killing himself." Mel stopped talking and swallowed from his glass. "You guys have been together eighteen months and you love each other. It shows all over you. You glow with it. But you both loved other people before you met each other. You've both been married before, just like us. And you probably loved other people before that too even. Terri and I have been together five years, been married for four. And the terrible thing, the terrible thing is, but the good thing, too, the saving grace, you might say, is that if something happened to one of us—excuse me for saying this—but if something happened to one of us tomorrow, I think the other one, the other person, would grieve for a while, you know, but then the surviving party would go out and love again, have someone else soon enough. All this, all of this love we're talking about, it would just be memory. Maybe not even a memory. Am I wrong? Am I way off base? Because I want you to set me straight if you think I'm wrong. I want to know. I mean, I don't know anything, and I'm the first one to admit it."

"Mel, for God's sake," Terri said. She reached out and took hold of his wrist. "Are you getting drunk? Honey? Are you drunk?"

"Honey, I'm just talking," Mel said. "All right? I don't have to be drunk to say what I think. I mean, we're all just talking, right?" Mel said. He fixed his eyes on her.

"Sweetie, I'm not criticizing," Terri said.

She picked up her glass.

"I'm not on call today," Mel said. "Let me remind you of that. I am not on call," he said.

"Mel, we love you," Laura said.

Mel looked at Laura. He looked at her as if he could not place her, as if she was not the woman she was.

"Love you too, Laura," Mel said. "And you, Nick, love you too. You know something?" Mel said. "You guys are our pals," Mel said.

He picked up his glass.

Mel said, "I was going to tell you about something. I mean, I was going to prove a point. You see, this happened a few months ago, but it's still going on right now, and it ought to make us feel ashamed when we talk like we know what we're talking about when we talk about love."

"Come on now," Terri said. "Don't talk like you're drunk if you're not drunk."

"Just shut up for once in your life," Mel said very quietly. "Will you do me a favor and do that for a minute? So as I was saying, there's this old couple who had this car wreck out on the interstate?

A kid hit them and they were all torn to shit and nobody was giving them much chance to pull through."

Terri looked at us and then back at Mel. She seemed anxious, or maybe that's too strong a word.

Mel was handing the bottle around the table.

"I was on call that night," Mel said. "It was May or maybe it was June. Terri and I had just sat down to dinner when the hospital called. There'd been this thing out on the interstate. Drunk kid, teen-ager, plowed his dad's pickup into this camper with this old couple in it. They were up in their mid-seventies, that couple. The kid—eighteen, nineteen, something— he was DOA. Taken the steering wheel through his sternum. The old couple, they were alive, you understand. I mean, just barely. But they had everything. Multiple fractures, internal injuries, hemorrhaging, contusions, lacerations, the works, and they each of them had themselves concussions. They were in a bad way, believe me. And, of course, their age was two strikes against them. I'd say she was worse off than he was. Ruptured spleen along with everything else. Both kneecaps broken. But they'd been wearing their seatbelts and, God knows, that's what saved them for the time being."

"Folks, this is an advertisement for the National Safety Council." Terri said. "This is your spokesman, Dr. Melvin R. McGinnis, talking." Terri laughed. "Mel," she said, "sometimes you're just too much. But I love you, honey," she said.

"Honey, I love you," Mel said.

He leaned across the table. Terri met him halfway. They kissed.

"Terri's right," Mel said as he settled himself again. "Get those seatbelts on. But seriously, they were in some shape, those oldsters. By the time I got down there, the kid was dead, as I said. He was off in a corner, laid out on a gurney. I took one look at the old couple and told the ER nurse to get me a neurologist and an orthopedic man and a couple of surgeons down there right away."

He drank from his glass. "I'll try to keep this short," he said. "So we took the two of them up to the OR and worked like fuck on them most of the night. They had these incredible reserves, those two. You see that once in a while. So we did everything that could be done, and toward morning we're giving them a fifty-fifty chance, maybe less than that for her. So here they are, still alive the next morning. So, okay, we move them into the ICU, which is where they both kept plugging away at it for two weeks, hitting it better and better on all the scopes. So we transfer them out to their own room."

Mel stopped talking. "Here," he said, "let's drink this cheapo gin the hell up. Then we're going to dinner, right? Terri and I know a new place. That's where we'll go, to this new place we know about. But we're not going until we finish up this cheap lousy gin."

Terri said, "We haven't actually eaten there yet. But it looks good. From the outside, you know."

"I like food," Mel said. "If I had it to do all over again, I'd be a chef, you know? Right, Terri?" Mel said.

He laughed. He twirled the ice in his glass.

"Terri knows," he said. "Terri can tell you. But let me say this. If I could come back again in a different life, a different time and all, you know what? I'd like to come back as a knight. You were pretty safe wearing all that armor. It was all right being a knight until gunpowder and muskets and pistols came along."

"Mel would like to ride a horse and carry a lance," Terri said.

"Carry a woman's scarf with you everywhere," Laura said.

"Or just a woman," Mel said.

"Shame on you," Laura said.

Terri said, "Suppose you came back as a serf? The serfs didn't have it so good in those days," Terri said.

"The serfs never had it good," Mel said. "But I guess even the knights were vessels to someone. Isn't that the way it worked? But then everyone is always a vessel to someone. Isn't that right? Terri? But what I liked about knights, besides their ladies, was that they had that suit of armor, you know, and they couldn't get hurt very easy. No cars in those days, you know? No drunk teen-agers to tear into your ass."

"Vassals," Terri said.

"What?" Mel said.

"Vassals," Terri said. "They were called vassals, not vessels."

"Vassals, vessels," Mel said, "what the fuck's the difference? You knew what I meant anyway. All right," Mel said. "So I'm not educated. I learned my stuff. I'm a heart surgeon, sure, but I'm just a mechanic. I go in and I fuck around and I fix things. Shit," Mel said.

"Modesty doesn't become you," Terri said.

"He's just a humble sawbones," I said. "But sometimes they suffocated in all that armor, Mel. They'd even have heart attacks if it got too hot and they were too tired and worn out. I read somewhere that they'd fall off their horses and not be able to get up because they were too tired to stand with all that armor on them. They got trampled by their own horses sometimes."

"That's terrible," Mel said. "That's a terrible thing, Nicky. I guess they'd just lay there and wait until somebody came along and made a shish kabob out of them."

"Some other vassal," Terri said.

"That's right," Mel said. "Some vassal would come along and spear the bastard in the name of love. Or whatever the fuck it was they fought over in those days."

"Same things we fight over these days," Terri said.

"Politics," Laura said. "Nothing's changed."

The color was still high in Laura's cheeks. Her eyes were bright. She brought her glass to her lips.

Mel poured himself another drink. He looked at the label closely as if studying a long row of numbers. Then he slowly put the bottle down on the table and reached for the tonic water.

"What about the old couple?" Laura said. "You didn't finish that story you started."

Laura was having a hard time lighting her cigarette. Her matches kept going out.

The sunshine inside the room was different now, changing, getting thinner. But the leaves outside the window were still shimmering, and I stared at the pattern they made on the panes and on the formica counter. They weren't the same patterns, of course.

"What about the old couple?" I said.

"Older but wiser," Terri said.

Mel stared at her.

Terri said, "Go on with your story, hon. I was only kidding. Then what happened?"

"Terri, sometimes," Mel said.

"Please, Mel," Terri said. "Don't always be so serious, sweetie. Can't you take a joke?"

"This is nothing to joke about," Mel said.

He held his glass and gazed steadily at his wife.

"What happened?" Laura said.

Mel fastened his eyes on Laura. He said, "Laura, if I didn't have Terri and if I didn't love her so much, and if Nick wasn't my best friend, I'd fall in love with you. I'd carry you off, honey," he said.

"Tell your story," Terri said. "Then we'll go to that new place, okay?"

"Okay," Mel said. "Where was I?" he said. He stared at the table and then he began again.

"I dropped in to see each of them every day, sometimes twice a day if I was up doing other calls anyway. Casts and bandages, head to foot, the both of them. You know, you've seen it in the movies. That's just the way they looked, just like in the movies. Little eye holes and nose holes and mouth holes. And she had to have her legs slung up on top of it. Well, the husband was very depressed for the longest while. Even after he found out that his wife was going to pull through, he was still very depressed. Not about the accident, though. I mean, the accident was one thing, but it wasn't everything. I'd get up to his mouth hole, you know, and he'd say no, it wasn't the accident exactly but it was because he couldn't see her through his eye holes. He said that was what was making him feel so bad. Can you imagine? I'm telling you, the man's heart was breaking because he couldn't turn his goddamn head and *see* his wife."

Mel looked around the table and shook his head at what he was going to say.

"I mean, it was killing the old fart just because he couldn't *look* at the goddamn woman."

We all looked at Mel.

"Do you see what I'm saying?" he said.

Maybe we were a little drunk by then. I know it was hard keeping things in focus. The light was draining out of the room, going back through the window where it had come from. Yet nobody made a move to get up from the table to turn on the juice inside.

"Listen," Mel said. "Let's finish this fucking gin. There's about enough left here for one shooter all around. Then let's go eat. Let's go to the new place."

"He's depressed," Terri said. "Mel, why don't you take a pill?"

Mel shook his head. "I've taken everything there is."

"We all need a pill now and then," I said.

"Some people are born needing them," Terri said.

She was using her finger to rub at something on the table. Then she stopped rubbing.

"I think I want to call my kids," Mel said. "Is that all right with everybody? I'll call my kids," he said.

Terri said, "What if Marjorie answers the phone? You guys, you've heard us on the subject of Marjorie? Honey, you know you don't want to talk to her. It'll make you feel even worse."

"I don't want to talk to Marjorie," Mel said. "But I want to talk to my kids."

"There isn't a day goes by that Mel doesn't say he wishes she'd get married again. Or else die," Terri said. "For one thing," Terri said, "she's bankrupting us. Mel says it's just to spite him that she won't get married again. She has a boyfriend who lives with her and the kids, so Mel is supporting the boyfriend too."

"She's allergic to bees," Mel said. "If I'm not praying she'll get married again, I'm praying she'll get herself stung to death by a swarm of fucking bees."

"Shame on you," Laura said.

"Bzzzzzzz," Mel said, turning his fingers into bees and buzzing them at Terri's throat. Then he let his hands drop all the way to his sides.

"She's vicious," Mel said. "Sometimes I think I'll go up there dressed like a beekeeper. You know, that hat that's like a helmet with the plate that comes down over your face, the big gloves and the padded coat? I'll knock on the door and let loose a hive of bees in the house. But first I'd make sure the kids were out, of course."

He crossed one leg over the other. It seemed to take him a lot of time to do it. Then he put both feet on the floor and leaned forward, elbows on the table, his chin cupped in his hands.

"Maybe I won't call the kids, after all. Maybe it isn't such a hot idea. Maybe we'll just go eat. How does that sound?"

"Sounds fine to me," I said. "Eat or not eat. Or keep drinking. I could head right on out into the sunset."

"What does that mean, honey?" Laura said.

"It just means what I said, honey," I said. "It means I could just keep going. That's all it means."

"I could eat something myself," Laura said. "I don't think I've ever been so hungry in my life. Is there something to nibble on?"

"I'll put out some cheese and crackers," Terri said.

But Terri just sat there. She did not get up to get anything.

Mel turned his glass over. He spilled it out on the table.

"Gin's gone," Mel said.

Terri said, "Now what?"

I could hear my heart beating. I could hear everyone's heart. I could hear the human noise we sat there making, not a one of us moving, not even when the room went totally dark.

GRAVEYARD DAY

BOBBIE ANN MASON

Holly, SWINGING HER LEGS FROM THE KITCHEN STOOL, lectures her mother on natural foods. Holly is ten.

Waldeen says, "I'll have to give your teacher a talking-to. She's put notions in your head. You've got to have meat to grow."

Waldeen is tenderizing liver, beating it with the edge of a saucer. Her daughter insists that she is a vegetarian. If Holly had said Rosicrucian, it would have sounded just as strange to Waldeen. Holly wants to eat peanuts, soyburgers, and yogurt. Waldeen is sure this new fixation has something to do with Holly's father, Joe Murdock, although Holly rarely mentions him. After Waldeen and Joe were divorced last September, Joe moved to Arizona and got a construction job. Joe sends Holly letters occasionally, but Holly won't let Waldeen see them. At Christmas he sent Holly a copper Indian bracelet with unusual marks on it. It is Indian language, Holly tells her. Waldeen sees Holly polishing the bracelet while she is watching TV.

Walden shudders when she thinks of Joe Murdock. If he weren't Holly's father, she might be able to forget him. Waldeen was too young when she married him, and he had a reputation for being wild, which he did not outgrow. Now she could marry Joe McClain, who comes over for supper almost every night, always bringing something special, such as roast or dessert. He seems to be oblivious to what things cost, and he frequently brings Holly presents. If Waldeen married Joe, then Holly would have a stepfather—something like a sugar substitute, Waldeen imagines. Shifting relationships confuse her. She doesn't know what marriage

53

means anymore. She tells Joe they must wait. Her ex-husband is still on her mind, like the lingering after-effects of an illness.

Joe McClain is punctual, considerate. Tonight he brings fudge ripple ice cream and a half-gallon of Coke in a plastic jug. He kisses Waldeen and hugs Holly.

Waldeen says, "We're having liver and onions, but Holly's mad 'cause I won't make Soybean Supreme."

"Soybean *Delight*," says Holly.

"Oh, excuse me!"

"Liver is full of poison. The poisons in the feed settle in the liver."

"Do you want to stunt your growth?" Joe asks, patting Holly on the head. He winks at Waldeen and waves his walking stick at her playfully, like a conductor. Joe collects walking sticks, and he has an antique one that belonged to Jefferson Davis. On a gold band, in italics, it says Jefferson Davis. Joe doesn't go anywhere without a walking stick, although he is only thirty. It embarrasses Waldeen to be seen with him.

"Sometimes a cow's liver just explodes from the poison," says Holly. "Poisons are *oozing* out."

"Oh, Holly, hush, that's disgusting." Waldeen plops the pieces of liver onto a plate of flour.

"There's this restaurant at the lake that has Liver Lovers' Night," Joe says to Holly. "Every Tuesday is Liver Lovers' Night."

"Really?" Holly is wide-eyed, as if Joe is about to tell a long story, but Waldeen suspects Joe is bringing up the restaurant—Sea's Breeze at Kentucky Lake—to remind her that it was the scene of his proposal. Waldeen, not accustomed to eating out, studied the menu carefully, wavering between pork chops and T-bone steak and then suddenly, without thinking, ordering catfish. She was disappointed to learn that the catfish was not even local, but frozen ocean cat. "Why would they do that," she kept saying, interrupting Joe, "when they've got all the fresh channel cat in the world right here at Kentucky Lake?"

During supper, Waldeen snaps at Holly for sneaking liver to the cat, but with Joe gently persuading her, Holly manages to eat three bites of liver without gagging. Holly is trying to please him, as though he were some TV game show host who happened to live in the neighborhood. In Waldeen's opinion, families shouldn't shift memberships, like clubs. But here they are, trying to be a family. Holly, Waldeen, Joe McClain. Sometimes Joe spends the weekend, but Holly prefers weekends at Joe's house because of his shiny wood floors and his parrot that tries to sing "Inka Dinka Doo." Holly likes the idea of packing an overnight bag.

Waldeen dishes out the ice cream. Suddenly inspired, she suggests a picnic Saturday. "The weather's fairing up," she says.

"I can't," says Joe. "Saturday's graveyard day."

"Graveyard day?" Holly and Waldeen say together.

"It's my turn to clean off the graveyard. Every spring and fall somebody has to rake it off." Joe explains that he is responsible for taking geraniums to his grandparents' graves. His grandmother always kept the pot in her basement during the winter, and in the spring she took it to her husband's grave, but she had died in November.

"Couldn't we have a picnic at the graveyard?" asks Waldeen.

"That's gruesome."

"We never get to go on picnics," says Holly. "Or anywhere." She gives Waldeen a look.

"Well, okay," Joe says. "But remember, it's serious. No fooling around."

"We'll be real quiet," says Holly.

"Far be it from me to disturb the dead," Waldeen says, wondering why she is speaking in a mocking tone.

After supper, Joe plays rummy with Holly while Waldeen cracks pecans for a cake. Pecan shells fly across the floor, and the cat pounces on them. Holly and Joe are laughing together, whooping loudly over the cards. They sound like contestants on "Let's Make a Deal." Joe Murdock wanted desperately to be on a game show and strike it rich. He wanted to go to California so he would have a chance to be on TV and so he could travel the freeways. He drove in the stock car races, and he had been drag racing since he learned to drive. Evel Knievel was his hero. Waldeen couldn't look when the TV showed Evel Knievel leaping over canyons. She told Joe many times, "He's nothing but a show-off. But if you want to break your fool neck, then go right ahead. Nobody's stopping you." She is better off without Joe Murdock. If he were still in town, he would do something to make her look foolish, such as paint her name on his car door. He once had WALDEEN painted in large red letters on the door of his LTD. It was like a tattoo. It is probably a good thing he is in Arizona. Still, she cannot really understand why he had to move so far away from home.

After Holly goes upstairs, carrying the cat, whose name is Mr. Spock, Waldeen says to Joe, "In China they have a law that the men have to help keep house." She is washing dishes.

Joe grins. "That's in China. This is *here*."

Waldeen slaps at him with the dish towel, and Joe jumps up and grabs her. "I'll do all the housework if you marry me," he says. "You can get the Chinese to arrest me if I don't."

"You sound just like my ex-husband. Full of promises."

"Guys named Joe are good at making promises." Joe laughs and hugs her.

"All the important men in my life were named Joe," says Waldeen, with pretended seriousness. "My first real boyfriend was named Joe. I was fourteen."

"You always bring that up," says Joe. "I wish you'd forget about them. You love *me*, don't you?"

"Of course, you idiot."

"Then why don't you marry me?"

"I just said I was going to think twice is all."

"But if you love me, what are you waiting for?"

"That's the easy part. Love is easy."

In the middle of "The Waltons," C. W. Redmon and Betty Mathis drop by. Betty, Waldeen's best friend, lives with C.W., who works with Joe on a construction crew. Waldeen turns off the TV and clears magazines from the couch. C. W. and Betty have just returned from Florida and they are full of news about Sea World. Betty shows Waldeen her new tote bag with a killer whale pictured on it.

"Guess who we saw at the Louisville airport," Betty says.

"I give up," says Waldeen.

"Colonel Sanders!"

"He's eighty-four if he's a day," C. W. adds.

"You couldn't miss him in that white suit," Betty says. "I'm sure it was him. Oh, Joe! He had a walking stick. He went strutting along—"

"No kidding!"

He probably beats chickens to death with it," says Holly, who is standing around.

"That would be something to have," says Joe. "Wow, one of the Colonel's walking sticks."

"Do you know what I read in a magazine?" says Betty. "That the Colonel Sanders outfit is trying to grow a three-legged chicken."

"No, a four-legged chicken," says C.W.

"Well, whatever."

Waldeen is startled by the conversation. She is rattling ice cubes, looking for glasses. She finds an opened Coke in the refrigerator, but it may have lost its fizz. Before she can decide whether to open the new one Joe brought, C.W. and Betty grab glasses of ice from her and hold them out. Waldeen pours the Coke. There is a little fizz.

"We went first class the whole way," says C.W. "I always say, what's vacation for if you don't splurge?"

"I thought we were going to buy *out* Florida," says Betty. "We spent a fortune. Plus, I gained a ton."

"Man, those jumbo jets are really nice," says C.W.

C.W. and Betty seem changed, exactly like all people who come back from Florida with tales of adventure and glowing tans, except that they did not get tans. It rained. Waldeen cannot imagine flying, or spending that much money. Her ex-husband tried to get her to go up in an airplane with him once—a $7.50 ride in a Cessna—but she refused. If Holly goes to Arizona to visit him, she will have to fly. Arizona is probably as far away as Florida.

When C.W. says he is going fishing on Saturday, Holly demands to go along. Waldeen reminds her about the picnic. "You're full of wants," she says.

"I just wanted to go somewhere."

"I'll take you fishing one of these days soon," says Joe.

"Joe's got to clean off his graveyard," says Waldeen. Before she realizes what she is saying, she has invited C.W. and Betty to come along on the picnic. She turns to Joe. "Is that okay?"

"I'll bring some beer," says C.W. "To hell with fishing."

"I never heard of a picnic at a graveyard," says Betty. "But it sounds neat."

Joe seems embarrassed. "I'll put you to work," he warns.

Later, in the kitchen, Waldeen pours more Coke for Betty. Holly is playing solitaire on the kitchen table. As Betty takes the

Coke, she says, "Let C.W. take Holly fishing if he wants a kid so bad." She has told Waldeen that she wants to marry C.W., but she does not want to ruin her figure by getting pregnant. Betty pets the cat. "Is this cat going to have kittens?"

Mr. Spock, sitting with his legs tucked under his stomach, is shaped somewhat like a turtle.

"Heavens, no," says Waldeen. "He's just fat because I had him nurtured."

"The word is *neutered!*" cries Holly, jumping up. She grabs Mr. Spock and marches up the stairs.

"That youngun," Waldeen says with a sigh. She feels suddenly afraid. Once, Holly's father, unemployed and drunk on whiskey and Seven-Up, snatched Holly from the school playground and took her on a wild ride around town, buying her ice cream at the Tastee-Freez, and stopping at Newberry's to buy her an "All in the Family" Joey doll, with correct private parts. Holly was eight. When Joe brought her home, both were tearful and quiet. The excitement had worn off, but Waldeen had vividly imagined how it was. She wouldn't be surprised if Joe tried the same trick again, this time carrying Holly off to Arizona. She has heard of divorced parents who kidnap their own children.

The next day Joe McClain brings a pizza at noon. He is working nearby and has a chance to eat lunch with Waldeen. The pizza is large enough for four people. Waldeen is not hungry.

"I'm afraid we'll end up horsing around and won't get the graveyard cleaned off," Joe says. "It's really a lot of work."

"Why's it so important, anyway?"

"It's a family thing."

"Family. Ha!"

"Why are you looking at me in that tone of voice?"

"I don't know what's what anymore," Waldeen wails. "I've got this kid that wants to live on peanuts and sleeps with a cat—and didn't even see her daddy at Christmas. And here *you* are, talking about family. What do you know about family? You don't know the half of it."

"What's got into you lately?"

Waldeen tries to explain. "Take Colonel Sanders, for instance. He was on 'I've Got A Secret' once, years ago, when nobody knew who he was. His secret was that he had a million-dollar check in his

pocket for selling Kentucky Fried Chicken to John Y. Brown. *Now*
look what's happened. Colonel Sanders sold it but didn't get rid of
it. He's still Colonel Sanders. John Y. sold it too and he can't get rid
of it either. Everybody calls him the Chicken King, even though
he's governor. That's not very dignified, if you ask me."

"What in Sam Hill are you talking about? What's that got to do
with families?"

"Oh, Colonel Sanders just came to mind because C.W. and
Betty saw him. What I mean is, you can't just do something by
itself. Everything else drags along. It's all *involved*. I can't get rid
of my ex-husband just by signing a paper. Even if he *is* in Arizona
and I never lay eyes on him again."

Joe stands up, takes Waldeen by the hand, and leads her to the
couch. They sit down and he holds her tightly for a moment.
Waldeen has the strange impression that Joe is an old friend who
moved away and returned, years later, radically changed. She
doesn't understand the walking sticks, or why he would buy such
an enormous pizza.

"One of these days you'll see," says Joe, kissing her.

"See what?" Waldeen mumbles.

"One of these days you'll see. I'm not such a bad catch."

Waldeen stares at a split in the wallpaper.

"Who would cut your hair if it wasn't for me?" he asks, rumpling
her curls. "I should have gone to beauty school."

"I don't know."

"Nobody else can do Jimmy Durante imitations like I can."

"I wouldn't brag about it."

On Saturday Waldeen is still in bed when Joe arrives. He
appears in the doorway of her bedroom, brandishing a shiny black
walking stick. It looks like a stiffened black racer snake.

"I overslept," Waldeen says, rubbing her eyes. "First I had
insomnia. Then I had bad dreams. Then—"

"You said you'd make a picnic."

"Just a minute. I'll go make it."

"There's not time now. We've got to pick up C.W. and Betty."

Waldeen pulls on her jeans and a shirt, then runs a brush
through her hair. In the mirror she sees blue pouches under her
eyes. She catches sight of Joe in the mirror. He looks like an actor
in a vaudeville show.

They go into the kitchen, where Holly is eating granola. "She promised me she'd make carrot cake," Holly tells Joe.

"I get blamed for everything," says Waldeen. She is rushing around, not sure why. She is hardly awake.

"How could you forget?" asks Joe. "It was your idea in the first place."

"I didn't forget. I just overslept." Waldeen opens the refrigerator. She is looking for something. She stares at a ham.

When Holly leaves the kitchen, Waldeen asks Joe, "Are you mad at me?" Joe is thumping his stick on the floor.

"No. I just want to get this show on the road."

"My ex-husband always said I was never dependable, and he was right. But *he* was one to talk. He had his head in the clouds."

"Forget your ex-husband."

"His name is Joe. Do you want some juice?" Waldeen is looking for orange juice, but she cannot find it.

"No." Joe leans on his stick. "He's over and done with. Why don't you just cross him off your list?"

"Why do you think I had bad dreams? Answer me that. I must be afraid of *something*."

There is no juice. Waldeen closes the refrigerator door. Joe is smiling at her enigmatically. What she is really afraid of, she realizes, is that he will turn out to be just like Joe Murdock. But it must be only the names, she reminds herself. She hates the thought of a string of husbands, and the idea of a step-father is like a substitute host on a talk show. It makes her think of Johnny Carson's many substitute hosts.

"You're just afraid to do anything new, Waldeen," Joe says. "You're afraid to cross the street. Why don't you get your ears pierced? Why don't you adopt a refugee? Why don't you get a dog?"

"You're crazy. You say the weirdest things." Waldeen searches the refrigerator again. She pours a glass of Coke and watches it foam.

It is afternoon before they reach the graveyard. They had to wait for C.W. to finish painting his garage door, and Betty was in the shower. On the way, they bought a bucket of fried chicken. Joe said little on the drive into the country. When he gets quiet,

Waldeen can never figure out if he is angry or calm. When he put the beer cooler in the trunk, she caught a glimpse of the geraniums in an ornate concrete pot with a handle. It looked like a petrified Easter basket. On the drive, she closed her eyes and imagined that they were in a funeral procession.

The graveyard is next to the woods on a small rise fenced in with barbed wire. A herd of Holsteins grazes in the pasture nearby, and in the distance the smokestacks of the new industrial park send up lazy swirls of smoke. Waldeen spreads out a blanket, and Betty opens beers and hands them around. Holly sits down under a tree, her back to the gravestones, and opens a Vicki Barr flight steward-ess book.

Joe won't sit down to eat until he has unloaded the geraniums. He fusses over the heavy basket, trying to find a level spot. The flowers are not yet blooming.

"Wouldn't plastic flowers keep better?" asks Waldeen. "Then you wouldn't have to lug that thing back and forth." There are several bunches of plastic flowers on the graves. Most of them have fallen out of their containers.

"Plastic, yuck!" cries Holly.

"I should have known I'd say the wrong thing," says Waldeen.

"My grandmother liked geraniums," Joe says.

At the picnic, Holly eats only slaw and the crust from a drum-stick. Waldeen remarks, "Mr. Spock is going to have a feast."

"You've got a treasure, Waldeen," says C.W. "Most kids just want to load up on junk."

"Wonder how long a person can survive without meat," says Waldeen, somewhat breezily. Suddenly, she feels miserable about the way she treats Holly. Everything Waldeen does is so round-about, so devious, a habit she is sure she acquired from Joe Murdock. Disgusted, Waldeen flings a chicken bone out among the graves. Once, her ex-husband wouldn't bury the dog that was hit by a car. It lay in a ditch for over a week. She remembers Joe saying several times, "Wonder if the dog is still there?" He wouldn't admit that he didn't want to bury it. Waldeen wouldn't do it because he had said he would do it. It was a war of nerves. She finally called the Highway Department to pick it up. Joe McClain, at least, would never be that barbaric.

Joe pats Holly on the head and says, "My girl's stubborn, but she knows what she likes." He makes a Jimmy Durante face which causes Holly to smile. Then he brings out a surprise for her, a bag of trail mix, which includes pecans and raisins. When Holly pounces on it, Waldeen notices that Holly is not wearing the Indian bracelet her father gave her. Waldeen wonders if there are vegetarians in Arizona.

Blue sky burns through the intricate spring leaves of the maples on the fence line. The light glances off the gravestones—a few thin slabs that date back to the last century and eleven sturdy blocks of marble and granite. Joe's grandmother's grave is a brown heap.

Waldeen opens another beer. She and Betty are stretched out under a maple tree and Holly is reading. Betty is talking idly about the diet she intends to go on. Waldeen feels too lazy to move. She watches the men work. While C.W. rakes leaves, Joe washes off the gravestones with water he brought in a camp carrier. He scrubs out the carvings with a brush. He seems as devoted as a man washing and polishing his car on a Saturday afternoon. Betty plays he-loves-me-he-loves-me-not with the fingers of a maple leaf. The fragments fly away in a soft breeze.

From her Sea World tote bag, Betty pulls out playing cards with Holly Hobbie pictures on them. The old-fashioned child with the bonnet hiding her face is just the opposite of Waldeen's own strange daughter. Waldeen sees Holly secretly watching the men. They pick up their beer cans from a pink, shiny tombstone and drink a toast to Joe's great-great-grandfather Joseph McClain, who was killed in the Civil War. His stone, almost hidden in dead grasses, says 1841-1862.

"When I die, they can burn me and dump the ashes in the lake," says C.W.

"Not me," says Joe. "I want to be buried right here."

"*Want* to be? You planning to die soon?"

Joe laughs. "No, but if it's my time, then it's my time. I wouldn't be afraid to go."

"I guess that's the right way to look at it."

Betty says to Waldeen, "He'd marry me if I'd have his kid."

"What made you decide you don't want a kid, anyhow?" Waldeen is shuffling the cards, fifty-two identical children in bonnets.

"Who says I decided? You just do whatever comes natural. Whatever's right for you." Betty has already had three beers and she looks sleepy.

"Most people do just the opposite. They have kids without thinking. Or get married."

"Talk about decisions," Betty goes on. "Did you see 'Sixty Minutes' when they were telling about Palm Springs? And how all those rich people live? One woman had hundreds of dresses and Morley Safer was asking her how she ever decided what on earth to wear. He was *strolling* through her closet. He could have played *golf* in her closet."

"Rich people don't know beans," says Waldeen. She drinks some beer, then deals out the cards for a game of hearts. Betty snatches each card eagerly. Waldeen does not look at her own cards right away. In the pasture, the cows are beginning to move. The sky is losing its blue. Holly seems lost in her book, and the men are laughing. C.W. stumbles over a footstone hidden in the grass and falls onto a grave. He rolls over, curled up with laughter.

"Y'all are going to kill yourselves," Waldeen says, calling to him across the graveyard.

Joe tells C.W. to shape up. "We've got work to do," he says.

Joe looks over at Waldeen and mouths something. "I love you"? Her ex-husband used to stand in front of the TV and pantomime singers. She suddenly remembers a Ku Klux Klansman she saw on TV. He was being arrested at a demonstration, and as he was led away in handcuffs, he spoke to someone off-camera, ending with a solemn message, "I *love* you." He was acting for the camera, as if to say, "Look what a nice guy I am." He gave Waldeen the creeps. That could have been Joe Murdock, Waldeen thinks. Not Joe McClain. Maybe she is beginning to get them straight in her mind. They have different ways of trying to get through to her. The differences are very subtle. Soon she will figure them out.

Waldeen and Betty play several hands of hearts and drink more beer. Betty is clumsy with the cards and loses three hands in a row. Waldeen cannot keep her mind on the cards either. She wins accidentally. She can't concentrate because of the graves, and Joe standing there saying "I love you." If she marries Joe, and doesn't get divorced again, they will be buried here together. She picks out a likely spot and imagines the headstone and the green carpet and the brown leaves that will someday cover the twin mounds. Joe and C.W. are bringing leaves to the center of the graveyard and piling them on the place she has chosen. Waldeen feels peculiar, as if the burial plot, not a diamond ring, symbolizes the promise of marriage. But there is something comforting about the thought, which she tries to explain to Betty.

"Ooh, that's gross," says Betty. She slaps down a heart and takes the trick.

Waldeen shuffles the cards for a long time. The pile of leaves is growing dramatically. Joe and C.W. have each claimed a side of the graveyard, and they are racing. It occurs to Waldeen that she has spent half her life watching guys named Joe show off for her. Once, when Waldeen was fourteen, she went out onto the lake with Joe Suiter in a rented pedal-boat. When Waldeen sees him at the bank, where he works, she always remembers the pedal-boat and how they stayed out in the silver-blue lake all afternoon, ignoring the people waving them in from the shore. When they finally returned, Joe owed ten dollars in overtime on the boat, so he worked Saturdays, mowing yards, to pay for their spree. Only recently in the bank, when they laughed over the memory, he told her that it was worth it, for it was one of the great adventures of his life, going out in a pedal-boat with Waldeen, with nothing but the lake and time.

Betty is saying, "We could have a nice bon-fire and a wienie roast—what *are* you doing?"

Waldeen has pulled her shoes off. And she is taking a long, running start, like a pole vaulter, and then with a flying leap she lands in the immense pile of leaves, up to her elbows. Leaves are flying and everyone is standing around her, forming a stern circle, and Holly, with her book closed on her fist, is saying, "Don't you know *any*thing?"

FAITH

ELLEN WILBUR

I WAS CHRISTENED Faith Marie after my mother's favorite sister, who died of Parkinson's disease the week before her 18th birthday, and whose memory has been preserved with stories of her courage and kindness that always inspired me as a girl. "The good die young," my mother used to sigh, whenever she mentioned Auntie Fay, and the saying always worried me. I wanted to be good. It was the one success I could imagine. While I was young, I tried to be as good as I could be, and for as long as my father lived, I gave him little trouble. I was his pride, my mother used to say. If he hadn't died of a stroke in his sleep that Sunday afternoon ten years ago, my life would never have taken the turn it did.

Were father and mother alive today, I know we'd be living just the same as always. We'd be rising at six and retiring at eleven seven days a week. Father would be winning at checkers, gin rummy, and hearts, and mother and I would still be trying to beat him. On Thursday nights we'd eat out at one of the same three restaurants we always went to, and father would be manager of Loudon Bank and Trust, where he hardly missed a day for 30 years. Wherever he went, he'd be making a grand impression with the profound conviction of his voice and the power of his penetrating eyes, which could see right into a man. And all the anger in him, which he rarely expressed, would still be stored at the back of his eyes or in the edge of his voice, so that even when he laughed you'd know he wasn't relaxed. He never was relaxed, no matter how he tried. I know I'd be dressed like a proper school girl, conservative and neat in cotton or wool dresses, never pants, my long hair pinned at the sides and rippling down my back or tied up in a braid for church or holidays or dinners out, but never short and boyish the way I wear it now. I'd be odorless and immaculate as ever, without an inkling of a body. And people would still be saying what a graceful girl I was. The way I moved was more like floating. The way I'd walk across our lawn, carrying a frosted glass of mother's minted tea out to the hammock where father read his evening paper in the summer before dinner. Sipping his drink and surveying the mowed yard and trimmed bushes and ever blooming flowers (which were my mother's work), he'd tousle my hair and sigh, "Now this is the life," as if he nearly believed it. Listening to him, I know I'd be as pale as ever with the face of a girl who lives as much in books as in the world. And I'd feel as far removed from father and that yard as if each page of history or poetry I'd ever read were another mile I'd walked away from home, and each word I learned another door that closed behind me. Though I'd know, no matter what I read, that my mind would never countermand my conscience or overrule my heart. Looking at me, my father's eyes would turn as warm as ever, the way they only seemed to do when he looked at me. Not even at my mother, whose whole mind and heart had been amended, geared to please him, would he ever look that way without a trace of anger or suspicion. But when he'd look at me I'd see the love he'd never put in words and the faith I'd never disappoint him. I hoped I never would. To keep the peace, his, my mother's and my own, was such a need I had that had they lived I'm sure the three of us would have passed from Christmas to Christmas, through the dips and peaks of every year, like a ship that's traveling the same circle where the view is always familiar.

I remember one Sunday father and I were walking home from church all finely dressed and fit to impress whomever we passed. We crossed the green at the center of town and were approached by a pretty girl no more than 20, who was singing at the top of her voice. She smiled at us as she went by, leaving a strong soprano trill in our ears. I wasn't surprised when father turned to look at her, outraged. "Now that's the kind of bitch I'd like to see run out of town," he said. I knew he'd say the same to mother or me if we ever crossed or disappointed him. Because he couldn't tolerate the slightest deviation from his rules. He loved me with all of his heart on the condition that I please him.

Poor mother couldn't live without father. He'd been the center of her life for 30 years. Unlike father, whose beliefs were sacred to him, she had no strong opinions of her own. When he died, she wept with fear as much as grief, as if his death had been a shattering explosion that left our house and town in ruins. She sat all day in his easy chair and couldn't be moved, as if all of her habits as well as her heart were permanently broken. My words and tears never touched her. Exactly like the garden flowers she used to cut to decorate the house, she faded a little more each day. And it was only two months after father was gone that she was laid beside him. She was buried in June, the week before our high school graduation.

Compton people who wouldn't speak to me today were concerned and kind when mother died. There were several families that offered me a home. But I was 18, old enough to be on my own, and more at ease in the drawing rooms of novels than I'd ever be in any Compton house. Today there are many in town who believe it was a great mistake, letting me live alone. But I was adamant about it, and I appeared to be as responsible and as mature as any valedictorian of her class is expected to be.

I was as shaken by my parents' death as if the colors of the world had all been changed. Having adjusted myself to my father's wishes for so many years, I had no other inclination. After he was gone, I continued to live exactly as he would have liked me to. If anything, I was more careful not to hurt him than before, as if in death his feelings had become more sensitive than ever and the burden of his

happiness was entirely left to me. After mother's death and the end
of school, I took the first available job in town at Compton library. I
was grateful that the work suited me, because I would have taken
any job to keep me busy.

Our town of Compton is a tourist town. For three months out of
every year the population triples, and Decatur street is a slow
parade of bodies and cars that doesn't end for 90 days. At the end of
June, the summer people come. In their enormous yachts and
their flashy cars, they arrive. Every year it is a relief to see them
come and then a relief to see them go. They are so different from
us.

Compton people are short on words. Even in private with their
closest kin, the talk is sparse and actions have more meaning.
Whenever father was troubled, mother made him a squash pie or
one of his other favorites to indicate her sympathy or support. She
never asked him to explain. If a man in Compton is well-liked, he'll
never have to buy himself a drink at the taverns. By the little
favors, by the number of nods he receives on the street, or by the
way he is ignored as much as if he were dead, he'll know exactly
what his measure is with people. And by the silences, by whether
there is comfort or communion in the long pauses between sentences, he'll know exactly how close he is to an acquaintance. I've
always known that Compton people were unique. Our women
never chattered the way the summer women do, as if there were
no end to what they'd say. I've seen the summer people's children
awed and muted by the grave reserve and the repressed emotion of
a Compton child. And I've seen the staring fascination of all
Compton with the open manner of the summer people, who
wander through the streets at noon, baring their wrinkled thighs,
their cleavage and their bulges to the sun for everyone to see—a
people whose feelings flash across their faces as obvious and naked
as if they had no secrets. As a child, I used to wander down to
watch them at the docks. They seemed as alien and entertaining as
a circus troupe. At five o'clock, from boat to boat, there was the
sound of ice and glasses, the smell of tonic water, shaving lotion,
lipstick, and perfume. For evening the women dressed in shocking
pink and turquoise, colors bright enough to make a Compton
woman blush. There was always laughter interwoven with their
conversation, and the liquor made the laughter louder and the talk
still freer until the people were leaning into each other's faces or

falling into embraces with little cries of "darling" or "my dear."
And as I watched them, the gaiety, the confidence, and the warmth
of these people always inspired me with affection and yearning for
the closeness and the freedom that they knew. It wasn't till I was
older I realized that all of their words and embraces brought them
no closer to each other than Compton people are—that the dis-
tances between them were just as painful and exactly as vast, in
spite of the happy illusion they created.

The summer mother died, I walked to work through the crowds
to the rhythm of the cash registers, which never stopped ringing
till ten o'clock at night in the restaurants and gift shops all along
Decatur Street. And all summer the library, which is a busy place
in winter, was nearly empty. I sat at the front desk in the still, dark
room, listening to the commotion of cars and voices in the streets.
And through the windows I could tell the weather in the patch of
sky above the heavy laden elms whose leaves were never still, but
trembled, bobbed, and shuddered to every slightest nuance of the
air. And seemed to capture and proclaim the whole vitality of every
day more truly and completely than any self-afflicted human soul
could ever hope to render it. I have no other memory of that
summer, which disappeared as quickly as it came. But the end of
every Compton summer is the same. Even the most greedy
merchants are frazzled and fatigued by the daily noise and the
rising exuberance of the tourists passing down the coast to home.
By then, the beaches and the streets are strewn with cans and
papers, as if the town had been a carnival or a zoo, and Compton is
glad to see the last of the crowd, whose refuse is only further
evidence of the corruption of their pleasure-happy souls.

My first winter alone there were many nights when I cried
myself to sleep. I missed my mother's quiet presence in the house,
and the smells which always rose from the warm, little kitchen
where she baked or washed or sat across from me on winter
afternoons when I came in from school. Even for a Compton
woman she was more than usually quiet, so shy that she had no
friends. She went to church on Sunday but the rest of the week she
hardly left the yard. My father shopped for all of our food to save
her the pain of going out in public. If she'd had her way, she'd
never have eaten out with us on Thursday nights. But father
insisted on it. "She needs the change," he used to say.

I don't remember mother ever raising her voice to me in anger.

All discipline was left to father. She didn't often kiss or hug me either. But she used to brush my hair one hundred strokes a night, and I remember the gentle touch of her hands. There were times when her shyness made her seem as self-effacing as a nun, and times when I thought I must be living with a saint, the way she read her Bible daily and seemed to have no selfish desires or worldly needs. She dressed in greys and browns, and her dresses hung loose on her bony frame. Though her face was usually serious if not sad, I always believed she was happy in her life with father and me. She couldn't do enough for us, particularly father. About her past I only knew that she was born of alcoholic parents who were now both dead, that she'd worshipped her sister, Faith, and that she never corresponded with her other sister, Mary, who lived in California and was also alcoholic. Most often mother didn't like to reminisce. If I asked her a question she didn't like, she didn't answer it. There were some weeks when she spoke so little that if she hadn't read aloud to me, I hardly would have heard her voice. It was her reading aloud at night that I missed the most after she was gone. It was a habit we kept from before I could read to myself, when to hear her speak page after page was a luxury as soothing and as riveting as any mystery unravelling itself to revelation. It was through the sound of her voice speaking someone else's words that I knew my mother best.

Many nights I cried with all the fear and passion of the child I was and would ever have remained had I been given a choice. And, with a child's love, I saw the images of my father and mother rise up in the dark above my bed as clear and painfully defined as the impression they had left upon my heart. For the simplicity of my old life, I also cried. The simple life of a child who wants to please. For I recognized myself among the spinster women of our town, of whom there are many. Women who never leave the houses of their stern fathers and their silent, sacrificing mothers, houses of a kind so prevalent in Compton. Daughters with all of the rebellion driven out of them at an early age, all of the rudeness skimmed away, severely lashed and molded by the father's anger and the mother's fear of all the changing values in the sinful world. Many of our Compton spinsters are sensitive, high strung. You can see they were the children who avoided pain, preferred endearments and affection. They rarely gossip the way the married women do. To their mothers and their fathers they are faithful and devoted to the end, loyal to the present and the past, forgetful of the future. So much I see about them now that I didn't know when I counted myself one of them.

I had one friend from childhood, Mary Everly, who was studying to be a nurse in a city 50 miles away. Though she sometimes wrote to me, she never came home, finding Compton a "stifling" place. I was close to no one else in town. A few months after mother died, the invitations to supper and the concerned calls from neighbors stopped. Like my mother, I was shy. I had no skill at small talk and was relieved to be left in peace. But I analyzed myself the way a lonely person wonders why he is not loved. And I studied my life until I was as far removed from it as if I had been carved and lifted out of Compton and left to hover like a stranger over everything familiar.

Two times I went to visit Father Ardley in his blue-walled office at the vestry, and twice the touch of his thumb on my forehead, where he signed the cross, brought me to tears. I was drawn to the love of the church. I had an unexamined faith in God, but a fear that His demands would be crushing, were I to take them to heart. It was an irrational fear I tried to explain to Father Ardley, whose eyes were as cold as a winter sky while his voice was like the sun warming it. "You are still in mourning Faith," he said to me. "Such a loss as you've suffered can't be gotten over quickly. You must pray to God and keep yourself busy, child," he said, though I had never been idle in my life, not ever then or now.

For seven years I was as busy as I could be. My conscience kept me well supplied with tasks, and there is no end to what a person ought to do. I worked at the library. I lived in my father's house. I baked for the church bazaars. I visited Father Ardley. The summer people came and left as regular as the tides. I had as many warm acquaintances as ever, and I had no close friends. I still wrote letters to Mary Everly, who was now a nurse, married, and living in Cincinnati with her second baby on the way. Though the memory of my parents' love sustained me, and my father's wishes continued to guide me, time diluted their power to comfort me. Some mornings, walking through the sunny streets to work, the thought of death would take me by surprise, and I knew that mine would mean no more to anyone in town than the sudden disappearance of a picket fence on Elm street or a missing bed of flowers in Gilbey Park.

I never went out with men. Not that I wasn't attractive. My father used to tell me I was pretty, and Mrs. Beggin at the library said I was a "lovely looking girl" and she couldn't see why I wasn't married yet. But Compton men knew different. Something they saw behind my shyness frightened them away. Something my mother and father had never seen. For beneath it all I wasn't a normal Compton woman, not typical no matter how I tried to be. Whether it was the influence of the summer people or the hours I had escaped in books, I was always "different" as far as Compton men could see, and they were just as strange to me.

It was the eighth summer after mother's death that I met Billy Tober. I was just 26. William Tober IV, his family had named him. He was a summer boy, four years younger than I, a college student, though his eyes were the shallow blue of a flier or a sailor. I noticed him before he ever noticed me. I'd always see him with a different girl with the same smile on his lips. He began to come to the library many afternoons. He liked poetry and novels, and he'd ask me for suggestions. I was surprised when he began to appear at the end of the day to walk me home. It wasn't long before we began to meet in the evenings too.

I wish I could say that I remember Billy well, and I wish that I could describe him clearly. But I can't remember much that he ever said and barely how he looked. I only remember the effect he had upon me. As if I knew how it would end, I never invited him to my house, and I'd only allow him to walk me halfway home, which made him laugh at first. In the evening, I'd meet him at Gilbey Park, which is just outside the center of Compton. It is a pretty hill of bushes, trees, and flowers which overlooks the harbor. On a hidden bench we sat and sipped the wine that Billy always brought. Though I'd never tasted liquor or sat and talked with a young man, I was completely at ease. The wine and dusky out-of-doors loosened my tongue until my hidden thoughts rose up as urgently as if my life depended on telling them. It often surprised me what I said, because whenever I was with Billy I was a different woman, so unlike my usual self I'm sure no one in Compton would have recognized me. It was as natural as breathing, the way I'd change into a giddy girl whenever I was with him. I fed on his flattery and couldn't get enough of it. "Where did you ever get such hair?" he asked about the curls my mother never let me cut. After that, it was my eyes he noticed. My neck was regal as a queen's, he said. And there was pride as well as grace in the way I walked. My hands, the smallness of my waist, my legs, my voice he also praised. I couldn't hear enough. For the month of July, we saw each other every night. At home, I'd often stare for an hour at the stranger in the mirror, this woman with a body that a man desired.

Whatever it is that attracts a man to a woman I've too little experience to know. But I believe that for Billy every woman was a challenge. To win her heart as well as her body was his goal. He was as restless and driven a person as I've known. Obsession with a woman must have soothed him. He used to tell me that he loved me, but I'm sure that if he'd heard the same from me, his feelings would have died. If I had loved him, I would have told him. He begged me often enough to say it. But I never was able to. "We're too different," I insisted. "I'm not myself when I'm with you." But I gloried in the power he'd given me. I was in love with his desire, which singled me out from all the world and made the world a painless kingdom where I ruled the more he wanted me. We met most nights in August. We drove out to Haskall Beach to a private place I knew. By then we hardly spoke, and there were times, with his breath hot on my face and his voice crying my name, I felt I'd be more comforted and serene if I were sitting there alone and free of all the yearning human arms can cause.

All those nights we spent together, I never took precautions. "Is it safe?" he asked me many times. But I ignored the question, as if it would have been the crowning sin if I'd been careful to prevent any meaning or possibility of love to come out of the fire of vanity and ignited pride which burned between us. Driving back to town, the silence in the car was so oppressive that it taunted us.

The day that Billy left, I felt relieved, and in the weeks that followed, I didn't miss him once, which surprised me. We wrote no letters to each other. Life went back to normal, and the longer he was gone the more I began to hope I'd never see him again.

When doctor Filser told me I was pregnant, I could see he was surprised the way all Compton would be. I saw the way he looked at me with new, appraising eyes, and I burned to think of all the other eyes that would be privy to scenes of Billy and me on

Haskall Beach. For I knew they'd piece it all together down to every detail.

When I told Father Ardley the news, I aimed the words and threw them at him one by one like darts. But his tone was not what I expected. He wasn't angry with me. "I suppose it was that summer boy you were seeing," he sighed, and he knew enough not to suggest the marriage he'd have insisted upon had Billy Tober been a Compton boy. Instead, he gave me the name of Brighton Adoption Agency.

For all of the nine months, I carried the child as if it were a sin beyond forgiveness and there was no forgetting or ignoring it. I felt my father's wrath in every room of the house, and I never visited his or my mother's graves, knowing the affront it would be. As if they had died again, I felt bereft. I was sure they wanted no part of me now and that I could never turn to them again.

Compton people were not so harsh. One hundred years ago they might have stoned me or run me out of town. Now, as much as they disapproved, they also pitied me. No one tried to deprive me of my job. Though there were some who would no longer speak to me, there were more whose pity moved them to be kinder than before. My humiliation was enough for them and lesson enough for their children. When they saw that my cross was sufficiently heavy, they approved. Even today, times when my heart is light and I'm tempted to laugh in public, I check myself. I know I'll always be on good behavior in Compton, and the more abject I appear the better off I'll be.

It is two o'clock, the last day of May, a Saturday, and all of the windows in the house are open for the first time this season. There is a cold breeze coming off the harbor, running through the rooms in currents which break against the walls and boil the curtains halfway to the ceiling. Every year it is the same, the day of opening the windows. The sea wind scours every corner of the house until its heavy atmosphere is broken. All of the memories which hang in odors are borne away until the rooms are only rooms and this woman, dreaming at a littered kitchen table, is just as relieved as if she'd just received communion, left all of her habits at the altar rail, and returned to her pew with no identity but her joy.

It is so quiet. The baby is asleep upstairs under a pink quilt. When he wakes, he will have roses in his cheeks. He is so blonde, his hair is nearly white. He bears no likeness to my family, and yet the night he was born I knew he was mine as surely as these arms or thoughts belong to me. After the pain of labor, as if I had been delivered of all shame, I asked to see the child. When I saw two waving arms, a tiny head, my heart rose up, amazed. And when they put him in my arms, it was love I held, all warmly wrapped, alive.

So many tired-looking mothers you see in Compton. They hardly seem to care how they appear. Wearing shabby clothes, herding their little broods across the streets, worried and snapping orders at them. But a Compton woman never shows her deepest feelings to the world. When Paul was first at home, I used to kiss his little face at least a hundred times a day. Who but an infant or God could stand so much affection? And all of those kisses were just the beginning of love, the first expression of my newly seeded heart which bloomed, expanded, and flowered with every kiss.

At five o'clock I'd pick the baby up from Mrs. Warren who cared for him the hours I worked. We'd ride home on a crowded bus of Compton women in their fifties, carefully dressed, who rested their heavy bodies behind a row of shopping bags. When they saw the child, their eyes grew soft and bright. "What a love," they'd say, all smiles, and they'd ask his name or age and touch the corner of his blanket so gingerly, with reverence, as if he were to them the fearful treasure he was to me, and they had forgotten all of the strain, the distraction, the heavy weight of care which had exalted them and only remembered how close they once had come to perfect love. I could see them in their kitchens years ago, bathing their babies in the little plastic tubs that Compton mothers use. I could imagine them, once so shy and bending to the will of the town, their fathers, and their husbands, becoming fierce and stubborn, demanding so much satisfaction, comfort, and such happiness for their little ones as they had never dreamed of for themselves.

By now I ought to have the kitchen clean, the wash brought in and folded, and the vegetables picked and washed. It is so rare I sit and dream that when I do the memories come fast and heavy as an avalanche. I've known some cynics who remember only pain and ugliness, as if the way a man remembers corresponds with what he hopes. When Paul was born, it changed my past as well as the future. Now, when I look back, I see beauty. The older the memory, the more beautiful it has become. Even moments of great pain or disappointment have been transformed, given an importance and a dignity they never had at the time, as if whatever happens and wherever I have failed may one day be redeemed in the far future. I pray it will be so.

DÉTENTE

JOYCE CAROL OATES

ALL OF LIFE IS REAL ENOUGH; but it's unevenly convincing.

Begin with a flat blunt bold statement. A platitude, a challenge, a wise folk saying. There are so many wise folk sayings. Hadn't the chairman of the Soviet delegation said, the other evening at the crowded reception, when everyone was being friendly and those who could not speak English were smiling eagerly, hopefully, squeezing their American hosts' hands with a pressure that seemed, well, too intense, hadn't the Chairman, the tall patrician silver-haired Yury Ilyin himself, a former ambassador to the Court of St. James, a former dean of the Gorky Institute, rumored to be an old, difficult, but highly respected friend and rival of the Soviet

President — hadn't he said, in impeccable English, with a certain half-lazy irony that chilled Antonia, who had been confused and charmed by the man's social manners: *"Nothing is more distant than that which is thought to be close. A Russian folk saying, very old. Very wise."*

All of life is real but it's unevenly convincing. There are incalculable blocks of time, days and even weeks, even months, that pass dimly, in a sort of buzzing silence; you sleepwalk through your life. Then the fog lifts. Abruptly. Rudely. You didn't realize you were sleeping and now you've been awakened and the sunshine hurts your eyes, the voices of other people hurt your ears, you find yourself astonished at what stands before you.

His name was Vassily Zurov. She rehearsed it, in silence. A tall, slightly stooped man in his mid-forties, lean, cautious, less given to mute strained smiles than his Soviet colleagues, but passionate in his speech, with a habit of widening his eyes so that the whites showed above the dark iris, fierce and glowering. Now he jabbed the air, and struck his chest, his heart, speaking so rapidly that Ilyin had to signal him to slow down, out of consideration for the interpreter. His metal-rimmed glasses had gone askew on his long thin nervous nose. A lank strand of dark lusterless hair had fallen across his rather furrowed forehead. He looked, Antonia thought, with that flash of irony and resentment that always preceded her reluctant interest in a man, like an old-fashioned divinity student. Wasn't there one in Dostoyevsky, in *The Possessed*, hadn't he been one of the demons. . . . If Antonia hadn't been told at last Saturday's briefing that all of the members of the Soviet delegation were probably members of the Communist Party, she would have thought nevertheless, A fanatic of some sort: look at that pale twisted mouth.

His language was, of course, incomprehensible. A massive, intimidating windstorm, a marvelous barrage of sounds, utterly alien. The Russian language: a language of giants, of legendary folk. Like something in a dream. Ungraspable. She stared and listened. She was a woman of some linguistic ability, she could speak fluent French and Italian, and could manage German, but though she had tried to learn some Russian in preparation for this conference she was forgetting it all: the slow stumbling childlike words, the somewhat preposterous sounds, the humble refuge in *Da, da*. She had forgotten everything. In fact it had turned out to be a perplexing chore for her simply to remember the pronunciations of the Soviet delegates' names. You must understand that these people are often quite sensitive, Antonia was told. It's important that we don't inadvertently insult them.

Vassily Zurov paused impatiently, and the interpreter — hidden at the far end of the room, inside a glass-fronted booth — said in a voice that managed uncannily to imitate, or perhaps to mimic, the Russian's florid style: *What is the function of art? From what does it spring in our hearts? Why do a people treasure certain works, which they transmit to the generations that follow? What significance does this have? Is it a human instinct? Is there a hunger for it, like a hunger for food, and love, and community? Without the continuity of tradition, what meaning is there in life? As our Chinese comrades discovered to their chagrin, after having tried to erase their entire heritage—*

But this was the interpreter's voice, this was another man's voice; and Antonia was having difficulty with her headphones. Somehow the mechanism would not work for her. When it worked, it was seemingly by accident: a few minutes later and the words sounding in her ears might be flooded by static. . . . *the writer's mission in our two great nations? Is there a historical inevitability in art that carries us all along.* . . . Vassily Zurov hadn't the diplomat's aplomb of Ilyin, or of several of the older, more distinguished members of the Soviet delegation; Antonia remembered, or half-remembered, from the briefing that he had not been allowed to visit the United States before. He had been, from time to time, in trouble with the authorities. Had he actually spent some time in a labor camp in the North, or had he been closely associated with a "liberal" magazine whose editor had been expelled from the Writers' Union and sent away. . . . Surreptitiously Antonia scanned the official list of the man's credits. It was part of a lengthy document prepared by the Soviet delegation's secretary, and listed only achievements that, she supposed, were impressive in another part of the world. *The Order of the Red Banner. Two Lenin Orders. Medal for Valiant Labour.* Two medals for prose fiction, 1971, 1975. Contributor to the journal *Literaturnoye Obozreniye.* Born in Novgorod, now a resident of Moscow.

How warmly, how guilelessly the man spoke . . .! His voice was somewhat hoarse, as if he were fighting a cold. During his fifteen-minute presentation he had led the discussion — "What Are the

Humanistic Values of Present-Day Literature?" — away from the naming of specific authors and titles and dates, which Matthew Burke, the chairman of the American delegation, had initiated, and into an abstract, inchoate region of ideas. Such speculations about life, and art, and the meaning of the universe, had fascinated Antonia many years ago, before she had grown up to become a professional, and surprisingly successful, writer; listening to Zurov now, she felt herself quite powerfully moved. It was all so child-like, so ludicrously appealing. The man's initial caution had fallen away and he was speaking with the urgency of an artist who has come halfway around the world to meet with fellow artists and to discuss matters of the gravest importance.

A photographer for the U.S. Information services was crouching before Zurov, preparing to take a picture. The man's head was hidden from Antonia by his camera: an eerie sight. Zurov paused, and the interpreter translated his words, blasting Antonia's ears in a flood of capricious static. She could not quite decipher what was being said. *Art is political. Art is apolitical . . .?*

The photographer took a number of pictures, rapidly, and Zurov, distracted by him, began to stammer. Antonia blushed. It was an old habit, an old weakness — she blushed scarlet when in the presence of someone who was himself embarrassed. The earphones went silent. Then Zurov mumbled a few more words, now staring down at the microphone before him, and the simulta-neous translation overlapped his faltering voice: *Thank you, that is all I wish to say.*

From her attractive third-floor room in the Rosedale Institute Antonia called her friends Martin and Vivian in Chicago. How are the Adirondacks this time of year, isn't June rather early for the mountains, they said, how is the conference going, how do you feel, do you expect to accomplish anything or is it just some sort of diplomatic game. . . . She heard her voice replying to their voices and it sounded normal enough.

How do you feel, Antonia, they asked.

Much better, she said.

After a while they said: Well, he isn't here. And he didn't call.

He didn't call?

One of us has been home the past three nights and he didn't call, are you absolutely certain he was headed this way . . .? You know

Whit sometimes exaggerates. He has such a . . . he has such a surrealistic sense of humor.

I didn't know that, Antonia said.

She spoke so gently, no one could have said whether she was being ironic or not.

They talked for a few more minutes, about the Russians, about the embarrassing political context — the President's highly-publicized stand on "human rights," the recent defection of a Soviet representative to the United Nations — and about mutual friends. As if to console her they offered news of Vera Cullen's divorce: Antonia thought the gesture a rather crude one.

What shall we say if he does call, or if he shows up . . .?

I don't know, Antonia said.

Give us your number there and we'll tell him to call. If he said he was coming here he must be on his way, unless of course something happened. . . . Should we have him call you at the conference?

I don't know, Antonia said, pouring an inch or two of cognac into a plastic glass. The cognac was a gift — a rather premature one, she thought — from a red-faced, gregarious, portly Ukranian who had been very attentive to her the previous evening, and at breakfast and lunch today. *All the way to my homeland,* he said, in careful English, and Antonia had not had the heart to correct him. His name was something like Kolevoy. According to the biographical sheet he was a poet, a writer of sketches, and a member of the board of the Soviet writers' Union. . . . I don't think so, she said.

How long has he been gone? When did he leave?

A few days before I did.

Did he take many clothes, did he take much money . . .?

No, Antonia said. But then he never does.

A pleasantly vulnerable feeling. As if convalescent. But it's been seven years now, Antonia thought reasonably. Surely I have recovered.

Numbness. Emptiness. She was not the sort of woman to refer everything to her femaleness, to her womb; the very thought bored her. Yet something circled, bat-like, nervous and fluttering, about the miscarriage of seven years ago, in the first year of her second marriage. Such things mean a great deal, she thought. Though probably they mean nothing.

It *did* bore her, she would never think of it again.

The problems inherent in a bourgeois existence, she would explain to Vassily Zurov, arise out of idleness. One must think about something in order to fill up time. So we think habitually of sex and death, of loss, of symbolic gestures, dismal anniversaries, failed connections. . . .

She was in retreat from her own life, which she might or might not explain to Zurov. There would be, after all, the problem of language: a common vocabulary. So far they had grinned at each other over glasses of sherry, and talked through one of the several interpreters — You are a poet? No? A writer of prose? Unfortunately your works are not available in my country. . . .

She had not wanted to participate in the Rosedale Conference on the Humanities, though the four-day meeting of Soviet and American writers, critics, and professors of literature did seem to her a worthwhile event. There were the usual promising words, and she liked them well enough to repeat them silently to herself, like a prayer: *unity, cooperation, universal understanding, East and West, friendship, sympathy, common plight, peace, hope for the future*. At the opening session the Soviet chairman Ilyin had even spoken, in English, of the need for Soviets and Americans to resist "our common enemy who seeks to tragically divide us." (The American chairman Burke called his delegation to a meeting room afterward, in order to speculate aloud, with the assistance of a Soviet specialist from Harvard and rapporteur named Lunt, on the possible meaning of Ilyin's carefully oblique words; but the words remained indecipherable, a kind of poetry.) Antonia had not wanted to participate though two friends of hers, or were they perhaps only acquaintances — the poet and translator Frank Webber, and the novelist Arnold Barry — were to be in attendance. In the end she said yes, for no particular reason.

She was a small-bodied woman of thirty-six who looked a great deal younger, mainly because of her shoulder-length, sumptuous brown hair. Which was grotesquely misleading: she did not feel sumptuous, had not felt sumptuous for many years. In fact the word puzzled her. Struck her as faintly comic. Her pale green eyes were slightly prominent and always a little damp. Her skin was an almost dead white: she hated it, and was made uneasy by well-intentioned compliments on her appearance. And by frequent half-accusatory remarks about her "youthfulness" — on the first morning of the conference a young woman journalist told Antonia with a beaming smile that she had pictured her as much older — in fact elderly.

She was the author of two slender novels, both written in her early twenties. They were fastidious and self-conscious, set in the upper-middle-class Catholic milieu of her girlhood in Boston. Obliquely autobiographical, but not stridently so, they were admired by the few critics who took the time to review them, but they were not commercially successful, and were reprinted in paperback only after Antonia achieved eminence for other work — essays on literature, art, and culture in general, some of them iconoclastic and devastatingly critical. Yet for the most part the essays were appreciative; they were certainly methodical, models of unobtrusive research and scholarship. In the world she customarily called "real" — that is, the world outside her imagination, her ceaselessly thinking and brooding self, her book- and music-cluttered apartment on East 72 Street — she was constantly meeting distorted images of herself which came to her with the blunt authority of seeming more real than the Antonia she knew. Though she was dismayingly shy, so quiet at large social gatherings that she might be mistaken for a mute, there was the widespread idea, evidently, that "Antonia Mason" was shrill and argumentative and maliciously — but, so her admirers claimed, *brilliantly* — unfair. She had published in the past decade interpretive and generally positive essays on John Cage, Octavio Paz, Iris Murdoch, Robert Rauschenberg, contemporary German films, contemporary American poetry, and other subjects, but it was for lengthy and perhaps somewhat sardonic assessments of the achievement of Tennessee Williams, Robert Motherwell, the works of Feminist novelists, and those of the "New Journalists" that she was most remembered. It must, she supposed, mean something significant: of six brief reviews she might publish in the New York *Times* in a year it was the one sarcastically negative review that would excite comment. Acquaintances telephoned to congratulate her on speaking honestly, people as far away as Spokane and Winnipeg might write to thank her for having made them laugh, friends alluded to her wit and courage and intelligence — as if these qualities, if they were hers at all, were not present in her more serious work. Even her husband, Whitney, complimented her when she was a "fighter" (his word) in public. If she complained that popular culture seems

to push individuals toward what is most aggressive, most comba-
tive, and least valuable, he brushed aside her remarks as disingen-
uous. "At heart you're really competitive, you're really a hostile
person," he often said, narrowing one eye in a mock wink. "Which
accounts for your astonishing *gentleness* . . . and your exasperating
charity. And your proclivity to forgive."

She could not help forgiving him: he was her husband, after all,
despite his infidelities. And she loved him. Or had loved him. Or,
at the very least, had consoled herself during a rather bad time
some years ago with the thought that she was capable of loving
someone after all — she would devote herself to this new relationship with Whitney Albright, she would meditate upon it, plunge
into it, make the old-fashioned sacrifices now being mocked by her
contemporaries, and thereby save herself. So she was, quite apart
from her promise as a novelist, and her uncontested brilliance as a
cultural critic, a genuine woman: divorced but remarried, once
again someone's wife. She was also someone's daughter and someone's sister. One of the Soviet delegates had referred to her as the
"leading American woman of letters" — or so the translation had
gone. Meanings hung on her like loose clothing.

Someone's estranged wife.

Someone's abandoned wife.

Is it so, Yury Ilyin's secretary, a plump, affable young man with
thick glasses, asked Antonia and several other Americans, that
each year in the United States there are between 700,000 and
1,000,000 children who run away from home . . .? We find this
hard to believe and wonder if the figure was not misreported.

It could not be said, however, that Whitney had "run away." For
one thing adults do not "run away"; they simply leave. And the
circumstances of his leaving were abrupt and dramatic enough to
suggest that the action was going to be temporary — his reply to
her reply, so to speak. (It was not the first time that Whitney had
left her. Several years ago, when driving to the West Coast, where
Antonia was scheduled to participate in an "arts festival" at one of
the state universities in California, Whitney had left her in the St.
Louis zoo, in front of the ocelot cage. The circumstances were
amusing, perhaps, though Antonia had not found them so at the
time. For weeks she and Whitney had been careful with each
other, gentle and solicitous and patient, and the long drive to
California was meant to be a vacation, a sort of second honeymoon;

perhaps the strain of being so unrelievedly nice precipitated a violent quarrel during which each accused the other of being incapable of love and "worthless" as human beings. Antonia had been admiring the ocelots, especially a lithe playful ocelot kitten named Sweetheart, and Whitney had liked them well enough—strolling through the zoo was something to do, after all, a way of killing time until late afternoon and cocktails—but he hadn't Antonia's concern about a penned-up ocelot that was crying angrily and plaintively to be released into the larger cage. The creature was hidden from sight, though by standing on the railing Antonia could *almost* see it. "My God," she said, nearly in tears, "listen to it crying, it sounds just like a child, have you ever heard anything so heartbreaking in your life. . . ." Whitney urged her to come away. After all, the cat must be quarantined for some reason: the zookeepers knew what they were doing. "But it's so cruel. It's so stupidly cruel," Antonia said. The ocelot's enraged full-throated miaows were really quite disturbing. Whitney said something further, Antonia said something further, and then they were shouting at each other, and could not stop. I suppose the goddam ocelot is a symbol of something, Whitney said, I suppose I'm meant to interpret all this in some personal way, a goddam fucking symbolic commentary on our marriage, and Antonia had screamed that it wasn't a symbol, it was a living creature, how could anyone listen to it howl like that and not feel pity and want to help. . . . In the end Whitney had walked away. Antonia did not follow him. An hour later, when she returned to their hotel, much calmer and ready to apologize if it seemed likely that he, for his part, would apologize, she discovered that he had checked out, had taken his suitcases, his share of the toiletries, and the car.)

It might be said that she was abandoned now, and had been so since Whitney disappeared twelve days before, after a quarrel at a friend's apartment; but she did not think of herself as abandoned. Talking with a group of Soviet writers, among them Vassily Zurov, she had answered a question about her marital status by saying with a smile that "such questions were no longer relevant"—she wanted to meet with them as a person, as a fellow writer, not as a woman. Perhaps the translation had been witty: they had all laughed, though not disrespectfully. Zurov said, "That's so, that's right," in fairly emphatic English.

Yet she could not resist, a while later, asking him if he was married. She asked him directly, not through an interpreter; his reply was a dismissive shoulder shrug.

Which, of course, she could not confidently translate, for perhaps he had not understood her question. And she hadn't the ability to ask it in his language.

He sat beside her in the Institute dining room, and hovered near at the cocktail gatherings, and frequently stared at her during the sessions, quite visibly not listening; his hair was bunched and spiky and disheveled by the earphones, with which he had a great deal of trouble. Once when several members of the Soviet delegation were laughing zestfully at a lengthy anecdote told to them by a stout, swarthy man from Georgia—it turned out to be, rather incredibly, about Stalin himself, Stalin as someone's old uncle, gruff but lovable—he pulled her aside and spoke emphatically, half in English, half in Russian, managing to communicate to her the need they had for exercise, for a walk around the lake before dinner, didn't she agree . . .?

She agreed. And halfway around the lake, as they stood on a grassy knoll staring at the glittering water and the Institute's fieldstone buildings on the far shore, he took her arm gently and slipped it through his. She did not resist, though she did not lean against him. "It's lovely, isn't it," she said. "Just at sunset. Just at this moment."

"Yes," he said doubtfully. He was obviously quite excited: she saw a flush on his throat, working its way unevenly up to his face.

At the American delegates' briefing Antonia and her colleagues had been told that the Soviet delegation was, of course, under strict control. They would be watching each other closely, spying on each other. They would above all be intimidated by their chairman and his aides. Yet it didn't seem to Antonia that this was the case. Vassily was his own man: it seemed quite clear that he was no more explicitly subservient to his chairman than the American delegates were to Matthew Burke. Wasn't it all rather exaggerated, Antonia wondered, this drama of East and West, Communists and American citizens, the outmoded vocabulary of the Cold War, the strain, the tension, the self-conscious gestures of brotherhood, the ballet of détente. . . . Walking with Vassily

Zurov she felt only a curious sort of elation. She could not help but be flattered by his interest in her; he was an attractive man, after all.

And it seemed to her that he was rapidly becoming more proficient in English.

At breakfast the next morning they sat together, alone together. She asked him about his stories: would they ever be translated into English, did he think? Were they political?

He asked her to repeat the question.

It would have been difficult for Antonia to determine precisely what, in him, attracted her so powerfully. For some time she had stopped thinking of men as men, she had stopped thinking of herself as a woman in terms of men, the whole thing had come to seem so futile, so upsetting. Adultery appealed intermittently, but only as a means of revenging herself upon Whitney; and as her love for Whitney waned her desire for revenge waned. There was, still, the incontestable value of adultery as a means of getting through a certain block of time: it was an activity charged with enough passion, enough recklessness, to absorb thought, to dissipate anxiety. If she allowed herself to be touched by a man, if she leaned forward to brush her lips against a man's lips, or to allow a man to kiss her, she would have no time to think of the usual vexing questions. Her husband. Her marriage. Her meandering "career." And there were the slightly tawdry, glamorous and melancholy questions of her girlhood: What is the meaning of life? Does God exist? Are we born only to die? Is there a means of achieving immortality . . . ? The Russians would not have jeered at such questions. Vassily Zurov would not have jeered.

At last he understood her question about his writing, and labored to reply in English. He leaned forward, gesturing broadly, staring fixedly at her as he spoke. "My stories are political, yes," he said with great care. ". . . As all art."

Antonia felt a sense of triumph.

"All art? Did you say art? . . . But all art isn't political," she said.

She was speaking too rapidly, he begged her to repeat what she had said.

"Art isn't political," she said slowly. "Not in its essence."

He stared at her, smiling, uncomprehending. She saw a dot of blood in his left eye. He adjusted his glasses, still staring. Antonia said, holding her hands out to him, palm upward, in an innocent, impulsive gesture whose meaning she could not have explained, "Of course some forms of art are political. Some writers are basically political writers. But in its essence art isn't political, it's above politics, it refers only to itself. I'm sure you understand, I'm sure you agree. Politics necessitates choosing sides, it excludes too much of life, life's nuances and subtleties, art can't be subservient to any dogma, it insists upon its own freedom. Political people are always superficial people. I couldn't be forced to choose sides — it's brutal, it isn't even human—"

He shook his head, baffled. He asked her to repeat her remarks.

She said only, blushing, that art isn't political. In its essence it isn't political.

He replied half in English and half in Russian, with a barking laugh that startled her. He seemed to be saying that art *is* political.

"Everything," he said firmly. He lifted a glass of water and gestured with it, as if toasting Antonia; he took a sip; he then extended it across the table to Antonia as if he wanted her to drink from it — but she drew away, baffled and a little annoyed. He was so demonstrative, so noisy. "Everything," he said with a queer wide smile, a half-mocking smile, "is political. You see, the water too. In the glass like this. Everything."

She shook her head to indicate that she didn't understand. And now that others were coming to join them, now that their intimate, edgily flirtatious conversation was becoming public, she felt suddenly drained of energy, unequal to his vehemence. She hadn't any appetite: she would have liked to go back to bed.

Vassily greeted the others in Russian and waved for them to sit down. He fairly pulled one of the English-speaking Soviets into the seat beside him, so that he could help with the conversation with Antonia. She looked from one to the other, smiling her strained polite smile, as Vassily spoke in rapid Russian, watching her cagily.

The interpreter — listed as a poet in the dossier, but named by Lunt as an *apparatchik*, a party hack — beamed at Antonia and translated in heavily-accented but correct English: "Mr. Zurov inquires — you do not think that art is political? But it is always political. It seeks to alter human consciousness, hence it is a political act. He says also that a mere glass of water is an occasion for politics. He says — but you see, we were talking about this last night, Miss Mason, some of us were talking about this last night, and Mr. Zurov insists upon bringing it up — perhaps you did not read the local newspaper yesterday? — no? Mr. Zurov refers to the front-page article about the poisons that have drained into the mountain lakes in this area. He says — through the winter, rain and snow have been blown into the mountains from somewhere to the west where there are coal and oil combustion plants, and nitric and sulfuric oxides have been concentrated in the snow, which has now melted, do you see? — and there are now toxins in the lakes — he is not certain of the technical terms, perhaps others here would know — and the fish, the trout, have died in great numbers. And so — "

Vassily interrupted him, speaking excitedly, watching Antonia's face. The man then translated, with a slight bow of his head in her direction: "Mr. Zurov does not mean to distress you on this lovely sunny day. He says — forgive me! But perhaps you did not know, perhaps it needed to be pointed out, that the simple act of drinking a glass of water can be related to politics and to history, if only you know the context in which it is performed, *and the quality of the water,* but of course if you are ignorant and do not know or choose to know, you will imagine it is above politics and you are un-touched. He says, however, to forgive him for being so blunt, but it is his way, it is his only way of speaking."

Impulsively Vassily reached out to seize Antonia's hand, for all to see. His smile was wide and anguished, showing irregular teeth. The gesture surprised Antonia but she hadn't the presence of mind to draw away. "Excuse me, Miss Mason? Yes? It is all right?"

"Of course it's all right," Antonia whispered. But she felt shaken: it was not an exaggeration to say that she felt almost ill. And there was the entire day to get through, the morning and afternoon sessions, and the usual lengthy dinner. . . . Staring at Vassily's slightly bloodshot eyes she knew herself on the very edge of an irreparable act: at the very least, she might burst into tears in public. But how trivial, how demeaning, even to care about such things! She drew her hand out of Vassily's dry, warm, eager grip. "Of course," she said faintly.

A long day of speeches. Prepared remarks. "Allow me to speak, I will be brief," said a thick-bodied swarthy critic and editor from a Soviet journal that translated, according to Antonia's notes, as *The Universe.* He then spoke, not quite spontaneously, for forty-five minutes. . . . Why do United States citizens know so little of

Soviet literature, why is there so much racist and pornographic material for sale in your country, why do you allow a "free market" for the peddling of such trash? Though it was a blatant attack, barely disguised by diplomatic language, the American delegation replied in civil, careful language: one of the novelists, whose books Antonia could never bring herself to read, managed to say something fairly convincing about the First Amendment, human rights, freedom of the press, democracy, the fear of censorship in any form. "And it's important, I think, for us to know, in a democracy, what people seem to want. Pornography disgusts me as much as it disgusts anyone, but I think . . . I think it might be valuable, in a democracy, simply to know what great masses of people seem to want." Antonia's colleague spoke softly but with a sophistication that pleased her.

Yes, freedom is desirable, certainly it is desirable, but racist trash, pornographic trash . . . ? "Such 'literature,' " one of the Soviets said, "strikes us as no more than a means of extracting money from the market."

The issue of dissident writers: tentatively, gingerly, brought up. But Yury Ilyin brushed it aside. Such a matter is not, strictly speaking, a literary or humanistic matter, it has to do with illegal activities, the right of a sovereign state to deal with its criminals, perhaps we will have time to discuss it later. With a chilly, impertinent smile Ilyin said he supposed the Americans were primarily interested in legitimate Soviet writers: otherwise why did the Rosedale Institute extend its generous invitation to this group to visit the United States and to meet with outstanding American writers, their colleagues and equals in the field of literature . . . ?

Vassily was sitting hunched over, peering short-sightedly at the table before him, or at his clasped hands. He had taken off his glasses; with his spiky, rumpled hair he looked like a man surprised in his sleep. Antonia had the impression that he was about to interrupt Ilyin. His pale mouth worked, his forehead was deeply furrowed. He had been, some years ago, a "dissident" writer himself—or at any rate he had gotten into trouble with Party officials. Perhaps he had even been sent away for a while, to a mental asylum or a labor camp. The rapporteur from Harvard, Lunt, hadn't offered much background information for Vassily Zurov, he was one of several "mysterious" members of the delegation, little known in the West, with only a few short stories translated and anthologized. . . . Suppose we become lovers, Antonia thought idly. Then he will tell me everything. Then he will tell me all his secrets.

Prolonged remarks, ostensibly "spontaneous." Frequent references to "the great Mayakovsky"—a poet of mediocre gifts, surely?—and to the concept of "socialist realism," which Antonia had supposed to be outmoded; but perhaps it was not, not entirely. Marxist metaphysics explained succinctly by a youngish Moscow novelist who was also First Secretary of his Writers' Union: we have first matter, there is no contesting that, and then comes spirit, and then comes "spirituality" (but there is no exact word for that concept in Russian) which is the activity of highly organized matter. . . . Antonia tried to take notes, it would be her turn to speak in a few minutes, she was becoming unusually nervous. *The activity of highly organized matter.* But perhaps the translation was only an approximate one? How could one know? How could one be certain?

Maxim Gorky, who is the "father of Soviet literature." Lenin, who stated clearly that the main function of the printed word is organizational. Jack London, Theodore Dreiser, Stephen Crane. Steinbeck. Chekhov. Dostoyevsky, now being reexamined. Vassily, who had spoken little, said a few words about "your great American poet William Carlos Williams." When it was Antonia's turn she spoke briefly of the "post-modern" novel, its movement inward, toward lyricism, toward poetry, away from the statistical world, the objectively historical or political world. . . . She twisted her pen nervously as the Soviets gazed at her with great interest. But when she finished only a single question was directed to her, by the Ukrainian Kolevoy, and it was clearly meant to be courteous, to show his appreciation of her words.

She wondered how those frail words were being translated.

Another photographer was taking pictures, crouching discreetly in the aisle, moving forward on his haunches. He took a number of pictures of Ambassador Ilyin, who gave the impression of ignoring him.

Antonia watched Vassily and wondered what he was thinking. What he had endured. Her delegation had been told that they must not mention certain things to the Soviets—under no circumstances should they inquire about certain books, written by Soviets but published outside the country, nor should they inquire about dissidents whose work they might know. Labor camps, prisons, mental asylums: don't bring the subjects up. Antonia had read that during Stalin's reign several hundred poets, playwrights, and prose writers were murdered by the secret police, in addition to the other thousands, or millions. . . . And in the sixties there was the highly-publicized case of Joseph Brodsky, put on trial for being an idler and a parasite without any socially useful work, sentenced originally to five years of forced labor in the North. And, more outrageous, even, the joint trial of Siniavsky and Yuli Daniel, who dared claim artistic freedom, the right to follow wherever one's imagination leads. . . . If Antonia remembered correctly the men were both sentenced to several years' hard labor in a "severe regime camp." There was also the example of a young man named Galanskov, the editor of a Moscow literary magazine of "experimental" tendencies, first sentenced to a mental institution, then to a concentration camp where he was allowed to die. Perhaps she would ask Vassily about him: it was quite likely that they were acquainted. . . . When she thought of how little she risked, in publishing her essays, even her autobiographical novels, she was stricken with a sense of guilt.

Matthew Burke was speaking, perhaps too slowly, on the "humanistic tradition" in the West. Yury Ilyin then spoke of the "humanistic tradition" in his country. Antonia's head began to ache. She rarely suffered from headaches, this was really quite extraordinary, it seemed to have to do with the simultaneous translation: the phenomenon of hearing Russian spoken and hearing, immediately, its English translation, the words often overlapping, one voice louder than the other and then suddenly subsiding in a buzz of static, only to surface again a few seconds later. And what was the reality behind the words, to what did they refer. . . ? In her world she had grown accustomed to the relative impotence of words: they might have *meaning*, but they rarely had *effect*. But in the Soviet world even the most innocent of words might have an immediate, profound effect. . . .

Ilyin was concluding the morning's "very fruitful discussion." He was speaking of brotherhood, of universal understanding, the hope for global peace. Antonia watched him guardedly, as did the others. One simply could not trust the man. He followed a script, a scenario, possibly prepared in advance; it was clear that most of the

members of his own delegation did not know what to expect from
him. Though he had proudly identified himself earlier as being the
son of "peasant stock" he was clearly an aristocrat in spirit, barely
tolerant of his colleagues, and contemptuously formal with the
American chairman, whom he challenged often and addressed as
"dear Matthew." They had said of him a few days before that he
was an anti-Semite. He was a neo-Stalinist. They had said . . . oh
they had said wicked things, but Antonia hadn't wanted to listen,
she hadn't wanted to believe, after all the conference was designed
to bring people together, weren't they all involved in literature, in
the humanities, wouldn't it serve the cause of "world peace" if she
and Eliot Harder and Arnold Barry sat at the same table in the
Institute's handsome dining room with their Soviet friends Vitaly
and Boris and Grigory and Vassily and Yury himself. . . . A popular
Leningrad poet named Kozanov, whose work Antonia had been
reading with admiration, had been withdrawn from the delegation
at the last moment and his place given to the mysterious Kolevoy,
according to Lunt; an obvious party hack. What this means about
Kozanov I wouldn't want to speculate, Lunt said with a conspira-
torial drop in his voice, it might mean nothing or it might indicate
bad news, very bad news. But I wouldn't want to speculate.

Ambassador Ilyin ended the session by expressing the hope that
the United States would someday come to the enlightened realiza-
tion that total freedom, in the arts as in any other sphere of life, is a
very ignorant, one might almost say a very naïve, condition. "We
aspire, after all, to the level of civilized man, we wish to leave
barbarism behind," he said with a smile.

In Antonia's room she said, far too rapidly, to Vassily: "I'm not
here to practice diplomacy, I'm a cultural critic, I think of myself as
an amateur even at that, I don't have the stamina, the nerves, for
this sort of thing—"
He had come to bring her gifts—a necklace, a slender bottle of
vodka, a box of candies with a reproduction of the Ural Mountains
on its cover, three slim, rather battered volumes of his short
stories, in Cyrillic. Now he stood perplexed and uncomprehending. "What is—? You are angry? You are not—" Here he paused,
squinting with effort. "—not leaving?"
"I came here to talk about literature, I didn't come to hear

debates about politics, it's very upsetting to me, to all of us, I mean the American delegation — I mean — "

Vassily seized her hands, staring urgently at her.

"You are not leaving?"

He kissed her hands, stooping over. She stared at the top of his head, at the thinning hair at the crown, feeling a sensation of . . . it must have been a wave of . . . something like love, or at least strong affection, emotion. He was so romantic, so passionate, he was an anachronism in her own world, she did love him, suddenly and absurdly. She could not understand his words — he was speaking now in Russian, excitedly — but there was no mistaking the earnest, almost anguished look in his eyes. She felt a sensation of vertigo, exactly as if she were standing at a great height with nothing to protect her from falling.

In an impulsive gesture she was to remember long afterward she reached out to hold him, to bring his head against her breasts. He was crouched over, one knee on the edge of her bed, gripping her tightly, murmuring something she could not understand. She felt him trembling; to her amazement she realized that he was crying. "You're so sweet," she murmured, hardly knowing what she said, wanting only to comfort him, "you're so kind, so tender, I love you, I wish I could help you, you don't know anyone here, you must be homesick, the strain of these past few days has been terrible, I wish we could go away somewhere and rest, and hide, I wish there were just the two of us, I've never met a man so kind, so tender. . . ." He held her close, desperately; she could feel his hot anxious breath against her breasts; he seemed to be trying to burrow into her, to hide his face in her. "I know you've suffered," she said softly, stroking his hair, stroking the back of his warm neck, "you can't be happily married, I know your life has been hard, they've tried to break you, I wish I could help you, I wish we could be alone together without all these other. . . ."

They would be lovers, Antonia thought wildly. Perhaps she would return with him to Moscow. Perhaps she would have a baby: it wasn't too late, she was only thirty-six. It wasn't too late. Stroking his neck and shoulders, embracing him awkwardly (she was thrown slightly off balance by the way they were standing), she felt tears sting her eyes, she was in danger of sobbing uncontrollably. Love. A lover. A Communist lover. Whitney would jeer at her: how can you be so deluded? You can't possibly love this man since you don't know him, you can't possibly love anyone since you're incapable of love. . . .

"You're so far from home," she murmured, confused. "We're all . . . we're all homesick. . . ."

He straightened to kiss her, and at that moment the telephone rang, and it was over. He jumped away from her, and she away from him, as the phone rang loudly, jarringly; and it was over.

Disheveled, flush-faced, Vassily backed out of her room like a frightened, guilty child, muttering words of apology she could not understand.

They were never alone together again.

The next morning, enlivened by a spirit of adventure, she and Vassily and one of the interpreters went for a rowboat ride before the session at nine o'clock, but the wind was chilly, Antonia regretted not having worn her heavy sweater and scarf, and even before the accident—though perhaps it could not be called an "accident," it was simply a consequence of their stupidity—she found Vassily's exuberant, expansive manner jarring. His dark blue shirt was partly unbuttoned, showing graying kinky hair; he looked at her too earnestly, too openly, with a fond broad smile that showed his crooked, rather stained teeth. Quite obviously he was in love with her: the interpreter laughed gaily, shaking his head as if he were being tickled, possibly not translating everything Vassily said. She began to worry about being late for the final session, she brushed her hair out of her watering eyes repeatedly, smiling a strained smile, wondering if this little adventure—there was a notice in the Institute lobby, on the bulletin board, warning against "unauthorized" boat rides on the lake—might get them into trouble.

"We should head for shore," Antonia said. Vassily was rowing, and he was so uncoordinated, so awkward, that the oars were splashing water onto her legs and ankles. Her feet felt damp. "Tell him," she pleaded with the interpreter, "to head for shore. It's getting late."

The interpreter, one of the more genial members of the Soviet delegation, spoke a few words in Russian, and Vassily replied with a gay shoulder shrug, and a torrent of Russian, and the interpreter leaned over to Antonia to translate, somewhat apologetically:

"Vassily says to tell you that we are all running away. An escape into the mountains. Into the woods. He says to tell you that he is very fond of you, he is very fond of you, perhaps you are aware of the fact, previous to this he has traveled in Northern Africa but not in Northern America, this is his first voyage, he is very grateful, he does not want the conference to end. . . . Just a joke, you know, a jest, running away into the mountains, Vassily is known for his humor, perhaps you have noted it."

Then Antonia noticed that her feet and ankles were wet because the boat was leaking.

There was a brief period of alarm, and consternation, though never any panic — for how could the three of them drown, so close to shore, in full view of anyone who chose to watch them from the Institute? The water was very cold. Antonia half-sobbed with the shock of it, and the discomfort, and the absurdity. Despite Vassily's spirited rowing they did not quite make it to the dock: they were forced to abandon the sinking rowboat in about three feet of freezing water, less than a dozen yards from safety. "I will save you — No danger — I will save — " Vassily cried, his teeth chattering from the cold. He tried to make a joke of it, though he was clearly chagrined. The interpreter cursed in Russian, his face gone hard and murderous, his skin dark with blood.

Vassily helped Antonia to shore, and insisted upon taking off his shirt to drape over her shoulders. Some of their colleagues came out to help; Lunt hurried to Antonia with a blanket, and one of the women connected with the Institute fussed over Vassily and the interpreter, who insisted, laughing, that they were all right, it was nothing, they would go change their clothes and that was that.

Antonia, blushing, saw a photographer on the veranda of the main lodge, his camera held up to his face, obscuring his face, as he took pictures. She pulled away from Vassily with an embarrassed murmur.

That was shortly before nine o'clock: by twelve-thirty, when the conference officially ended, her relationship with Vassily had ended as well.

The final session was tense, nearly everyone looked strained, or quite ordinarily exhausted; even Ilyin, taking up a great deal of time with an elegant expression of gratitude for the hospitality of the Institute, looked tired. Then, rather abruptly, certain issues resurfaced: a member of the Soviet delegation insisted upon speaking in response to Eliot Harder's statement of the other day concerning "freedom" of speech and of the marketplace, saying with ill-disguised contempt that one could package and sell human flesh, no doubt there would be some eager consumers, if you hold to a marketplace ideology where everything is for sale, everything is to be peddled, if you believe that in a "democracy" it is valuable to know what people want, what they will buy, why not package and sell human flesh, what is to stop you. . . ?

Another Soviet spoke of racist propaganda he had discovered in the American press. He had visited the United States many times, he said, as a guest of the government and of certain universities, and he had acquired astonishing publications, in order to study the mood of the United States, and it had shocked and disgusted him, anti-Negro propaganda published openly, in fact subsidized by leading capitalists, and there is the notorious instance of the American Nazis, defended by many, and their publications widely distributed, though perhaps it is not to be wondered at, for the United States has not suffered a war, it has not experienced a war like Russia experienced not long ago, when every family lost at least one member and many families of course were destroyed by the Germans under the madman Hitler, and in any case it is widely known, it is a matter of common knowledge, that the United States has no memory, it is the fashion to forget, to forgive and forget as the saying goes, and no doubt members of this American delegation would defend that point of view. . . .

Frank Webber insisted upon speaking, and in a trembling voice asked about the dissident writers, naming several names unfamiliar to Antonia, and going on to say, passionately, not quite coherently, that the humanistic tradition insists upon freedom of expression, freedom of the imagination, the enemy of the spirit is the totalitarian state, the supreme sovereign state, we have no tradition in the West of bowing down to authority, our writers and poets think for themselves, they are never censored, they speak out against the suppression of their fellow artists in all parts of the world. . . . It is complained by the Soviets, Webber went on, gripping his microphone, that we pay attention only to the dissident writers, we ignore the "real" writers, but no one would deny that the so-called dissident writers speak most truthfully, most forcefully, with the greatest aesthetic command, and in any case they would prefer to be published at home, they do not *want* to have their manuscripts smuggled out of their country, they do not *want* to be exiled or jailed. . . .

Matthew Burke intervened, and tried to restore calm, and Antonia sat staring at her hands, wondering why she was here, what pretext had she had for coming here, she remembered Vassily's head gripped against her breasts, she remembered the warmth, the urgency, the incredible unspeakable tenderness of their embrace, but what had it to do with anything else, how could it help them. . . ? Vivian had called to tell her that Whitney had called *them*, he did intend to drop by later in the week, so far as they could judge he sounded in good spirits, he didn't sound at all drunk, or bitter, once he got in Chicago they could persuade him to call her, perhaps she could even fly out, would she be willing, should they raise that possibility to Whit when he arrived. . . ?

Now Ilyin was speaking, now Ilyin had the floor and would not relinquish it. He spoke of Soviet anger over the fact that the American President always surrounded himself with Soviet "authorities" who were anti-Soviet, he spoke with irony of the fact that at the leading American universities contemporary Russian literature is represented by such writers as Solzhenitsyn, who is no longer a Soviet citizen, and Nabokov, who was an American, who is classified as an American, and now—the very latest—they are taking up the cause of the mentally disturbed Sokolov, and the criminal Siniavsky, and others whose works are worthless. . . . There is no genuine feeling of brotherhood between the Americans and the Russians, Ilyin said, or such outrages would not be permitted. Those who are called dissidents are criminals, nothing more. They are ordinary criminals. Why are such matters a concern for the United States, where criminals are dealt with harshly enough. . . ? It is none of your business, Ilyin said, and Antonia looked over to see Vassily staring at his hands, his clasped hands, and all around the table the Soviets sat motionless, silent. At the very moment that Frank Webber rose, not to protest but simply to walk out of the room, Antonia thought weakly, with a sickening certitude, We must leave, we must all leave, we can't sit here listening to this, but of course she did not move, she sat motionless as all the others.

"Problems of human rights are problems of sovereign states," Ilyin said, the interpreter said, droning in Antonia's ears, "not to be dealt with by outsiders. You would think that the Americans, priding themselves on their freedoms, would know enough to allow other states theirs. Why do you imagine that your views of human rights and freedom should be ours? Why do you even want to think so? . . . It is astonishing, I have always found it astonishing, even rather amusing, the tragic misconceptions of my American colleagues."

After Ilyin finished there was a brief silence, and then Matthew Burke repeated, gamely, with a strained courtesy Antonia found touching, a number of the points already made, and there were final remarks having to do with the "communication channels" that had been opened, and with the hope that the conference would be only the first of many. The Soviet chairman, speaking in exactly the same voice he had used a few minutes before, thanked the Rosedale Institute for their gracious and generous hospitality, and the American delegates for their generous friendship, and of course Matthew Burke who had labored to bring all this about, and he believed he spoke for the Soviet delegation in expressing the hope that they would all meet again, perhaps the following year, to discuss literary matters, and matters of humanistic interest, in order to bring together our two great nations, and to work for universal peace and brotherhood, and understanding. . . .

There was silence. Antonia saw out of the corner of her eye how Vassily sat, utterly immobile, still staring at his hands. He was not going to rise to his feet, he was not going to protest, or even to speak calmly and quietly: he was a Soviet writer who had learned his particular lesson.

And what blame could she assign to him, what privileged repugnance had *she* earned. . . ?

Despite her dark glasses the bright sunshine hurt her eyes: the pain was really quite piercing and intense. Yet she managed to say goodbye to everyone. She was sociable, she was unfailingly courteous, one of the friendlier Americans. There was a flurry of handshaking on all sides, and the lively presentation of gifts—mainly books ("Unfortunately I have not yet acquired an English translator") but also bottles of cognac and vodka, and boxes of candy in gaily-colored tins, and, for Mrs. Burke, and Antonia, and the several other women involved in the conference, hand-carved brooches made of walrus tusks. (Antonia, examining hers, thanking the Russians with a broad if numbed smile, wondered if she had heard correctly—walrus tusks? The brooch, approximately the size of a silver dollar, weighed very lightly in the hand and might well have been made of plastic. But it was quite attractive in any case and her admiration was sincere.)

The limousines were waiting. A small contingent to take the Soviet delegation to New York; two airport limousines to take Antonia and her companions away; but it seemed necessary—it seemed unavoidable—that everyone say goodbye yet another time, and repeat how beneficial the conference had been, how marvelous to become acquainted, to establish avenues of communication between like-minded persons. . . . Vassily stood near, smiling at her, though no longer with that hopeful, loving gaze: his expression had gone resigned, even somewhat bitter. He knew how she felt about him: he understood. Certainly he understood, he wasn't a fool, perhaps he wasn't even the amiable well-meaning romantic figure he had presented to Antonia, but quite another person altogether, a Soviet writer who had survived. Antonia smiled at him as she smiled at the others, shaking hands, retreating. Her anger had backed up everywhere in her, it throbbed throughout her body, beat cruelly behind her eyes. She dreaded crying because tears would be misunderstood.

Vassily squeezed her hand roughly and leaned toward her. "You will visit us someday?—soon?" His voice was edged subtly with shame and with anger as well, but Antonia took no notice. "You will be a guest of my government, a week, or a month sometime."

Vassily squeezed her hand roughly. "You will visit us soon? A week, a month in good weather, as a guest of my government?"

"That's possible, yes certainly," Antonia said, edging away. She was smiling her American smile but the corners of her mouth had begun to weaken. "You are very kind to invite me."

She backed away. Already things were shifting into episodes, acquiring anecdotal perspective. Vassily had clutched so eagerly at her, he had pressed his face against her breasts, and she had felt, hadn't she, such immediate, such extraordinary affection. . . . That episode had been genuine. It had really happened. She would remember it, she thought, for the rest of her life.

Vassily was still gripping her hand. He wanted to embrace her— but of course he didn't dare. Instead he pursued the subject of her coming to Russia to give lectures, to meet with fellow writers?— yes?—would she consent? She saw that Vassily chose to interpret her disdain for him as feminine shyness, or restraint; she understood he would not release her until she gave him the answer he required, that his companions might overhear. So she smiled and made an effort to return the pressure of his fingers, she murmured that helpful word, *"Da."*

SUMMER, AN ELEGY

ELLEN GILCHRIST

His name was Shelby after the town where his mother was born, and he was eight years old and all that summer he had to wear a little black sling around the index finger of his right hand. He had to wear the sling because his great-granddaddy had been a famous portrait painter and had paintings hanging in the White House.

Shelby was so high-strung his mother was certain he was destined to be an artist like his famous ancestor. So, when he broke his finger and it grew back crooked, of course they took him to a specialist. They weren't taking any chances on a deformity standing in his way.

All summer long he was supposed to wear the sling to limber up the finger, and in the fall the doctor was going to operate and straighten it. While he waited for his operation Shelby was brought to Bear Garden Plantation to spend the summer with his grandmother and as soon as he got up every morning he rode over to Esperanza to look for Matille.

He would come riding up in the yard and tie his saddle pony to the fence and start talking before he even got on the porch. He was a beautiful boy, five months younger than Matille and a head shorter, and he was the biggest liar she had ever met in her life.

Matille was a lonely little girl, the only child in a house full of widows. She was glad of this noisy companion fate had delivered to Issaquena County right in the middle of a World War.

Shelby would wait for her while she ate breakfast, helping himself to pinch-cake, or toast, or cold cornbread, or muffins, walking around the kitchen touching everything and talking a mile a minute to anyone who would listen, talking and eating at the same time.

"My daddy's a personal friend of General MacArthur's," he would be saying. "They were buddies at Auburn. General MacArthur wants him to come work in Washington but he can't go because what he does is too important." Shelby was standing in the pantry door making a pyramid out of the Campbell's Soup cans. "Every time my daddy talks about going to Washington my momma starts crying her head off and goes to bed with a backache." He topped off the pyramid with a can of tomato paste and returned to the present. "I don't know how anyone can sleep this late," he said. "I'm the first one up at Bear Garden every single morning."

Matille would eat breakfast as fast as she could and they would start out for the bayou that ran in front of the house at the end of a wide lawn.

"Did I tell you I'm engaged to be married," Shelby would begin, sitting next to Matille in the swing that went out over the water, pumping as hard as he could with his thin legs, staring off into the sky.

"Her daddy's a colonel in the Air Corps. They're real rich." A dark secret look crossed his face. "I already gave her a diamond ring. That's why I've got to find the pearl. So I can get enough money to get married. But don't tell anyone because my momma and daddy don't know about it yet."

"There aren't any pearls in mussels," Matille said. "Guy said so. He said we were wasting our time chopping open all those mussels."

"They do too have pearls," Shelby said coldly. "Better ones than oysters. My father told me all about it. Everyone in New Orleans knows about it."

"Well," Matille said, "I'm not looking for any pearls today. I'm going to the store and play the slot machine."

"You haven't got any nickels."

"I can get one. Guy'll give me one." Guy was Matille's uncle. He was 4-F. He had lost an eye in a crop-dusting accident and was having to miss the whole war because of it. He couldn't get into the Army, Navy, Marines or Air Corps. Even the Coast Guard had turned him down. He tried to keep up a cheerful face, running around Esperanza doing the work of three men, being extra nice to everyone, even the German war prisoners who were brought over from the Greenville Air Force Base to work in the fields.

He was always good for a nickel, sometimes two or three if Matille waited until after he had his evening toddies.

"If you help me with the mussels I'll give you two nickels," Shelby said.

"Let me see," Matille said, dragging her feet to slow the swing. It was nice in the swing with the sun beating down on the water below and the pecan trees casting a cool shade.

Shelby pulled a handkerchief from his pocket and untied a corner. Sure enough, there they were, three nickels and a quarter and a dime. Shelby always had money. He was the richest boy Matille had ever known. She stared down at the nickels, imagining the cold thrill of the slot machine handle throbbing beneath her touch.

"How long?" she said.

"Until I have to go home," Shelby said.

"All right," Matille said. "Let's get started."

They went out to the shed and found two rakes and a small hoe and picked their way through the weeds to the bayou bank. The mud along the bank was black and hard-packed and broken all along the water line by thick tree roots, cypress and willow and catalpa and water oak. They walked past the cleared-off place with its pier and rope swings and on down to where the banks of mussels began.

The mussels lay in the shallow water as far as the rake could reach, an endless supply, as plentiful as oak leaves, as plentiful as the fireflies that covered the lawn at evening, as plentiful as the minnows casting their tiny shadows all along the water's edge, or the gnats that buzzed around Matille's face as she worked, raking and digging and chopping, earning her nickels.

She would throw the rake down into the water and pull it back full of the dark-shelled, inedible, mud-covered creatures. Moments later, reaching into the same place, dozens more would have appeared to take their place.

They would rake in a pile of mussels, then set to work breaking them open with the hoe and screwdriver. When they had opened twenty or thirty, they would sit on the bank searching the soft flesh for the pearl. Behind them and all around them were piles of rotting shells left behind in the past weeks.

"I had my fortune told by a voodoo queen last Mardi Gras," Shelby said. "Did I ever tell you about that? She gave me a charm made out of a dead baby's bone. You want to see it?"

"I been to Ditty's house and had my fortune told," Matille said. "Ditty's real old. She's the oldest person in Issaquena County. She's older than Nannie-Mother. She's probably the oldest person in the whole state of Mississippi." Matille picked up a mussel and examined it, running her finger inside, then tossed it into the water. Where it landed a dragonfly hovered for a moment, then rose in the humid air, its electric-blue tail flashing.

"You want to see the charm or not?" Shelby said, pulling it out of his pocket.

"Sure," she said. "Give it here."

He opened his hand and held it out to her. It looked like the wishbone from a tiny chicken. "It's voodoo," Shelby said. He held it up in the air, turning to catch the sunlight. "You can touch it but you can't hold it. No one can hold it but the master of it. Here, go on and touch it if you want to."

Matille reached and stroked the little bone. "What's it good for?" she said.

"To make whatever you want to happen. It's white magic. Momma Ulaline is real famous. She's got a place on Royal Street right next to an antique store. My Aunt Katherine took me there when she was babysitting me last Mardi Gras."

Matille touched it again. She gave a little shudder.

"Well, let's get back to work," Shelby said, putting the charm into his pocket, wiping his hands on his playsuit. His little black sling was covered with mud. "I think we're getting someplace today. I think we're getting warm."

They went back to work. Shelby was quiet, dreaming of treasure, of the pearl that lay in wait for him, of riches beyond his wildest dreams, of mansions and fine automobiles and chauffeurs and butlers and maids and money, stacks and stacks of crisp five-dollar bills and ten-dollar bills and twenty-dollar bills. Somewhere in Steele's Bayou the pearl waited. It loomed in his dreams. It lay in wait for him beneath the roots of a cypress or water oak or willow.

Every morning when he woke he could see it, all morning as he dug and raked and chopped and Matille complained and the hot sun beat down on the sweating mud and the stagnant pools of minnows and the fast-moving, evil-looking gars swimming by like gunboats, all day the pearl shone in his mind, smooth and mysterious, cold to the touch.

They worked in silence for awhile, moving downstream until they were almost to the bridge.

"Looks like we could get something for all these shells," Matille said, examining the inside of one. It was all swirls of pink and white, like polished marble. "Looks like they ought to be worth something!"

"We could make dogfood out of the insides," Shelby said. "Mr. Green Bagett had a dog that ate mussels. My grandmother told me all about it. He would carry them up to the road in his mouth and when the sun made them open he would suck out the insides." Shelby leaned on his hoe, making a loud sucking noise. "He was a dog named Harry after Mr. Bagett's dentist and he would eat mussels all day long if nobody stopped him."

"Why don't we carry these mussels up to the road and let the sun open them?" Matille said.

"Because it takes too long that way," Shelby said. "This is quicker."

"We could make ashtrays out of the shells," Matille said.

"Yeah," Shelby said. "We could sell them in New Orleans. You can sell anything in the French Quarter."

"We could paint them and decorate them with flowers," Matille said, falling into a dream of her own, picturing herself wearing a long flowered dress, pushing a cart through the crowded streets of a city, selling ashtrays to satisfied customers.

Now they were almost underneath the bridge. Here the trees were thicker and festooned with vines that dropped into the water like swings. It was darker here, and secret.

The bridge was a fine one for such a small bayou. It was a drawbridge with high steel girders that gleamed like silver in the flat Delta countryside. The bridge had been built to connect the two parts of the county and anyone going from Grace to Baleshed or Esperanza or Panther Brake or Greenfields had to pass that way. Some mornings as many as seven cars and trucks passed over it. All day small black children played on the bridge and fished from it and leaned over its railings looking down into the brown water, chunking rocks at the mud turtles or trying to hit the mean-looking gars and catfish that swam by in twos or threes with their teeth showing.

This morning there were half a dozen little black boys on the bridge and one little black girl wearing a clean apron. Her hair was in neat cornrows with yellow yarn plaited into the braids. Her head looked like the wing of a butterfly, all yellow and black and brown and round as it could be.

"What y'all doing?" the girl called down when they got close enough to hear. "What y'all doing to them mussels?"

"We're doing an experiment," Shelby called back.

"Let's get Teentsy and Kale to help us," Matille said. "Hey, Teentsy," she called out, but Shelby grabbed her arm.

"Don't get them down here," he said. "I don't want everyone in the Delta in on this."

"They all know about it anyway," Matille said. "Guy told Granddaddy everyone at the store was laughing about us the other day. He said Baby Doll was busting a gut laughing at us for chopping all these mussels."

"I don't care," Shelby said, putting his hands on his hips and looking out across the water with the grim resignation of the born artist. "They don't know what we're doing it for."

"Well, I'm about worn out," Matille said. "Let's go up to the store and get Mavis to give us a drink."

"Let's open a few more first. Then we'll get a drink and go over to the other side. I think it's better over there anyway. There's sand over there. You got to have sand to make pearls."

"We can't go over there," Matille said. "That's not our property. That's Mr. Donleavy's place."

"He don't care if we dig some mussels on his bayou bank, does he?"

"I don't know. We got to ask him first. He's got a real bad temper."

"Let's try under this tree," Shelby said. "This looks like a good place. There's sand in this mud." He was bending down trying the mud between his fingers, rubbing it back and forth to test the consistency. "Yeah, let's try here. This feels good."

"What y'all tearing up all those mussels for," Kale called down from his perch on the bridge. "They ain't good for nothing. You can't even use them for bait."

"We're gonna make ashtrays out of them," Shelby said. "We're starting us an ashtray factory."

"Where about?" Kale said, getting interested, looking like he would come down and take a look for himself.

"Next to the store," Shelby said. "We're gonna decorate them and sell them in New Orleans. Rich folks will pay a lot for real mussel ashtrays."

"That ought to hold them for awhile," he said to Matille. "Let them talk about that at the store. Come on, let's open a few more. Then we'll get us a drink."

"All right," Matille said. "Let's try under this tree." She waded out into the water until it was up to her ankles, feeling the cold mud ooze up between her toes. She reached out with the rake. It caught, and she began pulling it up the shore, backing as she pulled, tearing the bark off the edges of the tree roots. The rake caught in the roots and she reached down to free it.

"Matille!" Shelby yelled. "Matille! Look out!" She heard his voice and saw the snake at the same moment, saw the snake and Shelby lifting the hoe and her hand outlined against the water, frozen and dappled with sunlight and the snake struggling to free itself and the hoe falling toward her hand, and she dropped the rake and turned and was running up the bank, stumbling and running, with Shelby yelling his head off behind her, and Teentsy and Kale and the other children rose up from the bridge like a flock of little blackbirds and came running down the hill to see what the excitement was.

"I got him," Shelby yelled. "I cut him in two. I cut him in two with the hoe. I got him."

Matille sank down on the edge of the road and put her head on her knees.

"She's fainting," Kale called out, running up to her. "Matille's fainting."

"No, she ain't." Teentsy said. "She's all right." Teentsy sat down by Matille and put a hand on her arm, patting her.

"It was a moccasin," Shelby yelled. "He was big around as my arm. After I killed him the top half was still alive. He struck at me four times. I don't know if I'm bit or not."

"Where's he gone to now?" Kale said.

"I don't know," Shelby said, pulling off his shirt. "Come look and see if he bit me." The children gathered around searching Shelby's skin for bite marks. His little chest was heaving with excitement and his face was shining. With his shirt off he looked about as big around as a blue jay. His little black sling was flopping around his wrist and his rib cage rose and fell beneath the straps of his seersucker playsuit.

"Here's one!" Teentsy screamed, touching a spot on Shelby's back, but it turned out to be an old mosquito bite.

"Lay down on the ground," Kale yelled, "where we can look at you better."

"Where do you *think* he bit you?" Teentsy said.

But Shelby was too excited to lay down on the ground. All he wanted to do was jump up and down and tell his story over and over.

Then the grown people heard the commotion and came out from the store. Mavis Findley and Mr. Beaumont and Baby Doll and R.C. and Overflow came hurrying down the road and grabbed hold of Shelby so they could see where the snake bit him.

"Didn't nothing bite him, Mr. Mavis," Kale said. "He kilt it. He kilt it with the hoe."

"He almost chopped my hand off," Matille said, but no one was listening.

Then Mavis and Baby Doll and Overflow escorted Matille and Shelby back to the big house with the black children skipping along beside and in front of them like a disorderly marching band.

By the time the procession reached the house the porch was full of ladies. Matille's mother and grandmother and great-grand-mother and several widowed aunts had materialized from their rooms and were standing in a circle. From a distance they looked like a great flowering shrub. The screen door was open and a wasp buzzed around their heads threatening to be caught in their hairnets.

The ladies all began talking at once, their voices rising above and riding over and falling into each other in a long chorus of mothering.

"Thank goodness you're all in one piece," Miss Babbie said, swooping up Matille and enfolding her in a cool fragrance of dotted

Swiss and soft yielding bosom and the smell of sandalwood and the smell of coffee and the smell of powder.

Miss Nannie-Mother, who was 96, kissed her on the forehead and called her Eloise, after a long-dead cousin. Miss Nannie-Mother had lived so long and grown so wise that everyone in the world had started to look alike to her.

The rest of the ladies swirled around Shelby. Matille struggled from her grandmother's embrace and watched disgustedly from the doorframe as Shelby told his story for the tenth time.

"I didn't care what happened to me," Shelby was saying. "No rattlesnake was biting a lady while I was in the neighborhood. After I chopped it in two the mouth part came at me like a chicken with its head cut off."

"He almost chopped my hand off," Matille said again, but the only ones listening to her were Teentsy and Kale, who stood by the steps picking petals off Miss Teddy's prize pansies and covering their mouths with their hands when they giggled to show what nice manners they had.

"This is what comes of letting children run loose like wild Indians," Miss Teddy was saying, brandishing a bottle of Windsor nail polish.

"Whatever will Rhode Hotchkiss think when she hears of this?" Miss Nell Grace said.

"She'll be terrified," Miss Babbie answered. "Then go straight to her knees to thank the Lord for the narrow escape."

"I knew something was going to happen," Miss Hannie Clay said, her hands still full of rickrack for the smock she was making for her daughter in Shreveport. "I knew something was coming. It was too quiet around here all morning if you ask my opinion."

Matille leaned into the door frame with her hands on her hips watching her chances of ever going near the bayou again as long as she lived growing slimmer and slimmer.

Sure enough, when Matille's grandfather came in from the fields for the noon meal he made his pronouncement before he even washed his hands or hung up his hat.

"Well, then," he said, looking down from his six feet four inches and furrowing his brow. "I want everyone in this house to stay away from the bayou until I can spare some men to clear the brush. Shelby, I'm counting on you to keep Matille away from there, you hear me?"

"Yes sir," Shelby said. He stood up very straight, stuck out his hand and shook on it.

Now he's done it, Matille thought. Now our luck's all gone. Now nothing will be the same.

Now the summer wore on into August, and Shelby and Matille made a laboratory in an old chicken house, and collected a lot of butterflies and chloroformed them with fingernail polish remover, and they taught a fox terrier puppy how to dance on his hind legs, and spent some time spying on the German prisoners, and read all the old love letters in the trunks under the house, and built a broad jump pit in the pasture, but it was not the same. Somehow the heart had gone out of the summer.

Then one morning the grown people decided it was time for typhoid shots, and no matter how Matille cried and beat her head against the floor she was bathed and dressed and sent off in the back seat of Miss Rhoda's Buick to Doctor Findley's little brick office overlooking Lake Washington.

As a reward Matille was to be allowed to stay over at Bear Garden until the pain and fever subsided.

In those days vaccinations were much stronger than they are now, and well cared-for children were kept in bed for twenty-four hours nursing their sore arms, taking aspirin dissolved in sugar water and being treated as though they were victims of the disease itself.

Miss Rhoda made up the twin beds in Shelby's mother's old room, made them up with her finest Belgian linens and decorated the headboards with Hero medals cut from cardboard and hand-painted with watercolors.

The bedroom was painted ivory and the chairs were covered with blue and white chintz imported from Paris. It was the finest room Matille had ever slept in. She snuggled down in the pillows admiring the tall bookcases filled with old dolls and mementos of Carrie Hotchkiss's brilliant career as a Rolling Fork cheerleader.

Miss Rhoda bathed their faces with lemon water, drew the Austrian blinds and went off for her nap.

"Does yours hurt yet?" Shelby said, rubbing his shot as hard as he could to get the pain going. "Mine's killing me already."

"It hurts some," Matille said, touching the swollen area. "Not too much." She was looking at Shelby's legs, remembering something Guy had shown her, something that had happened a long time ago, something hot and exciting, something that felt like fever, and like fever, made everything seem present, always present, so that she could not remember where or how it had happened or how long a time had passed since she had forgotten it.

"Just wait till tonight," Shelby rattled on. "You'll think your arm's fixing to fall off. I almost died from mine last year. One year a boy in New Orleans did die. They cut off his arm and did everything they could to save him but he died anyway. Think about that, being in a grave with only one arm." Shelby was talking faster than ever, to hide his embarrassment at the way Matille was looking at him.

"I can't stand to think about being buried, can you?" he continued, "all shut up in the ground with the worms eating you. I'm getting buried in a mausoleum if I die. They're these little houses up off the ground made out of concrete. Everyone in New Orleans that can afford it gets buried in mausoleums. That's one good thing about living here."

"You want to get in bed with me?" Matille said, surprised at the sound of her own voice, so clear and orderly in the still room.

"Sure," Shelby said, "if you're scared. It scares me to death to think about being buried and stuff like that. Are you scared?"

"I don't know," Matille said. "I just feel funny. I feel like doing something bad."

"Well, scoot over then," Shelby said, crawling in beside her.

"You're burning up," she said, putting a hand on his forehead to see if he had a fever. Then she put her hand on his chest as if to feel his heartbeat, and then, as if she had been doing it every day of her life, she reached down inside his pajamas for the strange hard secret of boys.

"I want to see it, Shelby," she said, and he lay back with his hands stiff by his sides while she touched and looked to her heart's content.

"Now you do it to me," she said, and she guided his fingers up and down, up and down, up and down the thick tight opening between her legs.

The afternoon was going on for a long time and the small bed was surrounded by yellow light and the room filled with the smell of mussels.

Long afterwards, as she lay in a cool bed in Acapulco, waiting for her third husband to claim her as his bride, Matille would remember that light and how, later that afternoon, the wind picked up and could be heard for miles away, moving toward Issaquena County with its lines of distant thunder, and how the cottonwood leaves outside the window had beat upon the house all night with their exotic crackling.

"You better not tell anyone about this ever, Shelby," Matille said, when she woke in the morning. "You can't tell anyone about it, not even in New Orleans."

"The moon's still up," Shelby said, as if he hadn't heard her. "I can see it out the window."

"How can the moon be up," Matille said. "It's daylight."

"It stays up when it wants to," Shelby said, "haven't you ever seen that before?"

It was Matille who made up the game now. They cleaned out an old playhouse that had belonged to Matille's mother and made a bed from a cot mattress. Matille would lie down on the mattress with her hand on her head pretending to have a sick headache.

"Come sit by me, Honey," she would say. "Pour me a glass of sherry and come lie down till I feel better."

"God can see in this playhouse," Shelby said, pulling his hand away.

"No, he can't, Shelby," Matille said, sitting up and looking him hard in the eye. "God can't see through tin. This is a tin roof and God can't see through it."

"He can see everywhere," Shelby said. "Father Godchaux said so."

"Well, he can't see through tin," Matille said. "He can't be everywhere at once. He's got enough to do helping out the Allies without watching little boys and girls every minute of the night and day." Matille was unbuttoning Shelby's playsuit. "Doesn't that feel good, Shelby?" she said. "Doesn't that make you feel better?"

"God can see everywhere," Shelby insisted. "He can see every single thing in the whole world."

"I don't care," Matille said. "I don't like God anyway. If God's so good why did he let Uncle Robert die. And why did he make alligators and snakes and send my daddy off to fight the Japs. If God's so good why'd he let the Jews kill his own little boy."

"You better not talk like that," Shelby said, buttoning his suit back together. "And we better get back before Baby Doll comes looking for us again."

"Just a little bit more," Matille said. "Just till we get to the part where the baby comes out."

August went by as if it had only lasted a moment. Then one afternoon Miss Rhoda drove Shelby over in the Buick to say goodbye. He was wearing long pants and had a clean sling on the finger and he had brought Matille the voodoo bone wrapped in tissue paper to keep for him.

"You might need this," he said, holding it out to her. He looked very grown up standing by the stairs in his city clothes and Matille thought that maybe she would marry Shelby when she grew up and be a fine married lady in New Orlenas.

Then it was September and the cotton went to the gin and Matille was in the third grade and rode to school on the bus.

One afternoon she was standing by the driver while the bus clattered across the bridge and came to a halt by the store. It was a cool day. A breeze was blowing from the northeast and the cypress trees were turning a dusty red and the wild persimmons and muscadines were making.

Matille felt the trouble before she even got off the bus. The trouble reached out and touched her before she even saw the ladies standing on the porch in their dark dresses. It fell across her shoulders like a cloak. It was as if she had touched a single strand of a web and felt the whole thing tremble and knew herself to be caught forever in its trembling.

They found out, she thought. Shelby told them. I knew he couldn't keep a secret, she said to herself. Now they'll kill me. Now they'll beat me like they did Guy.

She looked down the gravel road to the house, down the long line of pecan and elm trees and knew that she should turn and go back the other way, should run from this trouble, but something made her keep on moving toward the house. I'll say he lied, she thought. I'll say I didn't do it. I'll say he made it up, she said to herself. Everyone knows what a liar Shelby is.

Then her mother and grandmother and Miss Babbie came down off the porch and took her into the parlor and sat beside her on the sofa. And Miss Hannie and Miss Nell Grace and Overflow and

Baby Doll stood around her in a circle and told her the terrible news.

"Shelby is dead, Matille," her grandmother said. The words slid over her like water poured on stones.

Shelby had gone to the hospital to have his finger fixed and he had lain down on the table and put the gas mask over his face and the man who ran the gas machine made a mistake and Shelby had gone to sleep, and nothing could wake him up, not all the doctors or nurses or shots or slaps on the face or screams or prayers or remorse in the world could wake him. And that was the Lord's will, blessed be the name of the Lord, Amen.

Later the ladies went into the kitchen to make a cold supper for anyone who felt like eating and Matille walked down to the bayou and stood for a long time staring down into the water, feeling strangely elated, as though this were some wonderful joke Shelby dreamed up.

She stared down into the tree roots, deep down into the muddy water, down to the place where Shelby's pearl waited, grew and moved inside the soft watery flesh of its mother, luminous and perfect and alive, as cold as the moon in the winter sky.

AGE

JANET DESAULNIERS

LAST NIGHT I was seduced. "Lord," you must think, "this I've heard before." But then I could be wrong. I constantly overestimate my powers of intuition. Some days I walk to my store, my small shoebox of a bookshop, and feel the women near the bus stop stare at my balding head, my cracked shoes wound with electrical tape. I turn to face them and say, "It's not so bad." They look confused and I wonder: Were they really looking at me. Were they interested at all, or were they looking past me, to a store window, perhaps at a new pocketbook or spring coat. What do you think? I think you may not be interested in the seduction of a sixty-three year old man, that you may view the seduction of a man past his prime, past ambition, past desire's tap on the shoulder, as a shade perverse, slightly off the scheme of things.

You may be nowhere near sixty-three. Perhaps you are young—your body and mind firm and uncreased. Perhaps you think of seduction in terms of young men and women who move in and out of doorways as if always following some distant strain of music. If so, some day I think you'll find, as I did, those people have only a small role in the final order of things. Not that I don't appreciate them. Not that I don't see their long legs, their faces turned up and open—almost pious in their ease. I see, God, I see. But they are a diversion—bestseller fiction before bedtime. At sixty-three, you will be able to think of at least five things more important. I can: good wine, quiet sleep, easy digestion, less pain, something *new*.

Or perhaps you are older than sixty-three. Perhaps you think of seduction as that one bright glint in a shadowy past—the red scooter when you were nine, or the face of your wife the first morning she touched your arm as you rose from bed, the first time *she* took *you*—the trembling in your hands and knees. I take your hand in mine. To you, I offer comfort. To you, I say it can happen again.

I wonder if you believe me. I am balding, overweight, and alone. My body hangs from my shoulders like a coat that has lost its shape, its definition. From around my bald spot, my hair grows wild and unstyled. Often I don't comb it. I think, Why should I. I am poor—too poor for cars and clothes and casual drinks. My drinks, when I can afford them, are serious, meaningful. I wash my gray undershirts and socks in the bathtub and hang them to dry over my furniture. I read. That's all. I sit in my tiny, failing bookshop. I hear it sigh, give up and fail all around me, and I read. Otherwise, I do nothing. C.S. Lewis understood the dangers of nothing. He wrote: "Nothing is very strong: strong enough to steal away a man's best years not in sweet sin but in a dreary flickering of the mind over it knows not what and knows not why." C.S. Lewis is right more often than I am. Still, nothing is what I do most days. Like my shop, I gave up. I gave in. I sit quietly inside myself like a motionless pond. But this is important. This is what I'm trying to say: I am all these things, but last night I danced.

I suppose I should tell about the woman. I am impatient with the way this is going. The woman is not the most important thing. There are the places, the days, even the people who remind me of her—all scattered about in a shambles of significance. The woman is at the center, but alone, isolated, she'll look small, maybe ridiculous. Finally, though, she saved me—a save as clean and final and close to the heart of matters as any surgeon's stitch.

Lily is twenty-four. Perhaps I've been too abrupt. I can imagine the young people nodding and the old folks shaking their heads. But Lily is twenty-four, and though I'm hesitant to mention this now, she is also lovely though she's too thin like all the rest of the young ones. Women have lost respect for hips and breasts these days. I'm sure I'll suffer for saying that, but I don't understand. I have always envied women, praised them. Women are balanced, fluid, as if always something about them is in motion. Men are hard, clumsy, unyielding. Women can take men inside them. They can feel men grow inside them and feel themselves grow around the men.

A poet wrote those last two lines—a young poet with small

chapped hands who rented the room above my bookshop for two years and left his poems as a final payment of sorts. The sound of his typewriter came down to me through the vent over my cash register in fits and starts, like an animal fretting over a wound. He wrote only about women. Afternoons, when the lunch hour browsers abandoned me and the sun came through the front window to draw harsh edges around the clutter and the quiet, I imagined him up there, barechested in the heat, crossing his ankles and rocking in his chair, transfixed by the implications of his own words. He knew women though. In his poems, he knew them as I think they might choose to be known—tender and complex, opening slowly, over time, the way a small bud unfolds and unfolds until finally, it overwhelms. That young poet knew women's power; he held it in his mind, examined it. The sad part, the tragic part, is that all this was only on paper. Standing next to a real woman, he unraveled. I wanted to reach out and quiet his shoulders. He blinked, stammered, and the fear moved up in lines around his eyes. But on paper he found solace. There he could study women closely, impose an order upon them he could believe in, and though none of that order was real, none of it workable, its beauty was relentless and blinding. Finally, even I believed. It was a quiet, personal deception—one that caused my first disagreement with Plato, who argued that poets and painters should be denied a place in the City of the Good. I would save that young poet a place if it were my city. But I digress. The poet and what his poems did are a seduction of another kind.

Lily. Lily is a woman—a young one, thin and long-legged, with great eyes and a full but serious mouth. Her hair is long and auburn. She thinks she might cut it when she turns twenty-five. I hope she doesn't; you would, too, if you saw it. Its shine is like a mahogany cabinet. Everything about Lily wants to believe it's tough, unaffected—sensible sandals, no jewelry, never a pocketbook or a hat or a handkerchief, not even an umbrella on drizzly days. She says things like, "Hey. Howya doin'."—but softly, hesitating, as though the gangly familiarity is a ruse she hasn't fully accepted, and in her face there is something distant, quizzical, even sweet. When she stands among the stacks in my shop, I sometimes think if I reached out to touch her, she'd suddenly be gone. Her mouth is always open just a bit, and her eyes are always wide, as if she is standing just outside herself, viewing herself and her small life as a very interested, perhaps awestruck, spectator. She likes books (how else would we have met), mainly fiction, mainly contemporary, and works evenings as a waitress on the Square.

The Square brought Lily and me together. We both hate it—though she works in it and my bookshop leans against it like a poorly dressed cousin. I don't know quite how to describe the Square with fairness. It is a thorn in my side, a raucous painful reminder of the way things are, but it is important—the backdrop against which I've lived out my silly life. When I bought my bookshop in 1950, before the collapse of city neighborhoods, the buildings on the Square housed an upholstery shop, a bakery, a beauty salon, a tobacconist, a market, a movie house and a drugstore that doubled as neighborhood meeting place for the idle and garrulous. Now those same buildings accommodate clothing stores for the very young and very chic and countless bars and restaurants all bursting with overgrown ferns, brass fixtures and tinted glass. Lily works in a restaurant called the Soup Kitchen decorated in (it embarrasses me to say this) a Depression motif with blown up photographs of bread lines and Apple Annies and cold, hungry looking children. A bowl of split pea soup costs $3.95 there.

Sometimes I think I should have left the Square when I had the chance. During the Sixties, a group of young people pooled their tuition money and bought a few of the storefronts that had been abandoned in the rush to the suburbs. They worked hard—refinishing the doors and wood all around the windows, planting small gardens of herbs and flowers in the sooty dirt of the back alley. Sometimes, at dusk, when the cars and buses moved away from the city, when it seemed everyone was leaving, I would sit and have tea with the women who ran the sandwich shop. I liked those people. They were, for a time, fully young and fully earnest. One of them, a carpenter, helped me build new shelves for the north wall. Each morning, he'd arrive with his tools under one arm and his baby daughter under the other. Her name was Star, and she was a fat, good baby; her father used to say she was a baby of character. Mornings she'd sleep through the noise in a crate I'd used to store old magazines, and afternoons she'd sit up eating bananas and watching the door. It thrilled her to hear the bell over the door ring. Even then, my customers were few and far between, but Star was patient, and when one finally did come in, she'd laugh at him and laugh at us and then raise her banana in a kind of cheery salute. By the end of the first day of work, Star and her father and I were friends. When we finished the shelves, I gave them twenty dollars and they gave me a beret. I wore it every day. I let my hair grow. It had just reached the middle of my back when a developer decided he liked the site and offered to buy all of us out. I tried to convince the others to stay, but they had plans—a commune in Vermont, farmland in Arkansas. The carpenter asked me to join him, but I couldn't. This was the only place I knew. All right, I'll say it, I was afraid. I kissed Star goodbye and stayed. For months, I watched the renovation, and sometimes, even with a customer in the shop, I wept at my window.

Now I sit with a picture window view of the way things are. Lily agrees that people have changed less than I thought. I have changed more. The old drugstore came down last week. Late-night bar trade requires more parking than you can believe.

I did not mean to strike so bleak a note. As I tell women I imagine to be watching me in the street: It's not so bad. Lily. Lily waits tables in a tight jersey floor-length dress. It is a silly dress— meant to be sexy and demure at the same time. Lily knows this, but she wears the dress constantly, marketing and running errands in it before and after work. When I mention it, she holds the dress away from her hips as if it were diseased. "I sold out," she says. "Why should I try to hide it." Lily means she makes more money waiting tables four nights a week than I have made in any one week of my thirty-one years of bookselling.

Lily always seems to be caught up in some emotion. This is the part about her that angers me, frustrates me, and yes, even summons up desire. Some of you may think desire after sixty must be something like an echo trapped in a deep cave, but I tell you, if it is an echo at all, it is one that knows no logic, one that has lost its trajectory, its mathematical predictability. I hear it reverberate crazily, bouncing out of nowhere off the wall over my shoulder as I walk home at night, throwing itself up in front of me, randomly, in the shape of a simple dress in the window of Three Sisters or in the color of ripe oranges. Lily knows a similar kind of desire, but one less random, more pervasive. Always Lily seems to be longing for something—better cheekbones, a new job, wisdom, spontaneity.

In someone so young, such silliness is both maddening and charming. A young face touched with longing lights up; so does an old face, I suppose, but you must admit a lost look in young eyes is more appropriate, somehow prettier.

The problem is Lily tries to think about these emotions. Like the poet, she tries to order them, give one precedence over another. She is ill at ease with her longings. When she comes to me to talk about them, to think them out, I watch her grow heavy and careful right in front of me. I watch her pull her arms in, close secret doors, grow old. It angers me. She thinks about her longings so much that finally, before she has decided what to do about them, they pass. I can't help it—when this happens, I have to give her advice. I lean back in my chair until it squeaks, I put one hand on each knee, and then I tell her what to do. She never does it, but I think she believes I never notice that. I used to justify all this by telling myself she was saving all my advice, hoarding it in expectation of the one time she would really need it, and now I know she was.

A few weeks ago, Lily came into my shop with a decision that had to be made. Lily lightens my shop the way Star and her bananas used to. Without them, the shop is simply dark and quiet, and the only way I know to characterize it is to say that I lost control of the clutter years ago. The aisles are narrowing, and some have simply disappeared. I haven't been able to get through to the shelving against the back wall for at least two years. I've forgotten what's back there. But the shop just seems to recede and make room when Lily comes in. She sidles through the stacks and crawls over boxes and stands on crates, all the while crooking her neck so she can read titles. Every so often she'll call out an author she doesn't recognize and ask if she should read him. I pretend to think a moment but always say yes, and then she stands there, holding the book in her hand as if she's weighing it, before she puts it back and says, "I'll remember that."

The day of her decision she leaned against my counter and poked through a box of paperbacks I'd bought from a college kid that day. She said, "I waited on the director of that new dance company tonight. He said I should join. He said they have classes for beginners." I said, "Dance, Lily, you should," and thought of her in tights and leotard. I didn't tell her I thought that. Lily always catches me when I say things women don't like to hear anymore. I know she wouldn't like what I said about hips and breasts.

"I don't know though." She walked to the window and stared out into the street. "It's too late for me to be good. I'm already too old, and I never dance—not even socially. That sounds foolish, doesn't it. Social dancing. Maybe it's all foolish. Frivolous."

I had to interrupt her here. I mean, I thought of Martha Graham and Isadora Duncan.

"Lily, dance is movement," I said. "Movement is life. Everyone should move. Lord, Lily, Aquinas even defines God as the prime mover."

She turned from the window and looked at me.

"He does?"

"Yes."

"I don't know though—if I could do it."

"And you're not too old."

"Maybe. Not really, I guess. I don't know."

She walked around the shop, trailing her hand along the shelves and sometimes stopping to pat the spines of a row of books as if they were all lovely children. Lily punctuates all our conversation with wandering. Often she disappears behind the shelves for long periods. I can't see her. I can only hear her voice. That day she went behind the religion shelf. I think she was looking for Aquinas. Her voice floated out to me.

"But I was going to take that course in literature you told me about. I mean, I don't know a thing about books. I probably haven't read one-fifth of all the great ones."

"Maybe not even one-twentieth."

"See."

I think she was back in the corner when she said that. I began to get angry. I wanted her out in the open. I liked her to look at me when I gave her advice. I raised my voice and my chin, as if searching for her in a crowd.

"Then do it," I said. "Study literature. Go to the university and read the other four-fifths of all great books in the world."

"Maybe I will." She raised her voice to match mine. "I just might."

"Do it," I said and stopped looking for her. "Go."

She was silent for a time, long enough to have read a few pages.

The store was quiet without her voice, quiet the way it is in the afternoon—an oppressive quiet that seems to move in like heat and hover in the six inches of space between my tallest shelves and the ceiling. The quiet made me think of the poet and miss him. I even missed Lily. I knew she wasn't reading. I knew she was back behind a shelf imaging herself as someone else, as someone who had read all five-fifths of the great books in the world, perhaps as someone who said things like, "God is the prime mover."

"Lily."

"What."

"Why don't you just do both?"

"Oh—money."

"Money? You make lots of money. Enough for you and two more like you."

"I'm saving it."

I craned my neck and saw her peeking inside an old armoire I use to store books I want to read before I die.

"What are you saving for? What could you need?"

"I don't know. Something might come up."

"Lily, nothing is ever going to come up. Nothing ever comes up. You know what you should do with that money? I'm serious now. Are you listening?"

"Yes."

"Buy a little red sportscar, Lily. A convertible. Then find a young good man. Lord, buy one of those, too. You can buy anything these days. Then drive around, Lily. Drive around fast until you feel like dancing. Then do that. Dance. That's what you should do, Lily. That's what you should do with your money."

She poked her head from behind a shelf directly in front of me. She surprised me. I could never keep track of her when she was in the shop.

"Are you making fun of me?"

I didn't answer because I wasn't sure. I looked down into a box of books I'd traded for that week—criticism from the twenties. They'd never sell. Lily was out from behind the shelf and in front of me before I could look up.

"What would you do?" she said. Her voice trembled a little. "Would you drive around town, whistle at people and let your hair blow behind you in some silly damn car?"

"Lily, I'd do some silly damn thing."

I was tired of both of us when I said that, and I know I shouldn't have said it. Lily and I had a pact of sorts. You don't accuse someone of doing nothing when you have a pact. So I can't blame Lily for whispering, "You would not. You would not," and walking out the door. I do wish I could blame someone for the way the door closed behind her—quietly, slowly, like the end of some sad story. Even with the melodrama, it frightened me.

For ten days, she was gone; it rained for seven of them. People walked by under newspapers, plastic head scarfs and low, heavy clouds. I missed her. Lord, I read with one eye always on the door. Late last night after closing, she came back. I was reading behind the counter, and though I knew from the knock who it was, I walked to the door slowly. I composed my face. She stood there in her silly dress, swaying. She was out of breath and looked cold. Her face and dress seemed drawn, pulled tight against her, as if she had been running from something that stood right outside the door.

"Are you all right?" I said.

"I've been drinking. I'm cold."

She came into the shop, and I moved behind my counter to my chair, settling in like a judge.

"So what's the problem?" I said.

She looked at me hard until I felt a touch of foolishness at the way I sat, the way I crossed my arms on my chest. Then she said, "I think we should take your advice tonight."

"What advice?"

"I think we should go dancing."

How can I say what I felt when she said that. I was sixty-three years old, and hadn't danced, hadn't thought of it, in over thirty years. I leaned back in my chair, and for once, the squeak startled me. I was cold, and tense, as though some intruder were standing over me, armed with a weapon against which I had no choice. But I could feel the chair against my back. I was in my own shop. I told myself I was safe.

"No, Lily," I said, smiling and shaking my head. "I don't think we should."

"I do. Really."

She was still swaying, but her eyes were firm. I said, "Lily, sit down," but she didn't sit down. She put her hands on the counter and leaned over until her face was just inches from mine. For a moment, I thought she might kiss me. I was confused. I wanted her to. Instead, she looked into my eyes—a long unflinching look, a look that made me wonder what she saw there.

"I don't want to sit down," she said. "I think we should go dancing. Tonight. I think you should lock up this store and walk down the street with me. And I think we should go into that bar under the blinking purple sign. We should dance."

She took my hand. Maybe that's why I followed her out the door, or maybe I thought I could bolt down an alley, outrun her, or maybe she just overwhelmed me, her face that close to mine. We walked slowly down the street in a fine rain. Lily was looking straight ahead, as if expecting to meet someone, and she looked different than she had in the shop, moments before. She looked frightened and young. I put my mouth next to her ear and said quietly, "Come on, Lily. I'll walk you home." She raised her head, and her face was like a child's face.

"When we go in, we'll walk straight to the dance floor, okay? We won't stop or look around. We'll just walk straight up there. And I'd like you to hold my hands when we dance."

What could I say? Lord, she was standing in the rain and shivering. So we went into the bar under the blinking purple sign. I felt the stares, but I looked only at Lily's dress, drenched and dragging behind her like a tiny wake. We walked straight to the dance floor. I took her cold hands and looked at her face. She looked shy. The music was very loud. People all around us were dancing. They looked like they were born to dance, bred to dance. I thought of running again, and then I thought of standing very still in hope that I might disappear the way a telephone pole or a street sign can disappear in a landscape that is otherwise alive and in motion. But Lily said, "We have to move." So we moved, clumsily, drawing close for protection. I looked at my feet, concentrating only on moving them back and forth with Lily's, trying to remember anything about dancing. Gradually, the back and forth shuffling became comfortable, or at least automatic. The crowd moved in so close they didn't matter. I looked up to see Lily watching me, her mouth open, in surprise, as if the moon had just sat down next to her.

"We're dancing," she said.

Inside, I felt a delicate tug, the way healing aches when a scar forms, when the body makes peace with its wounds, and then I remembered something. I remembered it the way the blind must remember color or the way the dead must remember life—a memory rising strangely, all at once, like something buoyant moving up through water and exploding onto the surface. I raised my arm and, with it, Lily's hand, and I said to her, "Spin." She looked at me for a moment, and then she smiled and did it. She spun. At that moment, our lives cracked open and held out a small, very important opportunity. In the end, I did not seduce her and she did not seduce me, but something that lived in the very center of her and even of me, that breathed and moved, seduced us both.

THE ARTIFICIAL FAMILY

ANNE TYLER

THE FIRST FULL SENTENCE that Mary ever said to him was, "Did you know I have a daughter?" Toby was asking her to dinner. He had just met her at a party—a long-haired girl in a floor-length gingham dress—and the invitation was instant, offered out of desperation because she was already preparing to leave and he wasn't sure he could ever find her again. Now, how did her daughter enter into this? Was she telling him that she was married? Or that she couldn't go out in the evenings? "No," said Toby. "I didn't know."

"Well, now you do," she said. Then she wrote her address down for him and left, and Toby spent the rest of the evening clutching the scrap of paper in his pocket for fear of losing it.

The daughter was five years old. Her name was Samantha, and it suited her: she was an old-fashioned child with two thick braids and a solemn face. When she and her mother stood side by side, barefoot, wearing their long dresses, they might have been about to climb onto a covered wagon. They presented a solid front. Their eyes were a flat, matching blue. "Well!" Toby would say, after he and Samantha knew each other better. "Shall we all *three* go somewhere? Shall we take a picnic lunch? Visit the zoo?" Then the blue would break up into darker colors, and they would smile—but it was the mother who smiled first. The child was the older of the two. She took longer to think things over.

They would go to the Baltimore Zoo and ride the tiny passenger train. Sitting three abreast on the narrow seat—Toby's arm around Mary, Samantha scrunched between them—they rattled past dusty-looking deer fenced in among the woods, through a tunnel where the younger children screamed, alongside a parade of wooden cartoon animals which everyone tried to identify. "That's Bullmoose! There's Bugs Bunny!" Only Samantha said nothing. She had no television set. Bugs Bunny was a stranger to her. She sat very straight, with her hands clasped between her knees in her long skirt, and Toby looked down at her and tried to piece out her father from the curve of her cheek and the tilt of her nose. Her eyes were her mother's, but surely that rounded chin came from her father's side. Had her father had red hair? Was that what gave Samantha's brown braids that coppery sheen? He didn't feel that he could ask straight out because Mary had slammed a door on the subject. All she said was that she had run away with Samantha after two years of marriage. Then once, discussing some earlier stage in Samantha's life, she pulled out a wallet photo to show him: Samantha as a baby, in her mother's lap. "Look at you!" Toby said. "You had your hair up! You had lipstick on! You were wearing a sweater and skirt. Look at Samantha in her party dress!" The photo stunned him, but Mary hardly noticed. "Oh, yes," she said, closing her wallet, "I was very straight back then." And that was the last time she mentioned her marriage. Toby never saw the husband, or heard anything about him. There seemed to be no visiting arrangements for the child.

Mornings Mary worked in an art gallery. She had to leave Samantha with a teen-aged babysitter after kindergarten closed for the summer. "Summers! I hate them," she said. "All the time I'm at work I'm wondering how Samantha is." Toby said, "Why not let *me* stay with her. You know how Samantha and I get along." He was a graduate student with a flexible schedule; and besides, he seized on every excuse to entrench himself deeper in Mary's life. But Mary said, "No, I couldn't ask you to do that." And she went on paying Carol, and paying her again in the evenings when they went out somewhere. They went to dinner, or to movies, or to Toby's rambling apartment. They always came back early. "Carol's mother will kill me!" Mary would say, and she would gather up her belongings and run ahead of Toby to his car. When he returned from taking her home his apartment always smelled of her: a clean, straw smell, like burlap. Her bobby pins littered the bed and the crevices of the sofa. Strands of her long hairs tended to get wound around the rollers of his carpet sweeper. When he went to sleep the cracked bell of her voice threaded through all his dreams.

At the end of August, they were married in a civil ceremony. They had known each other five months. *Only* five months, Toby's parents said. They wrote him a letter pointing out all their objections. How would he support three on a university grant? How would he study? What did he want with someone else's child? The child: that was what they really minded. The ready-made grandchild. How could he love some other man's daughter? But Toby had never been sure he would know how to love his *own* children; so the question didn't bother him. He liked Samantha. And he liked the idea of her: the single, solitary treasure carried away from the disaster of the sweater-and-skirt marriage. If he himself ever ran away, what would he choose to take? His grandfather's watch, his favorite chamois shirt, eight cartons of books, some still unread, his cassette tape recorder—each object losing a little more worth as the list grew longer. Mary had taken Samantha, and nothing else. He envied both of them.

They lived in his apartment, which was more than big enough. Mary quit her job. Samantha started first grade. They were happy but guarded, still, working too hard at getting along. Mary turned the spare bedroom into a study for Toby, with a "Private" sign on the door. "Never go in there," she told Samantha. "That's Toby's place to be alone." "But I don't *want* to be alone," Toby said. "I'm alone all day at the lab." Nobody seemed to believe him. Samantha passed the doorway of his study on tiptoe, never even peeking inside. Mary scrupulously avoided littering the apartment with her own possessions. Toby was so conscientious a father that he might have written himself a timetable: At seven, play Old Maid. At seven-thirty, read a story. At eight o'clock, offer a piggyback ride to bed. Mary he treated like glass. He kept thinking of her first marriage; his greatest fear was that she would leave him.

Every evening, Samantha walked around to Toby's lab to call him for supper. In the midst of reaching for a beaker or making a notation he would look up to find her standing there, absolutely silent. Fellow students gave her curious looks. She ignored them. She concentrated on Toby, watching him with a steady blue gaze that gave all his actions a new importance. Would he feel this flattered if she were his own? He didn't think so. In their peculiar situation— nearly strangers, living in the same house, sharing Mary—they had not yet started to take each other for granted. Her coming for him each day was purely a matter of choice, which he imagined her spending some time over before deciding; and so were the sudden, rare smiles which lit her face when he glanced down at her during the walk home.

At Christmastime Toby's parents flew down for a visit. They stayed four days, each one longer than the day before. Toby's mother had a whole new manner which kept everyone at arm's length. She would look at Samantha and say, "My, she's thin! Is her father thin, Mary? Does her father have those long feet?" She would go out to the kitchen and say, "I see you've done something with Toby's little two-cup coffeepot. Is this *your* pot, Mary? May I use it?" Everything she said was meant to remind them of their artificiality: the wife was someone else's first, the child was not Toby's. But her effect was to draw them closer together. The three of them formed an alliance against Mrs. Scott and her silent husband, who lent her his support merely by not shutting her up. On the second evening Toby escaped to his study and Samantha and Mary joined him, one by one, sliding through the crack in his door to sit giggling silently with him over a game of dominoes. One afternoon they said they had to take Samantha to her art lesson and they snuck off to a Walt Disney movie instead, and stayed there in the dark for two hours eating popcorn and Baby Ruths and endless strings of licorice.

Toby's parents went home, but the alliance continued. The sense of effort had disappeared. Toby's study became the center of the apartment, and every evening while he read Mary sat with him and sewed and Samantha played with cut-outs at their feet. Mary's pottery began lining the mantel and bookshelves. She pounded in nails all over the kitchen and hung up her saucepans. Samantha's formal bedtime ritual changed to roughhousing, and she and Toby pounded through the rooms and pelted each other with sofa cushions and ended up in a tangle on the hallway carpet.

Now Samantha was growing unruly with her mother. Talking back. Disobeying. Toby was relieved to see it. Before she had been so good that she seemed pathetic. But Mary said, "I don't know what I'm going to do with that child. She's getting out of hand."

"She seems all right to *me*," said Toby.

"I knew you'd say that. It's your fault she's changed like this, too. You've spoiled her."

"*Spoiled* her?"

"You dote on her, and she knows it," Mary said. She was folding the laundry, moving crisply around the bedroom with armloads of sheets and towels. Nowadays she wore sweaters and skirts—more practical for housework—and her loafers tapped across the floor with an efficient sound that made him feel she knew what she was talking about. "You give her everything she asks for," she said. "Now she doesn't listen to *me* any more."

"But there's nothing wrong with giving her things. Is there?"

"If you had to live with her all day long," Mary said, "eighteen hours a day, the way I do, you'd think twice before you said that."

But how could he refuse anything to Samantha? With him, she was never disobedient. She shrieked with him over pointless riddles, she asked him unanswerable questions on their walks home from the lab, she punched at him ineffectually, her thumbs tucked inside her fists, when he called her Sam. The only time he was ever angry with her was once when she stepped into the path of a car without looking. "Samantha!" he yelled, and he yanked her back and shook her until she cried. Inside he had felt his stomach lurch, his heart sent out a wave of heat and his knees shook. The purple marks of his fingers stayed on Samantha's arm for days afterward. Would he have been any more terrified if the child were his own? New opportunities for fear were everywhere, now that he was a family man. Samantha's walk from school seemed long and underpoliced, and every time he called home without an answer he imagined that Mary had run away from him and he would have to get through life without her. "I think we should have another baby," he told Mary, although of course he knew that increasing the number of people he loved would not make any one of them more expendable. All Mary said was, "Do you?"

"I love that little girl. I really love her. I'd like to have a whole *armload* of little girls. Did you ever think I would be so good at loving people?"

"Yes," said Mary.

"I didn't. Not until I met you. I'd like to *give* you things. I'd like to sit you and Samantha down and pile things in your laps. Don't you ever feel that way?"

"Women don't," said Mary. She slid out of his hands and went to the sink, where she ran cold water over some potatoes. Lately she had started wearing her hair pinned up, out of the way. She looked carved, without a stray wisp or an extra line, smooth to the fingertips, but when Toby came up behind her again she ducked away and went to the stove. "Men are the only ones who have that much feeling left to spare," she said. "Women's love gets frittered away: every day a thousand little demands for milk and bandaids and swept floors and clean towels."

"I don't believe that," said Toby.

But Mary was busy regulating the flame under the potatoes now, and she didn't argue with him.

For Easter, Toby bought Samantha a giant prepacked Easter basket swaddled in pink cellophane. It was a spur-of-the-moment purchase—he had gone to the all-night drugstore for pipe tobacco, seen this basket and remembered suddenly that tomorrow was Easter Sunday. Wouldn't Samantha be expecting some sort of celebration? He hated to think of her returning to school empty-handed, when everyone else had chocolate eggs or stuffed rabbits. But when he brought the basket home—rang the doorbell and waited, obscured behind the masses of cellophane like some comical florist's-messenger—he saw that he had made a mistake. Mary didn't like the basket. "How come you bought a thing like that?" she asked him.

"Tomorrow's Easter."

"Easter? Why Easter? We don't even go to church."

"We celebrated Christmas, didn't we?"

"Yes, but—and Easter's not the question," Mary said. "It's the basket." She reached out and touched the cellophane, which shrank beneath her fingers. "We never *used* to buy baskets. Before I've always hidden eggs and let her hunt for them in the morning, and then she dyes them herself."

"Oh, I thought people had jellybeans and things," Toby said.

"*Other* people, maybe. Samantha and I do it differently."

"Wouldn't she like to have what her classmates have?"

"She isn't trying to keep up with the *Joneses*, Toby," Mary said. "And how about her teeth? How about her stomach? Do I always have to be the heavy, bringing these things up? Why is it you get to shower her with love and gifts, and then it's me that takes her to the dentist?"

"Oh, let's not go into *that* again," Toby said.

Then Mary, who could never be predicted, said, "All right," and stopped the argument. "It was nice of you to think of it, anyway," she said formally, taking the basket. "I know Samantha will like it."

Samantha did like it. She treasured every jellybean and marshmallow egg and plastic chick; she telephoned a friend at seven in the morning to tell her about it. But even when she threw her arms around Toby's neck, smelling of sugar and cellophane, all he felt was a sense of defeat. Mary's face was serene and beautiful, like a mask. She continued to move farther and farther away from him, with her lips perpetually curved in a smile and no explanations at all.

In June, when school closed, Mary left him for good. He came home one day to find a square of paper laid flat on a club sandwich. The sight of it thudded instantly against his chest, as if he had been expecting it all along. "I've gone," the note said. His name was nowhere on it. It might have been the same note she sent her first husband—retrieved, somehow, and saved in case she found another use for it. Toby sat down and read it again, analyzed each loop of handwriting for any sign of indecision or momentary, reversible anger. Then he ate the club sandwich, every last crumb, without realizing he was doing so, and after that he pushed his plate away and lowered his head into his hands. He sat that way for several minutes before he thought of Samantha.

It was Monday evening—the time when she would just be finishing with her art lesson. He ran all the way, jaywalking and dodging cars and waving blindly at the drivers who honked. When he arrived in the dingy building where the lessons were given he found he was too early. The teacher still murmured behind a closed door. Toby sat down, panting, on a bench beneath a row of coat hooks. Flashes of old TV programs passed through his head. He saw himself blurred and bluish on a round-cornered screen—one of those mysteriously partnerless television parents who rear their children with more grace and tact and unselfishness than any married couple could ever hope for. Then the classroom door opened. The teacher came out in her smock, ringed by six-year-olds. Toby stood up and said, "Mrs.—um. Is Samantha Glover here?"

The teacher turned. He knew what she was going to say as soon as she took a breath; he hated her so much he wanted to grab her by the neck and slam her head against the wall. "Samantha?" she said. "Why, no, Mr. Scott, Samantha didn't come today."

On the walk back, he kept his face stiff and his eyes unfocused. People stared at him. Women turned to look after him, frowning, curious to see the extent of the damage. He barely noticed them. He floundered up the stairs to his apartment, felt his way to the sofa and sat down heavily. There was no need to turn the lights on. He knew already what he would find: toys and saucepans, Mary's skirts and sweaters, Samantha's new short dresses. All they would have taken with them, he knew, was their long gingham gowns and each other.

TATTOO

BARBARA THOMPSON

THE SERVANT WOMAN rolls back the sleeves of her kurta, throws off the flimsy scarf and pours a dollop of oil into her small fleshy palm. Julia is already naked on the cotton mat, her light hair held away from the massage oil by a child's plastic barrette. Her face in company is alert, sharp, foxy, but now in repose, unobserved by anyone, it slips back into the mild formlessness of the time before her marriage.

Kishwar transfers oil to the other hand, automatically invoking the blessing of Allah on her enterprise, falling back on her haunches to gain momentum for the next lunge at Julia's vertebral ridge. Julia tells her friends Kishwar grunts like a sumo wrestler.

Kishwar has been in the household for more than a year. She was hired as Sherezad's ayah, and when the little girl began school last September, she became Julia's part-time masseuse. She is short for a Punjabi, fat and dark, and she has a light merry laugh. Kishwar's husband works somewhere as a driver.

It is mid-May. The foreigners spend whatever time they can manage in swimming suits around the Punjab Club pool. Julia has her massage every day at eleven and goes off, oiled and sleek, to lunch there. Three or four times every month she meets a man. He is Pakistani like her husband, but younger than Julia and still unmarried. His family maintains a huge house on the Canal Bank, but when he can contrive an excuse to come to Lahore from his post in Peshawar, he stays in one of the old-fashioned suites the Club maintains for out-of-station members. This is the first day of such a visit; earlier, after her husband left, Julia spoke with him on the telephone. Smiling, she closes her eyes for what is meant to be a short nap. When she wakens it is well past the hour. Kishwar is still working over her, mindless of time as a water-wheel. Julia jumps up, fumbling for her terrycloth robe on the floor—and sees the tattoos. Kishwar has no time to cover them.

"They're all over her arms," Julia tells Nazir later at the Club. "Hearts and flowers, flying birds. All blue."

Julia lies in a pink bikini at the edge of the Club pool. The day is as hot and dry as if the country were a tandoor, one of the mounded earthen ovens that dot the city. Few people are out, even here: two English children and their doughy mother storing up sun for the summer of home-leave; a crew-cut American who swims ten measured laps and hurries away. Pakistanis are always rare. Only love or lust or cultural alienation would bring a Pakistani to a communal swimming pool at noon in May.

Nazir Ahmad, who possesses all these qualifications, lies next to Julia. He spent ten years in America on a student visa and has sloughed off his origins sufficiently to admire an even tan and be willing to strip to a bit of colored latex in the presence of strangers. He came back five years ago, summoned by a spate of cables warning of his mother's imminent demise. Once he returned her heart condition improved miraculously and his Berkeley Ph.D. in Political Science served to ease his way through the Civil Service Exam. He has become the Deputy Commissioner in Peshawar.

And although he was sufficiently intimidated by his family not to bring back as wife the Jewish graduate student with whom he had been living, for the past ten months he has been seeing Julia. Today, as always, they will drink pink gins, lunch on kebabs and nan, and go up to his room. Julia will go separately, her arms full of brown shopping bags from the Mall, as though she is carrying parcels for some woman friend staying there. No one but the Club servants will know.

"She must have a past," Nazir says. "Your maidservant."

"Why?"

"Respectable 'desi' women don't go in for tattoos. But if one did, it wouldn't be the kind of design you see on British sailors."

"She has a perfectly respectable-looking husband," Julia says.

He is drowsy from the sun and gin and beginning to think of the cool dark room above. He calls the bearer and orders lunch. It is brought to them at the pool by two servants in starched white, their long coats cinched with cummerbands, their pugris stiff and tall above their heads. Julia and Nazir eat with their fingers, their movements quick, expectant.

That night at dinner Julia tells her husband about the tattoos. It is one of her duties as his wife to be entertaining at dinner. She spends a fair amount of time preparing herself—collecting gossip at bridge parties, going to family weddings and funerals and circumcisions, reading the air mail magazines at the Club. *The New Statesman* is best for her purposes, though its politics are not her husband's. He owns a complex of textile mills.

After six years of marriage, her own politics are non-existent, which Julia herself in reflective moments knows to be an odd neutrality in a woman who came here as an officer, however junior, in the U.S. Foreign Service. Lahore was her first overseas post, and nothing in her training or the talk of others had prepared her for the emotions she would feel at the work assigned her, refusing visas to the legion of the hopeless who were trying to emigrate. In time it numbed her: her real life began at twilight on the race course grounds, urging a long-maned polo pony around the perimeter of the field while the men, Pakistanis and a few foreigners, played their games. The horse was lent her by the man who later became her husband, a stocky middle-aged Punjabi from an old family who was at least partially married: his wife lived in the village. The second summer Julia found herself pregnant, and in the lassitude of that state, intensified by the flower-rich monsoon heat, let go of her life of demanding autonomy. With something like relief she let herself be married to him under the polygamous dispensation of Islamic law.

They are dining alone tonight and so her husband summons Kishwar into the dining room. Julia has aroused his curiosity; he will inspect the tattoos himself. The servant woman toddles in raking at the dopatta over her hair, self-conscious at this notice by the Sahib. He is pleasant, hearty, almost flirtatious with her—his habitual manner with women who could not possibly misunderstand.

Because of this manner and its contrast to the strict formality with which he treats the wives of his friends and business associates, Julia believed in the beginning that he had no interest in other women. Then when Sherezad was three, she discovered that every Thursday night, before the ritual bath that purified him for his Friday prayers, he visited a singing woman in a brothel in the Hira Mundi.

When Julia told him she was leaving, he was courteous and calm and offered, with regret at her decision, to take care of the travel arrangements if she was sure that was what she wanted. Of course, she could not take her jewelry, the rubies set with pearls, the heavy kundan earrings with the emerald drops: Customs would search her for any gold illegally exported. And she could not take Sherezad, who was without a valid passport.

Julia, with the wisdom of the weak, gave in immediately and made no terms. She knew he would not relent or be subverted. He loved Sherezad as he loved his Rajput miniatures, rarely looking at them but always conscious that they hung in fine gold frames in an air conditioned room with black cloths over the glass to keep the colors from fading.

They went on as before, but imperceptibly, without any volition on her part, Julia changed. She continued her Urdu lessons with the old Kashmiri ustad who came three mornings a week, but her early proficiency left her; she was lapsing into the kitchen Urdu of the other foreign women who had not been scholars and government officers. And after a time she braved the company of other Americans, steeling herself against a continuation of the coolness they had shown her at the time of Sherezad's birth. But those days and that cadre of diplomats had passed. Julia's husband was rich and clubbable; they were welcomed everywhere.

Her husband rarely accompanied her; he did not want to be officially perceived as a client of the Americans. But he seemed glad that Julia was back with 'her own kind' as though he understood it to mean that she was abandoning the excessive expectations with which she had begun their marriage, and was accepting the compromises her circumstance required.

A summer ago at the Consul General's reception for the Fourth of July, Julia met Nazir Ahmad. If her husband knows about the affair, he has elected to be complaisant. Julia's virtue was never a commodity of great value; he knew there had been men before him. And he knows too, as Julia did only when it was too late, that if he should ever want to do so, he can use this indiscretion to send her back to her own country, cut her off forever from Sherezad.

But there is nothing of that menace in the air tonight as they dine together under the whirring fans while Sherezad sleeps in the adjacent garden in a cocoon of mosquito netting. Julia can see that he is enjoying his interrogation of the maidservant, the flutter into which he has cast her by his courtliness and the range of his questions: Has she sons? What is her village? How does she come to be in Lahore? Kishwar answers in monosyllables, smiling shyly, her eyes downcast. The sleeves of her cotton shirt are tight at the wrists. He has not mentioned the tattoos, and after a while Julia realizes that he never will. That is not his way. He will lead her by indirection to tell him whatever he wants to know, either as an accidental self-betrayal or a free offering. His patience comes of knowing he has, at last resort, the power to command her. Julia feels a chill and goes out into the dark veranda to make sure that Sherezad has not thrown off her covers.

The next morning when she is again naked under Kishwar's kneading, Julia composes her questions in schoolbook Urdu, asking the woman where the markings came from, how she comes to have them. She cannot see Kishwar's face when she asks but she feels the woman's hands tighten. Then with a laugh, Kishwar gives Julia's buttock an affectionate slap. "Meri jan bahaut passand—"

Julia cannot follow the language. "Your husband likes it?" she asks tentatively in English.

Kishwar laughs again, a lazy laugh laced with contempt for the little dark husband about whom Julia could have such an unlikely idea. "Not husband," she says in English. "Meri jan." My Beloved. She says it comfortably, companionably.

Julia tells Nazir at lunch: "You can't believe it! She's so ugly. She's fat and gap-toothed and black as the Ace of Spades. And she has a lover!"

As she says it she is sorry. Slurs against color are acceptable from him, not from her. She has heard the tales of British memsahibs who undressed in front of their servants as they would have their poodles because, being black, they were not quite men. She is never sure what Nazir feels; he himself is quite dark, a dull cafe-au-lait.

"Think of Cleopatra," he says. "Swarthy, short-legged and with a hooked nose." He congratulates himself on finding an image that is racially neutral.

"If it's her lover who likes it, I wonder what her husband thinks," Julia muses.

That is a line of speculation Nazir prefers not to follow.

In the evening as Julia and Kishwar return from the bazaar, Kishwar's husband is waiting at the gate. Another man is with him, a tall lean Pathan with a sharp eye and the clothing of the Peshawar District. Julia hands over the parcels to the bearer, and Kishwar goes to her husband. There is a hasty exchange, monosyllabic and staccatto and then Kishwar comes to ask Julia for leave. Julia gives her the night but tells her to be back by breakfast time. Tomorrow is Nazir's last day. She wants to go to him scented and oiled, a sun-flushed houri. She likes the image of herself as a gift, and she dresses in bright soft colors—saffron, peach, aquamarine—layers of cloth to be unwrapped and inside, the firm soft flesh that Kishwar has prepared.

It is noon when Kishwar turns up. Julia is late already, and still on the telephone negotiating with her sister-in-law that Sherezad will be delivered to her house after school. There have been nasty incidents involving little girls left alone with menservants even in the best regulated households. Her husband does not permit her to leave Sherezad without a woman. Julia has explained this more than once, a little frantically she knows. She has the uncomfortable feeling that the other woman knows exactly why she is in such a hurry.

Kishwar looks worn and dirty, and she makes no apology at all for her tardiness, not even the conventional lies about sudden illness or family crisis. Julia has girded herself against the false-hoods but now she finds herself resenting Kishwar's disregard of the forms; it is a little insulting.

Kishwar trails her to the car as though she has more to say. Another request. "Not now," Julia says firmly. Her good nature is being imposed on.

Kishwar goes into halting English. "Memsahib, you speak to Lat'-sahib for me," she says, using the word "lord" that is reserved for governors and high officials. "Nazir-sahib." Her manner is sullen for somebody, especially a Punjabi, asking a favor.

"I can't stop now. I'm late."

Kishwar looks around. The house servants are busy elsewhere. Only two male figures lounging at the gate would see her—if they turn around—as she throws herself at Julia's feet, pressing her little round belly against Julia's shins. She hangs onto them sobbing. The sobs seem real. With a sigh and a glance at her watch, Julia urges Kishwar to her feet, and into the comparative privacy of the veranda.

Kishwar's husband has sent her. His honor is at stake. That much is clear; Julia can follow it even in the mix of Urdu, Punjabi and pidgin English. It is the usual story when some extraordinary request is about to be made. "Safarish," the favor that puts one eternally in somebody's debt, is a way of life here.

The details are difficult for Julia to follow. A Pathan tribesman—an Affridi from the hills outside Peshawar—came to Kishwar's husband yesterday morning. His only son is in jail in Peshawar, charged with murder. The boy is fifteen. He is accused of taking the gold earrings from a three-year-old girl of his village, and, when she said that she would tell her mother, of throwing her into the well. The earrings were knotted in the cord that fastened his baggy shelwar trousers. He said he had found them, but when the police beat him, he confessed. Now he will go to prison for life. The girl's family is willing to accept restitution—the blood-price: she was one of several daughters and the price includes not only gold but animals. But Government says the boy must go to trial. The Deputy Commissioner—Nazir Ahmad—has the power to release him.

"But he's guilty," Julia says. "Why should Nazir-sahib let him go free?" She is about to add, "and why do you plead for him?", when she understands. Of course, this Pathan, the sinewy man with the black moustache here yesterday in the courtyard is Kishwar's lover, the man for whom she had herself tattooed.

"If you want to, you can come with me to the Club. Nazir-sahib is likely to be there and you can speak with him yourself," she says. "I can't take any responsibility for it." She adds that for form; she has already taken on some responsibility just by listening.

The servant woman waits patiently at the edge of the Club lawn, a good distance from the swimming pool, where ayahs are permitted. She squats in the shade of the pink bougainvillea vine, every now and then getting up to look through the servants' gate at something or someone on the roadway. She has wrapped her sheer nylon dopatta over her head and neck, covering herself as much as possible. Near the pool the sahibs, in strength today because of the Friday holiday, lie glistening with sunoil on their bright terry towels. Occasionally a child dives off the board or paddles around the shallow end under the eye of his mother, but the real use of the blue water is to cool the tanning adults who float about on its surface in black trunk inner-tubes, drinks in hand.

Nazir tries to ignore the maidservant. He doesn't like refusing favors and he doesn't want to grant this one. From Julia's report, the boy seems clearly guilty, and any official interference would be not only wrong but conspicuous. So he sucks on his drink, splashing pool water on his shoulders to cool himself. But whatever he does he feels Kishwar's black eyes on him. He may as well hear her out. He throws a towel over his bare torso and walks to the gate.

She stands up and squints over her shoulder as he approaches. He sees two men, one in Peshawari dress, at the end of the servants' walk. "Ji, Mai?" He addresses her in the familiar form of 'mother', glancing without meaning to at her arms. Only the faint blue edge of the tattoo is visible at the buttoned wrist of her shirt.

"I told Memsahib," she says. "I will be beaten if you do not do this thing."

"Why do you plead for this boy? What is the father to you?" Nazir says it in as kindly a manner as possible. He asks not because he doubts Julia's interpretation but out of curiosity, to hear what a traditional Punjabi woman would answer in such a case.

"He did my husband a service once," the woman replies.

Nazir tries not to smile at that way of speaking of it.

She looks him straight in the face as though she reads his thoughts. "This Pathan killed a man for him."

Nazir shouts to the bearer to bring him a chair, slumps into it. He should have known the story was not as simple as Julia said.

Kishwar does not speak again until the bearer is out of earshot. "My husband was in prison," she begins. "It was nothing." She makes a gesture with open palms to indicate the absence of any guilt. "He was innocent. There was a quarrel between families. Someone had to confess. He had no job so he was chosen. He came to prison here in Lahore."

Nazir's work is administering the law; he does not take easily to her assumption that while justice must be served, it need not be served with any precision. For nothing, for his family's convenience, a man will serve seven years Rigorous Imprisonment?

"We were married only a little time. I had no child. I was prettier then. A man saw me. He would wait for me on the paths and give me sweets. He would come to the well and draw water for me. I was weak. I fell.

"When my husband's people came to know of it, they sent me away. I could not go back to my own people as I was, so I went to live with him. He was a good man, he never beat me. He kept me in the inner courtyard and never let me go anywhere, even to the shrine, but he bought me shiny cloth for clothes and pomegranates and wild honey so that I would conceive. Then at the end of the fourth year, he took me to Montgomery to the man who gives tattoos. He said it was so I could not run away. Where would I run to?"

She unfastens the buttons at the wrists of her shirt and rolls back the sleeves. Nazir sees that among the flowers and hearts, the birds in flight, are words in Urdu: a man's name, Asif Magid, and a date in the Islamic calendar. "Memsahib saw this."

"Memsahib can't read the Urdu," he says.

"It was the next year in the dry month before the rains. We were sleeping out on the roof, and on the night of the dark of the moon, someone came and killed him with a knife."

"Asif Magid?"

"Asif Magid, whom I loved. The man who killed him cut his throat so deeply that his head hung loose, and he cut the palms of his hands and his genitals. He must have done all that after he was dead because I did not wake until the flies began to buzz and the vultures circle over him. It was almost daybreak and he had been dead so long his blood was like river mud. I knew my husband had done it, or some of his kinfolk. When the constable came, I told him.

"But word came back that my husband was still in prison in Lahore, and that his kinfolk too had been locked up that night, taken in Lahore on suspicion of planning a burglary. So I went back to my husband's people and lived with them like a slave until my husband came out of prison. He beat me at first to take away the shame, but afterwards he brought me here to Lahore. He swore to me that he had no connection with the killing of Asif-sahib. I believed it because he swore on the heads of our unborn sons."

She smiles a queer smile. "I have no child to this day."

Nazir is impatient. "But what does all this have to do with that other business—the boy, the gold earrings?"

"Yesterday that Pathan came to my husband's quarters. He had shared my husband's prison cell those years ago. He knew—as everything, sahib is known—that I have a place with Memsahib, and that you will not refuse Memsahib's safarish. He asked my husband to obtain his son's freedom."

Nazir is annoyed at the implication that this affair with Julia is generally known. They have been unfailingly discreet. Julia has never even been to Peshawar. "Why should your husband ask you to plead, even if I were able to grant it?"

"This man did my husband a killing once, out of friendship." Her tone is heavy, implying it is something he already knows. "He is the one who came at the dark of the moon and killed Asif-sahib as he lay next to me."

Nazir shouts for another gin. This is like everything else in his official life in this place. He longs for the orderliness of America, where appetites are simple and simply satisfied, where killings are done out of need and anger, not out of duty and friendship.

Kishwar sees his weariness and presses. "This Pathan lived with my husband in his cell. They shared everything, their grief at having no sons, my husband's shame at the dishonor I had brought him. They were closer than brothers.

"He was released from prison a year before my husband. His own village was in the Frontier, a thousand miles away. He had never been to our village, but he knew from my husband's telling

"Once you start weighing things, nothing makes any sense," she says. "Kishwar gets beaten again, and the boy goes to jail forever—"

"Not forever. And if he's pretty he'll have an easy enough time." He knows this will shock her, will make it even more difficult for her to think in terms of abstract justice. "What do you think these prisons are?" He has lost the thread of his argument, of hers. Which side has he taken?

"Do what you think is right," she says almost primly. She does not want to think about Kishwar's story any longer; it contains a source of pain that she does not want to identify. She stands up and stretches herself. The sun is directly overhead now; it reflects off everything, the enamelled white table-tops, the aluminum frames of the chairs, the river-mica in the concrete.

When Julia comes out of the changing room, Nazir has already gone up. Kishwar is back under the pink bougainvillea and Julia gives her the bag of wet things to put into the car. They do not speak but Julia knows that she is conveying to Kishwar that everything is within her control.

Julia believes it herself. It is a small thing, really, that has been asked of him. Nazir will find extenuating circumstances to justify his action; there are always extenuating circumstances when someone has the will to find them. She wonders fleetingly why it has become so important that Nazir do this for her—do it without her making a direct request. Is it out of sympathy with Kishwar, who tends her daughter and who knows as no one else does her body when it is loose and undefended? Or does she simply crave proof that he will do anything at all for love of her?

Whatever it is, she feels intensely the power she has over him, and borne along upon it, she walks up the wide main stairs to his room without making any attempt at all to conceal her destination. She feels immune from the world's judgment.

It is only afterwards, coming down the stairs in her limp summer dress, that she reflects that Kishwar too must have felt that power, lying on the flat mud roof under the stars with the lover who was so afraid of losing her that he had his name etched in blue arabesques on her skin. And that tiny girl too, angry over the rings torn from her earlobes, reminding the big boy what punishment she can bring down upon him. The moment of power is brief and the danger abiding. Julia knows that and something in her falters, but she can still perfectly remember the elegant tracery of Nazir's ribcage under the wiry hair as he sprawled beside her on the wide bed. She does not yet feel the danger she knows is everywhere.

In the morning, Julia's sister-in-law drops by for coffee. She is a cool woman with streaks of bright henna covering her grey hair. She wastes no love on Julia, but she is invariably correct. This morning, among things of no importance at all, she tells Julia that Nazir Ahmad is to marry Inayutallah's daughter Shams. Julia remains composed but she does not summon the bearer for the usual second cups of Nescafe. When her caller leaves, Julia awards herself a tumbler of gin before she calls Kishwar for her massage.

The strong hands rest her. And as the muscles relax, Julia's mind, too, lets go a little. Nazir will do whatever she wants except—now the perimeters are known—in matters that concern his family.

This wife will not matter. She is one of his own kind and will never understand that part of him that needs Julia. For Julia knows, has known all along, the source of her power over him, and for just a moment she permits herself to think about it, to give it a name.

It has nothing to do with her prettiness, the soft supple body, her cultivated passion. She can age and wither, it will make no difference. He cleaves to her whiteness, the foreign smell—a lifetime of other foods, different rituals of hygiene—and the unfalsifiable paleness of her secret hair. Julia is proof to him that he is not altogether one of these people, that he was changed irrevocably in those ten years away. Nazir never thought to marry her, or to stay free for her, but what she has of him she can keep as long as she wants.

Kishwar sighs as she pours the warm oil onto the soles of Julia's feet. She too moves in a liquid drifting manner as though her mind is far away. Julia wonders if she is thinking of Asif Magid. Did Kishwar love him? And how could she know what love was in a life like that, when she had nowhere else to go? But she must have felt something—pride or power if not love—when he took her to Montgomery to have his name put on her.

The sun has reached the dusty pane of the high window and falls on her back and Kishwar's head. She can smell the pine massage oil and the heavier oil that Kishwar braids into her black hair.

Everything is still. Only Kishwar moves, her heavy rhythms a form of comforting.

Julia is half asleep when she hears her own rough sob like an infant's strangle, and wakes in time to bring back from sleep the image of a pale naked body engraved all over in an intricate calligraphy of fruits and flowers and the indelible names of men.

COPIES

MARY MORRIS

Beverly stands at the model 2200, wondering why Doug hasn't looked at her all day. Doug, the man Beverly has been dating for the past six weeks, is busy at the color xerox. He is her third boyfriend this year. That is one less boyfriend than last year but it is still more than she wants.

Beverly always meets her boyfriends on the job. She met Andy, the one before Doug, at the Actor's Hotline where they sat side by side, answering the phone for other people who were getting jobs. One day Beverly answered a call and handed the phone to Andy. "It's for you," she said. It was a producer he'd met at a party a long time ago who had found just the right part for him and he moved to L.A. in a matter of days. A week after he moved he sent her a postcard of the hills of Hollywood, saying he knew she'd get there sometime.

Beverly met Doug after working at the copy center for a few hours. He is a tall, skinny Columbia dropout who is "trying to find himself" and who sits at the edge of her bed at night, playing the guitar while she sleeps. Beverly learned to sleep through anything when she was a little girl and lived with her parents in a little split-level just beyond the northeast approach runway at LaGuardia. Her father wasn't a pilot but a sales representative for a shoe company and she hardly ever saw him.

Beverly hates the 2200 because there is nothing to do but watch and make certain it doesn't break down. The 2200 can print a hundred pages a minute. When it breaks down, it is a disaster. The Ektaprint is much better than the 2200 but Doug always works on the Ektaprint. Her favorite machine is the binder. She likes the way the frayed edges of paper fall like confetti into the little pouch at the back of the machine. Beverly collects this confetti. She plans to give a party when she leaves the copy center and toss these bits of paper into the air.

It is a Monday morning and there is already a long line of customers with numbers in their hands, waving them at the people who work behind the pale oak counter that separates customer from employee. They wave their tickets as if they were seeing people off who are about to depart on a long cruise. The copy center is done in California-style oak paneling with neatly painted signs that read "Express Pick-Up" or "Take a Number, Please." When Beverly came to work here six months ago, she thought it must be a very orderly place but it isn't very orderly at all.

A nervous homosexual has already been in to complain about the quality of the copies on his last teleplay. Every Monday he comes in to have something copied. He always refuses to drop it off and sometimes he will wait an hour. Usually he wants thirty copies of everything, done by hand, collated, bound, with a two-tone cover. He is a tedious client and Doug does his jobs. But it is Robert, the store manager, who listens to the complaints.

Andrea, Beverly's friend and assistant manager of the store, is crazy about Robert but Beverly doesn't see why. Robert is a pale, skinny man with stringy brown hair and jagged buck teeth. He is one hundred percent Italian and Andrea, who studied Italian literature for a term at Pomona College, thinks he is passionate. But Beverly finds him dull and self-absorbed; she thinks the only time Robert ever seems to react to anything is when Mrs. Grimsely comes into the store.

Mrs. Grimsley is an old Irish lady who always thinks other people are butting in line in front of her. She thinks that somehow people can slip a number in between hers and the one they are currently attending to. Mrs. Grimsley writes novels. She once brought in a copy of a novel that survived Hurricane Agnes. The novel was water-stained, the ink was smeared. It was virtually illegible. She told Robert she wanted it copied so that it would become legible.

Robert always gets a headache when he sees Mrs. Grimsley because Mrs. Grimsley wants the impossible. She wants things made bigger so she can read them with her failing eyesight but Robert has explained to her many times that he can't make a page bigger. Mrs. Grimsley doesn't understand. She wants things either if he didn't want to have children with Beverly. He has been in love with her since she walked into the store. He is short and Jewish and he always falls for tall, blond women who are not going to be interested in him.

As they are leaving, Steven asks Beverly if she wants to get a bite at Bagel Nosh. It is just around the corner and Beverly has nothing better to do so she says, "Why not." She wanted to go home and take a shower. Instead she goes to Bagel Nosh. She hopes Steven will not talk about the sperm bank over dinner. She gets an onion bagel with chicken liver and he gets a sesame bagel with lox.

Steven feels he is duty bound to level with Beverly. "Well, you know, Doug likes women, I guess. Lots of women, I mean. I'm looking for something a little more secure." Beverly knows this. Steven is the kind of man who would be looking for something more secure. Things don't come to him easily and he isn't likely to get what he wants out of life.

As they are about to leave Bagel Nosh, Robert walks in with Andrea. They were doing the books and decided to get a bite. Andrea stares at Robert wide-eyed as if she were a fish he just caught on a line. Robert smiles brightly at Beverly and she can tell that Andrea is jealous. Andrea thinks Robert likes Beverly. It would make sense. Everyone else does, except Doug. Beverly looks at Andrea in the Bagel Nosh reflecting glass. She is a rather dumpy brunette with frizzy brown hair. Andrea is the kind of woman most men would like to marry; they just don't want to date her.

Robert and Andrea sit down and Steven is disappointed. He wanted to go to Beverly's and drink wine. He wanted to tell her about his deprived childhood in Buffalo. Steven thinks he is a marvelous storyteller and that he can charm her with his yarns. Then he wants to get her into bed. Once he is able to convince a woman to go to bed with him, she usually has no regrets. Robert and Andrea order bagels and coffee.

Robert says, "Boy, this is copy center night, huh. We just ran into Doug going uptown."

Beverly takes this in carefully as Andrea nudges Robert. "Uptown?"

Andrea says, "Oh, we didn't know which way he was going." Andrea, who helped Beverly get her the job, has watched Doug go through many women at the copy center. Every time a new

darker than they are in reality. She wants fingerprint smudge
waterstains, ink blotches, removed from the page. She wants h
copies to come out perfect.

Mrs. Grimsley had a son who looked just like Robert who w
killed in one of the wars before Robert was born. Once she broug
in a picture of her son and everyone agreed that Robert did lo
like him. Mrs. Grimsley thinks Robert is her son. She wants t
impossible.

When Robert sees her come in, he shudders. He does not
along well with his own mother so the thought of having M
Grimsley as his mother irks him more. He has tried to explain
Mrs. Grimsley that he is not her son but she won't take no for
answer. "Around the eyes," she says. "And the hair. Just like
Billy." Andrea tries to wait on Mrs. Grimsley this morning but
will hear nothing of it. "I want Billy," she shrieks. "I want
Billy."

This particular Monday has been terrible. The 2200 broke do
twice and the repairman had to be called. It seems that ev
application to everything in the world is due by October 15
everyone wants his or her copies made on 25% rag. Beverly
barely stand toward the end of the day and all she wants to do i
go to bed with Doug. But Doug tells her he is going down to
Village to jam with some friends. Beverly is disappointed but
doesn't say anything. "O.K., so maybe tomorrow." Doug sm
"Maybe tomorrow." Beverly suspects Doug has another wo
but she doesn't say anything.

Steven can't take his eyes off Beverly as she tries to yank p
out of the 2200. Unlike Doug, Steven will never lose intere
her. He doesn't know what Beverly sees in Doug, but he kn
Doug has lost interest in her.

Steven thinks he is becoming sterile from the photocop
equipment. He is always careful not to get exposed to the li
Steven reads most of the information he copies and a few mo
ago he copied a report from the Journal of the AMA which susp
sterility from fluorescent lights. Once every few days Steven t
about going off to a sperm bank and putting some seeds on
"These machines are ruining us," Steven says in the middle
busy Monday morning. "Aren't you people concerned?"

No one is terribly concerned. Steven wouldn't be so conce

woman comes in, Doug, who has wonderful grey-green eyes and thick black hair, gets interested. But then, after a month or so, he will lose interest and usually the girl will have a broken heart.

Andrea has thought about firing Doug several times, but he is the fastest copier she has ever seen. Doug can keep three machines going at the same time and be hand-feeding another machine as well. Because the copy center is the busiest one in the neighborhood, Andrea can't really afford to fire him. She has tried to hint to Beverly that Doug has lost interest in her. Andrea knows the signs because Doug lost interest in her once a few years ago.

Robert is somewhat oblivious. "No, he said he was meeting a friend at Empire Szechuan, don't you remember?"

Andrea doesn't know what else to say. "Yes, I remember."

Robert is the only one who doesn't know exactly what is going on in his store. He doesn't know, for example, that every chance she gets, Andrea tries to work beside him. He has no idea that the reason why Andrea, who once had ambitions of going to law school, has stayed at the copy center for the past three years, is because she is hoping someday Robert will pay attention to her.

After a few minutes, Beverly gets up. "I'm going home." Steven gets up to go with her but Beverly waves him down and away, as if she were the trainer of an animal act.

As Beverly climbs the stairs to her apartment, she hears the phone ringing. She counts almost fifteen rings but she is not in a hurry to get the call. If it is not her mother, it is Doug. If it is Doug, she is not sure she wants to talk to him. When Beverly gets inside, she is glad to be alone. She is especially glad because her apartment is so quiet and the copy center is so noisy.

Beverly calls her service and tries not to be upset when she learns no one has phoned her for auditions. Like everyone in the copy center, she wants to be doing something else. In high school she was named "Most Likely to Appear on Saturday Night Live." Once a month she has new pictures of herself made up with new resumes and she mails them to all the agents in New York. Andrea thinks there is no other actress in the city with that much determination. Because she is very beautiful, sometimes Beverly gets calls, but she never gets a part.

The phone rings again and Beverly answers on the fifth ring. Doug sounds anxious on the other end. "Where've you been? We finished jamming a while ago. The tenor sax never showed. Can I come up?"

Beverly wants to say no, but she says all right. She wants to say no because the truth is that she want to be alone. She wants to read a book and wash her hair. She wants to watch *Family Feud* and call her mother. She wants to tell her mother she hasn't made it big yet and that she'd like to come home for Christmas but she can't afford it. Beverly's mother lives in a retirement village in Arizona; she always asks Beverly to visit but never sends her the money for a ticket.

There are a dozen things she wants to do but when Doug calls, she tells him to come on up. Beverly has always had a hard time saying no to men and she has spent too many nights with men she didn't want to be with. Doug arrives out of breath. He always runs up her steps, two steps at a time. She wonders why he does this since he is never all that happy to see her. Doug is seeing another woman as Beverly suspects. He was going to see her tonight but her husband called off his meeting so she had to be home.

Beverly kisses Doug perfunctorily on the cheek when he walks in. She wonders why she always falls for men who never pay much attention to her. Beverly's father died when she was fourteen and she's never felt so betrayed before or since. She knows Doug likes to be with more than one woman at a time. He has told her he has no desire to settle down. Doug's mother has been married three times and as far as Doug can tell, the new men were never improvements over the old ones.

After they make love, Beverly falls asleep and Doug strums his guitar. First he tunes it, then he plays "I Write the Songs That Make the Whole World Sing." In the middle of his tune, Beverly shoots out of bed. "Oh, my god," she cries.

Doug grabs her hand. "What was it?"

"Another DC 10." Since she was a little girl, growing up near LaGuardia, Beverly's dreams have been filled with airplanes crashing into her sheets. She can be in the middle of a dream about Yosemite, a place she visited with another boyfriend she met when she did mailings for the Sierra Club, and suddenly an airplane will crash into her sheets. Beverly always wakes up when there is a crash but otherwise she can sleep through anything.

He pulls the covers up over her chin. "You were just dreaming," he tells her. "Go back to sleep."

There are steady customers at the copy center and Beverly knows them all. She knows Mrs. Grimsley and she knows the homosexual playwright. She knows the Jehovah's witness, who sends prayers to his brother on Riker's Island, and the impatient woman who puts down her American Express gold card. She knows the music school teachers with dandruff on their collars, the desperate unemployed with their tattered resumes. And she knows a woman named Emily who has been coming to the copy center since she began working there.

Everyone who works at the copy center is jealous of at least one person who brings in work and stands at the other side of the oak counter. Robert is jealous of a graphic designer who does a lot of annual reports. Robert wants to have his own graphic design business some day. Doug is jealous of a musician who is always having his scores printed and bound for his publisher. Steven is jealous of a medical doctor and Andrea is jealous of a social worker. Beverly is jealous of Emily.

Emily comes in often. She has soft, doe-like eyes, and she cannot speak without smiling. She never comes up and says, "I'm 90. Why are you taking 91?" She always says, "Excuse me. Did you call 90?" Beverly knows Emily is happy and successful. Emily comes into the copy center calmly with the music for her newest concert to be run off. She has blurbs xeroxed in which Diana Ross says, "I'd be honored to sing any of Ms. Barkington's songs."

Beverly doesn't suspect that Emily curses the day she had her baby, that her work brings her no pleasure and she is married to a record producer for his money. She has no idea that Emily takes tranquilizers before going out and she has no idea that Emily is one of Doug's lovers. This isn't some strange coincidence. Emily and Doug worked together on a musical production in the Village two years ago and he's been her lover on and off ever since.

It is because of Emily that Beverly has decided to leave the copy center, give up her acting ambitions and go to school in public health. Beverly bought a copy of *Are You Really Creative?* and took the quiz in the book. Would you rather a) fix a clock, b) fly a plane, c) sit in a wild bird sanctuary? On New Year's Eve would you rather be a) the life of the party, b) the person who gives the party, c) the person who stays home from the party and reads a book?

Beverly has no idea how to answer these questions so she

answers at random. Then she adds up her score and learns that "You are too ambivalent about creativity but would work well with people. Why not try a helping profession?" Since she decided to go back to school in public health, her dreams of planes are increasing, only now she dreams of bombers, B-52s to be specific.

When Emily comes into the copy center in the afternoon, the mood is very tense. Mrs. Grimsley came in a little while ago. She wanted to make a hundred copies of a telegram from 1951 that read, "Dear Mr. and Mrs. Grimsley, We regret to inform you that your son, William, has been killed in action . . ." Mrs. Grimsley told Robert, whom she called Billy, that they were invitations to a party and she gave a copy to him. Even Robert who normally isn't shaken by anything was shaken by Mrs. Grimsley.

Beverly is a little upset when Emily walks in, and she calls out her number rather impatiently. "Forty-seven," Beverly snaps and Emily tells her she'd like to wait for Doug. Emily knows that Beverly and Doug are lovers, but Beverly has no suspicions at all. She does not even suspect when Emily hands Doug a note and Doug smiles. She thinks Doug is supposed to make a copy of the note.

That evening Doug tells Beverly he is going to jam downtown again and he'll be late so why don't they see one another the next night. She knows he is going to meet someone else, but she has no idea it is Emily. Doug and Emily could be drug dealers, they are so discrete. Beverly is disturbed but doesn't say a word. As she is leaving the store, Steven asks if she'd like to go to dinner with him uptown. Since she has no other plans, she agrees.

They go to a burger place near West 90th and Steven orders a bacon cheeseburger. Beverly orders the same thing because she can't make a decision. Even before their cokes arrive, Steven grabs Beverly's hand. "Listen," he says, "Doug Cransfield isn't worth this joint on your little finger." He extracts the joint from the mass of fingers he is holding. She pulls her hand away.

"It doesn't matter," she says. "I'm not looking for anything serious."

"Well, I am," Steven says boldly. "I'd like to see you more often."

"I already see you about eight hours a day." Beverly yawns and Steven frowns. "I just don't want to date much these days." She pats his hand gently. Steven and Beverly finish their burgers and walk downtown.

As they pass the 86th Street subway, they see Doug and Emily, coming out of the station. There is an odd moment of recognition as Beverly thinks to herself, "There's Doug with that woman." And Doug thinks he should do something but he doesn't know what. He smiles at Beverly and it is a strange mix of guilt and affection and confusion behind his smile. Beverly thinks he looks boyish, smiling at her, with Emily holding his arm.

Doug says, "Hello," and then Beverly says, "Hello." And not knowing what else to say, Doug says, "See you tomorrow."

Because she is somewhat disoriented, Beverly does something she would not ordinarily do. She asks Steven to come over. When they get to her apartment, a place Steven has wanted to get to for a long time, he praises her choice of furniture. He praises the posters that hang over her bed. He praises the cat, he praises a rather wilting lotus plant. Finally Beverly says, "Steven, let's face it. This place is a dump."

Beverly feeds the cat, named Walter, a can of Purina sardines, which he sniffs. Then he walks away. She dumps a glass of water on the plant. Then she puts on Keith Jarrett's Koln Concert and rolls a joint.

Steven is sure he will spend the night and he hardly knows what to do, he is so overjoyed. "I told you baby, that guy wasn't worth your tiny toenail."

Beverly doesn't want to think about Doug at all. She gets stoned and instead of thinking about Doug she thinks about her father. She thinks about how she used to be afraid of the airplanes that passed so closely over their house and so one day her father took her outside. He lay down in the grass and told her he was the runway and she should fly around the yard and come in for landings on his chest. So she spent the day running around their yard, making a buzzing noise, and then crashing into her father's rib cage.

Beverly is thinking about her father when Steven lunges across the candle between them and grabs her by the arm. He puts his thumb print into her muscle. Beverly pulls back, "I'm tired," she says. She gets up, goes into her bedroom, lies down and falls asleep.

Bewildered, Steven follows. He gets into bed with her and caresses her. Beverly wakes up screaming. "Oh, my god, two little private planes in mid-air." Then she looks at Steven, unsure of what he is doing there. "Please leave," she says, and Steven, because he has almost no will where she is concerned, gets up and leaves.

The next day when Beverly comes into work, Doug says "Hi" and Beverly says nothing. When Beverly is running off an actor's resume, Doug comes over. "How are you?" He waits but she doesn't reply. "Look, about last night . . ."

Beverly says, "There is nothing to say." And she says nothing.

She knows that Doug can stand anything but the silent treatment. His mother used to give him the silent treatment when he did anything she didn't like and it drove him crazy. Once his mother didn't talk to him for five days and they even ate their meals together. All afternoon Doug follows Beverly around, saying dumb things like, "You think they'd fix the fan in this place," that she won't respond to.

Beverly knows Robert and Andrea are watching her ignore Doug, but she doesn't care. She has decided to leave the copy center and go to school in public health. She can imagine herself working in a center for disease control. She knows Doug is exasperated. He stands next to her while she copies an entire book on how to grow a vegetable garden in a city apartment. "Don't be discouraged," one page reads. "You can grow fine tomato plants right in your window boxes."

Doug points to the line. "Isn't that stupid," he laughs. "You couldn't see out the window then."

Beverly doesn't say a word. Finally Doug says, "All right, so maybe I am a jerk but I'm trying to apologize."

She turns to him. "You are a jerk and I don't want your apology. I don't want to talk to you or see you. Just leave me alone."

When Doug walks away, Steven puts his machine on automatic. "Hey, Bev." He speaks loudly, hoping Doug will hear. "Can I see you tonight?"

She looks at Steven's small, frail body, his dark beard that hides his pock-marked face. He's not so terrible, she thinks, but she just can't stand him. "No," Beverly mumbles. "I've got plans."

Steven turns away in a huff and later when Beverly is leaving, he hands her an envelope. "Open this when you get home," he says to her. "It'll explain everything."

Beverly breathes a sigh of relief when she walks into her apartment. She puts a Weight Watchers veal with peppers TV dinner into the oven at 425 with the foil peeled back. She runs a bath. She calls her service and there are no messages. She gives herself a face sauna with honeysuckle herbs. She pours herself a glass of wine and gently eases her way into the bathtub.

Beverly often reads in the tub and so she dries her hands on a towel and opens the envelope Steven gave her as she left work. She opens it slowly, expecting to find a long letter, explaining why she should not care about Doug but about him. Instead what she finds is more to the point. What she finds is a color xerox of a portion of the male anatomy. At the bottom he has written, "You don't know what you're missing, baby."

The next morning Beverly walks into the copy center and screams at Steven. She holds up the color xerox so everyone in the store can see. "What is this? Is this your idea of a joke?"

Andrea is waiting on a customer and she turns around. Doug is making copies at two machines and he is stunned. Steven tries to grab the page out of her hand. "Of course it's a joke. What's your problem?"

Beverly pins the xerox to the bulletin board behind her. The place where she puts the pin makes all the men in the store wince. "This is no joke," Beverly shouts. "You're sick. I should call the police."

Doug smiles. He has never seen Beverly so passionate, so vital. Robert is not smiling. He rips the xerox off the board. "The customers are aware of what is going on," he says to them. "You're all fired if you don't get back to work."

"You should fire him," Beverly shouts. "He is sick."

Steven turns off his machine. "You can't even take a joke. I'll be back later." He slides out beneath the oak counter.

Just then Mrs. Grimsley comes in, checking numbers to make certain no one has butted in front of her. Everyone in the store is upset about Beverly's fight with Steven. Robert is especially upset because he is afraid he will lose business. When Mrs. Grimsley comes in, he decides to humor her. "How's my Billy today?" she says. She is an old woman with dark sunken eyes who probably hasn't long to live.

Robert reaches across the counter. "How'ya doing, Mom?" he pats her hand. "Boy've I missed you."

Mrs. Grimsley looks first stunned, then angry. She pulls her hand away. "Don't you call me that. You have no right. Only my son calls me Mom." And she walks out of the store, never to return.

Beverly also walks out of the store but she returns a few hours later. When she does, she finds a purple geranium, sitting on the 2200. She hopes it is from Doug, but she knows from the handwriting it is from Steven. She opens the card and reads, "Please accept this geranium for your apartment as an apology. I am sorry if I upset you." Beverly feels badly about having shouted at him. Sometimes she thinks, working here isn't so bad.

Because she took time off in the afternoon, Beverly agrees to stay late to finish up a doctoral dissertation. Doug decides to work late with her. It is dark out as they complete their jobs at different machines. They put on the radio and listen to a program of all Sinatra. Sinatra is singing "I Did It My Way."

They turn down the bright fluorescent lights which make them look pale green and now the lighting is amber. Doug works on a screenplay about corruption in the police department. He reads parts of it outloud to Beverly. They agree it sounds like all the police films they've ever seen.

Beverly is making seven copies of a dissertation on the abandonment/castration complex in men and women. As she is completing it, Doug comes up behind her. He puts his hands on her shoulders and kisses the back of her neck. He turns her to him. The green lights of the machines flash on and off. The amber lights are soothing. He takes her in his arms and pins her to the machine as he kisses her. She presses her body against Doug's and remembers what it was that made her like him in the first place. She feels the even, rhythmic pulsing of the 2200 against her spine. She prays it won't break down.

MILK IS VERY GOOD FOR YOU

STEPHEN DIXON

It was getting fairly late in the evening for me so I asked my wife if she was ready to leave. "Just a few minutes, love," she said, "I'm having such a good time." I wasn't. The party was a bore as it had been from the start. Another drinking contest taking place in the kitchen, some teachers and their wives turning on in the john, Phil somebody making eyes at Joe who's-it's wife, Joe trying to get Mary Mrs. to take a breath of fresh air with him as he said while Mary's husband was presently engaged with someone else's sweetheart or wife for a look at the constellation she was born under, and I felt alone, didn't want to turn on or drink another drink or walk another man's wife through the fresh air for some fresh caressing. I wanted to return home and my wife didn't as she was aching to turn on or drink with some other man but me and most especially to walk in the fresh air with Frank whatever his name was as Frank's wife had just taken that same stroll with Joe after Joe had learned that Mary had promised herself tonight to the dentist friend accompanying her and her husband to this house, so I decided to leave.

"Goodbye, Cindy," I said.

"Leaving now, love?"

"Leaving now, yes, are you going to come?"

"Not right this moment, Rick, though I'll find some way home."

"Take your time getting there," I said, "No need to rush. Even skip breakfast if that's what you've mind to—I'll see to the kids. Even pass up tomorrow's lunch and dinner if you want—things will work out. In fact, spend the weekend or week away if you'd like to—I'll take care of everything at home. Maybe two weeks or a month or even a year would be the time you need for a suitable vacation, it's all okay with me, dear," and I kissed her goodbye, drove home, relieved the babysitter who said, "You needn't have returned so early, Mr. Richardson, as the children never even made a peep. I like babysitting them so much it's almost a crime taking money for the job."

"So don't," I said, and Jane said, "Well, that wasn't exactly a statement of fact, Mr. Richardson," and pocketed her earnings and started for the door.

"Goodnight," I said on the porch, "and I really hope you don't mind my not walking you home tonight. I'm really too beat."

"It's only two blocks to the dorm, though I will miss those nice chats we have on the way."

Those nice chats. Those tedious six to seven minute monologues of Jane's on her boyfriends' inability to be mature enough for her or her inability to be unpretendingly immature for them or more likely she telling me about her school work, no doubt thinking I'd be interested because I taught the same subject she was majoring at in the same school she attended. "Tonight," Jane said, "I especially wanted your advice on a term paper I'm writing on the father-son if not latent or even overt homosexual relationship between Boswell and Johnson, since it's essential I get a good grade on my paper if I'm to get a B for the course."

"Bring it by the office and I'll correct it and even rewrite a few of the unclearer passages if you want."

"Would you do that, Mr. Richardson? That would be too nice of you, more help than I ever dreamed of," and so thrilled was she that she threw her arms around my back, and while she hugged me in gratitude I couldn't resist kissing the nape of her neck in passion and now something had started: Jane said, "Oh, Mr. Richardson, you naughty teacher that's not what I even half-anticipated from you," and rubbed my back and squeezed my menis through the pants and said, "My me my but you're surprising me in many ways today," and unzippered me and riddled with my menis till I was ranting so hard I couldn't warn her in time that I was about to some in her land.

"What funky rickety gush," she said, "do you have a hanky?"

"I'm sorry. And I think I also soiled your pretty skirt. ."

"This dinky old thing? Here, let me clean you off properly." And still in the dark of my porch she squatted down and wiped me dry with a hanky and then wobbled up my menis and before I could say anything rational to her, such as this was an extremely indiscreet setting for a young girl from the same college I didn't as yet have tenure at to be living read to the man whose children she just babysat for, I was on the floor myself, her south never letting go of my menis as I swiveled around underneath her, lowered her panties, stack my longue in her ragina and began rowing town on her also, slowly, loving the gradually increasing pace we had tacitly established when Jane said, "Go get the flit, Mr. Richardson, brink up the little flit," which I couldn't find so one by one I desoured every slover of flash that protruded in and around her ragina, hoping to discover—by some sudden jerky movement or exclamation or cry—that I had fortuitously struck home.

"That's it," she said, "right there, that's the little devil, you've got him right by the nose," and after several minutes of us both without letup living read to one another, we same at precisely the same time.

"Now for the real thing," Jane said, "though do you think we're in too much light? Screw it, nobody can hear us, you and Mrs. Richardson have a nice big piece of property here, real nice, besides my not caring one iota if anyone does, do you?" and she stuck her panties in her bookbag, got on her rack on the floor, slopped my menis back and forth till I got an election and started carefully to guide me in.

"Rick, you imbecile," my wife said. "I can hear you two hyenas howling from a block away."

"Good evening, Mrs. Richardson," Jane said, standing and adjusting her skirt.

"Good evening, Jane. Did the children behave themselves?"

"Angels, Mrs. Richardson. I was telling Mr. Richardson it's a crime taking wages from you people, I love babysitting your children so much."

"I told her, 'Well don't take the money' " I said.

"And I said, 'Well that wasn't exactly a statement of fact, Mr. Richardson,' meaning that like everybody else, I unfortunately need money to live."

"And what did you say to that?" Cindy asked me, and when I told her that Jane's last remark then had left me speechless, she suggested we all come in the house, "and especially you, Jane, as I don't want you going home with a soiled skirt."

We all went inside. Cindy, getting out the cleaning fluid and iron, said, "By the way. You two can go upstairs if you want while I clean Jane's skirt."

"I don't know how much I like the idea of that," I said, "or your blase attitude, Cindy."

"Oh it's all right, Mr. Richardson. Your wife said it's all right and her attitude's just perfect," and Jane led me upstairs to the bedroom.

We were in red, Jane heated on top of me, my sock deep in her funt and linger up her masspole, when Cindy said through the door, "You skirt is ready, Jane." "Is it?" Jane said, and Cindy entered the room without any clothes on, said, "Yes, it's cleaning store clean," got in red with us and after drawing us baking dove with me inder Jane for a whole, she put down her pen and pad and but her own funt over my mouth and in seconds all three of us were sounding up and down on the red, dewling, bailing, grubbing at each other's shoulders and hair, "Oh Rick," Cindy said, "Oh Mr. Richardson," Jane said. "Oh Janie," both Cindy and I said, "Oh Mrs. Richardson," Jane said, "Oh Cindybee," I said. And just as the thought came to me that my greatest fantasy for the last fifteen years of me with my longue and menis in the respective funts of two cotmassed magnificent women was about to be realized exactly as I had fantasized it and that was with the most spectacular some of my life, my oldest daughter, Dandy, entered the room and said, "Mommy, daddy, Janie, can I have some milk?"

"Go back to bed," Cindy said.

"I want some milk too," Beverly, my youngest daughter, said.

"There is no milk," Jane said. "I drank it all."

"You did what?" Cindy said. "You did what?"

"Drank it all."

Cindy hot off my lace and told me to sake alay my tick from Jane's funt and that I could also escort her to her dorm if I didn't mind as any babysitter who'd drink up the last of the milk when she knew the children she was sitting for like nothing better first thing in the morning than milk in their cereal and glasses, just shouldn't be allowed to remain another second in this house.

"How much milk was there?" I said.

"A quart at least," Cindy said.

"Two," Jane said, "—but two and a half to be exact. I simply got very thirsty and drank it all, though at several sittings."

Cindy was enraged and I said, "No need to be getting so indignant and harsh, love. So the young lady got thirsty. So it was an act of, let us say, imprudence."

"I want some milk," Dandy said. "Me too," Beverly said. "Drink some water if you're thirsty," Jane told them. "Drink water nothing," Cindy said. "Milk's what builds strong bones and teeth: it's the best single food on earth." "Well one morning without a glassful won't arrest their physical development," Jane said, and Cindy snapped back, "I'll be the judge of that," and put on her bathrobe, took the children by the hand and left the room. She was saying as she went downstairs: "The nerve of that girl. Two quarts. That cow. When your daddy comes down I'll have him drive straight to the all-night supermarket for some milk."

"I want some now," Dandy said. "Me too," Beverly said. "I have to go," I said to Jane.

"You don't think we can just finish up a bit?"

"The girls want their milk and Cindy's about to explode even more."

"You realize it was only this seizure of thirstiness I had. If you had had soda I would have drank that down instead—or at least only one of the quarts of milk and the rest soda."

"My wife won't have soda around the house. Says it's very bad for their teeth."

"She's probably right." Jane started to put on her panties, had one foot through a leg opening when she said, "I'm still feeling like

I'd like your sock and don't know when we'll have another chance for ic."

"I have to go to the market, Jane."

"Your wife has a nice funt, too. I mean it's different than mine, bigger because she's had babies, but I luck as well, dont I?" I said I thought she was very good, very nice. "And I know what to do with a menis when ic's in my south. I think I excell there, wouldn't you say?"

"Well I don't know. This is kind of a funny coversation."

"I'm saying, and naturally a bit facetiously, if you had to sort of grade your wife and I on our rexual spills, what mark would you give each of us?"

"The difficulty of grading there, is that I could only grade you on just our single experience this morning and not an entire term's work, while Cindy and I have had semesters together if not gotten a couple of degrees, if I'm to persist in this metaphorical comparison, so any comparison, so any grading would be out of the question."

"Well, grade on just what we'll call our class participation this morning."

"Then I'd give you both an A."

"You don't think I deserve an A plus?"

"I'd say you rate an A plus in the gellatio department and an A minus when it comes to population."

"And your wife?"

"Just the reverse, which comes to a very respectable A for you both."

"I was sort of hoping for an A plus. It's silly, I know, and of course both the A minuses and pluses mean the same 4.0 on your scholastic rating, but I've never gotten an A plus for anything except gym, which I got twice."

"Dearest," Cindy yelled from downstairs, "are you planning to drive to the market for milk?"

"In a second, love, I'm dressing."

"Daddy," Dandy said, "I'm starving, I want milk," and Beverly said, "Me too."

"Those are precious kids." Jane said, "and even though Mrs. Richardson got mad at me, I still like her a lot. I think she's very knowing, if not wise."

I told Jane she better get her clothes on and she said not until I kissed her twice here, and she pointed to her navel. "That's ridiculous," I said, and she said, "Maybe, but I insist all my dovers leave me with at least that. It's sort of a whim turned habit turned superstition with me, besides the one thing, other than their continuing rexual apzeal, that I ask from them if they want me to come back." I said, while making exaggerated gallant gestures with my hands, that in the case I'd submit to her ladyship and bent over and kissed her twice on the navel. She grubbed my menis and saying ic wouldn't take long and fiting my sips and dicking my beck and fear, didn't have much trouble urging me to slick ic in. I was on sop of her this time, my tody carried along by Jane's peverish hyrating covements till I same like a whunderflap and kept on soming till the girls ran into the room, asked if Daddy was dying of poison or something, and then Cindy right behind them, wanting to know whether I was aiming to be tossed into prison for disturbing the neighborhood's holy sabbath morning with my cries of otter ecstagy or Jane to be thrown out of school because a once well-respected professor could be heard from a few blocks off sailing out her fane.

"A plus," was all I could answer. "Milk," the girls said. Cindy threw the car keys on the red.

"What a luck," Jane said, "what a sock, what a day."

"Jane and I will have to run away for a month," I told Cindy. "I'm serious: there's no other way."

"And the milk?"

"I'll go to the market first."

"And your job?"

"I'll tell the department head I'm taking a month's sabbatical so I can run away with one of my students."

"And Jane's studies? And the children's sitter? Who'll I get now?"

"I'll provide you with a couple of names," Jane said. "Some very sweet reliable girls from my dorm."

"It's useless protesting against you too," Cindy said. "Just do what you want."

"You're a love," I said to Cindy, and hugged her. She sissed my boulder, right on the slot which excites me most of all and which only Cindy seems able to do right, so I mugged her lighter, clitched her mute rutt, and she began dicking my fear with her longue, holding my fair, pickling my falls, and said, "Let's go to red. Last time for a month, let's say."

"Milk, daddy," Dandy said. "Milk, daddy," Bev said.

"I'll go get the milk," Jane said, and Cindy, still ploying with me, said she thought that would be a very nice thing for Jane to do.

Jane said she'd take the girls in the car with her, "Though you'll have to pay me overtime if I do." "Doubletime," I shouted, but Cindy said that time and a half would be more than equitable—did I want to spoil Jane, besides fouling up the wage scale set up by all the other parents?

The car drove off, Cindy and I slopped onto red alm in alm, began joking about the variety and uniqueness of today's early morning experiences and then welt mery doving to each other, sissed, wetted, set town on one another, lade dove loftly till we both streamed, "Bow! Bow!" and had sibultaneous searly systical somes, Jane drove back with the car, honked twice, I went to the window, the girls were entering the house with a quart of milk each, Jane said she was leaving the keys in the car and going back to her dorm as she had to finish that term paper which she'd drop by my office after it was done. "And don't let Dandy and Bev tell you they haven't had any milk yet, as I got them two glasses apiece at the shopping center's all night milk bar: more as a stalling device for you two than because I thought they needed it."

Cindy was still weeping from her some. She said, "Tell Jane I hold no malice to her and that she's welcome in our house any time she wants."

"Cindy holds no malice to you," I said from the window.

"Nor I to her. By the way, did she get an A plus?"

"Plus plus plus," I said.

"Too much. It must've been very good."

"Very very very good."

"Well do you think I can come upstairs a moment. I've something important to tell you."

"Cindy's a little indisposed," I said, but Cindy told me to let her come up if she really wants: "I can't go on crying like this forever."

Jane came into our room. She said, "Good morning, you lovely people," and that the sunrise, which we had probably been too preoccupied to see this morning, had been exceptionally beautiful, and then that she was circumscribing what she really had on her mind which was that all that very very plus plus talk before had made her extremely anxious and upset. "Would you mind very much if we tried ic again, Mr. Richardson, Mrs. Richardson?"

"Mommy, daddy, Janie," Dandy said through the door, "we want some milk."

"Jane said you've already had two glasses apiece," I said.

"No we didn't, " Dandy said, and Bev said, "Me too."

"Let them have it," Cindy said. "Milk's very good for them and then maybe after they drink it they'll play down the street."

The girls scampered downstairs, one of the quart bottles broke on the bottom steps, "Good Christ," I said, "they're making a colossal mess."

"We can all clean it up together later," Jane said, and then Cindy suggested we lump into red before the girls disturbed us again. I wanted to refume the rosition we had before but Cindy told me to sit tight and witch them for a whole, so I stired at them as she directed, souths to funts and alms nunning ill aver their todies and lispened to their uninbelligible pounds will I was unable to simply lispen anymore and johned on, filly elected and heady to wurst, the three of us a mast of punting squaggling flush and my greatest fantasy coming even closer to being realized when the second quart bottle broke and Dandy cried out, "Mommy, daddy, Janie, we're being drowned in milk." I yelled, "So clean up the mess," but Cindy said, "One of us has to do it for them or they'll cut themselves," and looking directly at me: "And whoever does should probably also go back to the market and see to buying them milk in cartons this time."

I volunteered to go, then Jane said she'd go in place of me and clean up the downstairs mess besides, then Cindy said that she supposed she was being lazy and maybe derelict as a mother and that if anyone was to go she should go but she wanted me to come along with her. Cindy and I went downstairs, decided to save the cleaning job for later, and were in the car about to drive off when we heard Jane from our upstairs window asking us to bring some milk back for her also.

Seaing her, those dovely smell bound creasts so mutely but indisstreetly handing alove the till she beaned against bade me wont her alain and it reemed Cindy goo, because she said, "Let's chuck the milk, Jane already said the girls had two glasses," but I told her that she knew as well as me that Dandy and Bev's interfering whines would continue to hassle us till we were absolutely forced to get them more milk, so we might as well do it now.

"Then why don't you go upstairs and I'll get it," she said. "Call it my day's good deed."

Cindy drove off, I went upstairs and round Jane saiting for me with her begs aport and she stiftly flew my plick town to her funt and said. "I knew you'd never be able to resist my niny toobs, I know you by now, Rick Richardson."

I lofted her ap, pitted myself on, and married her abound the boom with me untide of her and in that rosition dently tressed against the ball, Janie tight as a teather, the two of us baking intermutent caughs and roans and ill wet to some when Cindy's car returned, she came upstairs and told us she had poured two glasses of milk apiece for the girls and had personally watched them drink the milk all the way down.

"Mommy's telling a fib," Dandy said, trailing behind her. "We want some milk."

"All you want you can have," I said. "Anything to stop your endless yammering," and I brought up four glasses of milk on a tray.

"Can I have some also?" Cindy said. "I've suddenly grown very thirsty."

"Jane, could you get a couple more glasses?" I said, and then ordered the kids to drink the milk they had clamoured for so much.

"Milk, milk, milk," Beverly said. "Yummy milk," Dandy said, "and now I won't get sick anymore," and they each drank two glasses of milk, Cindy drank one of the milks that Jane had brought up and I the other, and then Jane said she was also very thirsty now after having dealt with so much milk and watching us all guzzle down so many glassfuls, so I went to the kitchen for milk, there wasn't any left in the containers, "There's no milk," I yelled upstairs, "But I'm thirsty," Jane whined back. "do something then, Rick," Cindy said, "as Jane's been such a love about going to the market and taking care of the girls and all."

I went next door to the Morrisons and rang the bell. Mrs. Morrison answered, she only had a bathrobe on it seemed, and she said, "Well there's our handsome neighbor Mr. Richardson, I believe: what a grand surprise." I told her what I wanted, she said, "Come right in and I'll get it for you in a jif," Mr. Morrison yelled from the upstairs bedroom, "Who's there, Queen?" "Mr. Richardson." "Oh, Richardson," he said, "what's he want?" "Milk." "Milk? You sure that's all?" and she said, "I don't rightly know. Is that all you want, Mr. Richardson?" and let her bathrobe come apart, her long blonde hair spill down, smiled pleasantly, said they'd been watching us from their bedroom window and have truly enjoyed the performance, moved closer, extended her hand as if to give me something, I'd never known she had such a dovely tody, buddenly I was defiring her mery muck.

She said, "We're loth spill mery inferested in your seply, Mr. Richardson," and sissed my beck, light on the sagic slot, and snuck my land on her searly fairmess funt and said, "I think it'd first be desirable to shut the door, Mr. Richardson—our mutual neighbors and all?"

"He a rear, dove," Morrison said from upstairs while Mrs. Morrison was prying to untipper me, "and fake the yellow to the redboom." I died twat twat'd be mery vice rut my life was saiting far me ap dome. "Bell," Morrison laid, "rring her rere goo." I sold him she was deally mery fired, rut he laid, "I relieve save to incite earsalves to you mouse, ofay?" and they put on their raincoats, we went to my house, trooped upstairs to the redroom where Jane and Cindy were pitting on the red, beemingly saiting for us.

Jane asked if I brought the milk, and I told her I'd forgot. Morrison said he'd be glad to return to his house to get it but Mrs. Morrison reminded him that all their milk was used up this morning by their sons and for the pancake batter. "Hang the milk then," Morrison said, and we bent to red, ill hive of us—Dandy and Bev played outside with the two Morrison boys—and sparted to bake dove then Jane bayed, "I rant to lo bell thus tame, I rant to net twat A pluc pluc pluc, Y seed my bilk, I need my milk." "In that case," I said, "I'll go to the market." "I'll go with you," Jane said. "Why don't we all go," Morrison said. "Good idea for the four of you," Cindy said, "But I'm going to take a hot bath and be fresh and clean for you all when you return."

All of us except Cindy got in my car and were driving off when Cindy yelled from the bedroom window, "And get me some facial soap, dear. I want to take a facial." Banging but were her dovly mits, sigh and form as they were then we birst hot carried. "Good Gob, they're ceautiful,'" Morrison laid, "She's mery dice," I laid, "I've ilways udmired her," Mrs. Morrison laid, "Milk," Jane said, "I'm going to get very sick in the head unless I get my milk." "Right," I said, and to Cindy in the window: "Won't be long now, love." Samn," she laid, "Y won't snow twat Y man sait twat ling," so I asked Jane if she could wait till after for her milk but she told me she couldn't. "Oh, get the damn thing over with already," Morrison said, so I yelled to Cindy, "Sorry, love, but we'll be back in a flash," and we drove off, got Jane her milk, everybody in the car drank at least two glasses of milk apiece, bought six gallon containers of milk besides and drove home and went upstairs and johned Cindy and the pirls and the Morrison toys and ear fest triends Jack and Betty Slatter and my deportment read Professor Cotton and his life and a douple of Jane's formitory sals and my handlard Silas Edelberg in red.

"I'm thirsty," Silas Edelberg said.

"We've got plenty to drink in this house," I said.

"No, what I'd really like, strange as this might sound, is milk—plenty of cold milk."

"We have six gallons of it in our refrigerator," I said.

"I want milk too," Dandy and Bev said.

"More than enough for you also, loves. Everybody, including the children, can have as much milk as he wants."

"Yippee," Morrison boys shouted. "Three cheers for milk and Mr. Richardson."

"I'll certainly drink to that," Professor Cotton said, but all the milk in the containers turned out to be sour, so we decided to pack everybody into two cars and a station wagon and drive together to the shopping center for milk.

THE TIME, THE PLACE, THE LOVED ONE

SUSAN WELCH

I SPEND A LOT OF TIME ALONE NOW. It doesn't bother me. The others took up too much time. I am glad that they are gone. But it is January and now and then I think of January in Minnesota, how in late afternoon a rusty stain appears along the rim of the sky and creeps across the ice. The stain seems to stay there forever, spreading beneath the banked tiers of white sky, until it fades suddenly into the snowbanks and is gone. It is bleak then, as if the sun has just slipped off the edge of the world. Then there is only the ice and the freezing wind on the ice as the sky gets blacker and blacker through the long, deep night.

I hardly ever think of Minnesota now that I am content in Florida. There is a garden with a trellis and orange trees. The branches bend to me as I pluck the fruit, then spring back. As I bite into an orange I can taste the juice of the tree still in it, all its green leaves. The thorns on the rose bushes tear my skirt. The house has pillars and a courtyard; it is not far from the sea. Mal has given me all he promised. When Mal comes home he picks up my daughter at her school and she drinks lemonade while we drink scotch, sitting in the gazebo. By the time my head is clear again we have gotten through dinner and put the little girl to sleep and are upstairs, lying on the bed.

So I hardly ever think of Minnesota, how dark and still the winters are there. There was an apartment once, but I don't miss it, I just think about it sometimes when I consider how completely I have gotten out of the cold. From the street you could see a pale lamp shining through the window of the apartment, and the reflection of the lamp in the window; it was high up on the second floor above a store. Signs hung beneath the windows: Grimm's Hardware, Shaak Electronics—and together with the streetlights they cast a white glow into the big room all night long. Sometimes, coming home, we would see the snow falling silently in the beam of the streetlight, as if it were all a stage set.

Across the street was an all-night restaurant and sometimes people would leave there late, and yell to each other before they got into their cars. The first night I saw Matthew he was rushing down the stairs of our apartment building to confront some boys on the sidewalk near the restaurant. If I hadn't pressed against the railing he would have collided with me in his descent. I stood watching him through the glass of the door as he told the boys to be quiet, people were trying to sleep. They hooted and snickered as he turned to leave. As he came in the door, almost in tears, the boys were screaming in a mocking, falsetto chorus.

"They laughed at me," he said, bewildered, shutting the door against them, staring out. We started up the stairs together. He was tall and very thin, stooped even, pigeon-breasted in the t-shirt he wore in spite of the cold. His hair was a mass of ringlets and golden curlicues and it seemed full of its own motion like something alive at the bottom of the sea. For a moment, standing in the hallway, he looked very beautiful and strange.

'I live here now," I told him. "In that apartment, there."

His face was haggard, lantern-jawed, but his eyes were gentle as he stared at me. "Come over and visit me tomorrow night," he said. "I'll bake you some brownies."

All day long I thought I wouldn't go. I stood for a long time in the hallway, looking from Matthew's door to mine, before I turned to knock on his. When he called "Wait a minute," I thought he was a girl, that's how light and high his voice was.

His apartment was immaculate. The wooden floor gleamed. There was a rug made of swans' heads and necks, dark and light, facing in opposite directions—the neck of a dark swan provided the relief so you could see the neck of a white swan and so on. It was impossible to hold both the white and dark swans together in your mind at the same time. There was a bed at one end of the large room, a table with two chairs, and windows that faced the street all along the wall. There were no pictures up, just plants on a shelf, purple passion, jade plant, wandering jew, and a bulletin board studded with funny clippings, cartoons, a picture of a bald woman in a long smock.

"I see her all the time at school," Matthew said. "She goes to all the rallies and concerts and just walks around the university."

He was wearing a t-shirt that said "Minnesota" and a pair of jeans that hung on him. I saw that he was not handsome at all. He was bony and long and his joints, his elbows and wrists and probably his knees, were huge, like a puppet's.

"How old are you?" I asked.

"Twenty-one," he said, but he looked sixteen or seventeen. "You?"

"Twenty-five."

"I couldn't imagine what your age was," he said. "People are always drawn to you, your looks, aren't they?"

"My mother was beautiful. She's dead," I said.

I looked out the window and saw how the dark was settling in. When I was eighteen I won a beauty prize, Princess Kay of the Milky Way at the Minnesota State Fair. They sculpted my face in a thirty-pound block of butter, put the bust in a refrigerated glass case and ran it round and round on a kind of merry-go-round so people at the fair could look at it. I liked it and went every day to see it, standing on the dirt floor near the glass, wondering if anyone would recognize me, but they never did. My father told me I looked like my mother in the sculpture, but he thought it was dumb of me to stand around there all day. He made me come home.

"What in the world brought you to this place?" Matthew asked, and then I told him how I had come to be there. I must have been lonely, or starved for someone so nearly my own age, I know that's what made me pour out my feelings to him so. I told him how I had met Mal when I took a job in his publishing company, and how he had left his wife and children for me, and how he had taken me to live with him five years ago, right after my father died. I told him how Mal called me his suburban Botticelli and how he took care of me and taught me all he knew. Now Mal had sold out his interest in the Minneapolis company and we were moving to Florida, where he had a new business. But I had never been out of Minneapolis, my parents had died here, it was all too sudden. I begged him to let me have a couple of months here, work in the business as it changed hands, get used to the idea of leaving as he got our new life settled. I had found this apartment in a familiar area, near the university, where I, too, had gone to school. Matthew was looking at me so hard his jaw hung.

It was late autumn, just before Halloween, and Matthew and I watched out the window as the sky went down from copper to livery red to mother of pearl. The streetlights blinked on and so did the signs above the stores. The room darkened with the sky but the signs and streetlights shed pools of incandescent light on the bed, on the floor.

"What kind of person would leave his wife and children?" Matthew asked.

I sat with my head in my hands. "I don't know, he felt so awful about it. They'd been married twenty years. He told me not to think about it. He said it was my face; he loved my face." I pressed my fingers into my cheeks. The flesh gave like wax. But suddenly I was asking myself, what kind of person was Mal, to leave his wife and children. I had never thought of him in that way before.

Then slowly Matthew began to tell me about himself. It was hard for him to talk, he didn't charm me with what he said or the way he said it, no, not at all. His voice was a whisper and sometimes it cracked as it came out, no, not a man's voice at all. He had been in love with a girl and she hadn't loved him, but still he kept loving her and loving her and finally he had gone crazy.

He told me what it was like to be crazy. Everything seemed to have a secret meaning, cracks on the sidewalk, a phone that rang once but not again, the world was full of hidden messages.

"It sounds wonderful," I said. "I would love to feel that everything had a secret meaning."

He shook his head and his curls bounced. "You don't know what you're saying. No, it wasn't wonderful at all. It was horrible."

"And the girl?"

"She's gone. Gone a long time ago."

It was hard to talk to him, I had to strain to hear him, his murmurs. It was as if he were used to talking in whispers to himself. His father was a doctor, his mother wanted him to be a doctor, but he couldn't do it, his grades weren't good enough, he couldn't concentrate. So instead he was taking this degree in psychology, maybe something would come of that.

I don't know what it was, I didn't want to leave him. After a while he got up and turned on the lamp by the window, then he put on a record.

"I like that a lot," I said. "Mal and I don't listen to any rock, just classical. Bach. Vivaldi. Telemann. A lot of baroque."

"Don't you know any people your own age?"

I looked at him. "Hardly any. There are a few girls at work but I don't see them much."

It was late when I got up to go. I walked along the shiny dark floor to the door. The lamp shone on the green leaves of the plants and reflected white in the window. I could feel the cold on the street below seeping in around the window frames.

Matthew followed me and stood with me by the door. I thought I had never seen such a delicate-looking man. I could almost see the blood beating in his temples. He took my hands in his huge bony hands. I felt it only for an instant but my hands were throbbing where he had touched them.

A few days later I found a copy of the album we had been listening to wrapped and pushed under my door. When I walked over to Matthew's apartment I could hear the bass pounding in the record he was playing. I stood in the hall for a moment but the door opened.

"I heard your footsteps," he said. But how could he have heard me over the music? We stared at each other. He looked gawky and stupid. I wondered why I had come. "Listen, I've got a coupon for a pizza," he said. "Do you want to go?"

As we walked he took my hand in his. I couldn't take it back, his own hand trembled so.

"They removed a rat's memory surgically today," he said. And all through dinner we talked about how the rat experienced everything for the first time, every time.

When he himself had gone crazy, Matthew said, he thought about the same things over and over again. He had thought then that he was refining memories, getting down to their essence and their core. Now he realized that that was impossible.

His way of talking was innocent and strange. He thought differently from other people and I had to listen carefully to catch his meaning. Neither of us ate much. We pushed the pizza back and forth between us.

"Do you want to come back over?" he asked as we walked out into the bitter cold. He took my hand again. I just wanted to be with him, I don't know why. Perhaps I admired the sculpted, jutting angle of his cheekbones. He made some coffee and got out a box of fresh pastries from the bakery downstairs. He sat across the table from me, staring down at the coffee, his long legs stretched out until his feet nearly touched mine. The white light enclosed us in a long oval. He shook his head and ruffled his fingers fiercely through his curls.

"Your hair is so unusual," I said.

"I was helping my father give EEGs last summer," he said. "One lady saw me and wouldn't let them put the electrodes on. She thought that was what had happened to me."

We laughed. At that moment, I looked at him and he looked at me. I felt a dizziness, a tightness near my heart. I was snug, safe in his apartment against the cold—I'm sure that's what it was. I have thought about it since.

He put a record on and we were silent, sitting in the pool of light.

After a while he came over and knelt beside me and wrapped his arms around my waist. I could see the top of his head, his bobbing curls.

"Matthew, I have a lover."

He ignored me and put his cheek next to mine, holding my head. I could see the fine grain of his gold skin, how tight it was on the bone.

"Do you want to go lie down with me?" he asked and I nodded, yes.

I looked into his face as he undressed me and saw that his eyes were all pupil. For a long time he stroked the place where my hip met my thigh, running his fingers over the pale blue traceries of the veins.

"I love you," I said. Yes, I remember I said it, and I said it many times, I don't know what came over me. And I thought, this is the most wonderful night of my life, nothing will ever be this sweet again. We stared at each other in the light of the streetlamps and the Grimm's Hardware sign and we made love. All night long we looked into each other's eyes, He was so young I could see that his eyes were brand new, just budded in their sockets.

Sometimes even now I fancy I can feel Matthew's tongue, scratchy as a cat's, and the way he wrapped me up in his long, long arms. But I scarcely think of him at all now. In fact, I have entirely forgotten him. If it weren't for the little girl, considering her as much as I do, and the way the days are so long for me here, I doubt that I would think of him at all.

Three days later I went to work again. The phone was ringing as I walked into my office and I picked it up, knowing it was Mal. There had been a short circuit in one of the stereos in the electronics store and all night music from a rock station had pounded up to us through the floorboards. Elton John, Matthew told me they were playing. "Love Song." "Come Down in Time."

"What are you telling me?" Mal asked. "You were walking along, just minding your own business, and you got hit by a freight train?"

Light from the apartment flooded into my eyes and behind them as I held the receiver, the pure light on Matthew's face as he twined me with his legs and arms.

"I never should have left you alone, I knew it was a mistake," Mal said. And when I didn't answer he said: "I'm coming up there."

He was waiting for me in the office the next morning. For a long time he wouldn't believe that I was serious, that I wasn't coming down to Florida.

"I suppose his teeth are all white, not stained like mine," Mal said. "And I suppose he has all his hair and a flat belly, that's what you're thinking when you look at me, isn't it?"

"No, it's not," I said, but now that he'd said it it became true. All I was worried about was that he would kill me, and then I wouldn't be able to be with Matthew.

I wanted to tell him how fond I felt of him, how grateful I felt, how it hurt me to see his eyes glaze as he slumped against the window. But I stood speechless.

"I gave up everything for you. I can't let you go," he said.

For a moment I thought of the filthy warped floor in the hall of my apartment building, the way the brown paint on the floors bubbled and peeled. "I was a child then," I said. "That was for then."

I turned my face away as he held me.

"There's nothing I can do," he said. "I can't live without you." For an instant I prayed, begging that Mal would not die.

Then, miraculously, he was gone. He had me fired from my job but I found another where I just had to type. I bore no grudges. I was walking on love's good side. I had Matthew.

From our first night together Matthew was always in my thoughts. I suppose you could say I lived for him. He wanted us to be twins.

"One consciousness in two bodies," he said. "That's what we are." He looked at me in a way that made me feel holy. No one had ever paid this kind of attention to me, no, never. He painted our toenails the same color, green with silver dust. When I got a pimple he would often get one himself, in a similar spot. We wore each other's clothes, bought matching shoes. We copied each other, walked alike, talked alike. How I loved imitating Matthew. It was no longer lonely being me. We could be each other.

We had been together two months when I found out I was pregnant. Matthew had told me not to get another diaphragm, there could be no mistakes between us. Anything that happened was right.

When I told him, he smiled. "That's wonderful," he said. "I can't wait to tell my family. Now we'll get married."

We drove out to the suburbs for dinner so I could meet his parents. He had told them about me but they had resisted meeting me, until now. We drove to a ranch house with a swimming pool behind it, big as a gulch. His father was a tall, silent man who left in the middle of dinner to go to the hospital. His mother had Matthew's jagged features but none of his softness. She hated me on sight.

After dinner she took me aside.

"Do you realize what a sick boy he is?" she asked. "You're a grown woman, you should see these things. He's been institutionalized for long periods."

"I love him," I said calmly. "He loves me. He knows exactly what he's doing. And it's medieval to think of mental illness as a permanent condition. You get over it, like a cold."

"What do you know about it?" She stared until I dropped my gaze. "Have you ruined your life, eating your heart out over him?"

We left before dessert.

"Cheer up, honey. We have to go out and get some sour cream cherry pie, some cheesecake," Matthew said as we sat in the car in his mother's driveway. He started kissing me, digging his fingers into my thighs. "There's a great place near here. You'll love their hot fudge cake," he said. "I can't take my honey to bed before she has her dessert."

We went to a delicatessen where cakes and pies dipped up and down on little ferris wheels. "It tastes as good as it looks, too," Matthew said. We held hands and fed each other hot fudge and cherries on heaping spoons. The rich goo dripped like wax. We nudged and stepped on each other's feet the whole time, pressing each other's soles and toes till they hurt.

"Why doesn't she like me?" I asked. "Is it because I'm older?"

"She'll get over it, don't worry about her," Matthew said. "All she knows is her Bible. That time when I got sick—she thought it was God's rebuke to her. She's just going to have to get used to it."

I scraped some hot fudge on my plate with my spoon. It dried fast, sweet cement. "You're so old for your age, Matthew. I'm surprised she can't see it. I've always known I could depend on you."

He fed me the last bite of hot fudge cake. "How about some more?" he asked. "Come on, honey, you know you want it."

"Let's have the hazelnut torte," I said.

"Great," Matthew said. "Great. My mother would die. She believes in minimal sweets."

"Mal too," I said. "Seaweed and spinach. He made us eat seaweed and spinach every stupid day." We both grimaced, wrinkling our noses.

Matthew stared into my eyes and jammed my feet tight between his. "Hi, baby." I saw his mouth move but no sound escaped his lips. The waitress put the torte before him. Shrugging and rolling his eyes at me he plunged his fork into the crest of hazelnut lace.

We got married and I moved all my things into Matthew's apartment. Our lives went on much as before.

How did those days pass? They went by so quickly I swear I can't remember. We had everything in the world to find out about each other.

He took pictures of me with an expensive camera his parents had given him for his birthday. He gloated over the prints. "Look how you're smiling," he said. "How happy I must make you." He set the time adjustment so we could be in pictures at the same time, hugging or kissing or with our heads together, staring at the camera. "What a beautiful couple," he said.

He played his guitar as we sang duets of rock songs. He was charmed by my flat singing voice. He even admired my upper arms which had started to get pudgy from all our desserts. He flapped the loose flesh with delight. "That's one of the things I love about you most," he said. "Chubby arms, just like a little baby."

One freezing night as we walked home after a movie our boots crunched into the moonlight on the snow. Our gloved hands fitted into each other like the pieces of a puzzle.

"What should we name the baby?" he asked.

"I don't know," I said.

"If it's a girl how about Phoebe, after the moon," he said. "The moon is so beautiful, look how we're walking on silver, baby. And it always seems to have so many secrets."

"But we don't like secrets, Matthew," I said. "We don't believe in secrets."

"I bet she'll look like the moon," he said. "You'll get round like the moon and then the baby will come out and look like the moon."

I woke up once during the night. He was sleeping with his arms around my neck. He slept silently, like an infant. How could he be so quiet? The lights outside flooded his bulletin board, the shiny wooden floors, the carefully arranged cabinets. The radiators hissed then fizzled to stop. Outside the window the full moon shared the secret of the shadows on the dark street, his beating heart. I almost woke him up to tell him. I wanted to say, I could die now. I am so happy I could just die.

For Valentine's Day he wrote me a song. I sat on the bed while he played it for me on his guitar. He didn't need to breathe with my lungs filling his, the song said. He wanted to die from drinking my wonderful poison. I listened, filled with wonder.

As he played I watched his hands. For the first time I saw tiny scars on his wrists, fine and precise as hairs. When he finished playing I put my fingers to his pulse.

"Your wrists, Matthew," I said. "Look. Where did all those little marks come from?" He had never told me, yet he said he told me everything.

He withdrew his hands, fixing me with his long stare. "Let's stay in the here and now. Why talk about things that happened a long time ago, things you can't remember right anyway. What did my honey get for me?"

I had forgotten Valentine's Day. The next day I bought him a shirt and an expensive sweater. He thanked me but seemed disappointed. His mother could have given him the same. He had been involved in his gifts, mine were clichés.

The next day I got a valentine from Mal, forwarded from the old office. He loved me, he was thinking about me, he wanted me to come back to him. As I put it in the waste basket I found the valentine I had given Matthew folded at the bottom.

In the dead of winter it was fifty below for days at a time. We would sit on the bed and watch the smoke rise out of the chimneys in timid frozen curls. When we came home late at night, walking across the huge U of M campus, we would have to kiss and hold each other for twenty minutes before our noses and fingers thawed.

On Sunday mornings we would have breakfast at the restaurant across the street. We sat facing each other, our legs locked, talking about what was happening in our lives. I treasured my separate life for it provided me with stories to tell him. Nothing was real until I told Matthew about it.

After breakfast I walked him to his part-time job at the laboratory where he was working on a hearing experiment. Chinchillas were made deaf in one ear and then trained to jump to one side of a large revolving cage or another, on the basis of certain sounds. If the chinchillas didn't perform correctly they got a shock. That was Matthew's job, running them through tests and shocking them if they made mistakes.

I went with him once and saw the little animals in their cages. They were furry and adorable, bunnies without ears: how could Matthew, the gentlest of people, stand to shock them?

"They have to be shocked when they're not doing their job," he said. "It's horrible, but that's the way life is."

"Since when do you believe life is that way?"

One evening he came home shaking. A chinchilla had died when its eardrum was being punctured for the experiment.

"Matthew, why don't you quit that job?" I asked, looking up at him from where I sat at the table. "Don't you see what it's doing to you?"

"It's not doing anything to me. I'm fine," he said, standing there trembling. "Do you think you're better, that you wouldn't do that job?"

I stood up and rushed to him. "Matthew, are you angry at me? Please don't be angry at me. I just want you to be happy." I hugged him tighter, tighter. "Do I give you everything you want?" I whispered into his shoulder. "What can I give you?"

"You're everything I want," he said.

"But is it enough? You're so much better at being somebody's lover than I am."

"Yes, I am good at that, aren't I," Matthew said, and I could feel him thinking about it, there was a hum in him like currents in fluorescent tubes.

Then he held my shoulders and looked deeply into my eyes. "Come here, baby. Let me tell you about this experiment I've been thinking about all day."

We sat down at the table holding hands. "When they fasten electrodes to the pleasure centers of a rat's brain the rat will do nothing but push the bar that activates the electrode. It won't eat, it won't drink, it won't sleep, it just keeps pushing the bar for the pleasure sensation until it dies of starvation and dehydration."

We sat silent. "That's interesting," I said. I watched his hand as it moved slowly up my arm, to my shoulder, then curled around my neck.

"You," he said. "You."

Late afternoons Matthew would go to the bakery downstairs and come back with boxes of sweets. Then we would sit at the table, listening to the voices on the street, feeling how the winds lightened and the air became less bitter as spring blew in our windows. We watched the sun on the grain of the table. We cut eclairs with knives and fed them to each other. When Matthew ate chocolate he was in such ecstacy he had to close his eyes. I could see him shudder. It was like when we were in bed. Being around all those sweets made me greedier for them, it was strange. The more I ate the more I wanted. It was like being in bed.

I got fatter and fatter from the sweets.

"If you can't get fat when you are pregnant, when can you?" he asked, feeding me another pastry. Yet Matthew never got fat.

I ate cakes, petits fours, upside down tarts. At the soda fountain around the corner he fed me hot fudge sundaes.

"Eat, baby," he said. "I love to see your little tongue when you lick the syrup."

My breasts became huge. I swelled like an inflatable doll. All night long Matthew would lie in my arms as I lay there puffed with life and the splitting of my own cells. When we woke up he went downstairs and got doughnuts, filled and frosted pastries called honeymooners, pecan rolls.

Before long it was spring verging on summer and we took long walks along the Mississippi, breathing the crisp shocking air that rose from the torrents of icy water that came with the thaw. Sometimes we took sandwiches and stayed out till two in the morning. On one walk a pale, ovoid form approached us. It was the bald woman whose picture was on Matthew's bulletin board.

She stopped Matthew, held on to his arm, mumbled to him. She had been at the zoo, she said, and fed the elephant peanuts. It had lifted them out of her hand with its trunk, she said, holding up her palm, showing it. Its soft trunk had tickled and nudged her hand, gentle, tender. She could feel its hairs.

"Do you know her?" I asked Matthew, watching her as she disappeared. But Matthew wouldn't answer.

One afternoon after a rock concert we followed the path along a cliff near the river; below us the Mississippi glimmered like diamonds. We walked hand in hand but I was waddling fast to keep up with Matthew's long strides.

"Let me catch up," I said, and he stared at me, his eyes hard.

"You know I've been thinking," he said, walking faster. "We're really not that much alike."

I couldn't catch my breath. The air was freezing my fingertips even where Matthew held them.

"Like how so?"

"Like make-up," he said. "Like you wear make-up and I don't."

My eyes watered from the wind. "But I've always worn make-up," I said. "I'll stop wearing it if you don't like it."

"That won't do any good," he said. "And you take up a lot of the bed. It's hard for you to keep up with me when I walk."

"But I'm pregnant, I've got fat," I said, nearly in tears. "If I weren't pregnant and if you didn't force all that food on me, this wouldn't happen."

Tears were streaming down my face but Matthew was walking fast, not seeming to notice.

"I don't make enough to support a baby," Matthew said. "It's all going to be different. It seems cruel. Sometimes I think I can't do the job."

"You know I've got savings. And your parents will help." Now I couldn't stop crying. I halted in my tracks, jerking my hand out of his. The Mississippi roared below us. I waited for long moments by a tree, waiting for him to come back. And suddenly I knew that we would never again be as happy as we once were.

Finally he came back, retracing his steps, and looked at me.

"I'm sorry," he said. "I never want to hurt you."

I looked into his eyes and saw how young and frightened he was. I will never leave you, I said to myself. You need me and I will always take care of you.

That night in our room rainy air billowed the curtain inward on our long embrace. There was the smell of skin, warm salt flesh, clean.

"Please baby, whatever you say, never say you stopped loving me," Matthew said.

"Oh, never. I would never say that."

"You would never start hating me, would you? You would stop long before that."

Stop? He had never said anything about stop. "No. I would stop before that."

"We would stop while we still loved each other. And now . . . are you going to hug me all night long?"

The next day, on impulse, I called up Mal from work.

I couldn't even wait for him to get over his shock. I rushed into it. "You won't believe this, but I've just got to talk to someone. About Matthew. It's just interesting, you won't mind? He's absolutely terrified of getting fat. He is the skinniest man you've ever seen, yet he's worried about fat. Once he went on a fishing trip with his father and he ate a whole pound bag of M & Ms and he was so appalled he didn't eat anything else the whole trip. And by summer he had got so thin he could see the sun shining through his rib cage. Can you imagine anything so stupid?

"He loves sweets, you know, we live near a bakery, and sometimes he'll get so many good things and eat them, then do you know what he does? He sticks his finger down his throat and throws them up. Really, I've seen him do it."

Mal listened, silent, until I was done. "Why don't you leave him?" he said.

"Because I'm happy, that's why," I said, suddenly desperate to be off the phone. "Besides, I'm very fat, do you think you could like me fat?" He didn't answer. "I was just kidding about him throwing up. Do you believe me?" Mal was silent. "Well, maybe he did it once or twice when he was drunk."

"Do you know why I'm fat?" My voice grew shriller in the silence. "Because I'm pregnant. I'm going to have a baby in two months."

I pressed down the button, hoping he would think we'd been disconnected.

I came home from work one afternoon and found Matthew lying naked on the bed, his stereo earphones on, one leg propped straight up against the wall. He was so absorbed in the music he didn't see me coming up to him, see how I was staring at the long red marks on the inside of his thigh. As I sat down beside him he took his leg down quickly and removed the headset, smiling.

"It's spring," I said. "It's gorgeous out, Matthew."

"It's pretty," he said. "Have a good day?"

"Did you?" He said he hadn't been out and, leaning back again, he pulled me down with him. I moved away.

"Matthew, let me see your thigh." He watched me dociley as I lifted his leg. It was as if it were a specimen we were both going to examine.

"What are those red marks from?" I asked.

"Me."

"How did you do it?"

"With my own little fingernails," he said.

They weren't scratches, they were deeper than that. The gold hairs on his thighs spoked up innocently around.

"Matthew, why did you do it?" He took his leg down.

"Don't worry about it. It's nothing. It's something I do sometimes. I put iodine on it, it won't get infected."

"But why did you do it?"

"Because I was having evil thoughts."

"About what?"

He shook his head. "Don't worry about it." He eased me back

down. "Don't worry your little head," he said. "Baby. Double baby. Baby to the second power. Baby squared." He started moving his hands up and down my body.

I pulled away. "Wait."

"What's the matter, baby?" he asked, touching me all over. I felt his tongue in my mouth and I closed my eyes.

One night he came in late, very agitated.

"There was this guy following me down the street just now for about a mile. He was this weird, juiced-up black guy even skinnier than I am. He was muttering, calling me sweet cakes, doodle-bug, boney maroney. Can they tell about me?" he asked, looking into my face. "Can they tell I've been crazy? Do I give out special vibes?"

I thought of the tense air he always had, the speed of his walk on those long legs.

"He followed me all that way. He kept saying, 'Think you're pretty hot stuff, you creep, you creep.'"

And the bald lady, had he seen her? Matthew wouldn't answer.

"People can't tell," I said finally, but he wouldn't stop looking at me.

"Why are you staring?" I asked.

"Because you're so nice and fat," he said, still staring.

Behind that gaze there was an intensity that had nothing to do with me. I felt something ungiving in him, the tightness of his skin on the bone. "Stop making me eat," I said. "You're turning me into a monster."

"But honey," he said smiling. "I likes you fat." Then his expression changed. It was a dark look he gave me. "You're eating with your own mouth," he said.

I called up Mal again. "Can you imagine?" I said. "He washes his hair every morning because he doesn't want dirt to accumulate too close to his brain. He's afraid it will penetrate and sink in. And scratches himself with his fingernails when we have a fight. When I told him to stop buying me so many sweets he thought I hated him and you know what he did? He put a long cut down the top of his arm with a knife."

"He's crazy," Mal said. "Don't you know you've got a mental case on your hands? Why don't you get out before he does something to you?"

"He won't do anything to me," I said, but it was a long time before I could hang up the phone.

When I came home that night Matthew was sitting at the table with a stack of pictures. I sat down beside him.

"What are they of?" I asked.

He looked annoyed but said nothing. I slid the pictures over and started going through them. They were all of him. He had taken twenty-four pictures of his own face: laughing, smiling, stern, pensive, in profile, in three-quarter view, from the back.

"These are really good," I said. "When did you take them?"

"I've really changed a lot," he said. "I suspected it, but I can tell from the pictures how drastic it is."

"How have you changed?"

"In ways." He put his hand over his mouth, staring at me and then staring at nothing.

"Why are you so indifferent to me?" I said.

"I'm not indifferent." He took the stack of pictures and began looking through them again, humming to himself.

"Why don't you take my picture?"

He continued to sort through the pictures, humming.

"Why don't you take my picture, Matthew?"

There was a long silence. "Sure, I'll take your picture some-time," he said, and I saw how his hair flared out in the photo-graphs, like a sea fan.

I remember every detail of the next few days. It was the hottest part of the summer in Minnesota. Night after night I went sleepless in the motionless air, hanging over the side of the bed so Matthew would have more room. I was so huge and moist my nightgown clung to me like a membrane. I had to take it off and lie naked on top of the sheet. When I tried to meet Matthew's eyes he looked away.

"It will all be different after the baby comes," I whispered to him, but he pretended to be asleep.

One evening I could hardly walk when I got off the bus after work. With every step my fat thighs rubbed against each other.

They had become so sore and chapped they had begun to bleed. As I walked past the bakery the heat rose in waves; behind the window, a sheet of sunlight, I saw wedding cakes, gingerbread men, cookies with faces, shimmering.

I heard music coming from our apartment. I twisted my key again and again in the lock. Surely Matthew could hear me? I punched my knuckles against the door. I tried the key again and the lock gave suddenly.

The room was filled with smoke. Matthew was sitting on the bed with the bald woman and a short black man who was even skinnier than he was.

"We're tripping," Matthew said. "But there's nothing left for you."

"Who is that?" said the bald woman.

"She lives down the hall."

"I do not live down the hall and you know it, Matthew," I said. "I live here and I'm his wife." I stood there awhile and nobody looked at me. I put down my purse and sat down next to it on the floor.

"These are my friends. They're like me," Matthew said. He looked at me with the eyes of a little animal, eyes that were all pupil, the color black, absorbing everything and giving nothing back.

"He's a cabdriver," Matthew said. "You wouldn't think of having a cabdriver for a friend, would you? Or a busdriver? I like cabdrivers."

"I would so have a cabdriver for a friend," I said, but I couldn't think of a single friend I did have. Matthew was my only friend.

"You wear make-up and you're fat and you only want to be friends with editors," Matthew said. "Oh, yes, and friends with Uncle Mal." The bald woman edged closer to Matthew on the bed. Her hand brushed my pillow, the pillow I had brought to Matthew from my old bed. She whispered in his ear, moving her hand to his hip, to the front of his pants.

"We're going now," Matthew said, standing up.

"Wait a second, I'll come too," I said.

"Do you want her to come?"

"No way," said the bald woman.

"See? They don't want you to come," Matthew said. "They're my friends and they're like me and they don't want you to come."

I stood still as they passed, stupefied by my pain.

"Matthew, please don't go!" I said. "It's just a tough time now, baby. Isn't it?"

He stopped in the doorway, staring down at me. A vein like a root throbbed in his temple. His face blurred in my gaze and I saw his eyes staring wide at me as we made love on that bed, silver ghosts in the wash of pale neon. I saw the snow falling silently as we hurried home in the cold, looking high up for the glow of the lamp in our apartment.

He put his hands on my shoulders. His palms and fingers cut into me like brackets. "Stay here," he said.

I watched him from the window but he did not turn to look back up at me.

I lay on the bed watching the ceiling change as it got darker and darker. I don't know how long I lay there or when the pains in my back and stomach started, they blended so imperceptibly with the other things I was feeling, staring at the ceiling, lying on the bed. Then I lay down on the floor, on the rug of swans' heads and necks, hurting so much I imagined I felt them moving under me, nudging me with their bills. I waited and waited there for Matthew to come back, but he didn't come back. It must have been a couple of days later that I called a cab to take me to the hospital.

The baby was tiny. She was born feet first, the wrong way. They gave me a drug that put me in a twilight sleep, that turned everything pink until I saw her after she was born. She came out curled like a snail and stayed calm in her crib sleeping all the time. She fit over my shoulder like a chrysalis, a tight little cocoon.

It was Matthew's father and mother who came to see me at the hospital and who took me home. I wanted to go back to our apartment, but they wouldn't let me, they said Matthew wasn't there and I needed somebody to take care of me. They took me to the house in the suburbs, but Matthew wasn't there, either. He had taken too many drugs and hurt himself, they had to send him away somewhere, they wouldn't say where. His mother gave me the Bible to read.

He came to see me once, I was still lying down most of the time. He came and sat down beside me near the big swimming pool. He had seen the baby. "She wasn't like the moon," he whispered, or did I dream that? He sat down on a chair next to me in the sun for a little while and he cried.

He got up and started walking toward the house, muttering something.

"Matthew, I know you didn't mean to hurt me," I said, but he kept walking, shaking his head.

"He didn't even recognize you," his mother told me later, glaring at my face in the sunlight.

"Then why did he cry?" I asked. "If he didn't recognize me then why did he cry?" Words from her Bible swam in my head, he whom my soul loveth. We could do anything, be anything, with what we had. Hadn't he always told me that?

I rushed into the house, hoping I could still find Matthew, but he was gone. I took the keys to his mother's car off the kitchen table and ran to the garage, before she had a chance to stop me.

Then I went out to look for Matthew. I looked everywhere nearby, up and down the streets, and when I couldn't find him I drove back to our old neighborhood. I parked in front of the old apartment and went upstairs and knocked and knocked on the door but no one answered. I tried my key but it wouldn't fit into the lock. I pushed at the lock until the key had scratched my fingers and made them bleed. Then I sat down by the door on the floor in the hallway and remembered how there had been heaven in that apartment, time had stood still. No matter what he did, Matthew knew. We had made love all night, in the light of the streetlight and the Grimm's Hardware sign. If I put my cheek to the wood I could feel the vibrations of those nights, still singing in the floorboards of the apartment.

Mal came to the house in the suburbs after I called him. He cried when he saw me and I saw how his cheeks were now crosshatched with tiny red veins. Matthew's mother wanted to keep the baby for herself, but Mal wouldn't let her. He took me, and the baby, and brought us to this beautiful house where we have been so happy. It is not far from the ocean and we go sailing a couple of times a month if the wind is not blowing too hard. I am thin again and Mal has bought me wonderful new clothes. The little girl calls him Daddy and has never known another father.

I thought Mal would ask me to explain a lot of things, but mostly he hasn't.

"I know you've never loved anybody but me," he said. "I knew you'd come back. That's why I waited." That was four years ago. And more and more I think Mal was right.

Once we were sitting under the trellis and Mal asked me what I was thinking about when I looked so preoccupied and far away. I told him an apparition gripped my mind sometimes.

"It's a picture of man who looked like a boy and a girl at the same time, a man with hair like a sheaf of golden wires, with eyes as black and shiny as lava chips. You remember, it was a man who confused me, a man who studied the memory and even tried to look into his own head. I must be making it up, don't you think? For no real person could be anything like that."

Mal was annoyed, he said it was certainly something I had made up. I'd made a mistake and had altered the memory to turn it into something more compelling, so I didn't seem like quite such a fool. It was basic psychological theory, he said.

That was a long time ago. I am content with my life and light of heart. I know how evening rises up in the blue noon and I know every moment by the angle and quality of the sunlight spreading on my lawn and on my courtyard. I stand in the courtyard and watch the days and walk through my garden and wait for my daughter and Mal. For surely, as Mal tells me, I am the happiest of women. But it is always summer here and sometimes I remember how the winter was in Minnesota, how dark and drear. And it is just occasionally, as I watch Phoebe's copper hair growing into tighter and tighter curls with each passing year, that my mind strays back to that dead and gloomy time.

HEART LEAVES

BO BALL

WHEN SHE WAS NINE SHE BLED. She daubed the flow with leaves and didn't wonder till later when the better grainy wetness caught her by surprise. She was following the bells of the cows who had roamed into the woods and stubborned. She stopped to fondle rhododendron. The wetness came.

A bird's nest full of eggs could bring it on—the smell of heart leaves. But mostly rain. When thunder bassfiddled heaven, her fingers traveled to her thighs to play.

Pearl Duty said it was dying. For two years Bethel kept hands from thighs. Unless it rained.

Then after Christmas recess, she glanced up from her speller to the back of the room and saw the eyelashes of the new boy dance. She crossed her legs and tried to think of i before e. But she died.

Pearl said Doll Newberry's daddy killed a man in West Virginia and that his mama kept hounds in their house on Cherry Mountain. But he rode a spotted horse and Pearl petted its mane.

Her mama and her daddy said the Newberrys were no count— that his daddy shot a branch walker and was serving time. But Doll smelled of all her nose had taught her of perfume.

She gave her dinner bucket to Nez Wampler for the last desk in the seventh grade. It was right across from his, in the sixth.

He couldn't read. He couldn't spell. His talk was from tongues that hadn't learned from paper, but he could count in tens and he liked to hear the teacher tell of Abe Lincoln's eyes in lamplight.

While the grades—primer through seventh—followed their les-

219

sons, each different, his ears and eyes followed Mr. Armentrout and history.

The teacher plagued him only once. The first day he was asked to stand and read. He sat and stared red-faced into the book.

At dinner recess, those who brought food brushed snow from the well box to spread biscuits and sugar cake, to open lard cans filled with cornbread and milk.

Doll unhitched his spotted horse from the woodshed and rode off.

Bethel slipped a gingerbread baby in his desk. From the corner of an eye she saw his fingers pick crumbs to his mouth.

The next day her desk had walnuts, hickory, hazel. She kept some for a love box she was building.

She gave up the games of children. A farmer in the dell ground his heels in a circle to follow her eyes aimed upward at Doll Newberry on the big rock above the schoolyard. At "Hi-ye-o, my dearie-o," she broke circle and ran to the schoolhouse porch. She glanced upward. His nose and fingers were inspecting the winter sap of spruce. But he turned his face downward for her.

From then on, all games were just children in a ring.

At little recess, at dinner, and at big, her eyes stalked happy when they could catch a patch of him.

If a storm came up at free time, the scholars could play seat games or stand on the porch and flirt with fever.

Bethel flirted with Doll who made eyes at the sky. She let her whole face feast on half of his, and when his eyes shifted slightly to contain her, he would sigh and shift his weight, but she could see his britches grow as her thighs tightened to hold the wetness in.

At books, she learned how his page-turning finger caught spit. How, when he thought no one was looking, another finger joined to tug at a thin moustache. How at spelling his britches would sag, his legs bow to catch the belly of a horse that wasn't there.

But at history his legs would tighten when the teacher told of frozen Delawares.

It was in a morning drizzle she first touched him. She lingered on the porch till she heard hooves splash. She went to the little cloakroom and waited.

Mr. Armentrout cracked the Bible for devotion just as Doll's shoulders filled the cloakroom door.

Bethel's hand, fluffing dryness to her hair, caught the damp wool of his mackinaw. His fingers, fumbling for buttons, brushed hers.

"They's courtin' in a cloakroom," she heard Pearl Duty say above the teacher's "it shall come to pass."

Doll's hands darted to his pockets.

She took her seat for morning singing. She felt her cheeks fry.

She dared peep at him over a grade of history. The rose of a blush spotted his neck.

In February, she found an early violet blooming under a little rock that jutted out. She covered it from freeze at night, opened it to the thaw at day, and on the fourteenth, she picked it and put in it a red valentine of her own making—a boy and girl on a spotted horse in the middle of a heart. The horse was pretty. She traced that. The boy and girl she put on it looked squatty.

Her valentine came a day late—a bouquet of heart leaves tied with the bark of birch. All day long she breathed the sweetness of the gather. In geography, she forgot all her capitals.

Mr. Armentrout kept her after school to talk low. She was supposed to go away free to Normal next year. Bethel lowered her eyes and watched her right foot tap out no.

On her way home she put a heart leaf in her bosom. She hugged the bark of birches.

Doll started nodding to people and during big recess on a March day that played at being spring, he rode the primer on his horse. From the porch, she watched him gallop easy in the sun.

The next day, though a flurry made vague the horse's haunches, he rode the first grade in a circle around the schoolyard. When the last of five slid from the horse, Pearl Duty said, "When ye gone ride me an' Bethel?"

He nodded to Bethel. He pranced his horse to the well box. Her galoshes mounted. A hand swooped down to pull her for a side ride without a saddle.

She had made up how even her hair would flow. It would part in equal manes and tickle his neck as they rode off into the wilds.

But her hips kept the rest of her busy holding on. His left arm crooked for the same purpose. It gave her too much of a circle for bouncing.

When he let her down on the well box, she thought she felt her hair brush his face.

The long thaw came. He was absent more than present. The

government couldn't force him. He was over sixteen and they had his daddy. He had to stay home to plow.

Bethel smelled despair in the chalk. In the nests of mud daubers. In the over-ripe sweat of feet.

At home she paled and mumbled. Her mama boiled her spring tonics. Rolled rosin pills.

At school she kept her head on her desk. But she wouldn't miss a day in case he came.

He came for three rainy days in a row.

She left letters in his desk. He left in hers an Indian baby doll whittled from the sweet scented root of pine.

The last week in April he didn't come a single day.

She languished so that Mr. Armentrout sent her home with a note. She tore it up and stayed in the woods listening to the cow bells and talking to redbuds.

Though the last day of school was sunny, he came for his report card. She knew it would be fail. He could come back for two more years, if he wanted to.

Hers said pass, with no note for Normal. She could not come back.

Into his hands she placed pressed flowers and, for old time's sake, a fresh heart leaf.

In her desk was a bird's egg necklace—all blue and rounded to perfection. He rode off on his spotted horse before she could show him the neck it prided.

The first week away from school seemed longer than Moses' trip her mama made her read her every day. When Bethel came across a word she didn't know, she'd whisper Doll and lift her eyes toward Cherry Mountain and wonder what his hands and eyes were doing five miles away in wildness.

As a child she had fought sleep to catch fireflies or try to peep the dusky eyes of whippoorwills. Now she complained of aches and went to bed early. Katydids sawed their itch, night birds swelled their throats, but they blended with her dreams—wide-eyed and closed—of Doll and their twelve children who would escape snakebite and fever to grow up to take his image. When a storm came at night, she flailed love for him into the featherbed.

She asked to go herbing, but her mama and her daddy wouldn't let her. Galavanting they called it. They pointed out how Canady Crabtree lollagagged and ended up with a woods' colt at fourteen.

In late May she got to wear her necklace to a graveyard meeting to decorate her mama's dead. In early June to decorate her daddy's. She didn't catch a glimpse of Doll. His dead, she reckoned, were down in West Virginia.

When she could escape her mama's one good ear, she whispered to a schoolmate, "Seen Doll?"

Sardis Hess had seen him at the Jockey Grounds swapping the spotted horse for a mule.

Nez Wampler saw him digging May Apple root.

Pearl Duty said she saw him almost every day, but Bethel knew different.

At home she helped her mama in the garden. Found the cows and drove them home. Milked and churned. Read the kin of Moses past the Promised Land.

In early July, the oldest cow Piedy butted rails from the fence and roamed up the mountain. Clover and Cloudy followed. Her daddy walked the pasture fence to mend it, and though a red sky warned of rain, Bethel was sent to hunt the cows.

Two miles up the mountain she heard Piedy's old-timey bell clank tin. Another mile, the happy ring of Clover, like a handshook dinner bell. Cloudy wore a little brass one made for goats—a tinkle that hinted Christmas. Cloudy could not be told, but with the tin of Piedy in front and the iron of Clover in the middle, Bethel imagined the tiny bell baby out of the sound.

A half-mile away she could say what they were up to—the regular ring of walk. The unpatterned pause and ring of grass eating. The twisting side rings as their necks fought for buds. The more frantic clapper when they nudged away flies.

She knew a storm was brewing, for their bells became flaps of fear, hanging quiet for thunder.

She let them hide so she could follow another sound—the high whine of gee, the fall of haw, the bass of whoa, that came from a spur on the ridge above her.

She came to a clearing. She parted rhododendron to see Doll, naked to the waist, follow a black mule through corn rows. She caught the slight nod of his head right with the gees, left with the haws. The lift of chin upward for the whoas. She counted the knobs of muscles on his arms and back. The brave tremble of his chest.

She held her sides and rocked. She watched for two more rows, and when her knees stretched they could hold her, she answered her lips' say of go.

He stopped the mule in mid-field. He looked to the black clouds in the West, where the best storms came. A sudden breeze gathered leaves and turned them white.

She walked up beside him and said, "Ye ain't heard no bells?"

The belly of God rumbled. Dull lightning streaked the western sky.

"Best get 'fore hit pores," he said. He unhooked the mule and led it into the woods. She followed, around the spur on a small path that came to cliffs that jutted out to make a cave.

He tied the mule to a limb that elbowed inward for the shelter.

On rocks were whittled objects, dried and drying herbs, nuts from last year's swell. Her valentine in a high dry place.

He pointed to a bed of pine boughs. "To dream time 'way," he said.

She lay down on the bed and breathed the sweetness.

Thunder rolled. Lightning quickened.

He lay down beside her. He nibbled a heart leaf from her bosom. His lips played juice-harp on her breast. Minnowed her belly.

She smelled summer in him. She kissed the sweet lay of hair on his belly—up through naval to the little knob that said three ribs were passed, and then to the dark thickets that grew on both hills the nipples made, up to the ponds of collarbones where she lipped his salt. Then the ears that caught and held the seed of hay.

She kissed the lower lip in its tremble, the upper in its spread of joy, the whole mouth for the jerk his belly gave to her thighs that knew to open, knew to close.

"You killin' me," he said.

She sucked growth into his moustaches.

He rolled over on his back to let his muscles jerk. She waited for the apples on his shoulders to say fall. Then her chin caught the cup of a shoulder blade and her left hand babied navel.

The rain came down in heavy sheets.

He turned over to greet her snuggle.

"Let's die again," she said.

He straddled her to help them.

She ground her hips sideways and squeezed until the sweet hurt came.

"You killin' me," he said.

Her hips rose to meet the ride.

He slept. Through thunder. Through gulley washes.

She watched the two butt dimples rise and fall with his breathing. The storm darkened them from her eyes. Her fingers traced them through down.

He woke to breathe the sweet sourness sleep had fed him.

When a rainbow told them to, they rose to put on clothes. Doll reached out a hand to try to rake the color in. He settled for the new green that rain had given wildflowers.

She heard the clink of Piedy's tin, the clear ring of Clover, the tink of Cloudy.

"Day after tomar?" she asked.

He nodded.

"Noon?"

He nodded.

She gathered the cows and switched them into chimes. She laid her plan. She would cow hunt every other day on Cherry Mountain. She would stifle with rags the clappers of the cow bells. She would tie Piedy to a tree. Clover and Cloudy would linger beside her. She would slip all three forbidden winter hay at their milking to make up for lost graze.

She lied to her daddy that she had found the cows on Abner's Gap.

Her eyes were closed before the washed sky could blacken. Her thighs gathered feathers to pillow the burn past bruise into memory.

She woke to disappointment. Her daddy took one look at Piedy's tail and said, "Cuttin' up." He took her to a known bull in the valley. The silly daughters stuck their heads over the yard gate and mooed till milking time.

Bethel was fitful. Day after tomorrow would be delayed, for that night her daddy did the milking.

She sat on the front porch and read her mama the psalms of David and tried to catch the harps in her mind.

She couldn't hide the cows till Thursday evening's milking.

When they didn't come home by morning, her daddy said she would have to go find them. Once she was out of his sight, she followed a straight path up Cherry Mountain.

At the cave, the pine boughs were gone. In their place was a full bed of moss with blue-eyed grass and heart leaves duly spread. She let her face take their tickle.

She walked to the field. It was finished. She heard no gees, no haws.

She returned to the cave and prayed for him to come.

She rose to measure her shadow for noon.

She heard the nose of the black mule splutter, the click of Doll onward.

She quickly spread the heart leaves into pattern.

Her hand trembled when it helped him knot the strap of the bridle round the limb.

She told him how her daddy and Ole Pied had kept her from him.

They lay down together. Soreness made them gentle. His hands played pity-pat on her thighs. Her fingers forgot fumbles as they loosened his belt to trace down. She smelled the drip of work in him.

New blood drove away the blue from bruises.

They let the moss lip them, let the heart leaves slow impressions. Their thighs obeyed without a crop of thunder.

The day after tomorrow was Sunday. Her daddy would not violate the Sabbath for field work, but he would claim an ox in the ditch to hunt cows. She would have to hide them Sunday, see him Monday.

She led home the bewildered Piedy. Her bell, obedient to the fasting, told tin. Clover iron. Cloudy brass.

She milked them. Not much.

Stole them hay. A lot.

Her daddy deemed the bull's topping hadn't taken. On Sunday he led Piedy placid to the valley where the bull turned up his nose.

Yet Bethel's plan worked Monday, and for three weeks till her daddy sold Piedy. Said she taught them all to roam and stubborn. They were going dry.

Bethel tied Clover to a tree, but Cloudy traipsed home without her and lolled her head over the yard gate.

After three days away from Doll's eyes, she risked death.

She waited till snores told her she could gather dress from bed post. She held her breath for the count of fifty footfalls.

Bushes hugged for her hair. Sawbriars tried to tangle feet.

She slapped and kicked at thickets.

By midnight she crossed the field she knew. Then a tobacco patch. A stream. A garden. She saw his cabin stilled in moonlight.

She inched her way to the one window. She saw the face it gave her back—eyes rounded past recognition, lips pouted with fear. She heard the house hounds throat their warning. She jerked reflection away and waited behind the dahlias for what the dogs' teeth or Doll could give her.

She got Doll, his long fingers pushing at the noses of the dogs.

He took her elbow and they walked beyond the voice of his mother asking who.

The dogs, wagging now, smelled her out. She gave them her hands. They purposed tails and noses for night roam.

She told of the thwart. His arms answered she could count on him.

When the dew divided them, she said, "Come to me."

He came every other night through August. She held him under the crabapple tree, or when thunder squeezed the mountains into awe, in last year's corn shucks in the crib.

Once her mama rose to feel the bed and wonder where she was. Bethel claimed sleepwalking had taken her by surprise.

Her thighs caught wonder three months without daubing. She told Doll she was big. He replanted to be sure.

Her daddy found them and prized them apart before frost could. He threatened death and prison.

Bethel clutched her dress to her and said, "You kill three."

Her daddy lifted his right hand to the heavens and declared her dead.

"Go," he said. "With 'at woods' colt in yore belly."

She had only the one dress on her back. Her mama later slipped her others with love notes in the pockets.

They didn't marry. Doll and his mama didn't like the State. She asked his mama's blessing. She smiled through snuff and gave it in wide wink.

They stayed with her till the State gave back his daddy. Then they moved to a higher mountain where she taught wildflowers to grow in her yard, where he tilled fields and caught the bees in trees and told them to make honey.

The pregnancy was false. And every one thereafter. She would swell, but the egg would not ripen on her.

She made up the names and lives of twelve who escaped snakebite and fever to grow up to take his face. Doll would lie quiet in bed to listen to her tell what the children of her mind had done that day.

She grew too fat. He grew too thin. And they learned to snore many nights away. But when a storm would come, she'd rustle the bed clothes and turn to him.

And he'd say, "You gone kill me."

She did, in the flood of '52. At a clap of thunder, as he spent, he gave a gurgle she hadn't heard before. Then he lay heavy upon her.

She turned him over and, through lightning, she courted the skin time had blotched. Her lips traced the gray hairs to the knob that said three ribs were passed. Her arms cradled him till dawn.

She rose to see a rainbow. Her hands reached out to try to rake it in, but they settled on the new green rain had given.

She told them all—the flowers, the children, the bees—and, on her weak way down the mountain, the Queen's Lace, the Pennyroyal, heart leaves.

THE FAT GIRL

ANDRE DUBUS

HER NAME WAS LOUISE. Once when she was sixteen a boy kissed her at a barbecue; he was drunk and he jammed his tongue into her mouth and ran his hands up and down her hips. Her father kissed her often. He was thin and kind and she could see in his eyes when he looked at her the lights of love and pity.

It started when Louise was nine. You must start watching what you eat, her mother would say. I can see you have my metabolism. Louise also had her mother's pale blonde hair. Her mother was slim and pretty, carried herself erectly, and ate very little. The two of them would eat bare lunches, while her old brother ate sandwiches and potato chips, and then her mother would sit smoking while

Louise eyed the bread box, the pantry, the refrigerator. Wasn't that good, her mother would say. In five years you'll be in high school and if you're fat the boys won't like you; they won't ask you out. Boys were as far away as five years, and she would go to her room and wait for nearly an hour until she knew her mother was no longer thinking of her, then she would creep into the kitchen and, listening to her mother talking on the phone, or her footsteps upstairs, she would open the bread box, the pantry, the jar of peanut butter. She would put the sandwich under her shirt and go outside or to the bathroom to eat it.

Her father was a lawyer and made a lot of money and came home looking pale and happy. Martinis put color back in his face, and at dinner he talked to his wife and two children. Oh give her a potato, he would say to Louise's mother. She's a growing girl. Her mother's voice then became tense: If she has a potato she shouldn't have dessert. She should have both, her father would say, and he would reach over and touch Louise's check or hand or arm.

In high school she had two girl friends and at night and on week-ends they rode in a car or went to movies. In movies she was fascinated by fat actresses. She wondered why they were fat. She knew why she was fat: she was fat because she was Louise. Because God had made her that way. Because she wasn't like her friends Barbara and Marjorie, who drank milk shakes after school and were all bones and tight skin. But what about those actresses, with their talents, with their broad and profound faces? Did they eat as heedlessly as Bishop Humphries and his wife who sometimes came to dinner and, as Louise's mother said, gorged between amenities? Or did they try to lose weight, did they go about hungry and angry and thinking of food? She thought of them eating lean meats and salads with friends, and then going home and building strange large sandwiches with Italian bread. But mostly she believed they did not go through these failures; they were fat because they chose to be. And she was certain of something else too: she could see it in their faces: they did not eat secretly. Which she did: her creeping to the kitchen when she was nine became, in high school, a ritual of deceit and pleasure. She was a furtive eater of sweets. Even her two friends did not know her secret.

Barbara was thin, gangling, and flat-chested; she was attractive enough and all she needed was someone to take a second look at her face, but the school was large and there were pretty girls in every classroom and walking all the corridors, so no one ever needed to take a second look at Barbara. Marjorie was thin too, an intense, heavy-smoking girl with brittle laughter. She was very intelligent, and with boys she was shy because she knew she made them uncomfortable, and because she was smarter than they were and so could not understand or could not believe the levels they lived on. She was to have a nervous breakdown before earning her PhD. in philosophy at the University of California, where she met and married a physicist and discovered within herself an untrammelled passion: she made love with her husband on the couch, the carpet, in the bathtub, and on the washing machine. By that time much had happened to her and she never thought of Louise. Barbara would finally stop growing and begin moving with grace and confidence. In college she would have two lovers and then several more during the six years she spent in Boston before marrying a middleaged editor who had two sons in their early teens, who drank too much, who was tenderly, boyishly grateful for her love, and whose wife had been killed while rock-climbing in New Hampshire with her lover. She would not think of Louise either, except in an earlier time, when lovers were still new to her and she was ecstatically surprised each time one of them loved her and, sometimes at night, lying in a man's arms, she would tell how in high school no one dated her, she had been thin and plain (she would still believe that: that she had been plain; it had never been true) and so had been forced into the week-end and night-time company of a neurotic smart girl and a shy fat girl. She would say this with self-pity exaggerated by scotch and her need to be more deeply loved by the man who held her.

She never eats, Barbara and Marjorie said of Louise. They ate lunch with her at school, watched her refusing potatoes, ravioli, fried fish. Sometimes she got through the cafeteria line with only a salad. That is how they would remember her: a girl whose hapless body was destined to be fat. No one saw the sandwiches she made and took to her room when she came home from school. No one saw the store of Milky Ways, Butterfingers, Almond Joys, and Hersheys far back on her closet shelf, behind the stuffed animals of her childhood. She was not a hypocrite. When she was out of the house she truly believed she was dieting; she forgot about the candy, as a man speaking into his office dictaphone may forget the lewd photographs hidden in an old shoe in his closet. At other times, away from the home, she thought of the waiting candy with near lust. One night driving home from a movie, Marjorie said: 'You're lucky you don't smoke; it's *incredible* what I go through to hide it from my parents.' Louise turned to her a smile which was elusive and mysterious; she yearned to be home in bed, eating chocolate in the dark. She did not need to smoke; she already had a vice that was insular and destructive.

She brought it with her to college. She thought she would leave it behind. A move from one place to another, a new room without the haunted closet shelf, would do for her what she could not do for herself. She packed her large dresses and went. For two weeks she was busy with registration, with shyness, with classes; then she began to feel at home. Her room was no longer like a motel. Its walls had stopped watching her, she felt they were her friends, and she gave them her secret. Away from her mother, she did not have to be as elaborate; she kept the candy in her drawer now.

The school was in Massachusetts, a girls' school. When she chose it, when she and her father and mother talked about it in the evenings, everyone so carefully avoided the word boys that sometimes the conversations seemed to be about nothing but boys. There are no boys there, the neuter words said; you will not have to contend with that. In her father's eyes were pity and encouragement; in her mother's was disappointment, and her voice was crisp. They spoke of courses, of small classes where Louise would get more attention. She imagined herself in those small classes; she saw herself as a teacher would see her, as the other girls would; she would get no attention.

The girls at the school were from wealthy families, but most of them wore the uniform of another class: blue jeans and work shirts, and many wore overalls. Louise bought some overalls, washed them until the dark blue faded, and wore them to classes. In the cafeteria she ate as she had in high school, not to lose weight nor even to sustain her lie, but because eating lightly in public had become as habitual as good manners. Everyone had to take gym, and in the locker room with the other girls, and wearing shorts on the volleyball and badminton courts, she hated her body. She liked her body most when she was unaware of it: in bed at night, as sleep gently took her out of her day, out of herself. And she liked parts of her body. She liked her brown eyes and sometimes looked at them in the mirror: they were not shallow eyes, she thought; they were indeed windows of a tender soul, a good heart. She liked her lips and nose, and her chin, finely shaped between her wide and sagging cheeks. Most of all she liked her long pale blonde hair, she liked washing and drying it and lying naked on her bed, smelling of shampoo, and feeling the soft hair at her neck and shoulders and back.

Her friend at college was Carrie, who was thin and wore thick glasses and often at night she cried in Louise's room. She did not know why she was crying. She was crying, she said, because she was unhappy. She could say no more. Louise said she was unhappy too, and Carrie moved in with her. One night Carrie talked for hours, sadly and bitterly, about her parents and what they did to each other. When she finished she hugged Louise and they went to bed. Then in the dark Carrie spoke across the room: 'Louise? I just wanted to tell you. One night last week I woke up and smelled chocolate. You were eating chocolate, in your bed. I wish you'd eat it in front of me, Louise, whenever you feel like it.'

Stiffened in her bed, Louise could think of nothing to say. In the silence she was afraid Carrie would think she was asleep and would tell her again in the morning or tomorrow night. Finally she said Okay. Then after a moment she told Carrie if she ever wanted any she could feel free to help herself; the candy was in the top drawer. Then she said thank you.

They were roommates for four years and in the summers they exchanged letters. Each fall they greeted with embraces, laughter, tears, and moved into their old room, which had been stripped and cleansed of them for the summer. Neither girl enjoyed summer. Carrie did not like being at home because her parents did not love each other. Louise lived in a small city in Louisiana. She did not like summer because she had lost touch with Barbara and Marjorie; they saw each other, but it was not the same. She liked being with her father but with no one else. The flicker of disappointment in her mother's eyes at the airport was a vanguard of the army of relatives and acquaintances who awaited her: they would see her on the streets, in stores, at the country club, in her home, and in theirs; in the first moments of greeting, their eyes would tell her she was still fat Louise, who had been fat as long as they could remember, who had gone to college and returned as fat as ever. Then their eyes dismissed her, and she longed for school and Carrie, and she wrote letters to her friend. But that saddened her too. It wasn't simply that Carrie was her only friend, and when they finished college they might never see each other again. It was that her existence in the world was so divided; it had begun when she was a child creeping to the kitchen; now that division was much sharper, and her friendship with Carrie seemed disproportionate and perilous. The world she was destined to live in had nothing to do with the intimate nights in their room at school.

In the summer before their senior year, Carrie fell in love. She wrote to Louise about him, but she did not write much, and this hurt Louise more than if Carrie had shown the joy her writing tried to conceal. That fall they returned to their room; they were still close and warm, Carrie still needed Louise's ears and heart at night as she spoke of her parents and her recurring malaise whose source the two friends never discovered. But on most week-ends Carrie left, and caught a bus to Boston where her boy friend studied music. During the week she often spoke hesitantly of sex; she was not sure if she liked it. But Louise, eating candy and listening, did not know whether Carrie was telling the truth or whether, as in her letters of the past summer, Carrie was keeping from her those delights she may never experience.

Then one Sunday night when Carrie had just returned from Boston and was unpacking her overnight bag, she looked at Louise and said: 'I was thinking about you. On the bus coming home tonight.' Looking at Carrie's concerned, determined face, Louise prepared herself for humiliation. 'I was thinking about when we graduate. What you're going to do. What's to become of you. I want you to be loved the way I love you. Louise, if I help you, *really* help you, will you go on a diet?'

Louise entered a period of her life she would remember always, the way some people remember having endured poverty. Her diet did not begin the next day. Carrie told her to eat on Monday as though it were the last day of her life. So for the first time since grammar school Louise went into a school cafeteria and ate everything she wanted. At breakfast and lunch and dinner she glanced around the table to see if the other girls noticed the food on her tray. They did not. She felt there was a lesson in this, but it lay beyond her grasp. That night in their room she ate the four remaining candy bars. During the day Carrie rented a small refrigerator, bought an electric skillet, an electric broiler, and bathroom scales.

On Tuesday morning Louise stood on the scales, and Carrie wrote in her notebook: *October 14: 184 lbs.* Then she made Louise a cup of black coffee and scrambled one egg and sat with her while she ate. When Carrie went to the dining room for breakfast, Louise walked about the campus for thirty minutes. That was part of the plan. The campus was pretty, on its lawns grew at least one of every tree native to New England, and in the warm morning sun Louise felt a new hope. At noon they met in their room, and Carrie broiled her a piece of hamburger and served it with lettuce. Then while Carrie ate in the dining room Louise walked again. She was weak with hunger and she felt queasy. During her afternoon classes she was nervous and tense, and she chewed her pencil and tapped her heels on the floor and tightened her calves. When she returned to her room late that afternoon, she was so glad to see Carrie that she embraced her; she had felt she could not bear another minute of hunger, but now with Carrie she knew she could make it at least through tonight. Then she would sleep and face tomorrow when it came. Carrie broiled her a steak and served it with lettuce. Louise studied while Carrie ate dinner, then they went for a walk.

That was her ritual and her diet for the rest of the year, Carrie alternating fish and chicken breasts with the steaks for dinner, and every day was nearly as bad as the first. In the evenings she was irritable. In all her life she had never been afflicted by ill temper and she looked upon it now as a demon which, along with hunger, was taking possession of her soul. Often she spoke sharply to Carrie. One night during their after-dinner walk Carrie talked sadly of night, of how darkness made her more aware of herself, and at night she did not know why she was in college, why she studied, why she was walking the earth with other people. They were standing on a wooden foot bridge, looking down at a dark pond. Carrie kept talking; perhaps soon she would cry. Suddenly Louise said; 'I'm sick of lettuce. I never want to see a piece of lettuce for the rest of my life. I hate it. We shouldn't even buy it, it's immoral.'

Carrie was quiet. Louise glanced at her, and the pain and irritation in Carrie's face soothed her. Then she was ashamed. Before she could say she was sorry, Carrie turned to her and said gently: 'I know. I know how terrible it is.'

Carrie did all the shopping, telling Louise she knew how hard it was to go into a supermarket when you were hungry. And Louise was always hungry. She drank diet soft drinks and started smoking Carrie's cigarettes, learned to enjoy inhaling, thought of cancer and emphysema but they were as far away as those boys her mother had talked about when she was nine. By Thanksgiving she was smoking over a pack a day and her weight in Carrie's notebook was one hundred and sixty-two pounds. Carrie was afraid if Louise went home at Thanksgiving she would lapse from the diet, so Louise spent the vacation with Carrie, in Philadelphia. Carrie wrote her family about the diet, and told Louise that she had. On the plane to Philadelphia, Louise said: 'I feel like a bedwetter. When I was a little girl I had a friend who used to come spend the night and Mother would put a rubber sheet on the bed and we all pretended there wasn't a rubber sheet and that she hadn't wet the bed. Even me, and I slept with her.' At Thanksgiving dinner she lowered her eyes as Carrie's father put two slices of white meat on her plate and passed it to her over the bowls of steaming food.

When she went home at Christmas she weighed a hundred and fifty-five pounds; at the airport her mother marvelled. Her father laughed and hugged her and said: 'But now there's less of you to love.' He was troubled by her smoking but only mentioned it once; he told her she was beautiful and, as always, his eyes bathed her with love. During the long vacation her mother cooked for her as Carrie had, and Louise returned to school weighing a hundred and forty-six pounds.

Flying north on the plane she warmly recalled the surprised and congratulatory eyes of her relatives and acquaintances. She had not seen Barbara or Marjorie. She thought of returning home in May, weighing the hundred and fifteen pounds which Carrie had in October set as their goal. Looking toward the stoic days ahead, she felt strong. She thought of those hungry days of fall and early winter (and now: she was hungry now: with almost a frown, almost a brusque shake of the head, she refused peanuts from the stewardess): those first weeks of the diet when she was the pawn of an irascibility which still, conditioned to her ritual as she was, could at any moment take command of her. She thought of the nights of trying to sleep while her stomach growled. She thought of her addiction to cigarettes. She thought of the people at school: not one teacher, not one girl, had spoken to her about her loss of weight, not even about her absence from meals. And without warning her spirit collapsed. She did not feel strong, she did not feel she was committed to and within reach of achieving a valuable goal. She felt that somehow she had lost more than pounds of fat; that some time

But she knew the story meant very little to him. She could have been telling him of a childhood illness, or wearing braces, or a broken heart at sixteen. He could not see her as she was when she was fat. She felt as though she were trying to tell a foreign lover about her life in the United States, and if only she could command the language he would know and love all of her and she would feel complete. Some of the acquaintances of her childhood were her friends now, and even they did not seem to remember her when she was fat.

Now her body was growing again, and when she put on a maternity dress for the first time she shivered with fear. Richard did not smoke and he asked her, in a voice just short of demand, to stop during her pregnancy. She did. She ate carrots and celery instead of smoking, and at cocktail parties she tried to eat nothing, but after her first drink she ate nuts and cheese and crackers and dips. Always at these parties Richard had talked with his friends and she had rarely spoken to him until they drove home. But now when he noticed her at the hors d'oeuvres table he crossed the room and, smiling, led her back to his group. His smile and his hand on her arm told her he was doing his clumsy, husbandly best to help her through a time of female mystery.

She was gaining weight but she told herself it was only the baby, and would leave with its birth. But at other times she knew quite clearly that she was losing the discipline she had fought so hard to gain during her last year with Carrie. She was hungry now as she had been in college, and she ate between meals and after dinner and tried to eat only carrots and celery, but she grew to hate them, and her desire for sweets was as vicious as it had been long ago. At home she ate bread and jam and when she shopped for groceries she bought a candy bar and ate it driving home and put the wrapper in her purse and then in the garbage can under the sink. Her cheeks had filled out, there was loose flesh under her chin, her arms and legs were plump, and her mother was concerned. So was Richard. One night when she brought pie and milk to the living room where they were watching television, he said: 'You already had a piece. At dinner.'

She did not look at him.

'You're gaining weight. It's not all water, either. It's fat. It'll be summertime. You'll want to get into your bathing suit.'

The pie was cherry. She looked at it as her fork cut through it; she

during her dieting she had lost herself too. She tried to remember what it had felt like to be Louise before she had started living on meat and fish, as an unhappy adult may look sadly in the memory of childhood for lost virtues and hopes. She looked down at the earth far below, and it seemed to her that her soul, like her body aboard the plane, was in some rootless flight. She neither knew its destination nor where it had departed from; it was on some passage she could not even define.

During the next few weeks she lost weight more slowly and once for eight days Carrie's daily recording stayed at a hundred and thirty-six. Louise woke in the morning thinking of one hundred and thirty-six and then she stood on the scales and they echoed her. She became obsessed with that number, and there wasn't a day when she didn't say it aloud, and through the days and nights the number stayed in her mind, and if a teacher had spoken those digits in a classroom she would have opened her mouth to speak. What if that's me, she said to Carrie. I mean what if a hundred and thirty-six is my real weight and I just can't lose anymore. Walking hand-in-hand with her despair was a longing for this to be true, and that longing angered her and wearied her, and every day she was gloomy. On the ninth day she weighed a hundred and thirty-five and a half pounds. She was not relieved; she thought bitterly of the months ahead, the shedding of the last twenty and a half pounds.

On Easter Sunday, which she spent at Carrie's, she weighed one hundred and twenty pounds, and she ate one slice of glazed pineapple with her ham and lettuce. She did not enjoy it: she felt she was being friendly with a recalcitrant enemy who had once tried to destroy her. Carrie's parents were laudative. She liked them and she wished they would touch sometimes, and look at each other when they spoke. She guessed they would divorce when Carrie left home, and she vowed that her own marriage would be one of affection and tenderness. She could think about that now: marriage. At school she had read in a Boston paper that this summer the cicadas would come out of their seventeen year hibernation on Cape Cod, for a month they would mate and then die, leaving their young to burrow into the ground where they would stay for seventeen years. That's me, she had said to Carrie. Only my hibernation lasted twenty-one years.

Often her mother asked in letters and on the phone about the diet, but Louise answered vaguely. When she flew home in late May she weighed a hundred and thirteen pounds, and at the airport her mother cried and hugged her and said again and again: You're so *beaut*iful. Her father blushed and bought her a martini. For days her relatives and acquaintances congratulated her, and the applause in their eyes lasted the entire summer, and she loved their eyes, and swam in the country club pool, the first time she had done this since she was a child.

She lived at home and ate the way her mother did and every morning she weighed. Her mother liked to take her shopping and buy her dresses and they put her old ones in the Goodwill box at the shopping center; Louise thought of them existing on the body of a poor woman whose cheap meals kept her fat. Louise's mother had a photographer come to the house, and Louise posed on the couch and standing beneath a live oak and sitting in a wicker lawn chair next to an azalea bush. The new clothes and the photographer made her feel she was going to another country or becoming a citizen of a new one. In the fall she took a job of no consequence, to give her something to do.

Also in the fall a young lawyer joined her father's firm, he came one night to dinner, and they started seeing each other. He was the first man outside her family to kiss her since the barbecue when she was sixteen. Louise celebrated Thanksgiving not with rice dressing and candied sweet potatoes and mince meat and pumpkin pies, but by giving Richard her virginity which she realized, at the very last moment of its existence, she had embarked on giving him over thirteen months ago, on that Tuesday in October when Carrie had made her a cup of black coffee and scrambled one egg. She wrote this to Carrie, who replied happily by return mail. She also, through glance and smile and innuendo, tried to tell her mother too. But finally she controlled that impulse, because Richard felt guilty about making love with the daughter of his partner and friend. In the spring they married. The wedding was a large one, in the Episcopal church, and Carrie flew from Boston to be maid of honor. Her parents had recently separated and she was living with the musician and was still victim of her unpredictable malaise. It overcame her on the night before the wedding, so Louise was up with her until past three and woke next morning from a sleep so heavy that she did not want to leave it.

Richard was a lean, tall, energetic man with the metabolism of a pencil sharpener. Louise fed him everything he wanted. He Italian food and she got recipes from her mother and watche eating spaghetti with the sauce she had only tasted, and ravio lasagna, while she ate antipasto with her chianti. He made a money and borrowed more and they bought a house whose sloped down to the shore of a lake; they had a wharf and a boath and Richard bought a boat and they took friends watersk Richard bought her a car and they spent his vacations in Me Canada, the Bahamas, and in the fifth year of their marriage went to Europe and, according to their plan, she conceived a chi Paris. On the plane back, as she looked out the window and bey the sparkling sea and saw her country, she felt that it was waitin her, as her home by the lake was, and her parents, and her g friends who rode in the boat and waterskied; she thought of accumulated warmth and pelf of her marriage, and how by slimn her body she had bought into the pleasures of the nation. She cunning, and she smiled to herself, and took Richard's hand.

But these moments of triumph were sparse. On most days went about her routine of leisure with a sense of certainty ab herself that came merely from not thinking. But there were tim with her friends, or with Richard, or alone in the house, when s was suddenly assaulted by the feeling that she had taken the wro train and arrived at a place where no one knew her, and where s ought not to be. Often, in bed with Richard, she talked of being fat was the one who started the friendship with Carrie, I chose her, started the conversations. When I understood that she was m friend I understood something else: I had chosen her for the sam reason I'd chosen Barbara and Marjorie. They were all thin. I wa always thinking about what people saw when they looked at me and didn't want them to see two fat girls. When I was alone I didn't mind being fat but then I'd have to leave the house again and then I didn' want to look like me. But at home I didn't mind except when I was getting dressed to go out of the house and when Mother looked at me. But I stopped looking at her when she looked at me. And in college I felt good with Carrie; there weren't any boys and I didn't have any other friends and so when I wasn't with Carrie I thought about her and I tried to ignore the other people around me, I tried to make them not exist. A lot of the time I could do that. It was strange, and I felt like a spy.'

If Richard was bored by her repetition he pretended not to be.

speared the piece and rubbed it in the red juice on the plate before lifting it to her mouth.

'You never used to eat pie,' he said. 'I just think you ought to watch it a bit. It's going to be tough on you this summer.'

In her seventh month, with a delight reminiscent of climbing the stairs to Richard's apartment before they were married, she returned to her world of secret gratification. She began hiding candy in her underwear drawer. She ate it during the day and at night while Richard slept, and at breakfast she was distracted, waiting for him to leave.

She gave birth to a son, brought him home, and nursed both him and her appetites. During this time of celibacy she enjoyed her body through her son's mouth; while he suckled she stroked his small head and back. She was hiding candy but she did not conceal her other indulgences: she was smoking again but still she ate between meals, and at dinner she ate what Richard did, and coldly he watched her, he grew petulant, and when the date marking the end of their celibacy came they let it pass. Often in the afternoons her mother visited and scolded her and Louise sat looking at the baby and said nothing until finally, to end it, she promised to diet. When her mother and father came for dinners, her father kissed her and held the baby and her mother said nothing about Louise's body, and her voice was tense. Returning from work in the evenings Richard looked at a soiled plate and glass on the table beside her chair as if detecting traces of infidelity, and at every dinner they fought.

'Look at you,' he said. 'Lasagna, for God's sake. When are you going to start? It's not simply that you haven't lost any weight. You're gaining. I can see it. I can feel it when you get in bed. Pretty soon you'll weigh more than I do and I'll be sleeping on a trampoline.'

'You never touch me anymore.'

'I don't want to touch you. Why should I? Have you *looked* at yourself?'

'You're cruel,' she said. 'I never knew how cruel you were.'

She ate, watching him. He did not look at her. Glaring at his plate, he worked with fork and knife like a hurried man at a lunch counter.

'I bet you didn't either,' she said.

That night when he was asleep she took a Milky Way to the bathroom. For a while she stood eating in the dark, then she turned on the light. Chewing, she looked at herself in the mirror; she looked at her eyes and hair. Then she stood on the scales and looking at the numbers between her feet, one hundred and sixty-two, she remembered when she had weighed a hundred and thirty-six pounds for eight days. Her memory of those eight days was fond and amusing, as though she were recalling an Easter egg hunt when she was six. She stepped off the scales and pushed them under the lavatory and did not stand on them again.

It was summer and she bought loose dresses and when Richard took friends out on the boat she did not wear a bathing suit or shorts; her friends gave her mischievous glances, and Richard did not look at her. She stopped riding on the boat. She told them she wanted to stay with the baby, and she sat inside holding him until she heard the boat leave the wharf. Then she took him to the front lawn and walked with him in the shade of the trees and talked to him about the blue jays and mockingbirds and cardinals she saw on their branches. Sometimes she stopped and watched the boat out on the lake and the friend skiing behind it.

Every day Richard quarrelled, and because his rage went no further than her weight and shape, she felt excluded from it, and she remained calm within layers of flesh and spirit, and watched his frustration, his impotence. He truly believed they were arguing about her weight. She knew better: she knew that beneath the argument lay the question of who Richard was. She thought of him smiling at the wheel of his boat, and long ago courting his slender girl, the daughter of his partner and friend. She thought of Carrie telling her of smelling chocolate in the dark and, after that, watching her eat it night after night. She smiled at Richard, teasing his anger.

He is angry now. He stands in the center of the living room, raging at her, and he wakes the baby. Beneath Richard's voice she hears the soft crying, feels it in her heart, and quietly she rises from her chair and goes upstairs to the child's room and takes him from the crib. She brings him to the living room and sits holding him in her lap, pressing him gently against the folds of fat at her waist. Now Richard is pleading with her. Louise thinks tenderly of Carrie broiling meat and fish in their room, and walking with her in the evenings. She wonders if Carrie still has the malaise. Perhaps she will come for a visit. In Louise's arms now the boy sleeps.

'I'll help you,' Richard says. 'I'll eat the same things you eat.'

But his face does not approach the compassion and determination and love she had seen in Carrie's during what she now recognizes as the worst year of her life. She can remember nothing about that year except hunger, and the meals in her room. She is hungry now. When she puts the boy to bed she will get a candy bar from her room. She will eat it here, in front of Richard. This room will be hers soon. She considers the possibilities: all these rooms and the lawn where she can do whatever she wishes. She knows he will leave soon. It has been in his eyes all summer. She stands, using one hand to pull herself out of the chair. She carries the boy to his crib, feels him against her large breasts, feels that his sleeping body touches her soul. With a surge of vindication and relief she holds him. Then she kisses his forehead and places him in the crib. She goes to the bedroom and in the dark takes a bar of candy from her drawer. Slowly she descends the stairs. She knows Richard is waiting but she feels his departure so happily that, when she enters the living room, unwrapping the candy, she is surprised to see him standing there.

THE INFINITE PASSION OF EXPECTATION

OF EXPECTATION

GINA BERRIAULT

THE GIRL AND THE ELDERLY MAN descended the steep stairs to the channel's narrow beach and walked along by the water's edge. Several small fishing boats were moving out to sea, passing a freighter entering the bay, booms raised, a foreign name at her bow. His sturdy hiking boots came down flatly on the firm sand, the same way they came down on the trails of the mountain that he climbed, staff in hand, every Sunday. Up in his elegant neighborhood, on the cliff above the channel, he stamped along the sidewalks in the same way, his long, stiff legs attempting ease and flair. He appeared to feel no differences in terrain. The day was cold, and every time the little transparent fans of water swept in and drew back, the wet sand mirrored a clear sky and the sun on its way down. He wore an overcoat, a cap, and a thick muffler, and, with his head high, his large, arched nose set into the currents of air from off the ocean, he described for her his fantasy of their honeymoon in Mexico.

He was jovial, he laughed his English laugh that was like a bird's hooting, like a very sincere imitation of a laugh. If she married him, he said, she, so many years younger, could take a young lover and he would not protest. The psychologist was seventy-nine, but he allowed himself great expectations of love and other pleasures, and advised her to do the same. She always mocked herself for dreams, because to dream was to delude herself. She was a waitress and lived in a neighborhood of littered streets, where rusting cars stood unmoved for months. She brought him ten dollars each visit, sometimes more, sometimes less; he asked of her only a fee she could afford. Since she always looked downward in her own surroundings, avoiding the scene that might be all there was to her future, she could not look upward in his surroundings, resisting its dazzling diminishment of her. But out on these walks with him she tried looking up. It was what she had come to see him for—that he might reveal to her how to look up and around.

On their other walks and now, he told her about his life. She had only to ask, and he was off into memory, and memory took on a prophetic sound. His life seemed like a life expected and not yet lived, and it sounded that way because, within the overcoat, was a youth, someone always looking forward. The girl wondered if he were outstripping time, with his long stride and emphatic soles, and if his expectation of love and other pleasures served the same purpose. He was born in Pontefract, in England, a Roman name, meaning broken bridge. He had been a sick child, suffering from rheumatic fever. In his twenties he was a rector, and he and his first wife, emancipated from their time, each had a lover, and some very modern nights went on in the rectory. They traveled to Vienna to see what psycho-analysis was all about. Freud was ill and referred them to Rank, and as soon as introductions were over, his wife and Rank were lovers. "She divorced me," he said, "and had a child by that fellow. But since he wasn't the marrying kind, I gave his son my family name, and they came with me to America. She hallucinates her Otto," he told her. "Otto guides her to wise decisions."

The wife of his youth lived in a small town across the bay, and he often went over to work in her garden. Once, the girl passed her on the path, and the woman, going hastily to her car, stepped shyly aside like a country schoolteacher afraid of a student; and the girl, too, stepped sideways shyly, knowing, without ever having seen her, who she was, even though the woman—tall, broad-hipped, freckled, a gray braid fuzzed with amber wound around her head—failed to answer the description in the girl's imagination. Some days after, the girl encountered her again, in a dream, as she was years ago: a very slender young woman in a long white skirt, her amber hair to her waist, her pale eyes coal-black with ardor.

On the way home through his neighborhood, he took her hand and tucked it into the crook of his arm, and this gesture, by drawing her up against him, hindered her step and his and slowed them down. His house was Spanish style, common to that vanward section of San Francisco. Inside, everything was heavily antique—carven furniture and cloisonné vases and thin and dusty Oriental carpets. With him lived the family that was to inherit his estate—friends who had moved in with him when his second wife died; but the atmosphere the family provided seemed, to the girl, a turnabout one, as if he were an adventurous uncle, long away and now come home to them at last, cheerily grateful, bearing a fortune. He had no children, he had no brother, and his only sister, older than he and unmarried, lived in a village in England and was in no need of an inheritance. For several months after the family moved in, the husband, who was an organist in the Episcopal Church, gave piano lessons at home, and the innocent banality of repeated notes sounded from a far room while the psychologist sat in the study with his clients. A month ago the husband left, and everthing grew quiet. Occasionally, the son was seen about the house—a high school track star, small and blond like his mother, impassive like his father, his legs usually bare.

The psychologist took off his overcoat and cap, left on his muffler, and went into his study. The girl was offered tea by the mother, and they sat down at the dining table, by sunstruck windows. The woman pushed her sewing aside, and they sat in tete-a-tete position at a corner of the table.

The woman's face was too close. Now that the girl was a companion on his walks, the woman expected a womanly intimacy with her. They were going away for a week, she and her son, and would the girl please stay with the old man and take care of him? He couldn't even boil an egg or make a pot of tea, and two months ago he'd had a spell, he had fainted as he was climbing the stairs to bed. They were going to visit her sister in Kansas. She had composed a song about the loss of her husband's love, and she was taking the song to her sister. Her sister, she said, had a beautiful voice.

The sun over the woman's shoulder was like an accomplice's face, striking down the girl's resistance. And she heard herself confiding—"He asked me to marry him"—knowing that she would not and knowing why she had told the woman. Because to speculate about the possibility was to accept his esteem of her. At times it was necessary to grant the name of love to something less than love.

On the day the woman and her son left, the girl came half-an-hour before their departure. The woman, already wearing a coat and hat, led the way upstairs and opened, first, the door to the psychologist's bedroom. It seemed a trespass, entering that very small room, its space taken up by a mirrorless bureau and a bed of bird's-eye maple that appeared higher than most and was covered by a faded red quilt. On the bureau was a doilie, a tin box of watercolors, a nautilus shell, and a shallow drawer from a cabinet, in which lay, under glass, several tiny bird's-eggs of delicate tints. And pinned to the wallpaper were pages cut from magazines of another decade—the faces of young and wholesome beauties, girls with short, marcelled hair, cherry-red lips, plump cheeks, and little white collars. She had expected the faces of the mentors of his spirit, of Thoreau, of Gandhi, of the other great men whose words he quoted for her like passwords into the realm of wisdom.

The woman led the way across the hall and into the master bedroom. It was the woman's room and would be the girl's. A large, almost empty room, with a double bed no longer shared by her husband, a spindly dresser, a fireplace never used. It was as if a servant, or someone awaiting a more prosperous time, had moved into a room whose call for elegance she could not yet answer. The woman stood with her back to the narrow glass doors that led onto a balcony, her eyes the same cold blue of the winter sky in the row of panes.

"This house is ours," the woman said. "What's his is ours."

There was a cringe in the woman's body, so slight a cringe it would have gone unnoticed by the girl, but the open coat seemed hung upon a sudden emptiness. The girl was being told that the old man's fantasies were shaking the foundation of the house, of the son's future, and of the woman's own fantasies of an affluent old age. It was an accusation, and she chose not to answer it and not to ease the woman's fears. If she were to assure the woman that her desires had no bearing on anyone living in that house, her denial would seem untrue and go unheard, because the woman saw her now as the man saw her: a figure fortified by her youth and by her appeal and by her future, a time when all that she would want of life might come about.

Alone, she set her suitcase on a chair, refusing the drawer the woman had emptied and left open. The woman and her son were gone, after a flurry of banging doors and goodbyes. Faintly, up through the floor, came the murmur of the two men down in the study. A burst of emotion—the client's voice raised in anger or anguish and the psychologist's voice rising in order to calm. Silence again, the silence of the substantiality of the house and of the triumph of reason.

"We're both so thin," he said when he embraced her and they were alone, by the table set for supper. The remark was a jocular hint of intimacy to come. He poured a sweet blackberry wine, and was sipping the last of his second glass when she began to sip her first glass. "She offered herself to me," he said. "She came into my room not long after her husband left her. She had only her kimono on and it was open to her naval. She said she just wanted to say goodnight, but I knew what was on her mind. But she doesn't attract me. No." How lightly he told it. She felt shame, hearing about the woman's secret dismissal.

After supper he went into his study with a client, and she left a note on the table, telling him she had gone to pick up something she had forgotten to bring. Roaming out into the night to avoid as long as possible the confrontation with the unknown person within his familiar person, she rode a streetcar that went toward the ocean and, at the end of the line, remained in her seat while the motorman drank coffee from a thermos and read a newspaper. From over the sand dunes came the sound of heavy breakers. She gazed out into the dark, avoiding the reflection of her face in the glass, but after a time she turned toward it, because, half-dark and obscure her face seemed to be enticing into itself a future of love and wisdom, like a future beauty.

By the time she returned to his neighborhood the lights were out in most of the houses. The leaves of the birch in his yard shone like gold in the light from his living room window; either he had left the lamps on for her and was upstairs, asleep, or he was in the living room, waiting for the turn of her key. He was lying on the sofa.

He sat up, very erect, curving his long, bony, graceful hands one upon the other on his crossed knees. "Now I know you," he said. "You are cold. You may never be able to love anyone and so you will never be loved."

In terror, trembling, she sat down in a chair distant from him. She believed that he had perceived a fatal flaw, at last. The present moment seemed a lifetime later, and all that she had wanted of herself, of life, had never come about, because of that fatal flaw.

"You can change, however," he said. "There's time enough to change. That's why I prefer to work with the young."

She went up the stairs and into her room, closing the door. She sat on the bed, unable to stop the trembling that became even more severe in the large, humble bedroom, unable to believe that he would resort to trickery, this man who had spent so many years revealing to others the trickery of their minds. She heard him in the hallway and in his room, fussing sounds, discordant with his familiar presence. He knocked, waited a moment, and opened the door.

He had removed his shirt, and the lamp shone on the smooth flesh of his long chest, on flesh made slack by the downward pull of age. He stood in the doorway, silent, awkward, as if preoccupied with more important matters than this muddled seduction.

"We ought at least to say goodnight," he said, and when she complied he remained where he was, and she knew that he wanted her to glance up again at his naked chest to see how young it appeared and how yearning. "My door remains open," he said, and left hers open.

She closed the door, undressed, and lay down, and in the dark the call within herself to respond to him flared up. She imagined herself leaving her bed and lying down beside him. But, lying alone, observing through the narrow panes the clusters of lights atop the dark mountains across the channel, she knew that the weighed a hundred and thirteen pounds, and at the airport her mother cried and hugged her and said again and again: You're so *beautiful.* Her father blushed and bought her a martini. For days her relatives and acquaintances congratulated her, and the applause in their eyes lasted the entire summer, and she loved their eyes, and swam in the country club pool, the first time she had done this since she was a child.

She lived at home and ate the way her mother did and every morning she weighed. Her mother liked to take her shopping and buy her dresses and they put her old ones in the Goodwill box at the shopping center; Louise thought of them existing on the body of a poor woman whose cheap meals kept her fat. Louise's mother had a photographer come to the house, and Louise posed on the couch and standing beneath a live oak and sitting in a wicker lawn chair next to an azalea bush. The new clothes and the photographer made her feel she was going to another country or becoming a citizen of a new one.

In the fall she took a job of no consequence, to give her something to do.

Also in the fall a young lawyer joined her father's firm, he came one night to dinner, and they started seeing each other. He was the first man outside her family to kiss her since the barbecue when she was sixteen. Louise celebrated Thanksgiving not with rice dressing and candied sweet potatoes and mince meat and pumpkin pies, but by giving Richard her virginity which she realized, at the very last moment of its existence, she had embarked on giving him over thirteen months ago, on that Tuesday in October when Carrie had made her a cup of black coffee and scrambled one egg. She wrote this to Carrie, who replied happily by return mail. She also, through glance and smile and innuendo, tried to tell her mother too. But finally she controlled that impulse, because Richard felt guilty about making love with the daughter of his partner and friend. In the spring they married. The wedding was a large one, in the Episcopal church, and Carrie flew from Boston to be maid of honor. Her parents had recently separated and she was living with the musician and was still victim of her unpredictable malaise. It overcame her on the night before the wedding, so Louise was up with her until past three and woke next morning from a sleep so heavy that she did not want to leave it.

Richard was a lean, tall, energetic man with the metabolism of a during her dieting she had lost herself too. She tried to remember what it had felt like to be Louise before she had started living on meat and fish, as an unhappy adult may look sadly in the memory of childhood for lost virtues and hopes. She looked down at the earth far below, and it seemed to her that her soul, like her body aboard the plane, was in some rootless flight. She neither knew its destination nor where it had departed from; it was on some passage she could not even define.

During the next few weeks she lost weight more slowly and once for eight days Carrie's daily recording stayed at a hundred and thirty-six. Louise woke in the morning thinking of one hundred and thirty-six and then she stood on the scales and they echoed her. She became obsessed with that number, and there wasn't a day when she didn't say it aloud, and through the days and nights the number stayed in her mind, and if a teacher had spoken those digits in a classroom she would have opened her mouth to speak. What if that's me, she said to Carrie. I mean what if a hundred and thirty-six is my real weight and I just can't lose anymore. Walking hand-in-hand with her despair was a longing for this to be true, and that longing angered her and wearied her, and every day she was gloomy. On the ninth day she weighed a hundred and thirty-five and a half pounds. She was not relieved; she thought bitterly of the months ahead, the shedding of the last twenty and a half pounds.

On Easter Sunday, which she spent at Carrie's, she weighed one hundred and twenty pounds, and she ate one slice of glazed pine-apple with her ham and lettuce. She did not enjoy it: she felt she was being friendly with a recalcitrant enemy who had once tried to destroy her. Carrie's parents were laudative. She liked them and she wished they would touch sometimes, and look at each other when they spoke. She guessed they would divorce when Carrie left home, and she vowed that her own marriage would be one of affection and tenderness. She could think about that now: marriage. At school she had read in a Boston paper that this summer the cicadas would come out of their seventeen year hibernation on Cape Cod, for a month they would mate and then die, leaving their young to burrow into the ground where they would stay for seventeen years. That's me, she had said to Carrie. Only my hibernation lasted twenty-one years.

Often her mother asked in letters and on the phone about the diet, but Louise answered vaguely. When she flew home in late May she longing was not for him but for a life of love and wisdom. There was another way to prove him wrong about her. There was another way to prove that she was a loving woman, that there was no fatal flaw, that she was filled with love, and the other way was to give herself over to expectation, as to a passion.

Rising early, she found a note under her door. His handwriting was of many peaks, the aspiring style of a century ago. He likened her behavior to that of his first wife, way back before they were married, when she had tantalized him so frequently and always fled. It was a humorous, forgiving note, changing her into that other girl of sixty years ago. The weather was fair, he wrote, and he was off by early bus to his mountain across the bay, there to climb his trails, staff in hand and knapsack on his back. *And I still love you.*

That evening he was jovial again. He drank his blackberry wine at supper; sat with her on the sofa and read aloud from his collected essays, *Religion and Science in the Light of Psychoanalysis,* often closing the small, red leather book to repudiate the theories of his youth; gave her, as gifts, Kierkegaard's *Purity of Heart* and three novels of Conrad in leather bindings; and appeared again, briefly, at her door, his chest bare.

She went out again, a few nights later, to visit a friend, and he escorted her graciously to the door. "Come back any time you need to see me," he called after her. Puzzled, she turned on the path. The light from within the house shone around his dark figure in the rectangle of the open door. "But I live here for now," she called back, flapping her coat out on both sides to make herself more evident to him. "Of course! Of course! I forgot!" he laughed, stamping his foot, dismayed with himself. And she knew that her presence was not so intense a presence as they thought. It would not matter to him as the days went by, as the years left to him went by, that she had not come into his bed.

On the last night, before they went upstairs and after switching off the lamps, he stood at a distance from her, gazing down. "I am senile now, I think," he said. "I see signs of it. Landslides go on in there." The declaration in the dark, the shifting feet, the gazing down, all were disclosures of his fear that she might, on this last night, come to him at last.

The girl left the house early, before the woman and her son

appeared. She looked for him through the house and found him at a window downstairs, almost obscured at first sight by the swath of morning light in which he stood. With shaving brush in hand and a white linen handtowel around his neck, he was watching a flock of birds in branches close to the pane, birds so tiny she mistook them for fluttering leaves. He told her their name, speaking in a whisper toward the birds, his profile entranced as if by his whole life.

The girl never entered the house again, and she did not see him for a year. In that year she got along by remembering his words of wisdom, lifting her head again and again above deep waters to hear his voice. When she could not hear him anymore, she phoned him and they arranged to meet on the beach below his house. The only difference she could see, watching him from below, was that he descended the long stairs with more care, as if time were now underfoot. Other than that, he seemed the same. But as they talked, seated side by side on a rock, she saw that he had drawn back unto himself his life's expectations. They were way inside, and they required, now, no other person for their fulfilling.

LOST TIME ACCIDENT

GAYLE BANEY WHITTIER

Don't get that stuff near your mouth!"

"Why not? What'd happen?"

"It could kill you." But he deals this out easily, a man who moves daily among fatalities. My mother, fixing dinner, frowns: "I simply fail to see why you bring that poison home!"

He winks at me. "Why, that's not poison you're lookin' at, Lizzie, that's money."

"Oh, *sure*."

"Besides, Annie'll be the only kid in her class who's got *samples* for her project," he justifies. "Even Old Brown's daughter won't have nothin' like this!" A smile bonds him, the father, me the girlchild: Old Brown may be his boss's boss, but in school I get higher marks than Nancy Brown in every subject. In school, we get even. "Brown wouldn't even know where to *look for* samples," my father adds complacently.

"I still don't like it."

What she doesn't like lies in front of me: little vials of soft-looking abrasive dust, in various grinds like coffee or like spice; the lethal bead of mercury which, if smashed, reforms itself at once into a chain of smaller spheres; sharp green and black and rose-colored, manmade crystals, products of Diamonid, where my father works. A public relations booklet, "How Diamonid is Made," lies on the kitchen table too. But I already know that story.

"They heat up all them chemicals in furnaces—you know, you seen 'em—till it gets harder than diamonds. They even use this stuff to *cut* diamonds. What d'ya think of *that*?"

Reverently, my finger tries the needle tip of one of the crystals. It feels true: HARDER THAN DIAMONDS. That is the electric promise on a big sign between the factory's twin chimneys. Below it, a smaller legend swings in the cloudy wind along the riverfront:"—Days Since the Last LTA." LTA stands for "Lost Time Accident," my father says. As the crystal dimples my fingertip, imminent danger draws me nearer to my father and my father's world. I imagine how close to the surface our blood is.

He works in dangers, where a man should work, and wears the steel-toed "safety shoes" to prove it. So do my uncles and my male cousins, those who are old enough to quit school and get a job. "Wouldn't catch me in no office!" they all boast. Looking down now at the luminous bead of mercury, a bead pregnant with my own suddenly possible death, I feel the strict enchantment of my father's otherness; and I divine the high and final line where violence marries beauty. Risk is my father's legacy to me: my mother's will be different.

"Don't breathe!" she always cries out, in those nights when we drive homeward from a family party or a movie, following the ancient crescent of the Niagara River which will outlast us all. "Don't breathe it! Hold your breath!"—distrustful of the silicon and pungent air around the factories, blind to the terrible loveliness of their smoking, glowing slagheaps in our ordinary night. When the stench begins, my mother and father both take big, ostentatious breaths; he plants his foot down hard on the gas pedal;

the car jumps forward as if at the sound of a starting gun. A mile later, just beyond the row of factories, they surface, gasping. But although I always join them at the start, always draw my deep underwater-swimmer's breath too, I can't resist knowing what danger tastes like. Surreptitiously, I breathe them in: rancid, acid, strange odors that beg analysis even when they most disgust me. My throat is full of them, their sharpness and their exotic new complexities. Tasting them, I taste as well my coming sensuality, which will set experiment ahead of judgment, pleasure above safety, every time. That is why I disobey them both so secretly, seeming to gasp too, for the air which we pretend is safe again.

They would be worth a life or two, those alchemical fires glimpsed over my shoulder as we drive away. I try to read by colors what is smelted there: yellow for sulphur, framed in blue; the neon green, leafbright, to speak for copper; and a mysterious quiet mound, banked and smouldering pink as roses. Full of wonder, I feel myself moving towards a prayer in praise of my own human-kind, rash dreamers and builders of all that I behold. The words of awe rise upward on my young but going breath. In my mouth they turn back into air just as I start to speak them. Music, sometimes, even now, revives those visions and the troubling, stubborn vener-ation that I feel yet before the face of power.

Power is my native city's rightful name. The Power City. It rides on the neck of the rough white river, deadly too, like a leash on the leviathan. My father's maleness goes with it in its power, runs outward from the city's metal core into the country's infinite iron body. The river clasps Grand Island in a dread embrace, then parts like the branches of the human heart. But it feels nothing. America—this was my earliest lesson after God—is built on what he does.

But what exactly *does* he do? Like all my other childhood mysteries, this one will never yield its final name. "My husband works for the Diamonid," my mother merely says. Her brothers and his do, too—or for Hooker or Dupont or Olin. "He works at Olin." That's my Uncle Joe.

"What does he do?" I ask.

Her answer trades me word for unknown word. "He works in Shipping and Receiving. On the night shift now." Or, "Why, he makes *big money*. He's getting star rate now."

But what does he do? The proud-eyed men in my family come

back to mind: their serious, important look, the rare and hefty laughter salvaged when they "let themselves go": Thinking of their splendor, physical and brief, their dignity mined somehow from a day of taking orders—thinking of my childhood love which has outlasted them, I see that I am blessed not to know. They sold the only thing the poor have to sell, their breath and blood. And I confess the child I was. I would have loved my Uncle Casey, that night singer, less if I had known he spent the workday heaving sacks of concrete from a platform to a shed. And what if I had numbered, even once, my own father's compromises, counted out the daily spirit-killing facts behind his "steady job?" His pride is my pride too. If I had known, I could not have volunteered, when the teacher went around the room asking what all the fathers did, I could not have answered with such easy, innocent pride, "*My* father works for Diamonid."

"That filthy place!"

Whenever the industrial stench, the greasy dust, invades our house, my mother curses and mourns her missed life elsewhere, with another sort of man, in another sort of place. "I could have married Leonard Price. My mother *begged* me to. And he's a lawyer now, he lives on the Escarpment. Oh, I was beautiful, just beautiful. . . ."

"Goddamighty," my father reminds her wearily, "that dust is what we live off, Lizzie. You can thank your lucky stars for it, if you got any sense." He has "seniority" now, then a promotion and another one. No longer paid from week to slender week, he gets his paycheck once a month, like the management. "Unless there's a big layoff," my father promises, he will always bring home his paycheck and his bonus at Christmas, every month, every year, for as long as I need him. Forever.

"Oh, they just give you a fancy title and less money," my mother sneers. "Why, my baby brother on the assembly line's earning more than you."

"Yeah, and doin' what?" he counters.

"Don't you insult my brother! Good honest work and nobody can say it ain't!" I listen to her slip back into the dialect she hoped to leave behind her.

"I'm sorry, Liz. By God, I'm sorry."

"I should hope so!" she tells him. "That filthy place. Why. . . ."

"Ahh, stop bitin' the hand that feeds you." He strides out of the room.

"Mr. High-and-Mighty," she mutters behind his back. Then she notices me. "Why, that man owes everything he is to me! When we got married, he couldn't even read. I used to teach him. Don't you ever tell him that I told you."

"I won't," I swear, I who will remember this forever.

Our day turns as evenly to the whistles of Diamonid as a monk's day to bells. It opens in my sleep. Sometimes I rouse myself dimly when my father leaves. The noise of his Studebaker unsettles my deep child's sleep long enough for me to feel and mourn his absence in the house. Later I wake up to find him gone. And until he comes home again, nothing sits in its right minute or right place.

"When's supper? What're we having?"

"Don't call it 'supper.' It's dinner; we aren't farmers."

No. Coal miners, my father's people were, used to laboring in blackness and in early deaths. Hers marched a safe and charted course as civil servants. The stamp of these ancestral trades imprints them both, but she has married him, drawn to that breakfree energy that sent him to Diamonid, that promoted him through the war, that brought him, finally, a crew of men.

Our family begins, then, only at four-fifteen in the afternoon, on the shrill distant note of the quitting whistle. My mother, newly fragrant with Friendship Garden, her pincurled hair unfurled around her solemn face, pretends to leisure, ties a ruffled apron over her clean dress. Then his car rushes into the driveway, the door's lock gives way with a click of metal like a broken bone. His footsteps. They are unique; the man himself is in them—a man no longer young, a man too old, really to have a child as small as I, an accidental blessing.

"*Was* I an accident?" I dare to ask my mother once.

"Who told you that?"

"Nobody. *Was* I?"

"You were a big *surprise*," she finally allows.

"Surprise!" my father shouts, bursting through the door. Behind it, almost flattened, we stand silently, SHHH, pantomimes my mother, raising a newly manicured finger to her lips. Something like an old, remembered joy brightens her features momentarily.

"Hey, anybody home?" he asks, pretending to look for us. "Hey, where is everybody? Ain't nobody here?" Mock worries. Then "BOO!" he's found us. And in his hand, a chocolate bar, a suitor's rose: for me, a sunset sheath of scrap papers, or carbons the color of midnight. Out of the giving and his old return, even my obdurate loneliness melts. "Daddy!" I shout, and we are home.

"Well, will you just look at my two beautiful ladies!" he lies. "Don't you look good enough to eat!"

"Oh, blarney," my mother says, but smiles a younger smile. I feel his lie, a long one by the time that I am born and stand beside her, sharing unevenly in all of his old compliments.

"Somethin' smells good! You got somethin' in the oven, Lizzie?" And he winks a broad vaudevillian wink.

"Herb!"

"Well, have ya?"

"Don't you hold your breath," she tells him, eyes snapping.

I understand them just enough to know that their teasing predates me, that they are remembering each other as they were alone. I am lonely again myself. What does he mean? What could be in the oven except one of my mother's thrifty casseroles, almost unsalted and tending towards one even color? Suspicious of daily pleasure, she cooks "plain." But we must be grateful for it because of all the children who are starving in Europe. Not even Grace can sweeten what she serves.

Now, "Don't get any of that filth on my clean floor!" she warns, as he pretends to lunge at her. "And don't get *near* that carpet! Why, it'd cut it all to pieces. Go wash up," she commands, turning into his mother too. And their flirtation is over for the day.

The Company follows him home. *Don't breathe it.* But the silent, ubiquitous black Diamonid dust collects invisibly in the folds of his clothing, sifts out unseen into a fine glittering shadow which outlines the place where he has stood. All at once you look down and see it there, pooled around his safety shoes with their steelcapped toes ("Company rule, cuts down on accidents") covering his own crooked, comical ones. Diamonid dust destroys whatever it touches; but every night my father comes back to us preserved, saved by his safety shoes and by his ready Irish wits. He comes home "on the dot," my mother boasts to her less-fortunately married friends, the wives of "ladies' men" or drunkards—which is the worst thing a man can be, because if he drinks he will not be a "good provider."

"I'd trust him anywhere," my mother sings. But she too clocks his fifteen minutes between the company gates and our back door. Suddenly, in the midst of one of their quarrels, I will hear her cry, "You work in a filthy place! Your secretary. . ." before his hand bruises her into silence. And I understand that there is moral filth, too, just outside her jurisdiction, in the subtle colors of the air where our livelihood inhales and exhales.

"Back in a jiffy," he tells us now, disappearing into the cellar. Bent over the washtub, he violently scrubs away the company dirt, puts on fresh clothes for the second half of his daily life.

Above him, just as energetically, my mother sweeps up the dark dust. It winks and glistens in her dustpan among our duller household kind. "I want to be sure I get it all," my mother says, as if acknowledging that it is aristocratic, powerful as if it had fallen from a magician's pack stamped with an open trademark diamond around the letter D.

"Diamonid," I try the latinate word, echoing an inventor who named, but did not make, that terrible powder with his own two hands, his nostrils, or his broken lungs. "Diamonid." I am softly in love with its strangeness. When I touch the dust my finger leaves its print, and the dust sets its shiny smudge against my skin.

He washes it away with a soap hard and yellow as a brick of amber. Coming back upstairs, he smells of the soap, acid and golden-brown and potent as the man himself. "Clean as a whistle," he supposes.

But in my father's lungs, invisibly, the black pollen settles, cutting and hardening into what will be his distant death. Some other day, coming back ashen from the doctor's office, "Oh, my God," he'll cry to us, "I got emphysema. Advanced, he says. Do you know what that is? That's just a new name for Black Lung, that's all. That's all." And he will recount, over and over, his grandfather's tortured death, the miner's death he thought he had outrun, until my mother ends it: "For the love of God, shut up! You think that you're the only one. . .?"

Now, that day unguessed, my mother serves dinner to us, I set the table, he lifts up his voice to tell us about Work. He spins stories out of it, takes male sustenance there, and somehow, miraculously, dreams a tall and fugitive pride in what he does. After the second story, or the third, I imagine that I stand in the stone and concrete of his masculine world. Sometimes, crushed, he seconds my mother's bitter knowledge: "Christ, what a hole that place is!" But, "You'll never have to work in a place like that, Annie," he promises us both. "You're real smart. Your teacher said. *You* won't end up in there."

It puzzles me. No other woman in my family works anywhere at all, except the wife of my uncle-the-gambler. *Men* work. Women marry them. Why would I ever have to work? Listening to my father, I suddenly guess that I am not pretty. I feel a confused shame, but he goes on: "You're college material. Get yourself a real good job," he is advising me. "Something clean. You got what it takes . . . I'd be right up there now, if I got an education."

Briefly, our lives ascend together. We exchange laurels. I recount the prizes that I win in school; he, a boss, tells stories about his men.

"What'd you do in school today? What's that you're reading?"

"French. I'm reading French."

"I'll be damned! Go on, say something in French for me."

"Ma plume est sur le bureau," I tell him, waiting until I make him ask for the translation, then: "My pen is on the desk."

"Me, I know some Polack and a lot of Eyetalian," he boasts. Then he says, "Eh! Ven'aca!" which means "Come over here," or "No capeesh?" for "Don't you get it?"

"You say it after me," he instructs, proud of my agile tongue and that textbook-stilted French, passwords into a world unlike his own, where he will not be welcome. Obeying him, I taste the flavor of my father's role at Work. The spoken phrases teach him to me. I see him merciful but just, commanding them in their homespoken tongues: *Come over here. Hey, buddy, don't you get it?*

"I got my men's respect," he always finishes.

They have simple, children's names, those men: Little, Big, Young, Old. Little Carl brings in the spring each Easter. He brings it tied up in a stout bag full of hard anise-seed cookies, the predictable chocolate rabbit that I am too old for now; a big bottle of bright red wine for my father, and a littler blue bottle of Evening in Paris perfume for my smiling mother. My father laughs, holding the wine up to the light. "Dago red!" And Little Carl laughs at himself, too, while my father claps him on his rounded back. "He's a pain in the ass, that guy," my father says, but says it chuckling.

"Why don't you fire him? *I* would," my mother vows.

"Ah, he's all right," my father redetermines.

Then the war lets go of us, and one day—no holiday at all—little Carl runs shouting and weeping towards our house, waving the first telegram from a brother he had thought was dead. In our staid Northern European neighborhood, people come defensively to the railings of their porches, grimace at him, and go back inside. Final judgment. But, "Hey, buddy! Eh, paysan!" my father is already running out to meet him, infected with his joy. They embrace, Italians together, in the back yard, while indoors my mother hardly needs to ask, but does, "What will people think?"

I watch them through the glass. They are clasping and dancing their fellowship. "You get damned close to guys, workin' with 'em," he has often said. But men don't hug each other like that, do they? Do they? I ask myself if what I see is love, workborn. My mother, as if she has heard my silent question, states, "Blood is stronger," looking at them too. Jealous now, "Blood can't be broken," she reminds us both. "*His* men indeed!"

She herself maintains a distance which my French lessons have not yet taught me to name *noblesse oblige.*

"Wouldn't you like a nice cup of coffee?" she asks, moving already towards the speckled coffee pot on a back burner. "It's only this morning's heated up, but I think it's still O.K."

A bearish blond giant stands shy and huge against our kitchen door. One black-mittened hand wrings another, warming him against the late November cold. He has just delivered our winter kindling.

"No, t'ank you, missus," he says roundly and severely.

"Oh, dear! Well, at least sit down for a minute. You look chilled to the bone!"

Wearing a darker shadow even than my father's, he maintains his statue's pose against the yellow door.

"No, t'ank you, I get your floor all dirty. Anyway, got to get to another job." Only, "chob" he says.

"They sure keep you busy, don't they? What's the next one?"

The silence lengthens. I wonder whether his language or his wits can run so slowly. At last, "We dump barrels in that old canal," he remembers.

"Oh? What're they dumping?"

"They don't tell *me*, missus."

"Well. Well, I guess you've got to run, then," she dismisses him. "Now you tell 'the boss,'" my mother winks, "I said, 'Hello there!'" She thinks it is a joke that both of them work for the same boss. He does not.

"Be seein' you, missus," he tells her. Then, still unsmiling, he lifts his denim cap, work-blackened, to make a courtly gesture that starts me laughing inwardly. But my laughter dies unborn. I take in the strip of forehead underneath the brim: pure and white as day. Beneath the dusty skin, the shadow of his livelihood, another man is hiding, a man all pale and gold: a Viking or a lion.

Only one of the men, Shorty, ever stays. Anomalously black as a junebug, delicate and maimed, with a glass eye to match his equally freakish blue one, and one elegant leg made out of wood, he calls my mother "Miz Elizabeth." His stump is aching, he tells her, as she pours her coffee in his cup; he thinks that it will rain or snow, that's how he knows.

My mother bends, easy in her sure superiority. From below the cupboard she lifts up an almost-full bottle of brandy for emergencies. She adds a dollop to the black coffee in his cup. "Don't you tell a soul!"

One September afternoon, while my mother was taking down her steel-colored hair, the telephone rang. "Your father!" she knew, although he never called home.

For once she loved him, she rushed so quickly to the telephone. But she let it ring one more shrill time, while her hand endorsed her breastbone with the sign of the cross, as if she were putting on perfume.

"I just knew it was you! What's happened?" she spilled into the receiver. ". . .Oh, *no*! Who is it? . . . No, I didn't, *don't* . . . Just where is he now? Is he still. . .? Oh, Oh. . . . I see. And when are you coming home?" Just as I thought she was about to hang up, she added gently, "Honey," as if her love must make some kind of difference now.

"What is it? Is there a strike?" I asked excitedly.

"No, there's been an accident at Work. Oh, your father's O.K., just shook up," she said. "But one of his men got badly hurt."

"Which one?" I warmed to the drama, selecting a victim in my imagination. "Shorty? Little Carl?"

"No. His name is Stash, Stanley . . . Wuh . . . I don't know how to say it," She added, "Be awful good to your father when he gets home."

But I hardly had the chance. He walked in, giftless and mad, deliberately striding right onto the forbidden linoleum with his abrasive dust, then even into the hallway where my mother's sacred expanse of new carpet started. He moved tight and fast, dramatically ignoring us. Then, angrily too, he tore a number into the telephone dial.

"Hello, is Mrs. Wyczolaski there? . . . Oh. Well, this here's Herb O'Connor. I'm Stash's . . . Stash and me, we work together," he said. "You just tell Stella if there's anything she wants, *anything*, why, us boys'll give blood or whatever else. . .? I see. Yeah, I understand. I'd feel the same damned way. Well, like I said, *anything*. I'll call back later."

In the kitchen my mother was already sweeping up the fine black silt behind his rage. But she swept slowly and gently, so as not to anger him, I felt, or, perhaps, so as not to remind him that it was there. It made a dark and gritty sound in her dustpan.

"There's dirt all over here!" I imitated her.

But, "Never mind," she said. And when he returned to the kitchen, my mother did not mention it, only, "Tell me what happened," and a moment later, "Your paper's over there on the chair," as she always said, as it always was.

"Yes, tell us about it!" but I felt my enthusiasm for a story thrown back at me by their silence. Ashamed, I stopped, and heard my father speak only to my mother, to himself.

He documented it, how in the hot September afternoon, Stash and the other men were out in the yard, "sweatin' like pigs," he said. He would have called to them to quit work early, it was so damned hot, only a bigger boss walked through, inspecting. Just as the whistle blew, "Put 'er down!" he shouted. And Stash, tired, hot himself, carelessly leaned over the pallet of the forklift and pushed the release button. The whole load flattened him.

"Oh, Jesus," my father recalled. "Everybody's shoutin' and yellin', nobody even remembered to get that fuckin' thing off of him. 'Herb, help me!' he's screamin'. I push this button and it lifts up in the air, takin' part of him with it, I swear to God. Joe Vetucci, he fainted. And there's this sound out of him when I did it, like a crunch, only. . ."

"Oh, don't!" my mother cried. "No, no, that's all right. No. Tell me."

"Softer," he said. "Like a deep breath when it goes out." His face sealed itself over the trace of the mystery, the failure of his own description of it.

My mother's hand reached out for him as over greater space, but his words bore him away, back to the yard, miles from us, back to quitting time, centuries ago.

"You couldn't tell his shirt from his chest. Blood everywhere. Mrs. Prince, she's the company nurse, she come runnin' from the clinic with her bag and give him oxygen. They called the ambulance. Then she started cuttin' his shirt away, and he was screamin'. No. It wasn't a *scream,*" he corrected. "He couldn't scream. It was more. . . ." And his voice left off in a chugging sound as his own mouth filled up with vomit. Keeping it back with an unwashed hand, he rushed into the bathroom. We could hear him vomiting there, wildly trying to get rid of what he had seen that day, or saying it.

"Shouldn't we go in?" I asked.

"No, leave him alone," my mother said.

After a while the vomiting dried off into sobs. The sobs stopped too. Finally, he came out angry.

"I'm gettin' the hell outta here! I'm goin' for a ride!" he shouted in my mother's direction, as if she meant to stop him.

"Herb, be careful! Please!" Futile. The door slammed; he punished the car, its parts shrieking and grinding against each other; it squealed down the street, him in it.

In the silence that gathered thickly where he had stood, I asked, "Can't that man get better? Can't they fix him?"

"Now, what do you *think*!" I heard my mother cry. Then, seeing that my question had for once been almost innocent, she added more kindly, "Oh, I doubt it." She took my father's plate away from the table, heaping it with portions of dinner, then putting it in the oven to keep it warm. She glanced at the kitchen clock, adjusted a dial, then moved our two remaining plates side by side. "Why, it would be a miracle if that man got well!" she afterthought.

But I lived then in a climate of miracles as of dust. First there were the stained-glass cures that had entertained my Sundays since my babyhood: "Take up thy bed and walk." These, however, I had recently understood to be ancient, outgrown events, mere precursors of the newer miracles, which my century's god, science, was dispensing. Through science—they told me so at school—we were getting an edge on death and illiteracy: also on other kinds of darknesses, bigotry, for example, and communism. Surely one of these hoarded miracles could save Stash.

Out of the clustered silence, my mother's voice awoke me. "Of course, *his* wife'll get a bundle."

"What? Oh."

"Because he died on the job," she explained. "That's why."

"Even if it was an accident?"

"Why, that's true," she considered. "He was *careless,* after all. Maybe she won't get anything." And now her voice took on vindication. "After all, it was his own fault, he didn't look what he was doing." *Careless.* I startled into shame, I who was accused daily of negligence and a child's innocent amnesia before the world. She had called me by my own secret name. Was death a kind of carelessness too?

Eight o'clock. Nine. The night went on without my being sent to bed. My mother turned on the radio, sat sewing against its background of ventriloquists and organ chords. I, defying sleep, lay listening, raised my head to see her golden thimble twinkle as she stitched, magically recalling my father, thread by thread. At last her simple magic worked, and he came home.

The car gently ("Don't wake the neighbors") in the driveway; the careful clasping of the garage doors; the snap of the familiar lock. His older, lonelier steps came towards us.

"Are you feeling any better, Herb?" she asked.

"Oh, shit," he said. "Shit. I seen him. I went to the hospital and seen him."

"How . . uh, what hospital is he in?"

"Memorial. It was nearest. She wanted St. Catherine's 'cause they're Catholics. But they can't move him anyplace, shape he's in. I seen him. He's so bad off they got him strapped to the bed, tubes goin' in and out. Givin' him blood. . . ." The uncaring tone began to take him away from us. Perhaps to prevent it, my mother cried too empathetically, *"Oh that poor man!"*

"He says to me, he says, 'Herb, I wanna die. Honest to God, I just wanna die,' is what he said. 'Just let me go.' Well, he mouthed it. I couldn't hardly make it out."

"Why, for heaven's sake!" My mother strung out her words like counted beads. "Didn't they give him something for the pain, those people?" An alert, outraged expression stuck to her face.

"Oh, sure, sure," my father answered bitterly. "But they can't give him enough, is all. I seen his doctor, I says to him, 'Doc, why the hell can't you people deaden this man's pain?' What were they there for, I asked him. And you know what? He told me they *would*, only that much pain-killer might kill Stash too. Dying anyway, I says. And the doctor just froze me out, said that's *different*, it's the *law*."

At the word "law" my mother faltered. "Well, maybe he's right, Herb. I mean, it probably *is* the law, isn't it?"

"The law can go fuck itself, far as I'm concerned."

"Now, Herb," my mother went on academically, "you have to see it from the doctor's side. . ."

"No, I don't. Why should I? Goddamned legalized thieves's all they are!"

My mother touched his arm. "Maybe he's got a chance, though . . . Stash, I mean."

"Oh, hell, Lizzie, you'd a seen him you wouldn't talk like that. The man's crushed to a pulp, that's what. A pulp." (The cliché tried to come alive in my mind, but didn't.) "And his wife's standin' out in the hall cryin', and his son . . . well, Jesus. 'I just wanna die,' he says to me."

"Son? I didn't know the . . . Wuh. . . ."

"Wyczolaski," he spat at her.

"I didn't know they had *two* children," my mother said almost brightly. "I thought there was only that one girl who goes to school with Annie. Annie, what's her name?"

"Wanda," I replied, disliking my mother. "Her name is Wanda."

"Of course," my mother acknowledged with the littlest of her smiles.

"Yeah, two kids. That poor woman. What's she gonna do now?"

My mother suppressed something sharper than she said. "Why, she's got Compensation coming, hasn't she? She'll do all right."

"Well, she gets it if I testify it happened on company time, before quitting," he said. "Or that the machine slipped."

In the length of silence my mother picked her way among the thickets where we lived. "A lot of people saw what happened, though," she finally ventured. "I mean, they'd know if you were lying, if you swore it happened on company time. Or was the equipment." His look, which I could not see from where I sat, must have embarrassed her. "Well, I *mean*, he *was* careless, really. It was his own fault."

"Own fault! Who the hell wouldn't get careless, all day in that heat?" He brought his fist down against the table. There was an interval of tiny chimes as her porcelain knick-knacks trembled against each other. "Anybody'd get 'careless,' that's all. That's *all*."

"But suppose you lose *your* job? You're not even in the union any more. There's witnesses."

"Now, Lizzie. . ."

"What about us? Have you ever thought of that? Oh, no; not you. And there's *witnesses*," she repeated, her voice rising. Her finger rose too and pointed him out, one red nail gleaming blood-drop pure.

"You make a better lawyer than a wife, Lizzie. Now shut up. It was on company time, and that's that."

"But it wasn't. . . ."

"I said shut up, Lizzie, and I meant it," he commanded in a stonedust voice. Then my father's eye caught sight of me. "What the hell are *you* doin' up? Ain't you got school tomorrow?"

"It's not her fault."

"Well, go on. Scoot. Go get your beauty sleep," my father said. As I escaped the room, his large hand lightly told me of the shape of my child's head.

Through my door, half open to let in the whisper of the cooler early autumn night, a long finger of light crossed the thin yellow varnished floorboards and pillared up the wall. There a wallpaper lattice lifted up its repeated clusters of white roses, stale and old.

I slept a white sleep.

Later in the night, half conscious and alone, I heard the customary thunder of their household quarrel. It no longer frightened me. I could identify their cadences like phrases in a symphony. Sometimes I even fell asleep, while they still raged, as constant and as changing as the sea, beneath my painted bed. This time, sitting up alive, I sorted out new and different sounds.

Against the rocking of their human voices, he was throwing

things. Their dense thuds declared them heavy, breakable. They rang out dully. They reverberated against the floor. Once, I remembered, he had gotten angry at my mother and had thrown his breakfast at the wall. The plate splintered. But the fried egg slid slowly downward to the baseboard, a cartoon sun. Watching its descent, I held back my laughter, lest I disrespect the enchantment of my father's violence. But fear brought more laughter bubbling to my nervous lips. He had only broken the plate that one time, though. This breakage went on and on.

Where usually my mother's voice climbed, sickening, to half-evasive pleas, it kept instead a low and reasonable horizon note, a stranger's tone. They walked the circle of the rooms below, my father pacing heavily, erratically, my mother keeping up while he shouted: "That goddamn bastard! Polack son-of-a-bitch!" Crash—an object seconded his rage. "Stupid fucking idiot! If I told him once, I told him a hundred times: *One slip* and it's curtains, buddy! Yeah, I told him. . . ." Something struck the floor. "You, you gold-crowned son-of-a-bitch . . ." (even my mother's voice protested it) "Be-all, know-all fucker of the rest of us! . . . No, no, I won't, I won't . . ." And his body bore his words away, stepping through the stairwell to the kitchen to the dining room, almost never used, then the circuit of the downstairs floor. His muffled voice remained; against it, my mother's preserving obbligato. From time to time he climbed above language, and then I heard another heavy thud, and tried to imagine what it was he threw.

Slowly the intervals lengthened. At last, exhausting things to throw, he broke himself and cried. I lay in my changed bed, shocked in my hearing and my heart, while the night air carried up to me his foreign male weeping, wholly of this earth. I felt that my father's sobs would go on unbearably forever, but he was diminished too. In astonished meditation on the edge of sleep, I knew that he was less my father than he had been before. Aware of his abandonment, I abandoned myself to dreams.

There was a next day, and on it, everything resumed functionally but awkwardly, like a broken machine. Breakfast brought gluey oatmeal, acid orange juice, and lukewarm milk in the old chipped cup with a hair-thin crack through its pale wall. A lump of breakfast in me, I underwent my regimented schoolday. But through getting dressed and the roll call, through the Products of Peru and our spiritless public school singing of "The Volga Boatman," I waited. Something else must happen, I assumed. Nothing did.

When I got home from school, home was still there, a semaphore of well-known laundry strung behind it. My mother, newly powdered, wearing the set, severe expression of a woman living out a holy but mistaken life, ran her finger over a few inches of window-sill: "Just look at that! Third time today I dusted it!" she said. Then, at four o'clock exactly, she disappeared to put on a fresh dress, to brush out her cold hair. Even her face in the center of it all was her old face, rigid and alone, the face I remember her by, even now: my mother.

"Wash your hands, Annie," she commanded absently." And put on another blouse; that one's just covered with ink. How do you ever do it?"

Coming in to us, me with my clean hands, my mother in her unmarked apron, my father made no jokes at all that night, but went downstairs at once to scrub himself. I could hear the water rushing into the washtub, could sense his muted gestures as he changed into clean clothes. I felt his feet, my father's feet, measuring the steps deliberately as he climbed, purified, to the kitchen. Only then did my mother look at him questioningly, gently.

He shook his head. No. And again, as she asked, "Is he. . .?" No, but only with his eyes.

"Is Stash dead?" I asked, voicing what I knew must be her question too.

"Mr. Wyczolaski," he corrected me. "No."

"I suppose he's in a coma," my mother said.

"Still conscious."

"Oh, that's good," I tried.

"It isn't good at all! What do *you* know . . . !" my mother scowled.

"Somebody oughta do something," my father said only to her.

"Well, they won't," she answered him. "You know it and I know it. Your paper's over there on the chair," she said.

Proving what nobody would do, they separated their lives from the dying man's. Humming a little, even, she set out dinner plates in their three places; we thanked our same God for her utilitarian food, which was not really the same every night, but seemed so. Only our voices, by an unspoken accord, stayed deep inside us, and we did not talk.

After dinner, while I laid out my assignment book and papers to do homework, my parents briefly whispered together in the kitchen, murmuring low enough for mourning in our altered house. ". . . a collection?" I caught, and then my father said, "Oh, flowers, sure," loud enough to carry easily to me. "Hey, Lizzie, did you know they put coins on their eyes, them Polacks? Honest to God. It's to pay their way into heaven."

In the outer room, always my room, with my books and my unbidden fear spread out around me, I felt myself only fraudulently theirs: my untapped excitement, my young urgency against their casual resumption of our life. A man was dying. And it was their fault, I decided. Too easily, too carelessly, they had let go of him, just as if they had let go of my hand in a crowd and I was lost forever. They had not kept him in their minds, they had excluded him. I felt a spirit sympathy between the man and myself; but even more warmly, a learned and rancid sense of drama took possession of my imagination, phrase by rehearsed phrase, as I tried to encompass him. "He's in God's hands now." "His life is hanging by a thread!" Where had I heard those words, those keys to my unwritten drama? Which would work, would open it? "Nothing tried, nothing gained. . ." "Perseverance wins the crown" (my mother's favorite). And "if at first you don't succeed. . . ." So that was it. They hadn't cared to try for the magical third time. And that was why he was dying so invisibly.

"Somebody should do something," my father had admitted. *I* would, I answered to myself.

I did. Leaving my homework and my parents' voices in the rooms below, I put my own small upstairs bedroom in close to perfect order. The rug, a worn pink pile, I placed equidistant from the headboard and the footboard of my narrow bed. I spat on a turned-up corner of the chenille bedspread for luck, as if it were my skirt hem, and then I smoothed it into place. The window-shades, I saw, jogged awkwardly, one up, one down: I evened them.

Then I took up my last thing, my prayerbook, white leather stamped with a delicate gold cross. A recent Christmas present, it smelled like nothing else in the house, papery and new. Its thin pages clung to my clumsy fingers, and its scarlet bookmark lay silkenly against last Sunday's portion of the Psalter, accusing me of the early place where I had let my attention wander from the text. I was sorry now that I did not pray every day. I promised myself and God that, starting now, I would. I would read the Bible too, each morning, if only—but even I stopped sort of bribery.

Almost at once, I turned to the right prayer, but, like any browser, kept my finger there to scan the nearby titles. "For Social Justice," I read, "For the Navy," "For Rain." And I kept on reading, delaying as long as possible the moment of what I now suddenly saw to be a test. At last nothing but the moment of my trial remained, and I resorted to my destined prayer: "For a Sick Person." Briefly its Renaissance cadences helped me on, but then I stumbled from the archaic words, falling back into my century and my place. Perhaps, I reconsidered, spontaneous prayer would be better? Yes.

Still I had to find the name of God.

I meant to choose a title which best suited my petition and my own unaccustomed voice, used only to a bedside "Our-Father-who-art-in-heaven" run off proudly and not even consciously, the same way I recited muliplication tables or conjugated French verbs. But by now my knees reminded me of time, and all the names of God began to sound ponderous and strange. I could not even repeat some of them without hearing, over mine, the priest's majestic voice drawing out vowels and clicking consonants shut to speak God's grandeur—or his own.

"Most Gracious God," I imitated. But I felt at once remoter from Him than I had ever known myself to be. "Our Heavenly Father," then. No. I was only one abashed person speaking, no "we" at all; and anyway, "heavenly" felt too distant, and "father" too close in. "Lord" avoided these degrees, but struck me as bare and abrupt, almost rude. And I passed over "God Almighty" embarrassedly. Except when a priest said it, it was a curse. In our household, where everyone but me blasphemed with Celtic latitude, I had often heard that title eased into a punctuating "Goddamighty!" I could not now make my own tongue disobey these family cadences, replace them with the unctious elevation of the priest's. They were in me, my people's voices. Hearing them, the others, I stopped altogether, afraid that my mouth might name God wrongly and undo my prayer.

Finally, on my numb knees and exhausting God's known names, I shifted my felt weight and got familiar: "God," I said, "please. . ." (minding my manners), "please take care of, of. . ." But here again I hesitated like a child in a spelling bee. I practiced the word in my head, then spoke, "Mr. Wyczolaski," out loud, fast and right. Borne on my confidence in the victim's name, and in my own power to pronounce it, I next told God why he should save Stash, "*Stanley*," I reminded God, although He would know a nickname, too, I reasoned to myself. "Save him for his daughter Wanda, who's the same age as me, and for his wife. . ." I had forgotten her name, but chanted bravely on, since God knew everything, "and for himself," I said. After a moment I added, "In Thy Infinite Mercy. . ." I felt the thrill of my translation. The extemporaneous prayer sounded almost like those in my book: I knew that it was good. But with this recognition of my composition's quality, I almost praised myself, the speaker: suddenly I knew that God must save Stash for my own sake most of all. It was for my words that I wanted the miracle to happen: to make them good. The prayer was for myself. Before this forbidden fact, I arrested: and the prayer's lost momentum fell away from me, inexorable as dust.

"Not just for *me*," I tried to get it back. "For everyone, O God." But I doubted that He would be taken in by this patchwork charity: I did not believe it myself. It opened falsely onto my new world, which was flat, not round, no matter what they said, and had an edge where heaven ought to be, and big deaths even for its smallest, most accidental men.

Almost dumb with loss, I waited out my first time of nothingness. It felt like death, that space between the outgrown child who had dared to pray and this self-conscious stranger who suddenly could not. Then the image of the careless, crushed man formed itself in my mind, textbook clear. I knew he must lay smashed— "like an egg," my father had described him—beneath a hospital sheet; and so I started there. I envisioned it whiter and coarser than my mother's sheets, decently containing him. The room around him smelled of purity and pain.

I drew nearer to that invented bed. But I did not open his eyes. They closed on his unimaginable expression, which I did not know how to see. His iconic head, I saw, resembled my father's, was not a young man's head; and his imagined features came to view both personal and sure, as if I had seen him many times before.

Then—even now—I knew I really saw Stanley Wyczolaski's face. Safe white bandages held back his damage, like the swaddling on the porcelain Della Robbia in my new classroom.

I wanted to know more. In my mind's chamber still, I folded the silver bandages aside, neat as a lifted page. Underneath, everything showed itself smooth and charted, the proud high cage of ribs, the shadow of male hair. "There, there, you'll be all right," I comforted. Then, for the first time, I heard my own voice say, "Darling," in a whisper. At the word his body, a lattice in a birthday card, answered me by opening up. I saw all the mysteries that I had only read of: this, the four-chambered heart, but still, so still; here the arteries and veins running blue into it and red away; there the lungs, pink as shell. They lay as real as my eye, but unreal, too.

By now I had forgotten God. My dreaming hands moved in circles over the dying man, and in my vision they restored his life. Veins and arteries, collapsed, sprang full and fresh as stems after rainfall. I bent to kiss him better, and my borrowed breath lifted new roundness in his flattened lungs. I gave him my voice, too. "There, you see," I proved to him out loud.

Then my real hands began to move tenderly over the chenille ridges of my bed's coverlet. I breathed faster, conscious of a drum of pulse, my own, and of my will contracted tightly to a concrete thing meant to uphold him. The unguessed power of my life ran free, and with it, sadness older than the earth.

I could not know yet that my caresses, my reverence, and—when I moved—my newfound exactitude of care, made me a lover. But I knew that everything I did was futile, that I could not really mend: only I made the gestures of the healer all the same, defiantly. I felt my own bones age against the hardness of the floor, and, breathing for us both, for myself and for the dying man, I tasted my own mystery. In that dark way, among my vanquished gods, I began my work in the world.

A CHRONICLE OF LOVE

H.E. FRANCIS

THE CLUB WANDERER IS ALWAYS IN near darkness. Lights burn from invisible places. A crystal globe revolving over the dance floor sends out shafts, steady as a light at sea. Against the sunken glow the band becomes four living shadows. Front spots now and then thrust them close. During breaks, the juke blinks on for ten minutes, coiling blue-green-yellow-purple-orange over the faces clustered around the tables. At the entrance three figures, two women and the doorman, come stark against the lights whenever the door swings open. Through an arch, dim lights over the bar glitter—bottles and glasses, sometimes the flash of eyes or teeth.

The dancers are dark against the lights, silhouettes whose motion the music dictates as if with unseen strings, now leaping and veering, now drifting, swaying, or standing in a quivering freeze—but always moving, moving. The pianist's arms leap, the guitarists sway, the drummer goes frenzied, the vocalist breaks into the flood. Sounds drown over. From all the country around—and all the way from Nashville or Birmingham or even Atlanta, when there is a big-time guest star—the swingers come to hear the country western of the SOUNDS.

The day he was twenty-one, Lawton Wingfield's buddies said, "Field, tonight we're carrying you to a real place. Wow! We'll celebrate this here birthday like it's the *last*. If you don't get you a good drunk and fun and laid all to one time, we been sure miscalculating. . . ." And Field did. Then, come every Friday, he was back at the Wanderer as regular as work or church, a thing not to be omitted without breaking his new rhythm. His whole self came to be attuned to it. Going to the club was how he knew it was the end of work week and the beginning. That's what he told everybody: "Man, when you walk in there, it's the beginning."

(*John Paul Vincent:* When I heard Field's sick in the city, I went; but he wasn't in no room. Mrs. Warner said he didn't hardly stay there a minute after he come from work, got him a shower and changed clothes and gone—she didn't know where—cept she knew he drank, but never said a word to him cause he was good and quiet, paid on the button, and she knew something was bugging him. You all right, Field? she'd say. Right as the day I was born, was all she'd get out of him. Field never was much for talking, after Alice. Don't believe nobody ever heard him say that name, Alice, one time neither, after, like the name died with her too, or her name's just for him, I don't know. Can't be far, Mrs. Warner said, he's got no car. Had a wreck, Field did, and lost it. But you know, she said, I don't think he had no wreck. I think, the way he looks sometimes, I think he let that car go, just let it go, she said. What his friend Hadley said was: he didn't even hear sometimes; and Field told Hadley: I don't know, Had, if it was accident nor not, it just happened like I wasn't there. I seen—But he'd never tell what he seen. That's how come I think he didn't have no accident. I went looking—Field wasn't far: that club one block off, the Wanderer, that's where. Says: Well, John Paul, agrabbing me, and I seen that whole place come up in his eyes like he's not going to make it, like I was something I wasn't or maybe all of Greenville come in with me and surprised him, maybe like it was Alice; but in a minute he's turned on again—gone, way out, sailing like I never seen nobody. And *skinny!* Only I was afraid to say, but after I did: you got to take care now, Field, I said. Hooo, I'm in the best shape I ever been in, not a ounce of fat and all hard's a rock, he says, never was this way on the farm—*feel* that. But his face was like jaundice, no matter what he said; like a ha'nt he was; and I thought, He'll die right here this night, he ain't going nowhere or moving in about a hour, but he's on his pins, high up like a jack, and Je-*sus*, you should of seen that mother! I sure in a hurry changed my mind. And he didn't stop neither. He went at it till the last lick, only I don't know what happened, he all of a sudden went, passed out. We had to carry him home, they got a doctor, he said You bring him around in the morning; but there wasn't no disease nor nothing he could see, but says That boy's so weak he maybe won't get up again if you don't see that he gets to the hospital in the morning. The doctor began to ask about family and all. I told him too, but looked like they'd do him no good here. Only Field came round after—I sat watching him like he was going to fade out—he said You better sleep, hoss—hear? The boys pick me up for work at six. And I slept too—I didn't mean to—and when I come to he was gone. Jesus, who'd of believed it—gone to work and back and that night dancing again! I had to go to Greenville. I had to tell his folks. He couldn't go on too much like that.

Reta: Where are you going, Field? I'd ask him, cause he was already smiling, he was on his way—like doped up or loaded or Jesus-bit. I couldn't think of anything else to say. He looked like traveling, he'd never stop, his eyes were seeing things—he had that look—and I wanted to reach up and jerk his head down and tell him Me me me, look at *me*, but he'd study that globe or the long lights. His eyes followed like they were real and he'd lose them. He made me feel like a *thing*, just nothing. I hated him. I did, I did, I did.

Marylou: Nobody ever danced like Field. I followed him around. I'd sit and watch all night, thinking he'd ask me, but once he picked somebody it was her all the time, he most never let up, held onto her like she's his life, and dance dance dance. When the band took a break, it was the juke, and he'd even bend and bob when he wasn't dancing, aswaying, like he was rubber and couldn't stop. Sometimes it was funny—I wanted to push him like one of them toy clowns with a round bottom.

Reverend Bullard: Lawton used to come to Greenville, to the church—I'd seen him from the rectory window—never when there was service, always Saturday—and stand outside and stare. He'd been there a long time, walk around the grounds, and go back and look at that door, then go away. He never set foot in the church. Perhaps he'd stay fifteen minutes, half an hour. He never looked sad, no—but quiet and natural, a bit at home even. I never went to disturb him.

Wendy: Call me his Tuesday girl. Every Tuesday, like clockwork. And all night. How'd Field ever get to work? Who knows? He'd leave me in bed. I don't think he even knew who I was by then. Sometimes he'd slip and call me Alice. Who cares? He gave me a good time and if I had to be Alice for him to make it that good, okay, so I'm Alice.

Friday night

FIELD: Like it says in the Bible, Alice, I come to a city over five months now, only it ain't like you think. Oh, it's all shining all right, them neons make it so bright you see it miles, yeah, it makes a great big whale of a light in the sky, a mountain you're going to big as a promise, like driving fast to, only when you get there, it come down, you're on it and can't see it anymore, just a couple of miles of neons, and they're pretty, they sure are, like an invite to anything you ever dreamed could be, you know, like the sun at home daytime only this here's here, makes you feel the things are so close you can grab them. Grab what? Well, I had to find out, you gone and all, and came here. It's a stone city, and days, when the neons are gone, it's like they just died quiet come morning, and the city's not even there, not the same one, it's a whole different thing, like it's got a mind of its own and a body too, you know what I mean? And days I get a hankering for green and dirt under my feet, not cement, stone, asphalt and all—makes your feet hurt, cept when you're dancing. I'm dancing all the time now, Alice, like I'm with you and loving dancing the way you did,

and got me some prizes even, they're yours, they really are; if it
wasn't for you, I'd never of danced anyway, not one time, I don't
know—maybe that's a lie, but how do you know? Anyway I'm
telling you, that's how come you know. *You* taught me—
remember? Daddy said no, not to go, he'd give me the farm,
always said I'd be him someday and my kids me standing in that
same doorway and looking at the view, and I swear to God I can
see the view right now bigger than the ceiling and high and wide
and so fresh with air, Alice; and Momma she said I'll not have a
body to cook for f-you go, son, and that almost broke me up. I
couldn't tell them why, why I was going, and you got to hand it to
them, they didn't prize it out of me, not even try cept Momma's
hangdog look when she wants to get her way, only I still wouldn't
tell them, in their hearts they know I guess, I don't know, and I'm
getting letters all the time—oh, it ain't but a hour from here,
sometimes Daddy comes in to business, I seen him bout a month
ago, and he said Son, you looking bad, you better come home, this
life ain't doing you no good, but I said Got me a steady job in
construction almost five months now, I can't go back on that, and
he said Guess you cain't if you feel that way, son. It's that *son* got
me. Daddy he don't use it like that all the time, son son son, like
he got a hankering to. Well, ain't we all? And he give me all the
news, said the Hansons moved to town, mister got too old to keep
things going; Whip McCord gone to college—imagine, Whip!—
and Bethanne McCune married ole Jimmie Haley—*Jimmie*,
what never settled down one minute in his life, and Willa Mae
took a job as a librarian in town; seven boys gone to Vietnam; and
Wick—you remember how he pestered me to go with him hunt-
ing all the same times I was sneaking off with you?—the Viet
Cong got him; and all the news, only nothing from your house—
that's how come I know Momma and Daddy's sure why I come
here without one time saying it; it made me feel better I tell you,
Alice, only cept when Daddy went; he said I'll tell Momma we
had a long talk; and I give him a linen handkerchief for Momma I
bought one time for when she'd go to church, you know when she
gets to hacking and one of Daddy's won't do; and then he got in the
truck, he said Better be careful, boy, you look mighty bad, I won't
tell your momma that; and I almost couldn't see him when he said
that, but it don't matter none's long's I can dance, I got to keep
dancing, it's the time you're there, Alice, I feel you—you know

that—and you know something, Alice—course you do!—you know that ball hangs right smack there in the center of the dance floor, it makes colored lights moving slow, every color, and when it hits, you see faces just one sec, like it's all a dream and you drifting like water's carrying you past everything far far. Last night I sure got going good, you know, I mean that music tore right through me and made my blood sing to it's going like that rhythm abeat and abeat taking me right up there, agoing so my feet's dancing on fire and my arms touching the sky and me like getting longer and longer till my hands near touched that light and it come in my eyes and made me feel all lit up inside and about to bust into it all and—you know what, Alice!—them faces bobbed and bobbed, I got like dizzy and that light white as fire and I seen your face just as clear, it tore me up, and I reached out quick and all that music saying *Alice* and me too *Alice, Alice*, and I must of passed out, I couldn't dance any more, or I fell or something, but my whole heart's to bust I'm so happy cause I seen you, I seen your face.

Six nights a week the band plays. They give the place a soul, slow and fast, always loud, a vibrating voice that trembles everything. All the place keeps moving, the juke instantly merging into their last struck note. One of the three owners is always at the entrance, a smile of welcome. Weekends Jaw sells tickets, fifty cents cover charge, for the whole long night; and Willyjo, the doorman, a kind-faced, ox-broad man not very tall, pounds his fist into his palm rhythmically, and taps, and rolls on heels and toes, arock half the night in a partnerless dance. When the door swings out, the neon freeway pours scorching bright light in. "Hey, Freddie!" What say, Jumbo?" "You're sure lookin' cool, honey." "Man, get a load-a that!" "You'd cream just lookin' at her!" "Which side is up?" They laugh in the warm, near air and cigarette smoke and wafted alcohol. From a side room, especially during band breaks, comes the familiar clack of pool balls. Cries, laughs, jeers fill the room—JoePeteMiriam WaltBickWillaMaeLoisJimmieMurphyAngieRoberta.

Each entry shuts a door. Outside, a hundred rooms vanish. The world recedes into deep and endless dark. The Wanderer holds its own lights, faces, past—familiar. Benn, one of the owners, smiles. "Ready, Will? Say, Gert, another screwdriver here." The bartender, Bob, knows them all inside out and backwards ("You heard about ole Harry's pullin' a gun on that drummer last night? One o'clock in the a.m. the cops come, askin' where he headed—"). And the waitresses, Gert and Eula, are faces constant as drink, despite the shifting wigs and eyes and lashes and gewgaws and rage of outfits. And the other constants are there: the half-drunk little carpetlayer hanging on the end of the bar; the NASA engineer; the Fayetteville carpenter; the long-haired, dark girl from the Studebaker place; Alton, the Vietnam vet; Paul, the bootlegger from New Hope.

Whenever Field looked around they were all there. He breathed it all in deep. "Hey, Field!" "Hey, Ben. Hey, Eula," he said. "Bud?" Bob said, bottle and glass ready. "And a double shot of E.T.," Field said. He relaxed—back, as if at home, a family. Light glowed. The dark burned.

(Roanna: Met him downtown by Grant's this one Friday morning and I don't know what but something just stopped him cold when he saw me like he thought I was somebody—you know, somebody not me. He near flipped when he came to. Me, Roanna Wilcox, I said. I know Roanna, he said, looking like he still didn't but looking hard too, and I put it out for'm to see too. Sure don't look like no country girl right now, he said. Pure country, I said, you know it—he ought to, coming from right down my way there by the Piggly-Wiggly sign—and I touched his arm, quick: You doing all right, Lawton? And just that quick li'l ole touch did it, he came round, he came right close like he's going to have me right there against Grant's window, and I laughed and said Now, Lawton, and quick he said How bout dancing tomorrow night, it's Sat'dy, and we can go down to the River Club after and never stop, what say? Why, Lawton, I said. Only he ain't so dumb; this time he reached out and touched my shoulder and his hand hard and rough-skinned it just sent shivers down me. You're from my town, he said, like it was the sweetest thing. And he made it that way all night too at the club and me thinking every minute Pretty soon we'll leave, we'll go it somewhere—in the car or the grass or back of my place, or he got a place, about to die with him rubbing me like that sometimes, and when it's over, him near passing out from dancing and drinking, and fell asleep on me and me on top of him to wake him up and go at it, I couldn't stand it, and drove back home alone without a thing, Goddamn it.

*　　*　　*

Reddick Farr: His daddy was the only one came. Mrs. Warner couldn't say a word to him. I said Field wouldn't have nobody around, a loner he was since he came here, only he didn't seem alone, he had something in his head, I don't know what. His daddy just looked at him. Said How'll I tell his momma? And it Sunday too. Jesus!

Kim: Always did prefer ectomorphs, and he certainly was that. Field was on the construction crew for the new building. He told me how he went dancing at the Club Wanderer. I got the hint and couldn't resist. And he did dance. You're a little out of my class, he said. And you out of my orbit, I said. He laughed, a rather boyish innocent laugh too. There was something terribly moving about him. I wanted to hold him and comfort him, tell him it was all right. And in bed when he was sleeping, I did hold his head, so thin and long his face, with long dark lashes, and long brown hair. But the rest of him was all hard, wiry, all energy—maddening in bed, with a terrible impersonal drive. I felt used, used, with an enormous indifference by him—and I wanted that.)

Saturday night

FIELD: Oh, Alice, I'm telling you this every night, honey, only what can I do, me not wanting to talk to nobody, everybody's you—I can't help it—I'm looking at them, but it's you. Pretty soon I'm dancing up a storm. I know how it is: I try—I say I'm going out with Sue, Alice wouldn't want me to just moon like this; but it's because that—you wouldn't want me to do it—that's why I do it: If you wanted me to it wouldn't mean the same thing, now would it, Alice, honest? It's cause you don't. Maybe that don't make no sense, but it's the onliest way I know. Mornings—not just one time, Alice, but every morning—since you gone I been waking up like I died and come back and it ain't real. First thing, I think The bed's real, I ain't dead, Alice's here; and for a sec I believe it too, I leap out and get in my clothes—it's like back on the farm with Daddy and Momma, and I know if I look out the kitchen window I can see straight out to the sun smack on your bedroom window just the way I could nighttime fore you put your light out, and me watching, like it's the moon right inside your room shining for me—you saying Field, I'm never going to pull the shade down

so's you can't stop seeing me—ever. And I ain't—I ain't stopped
one second since I seen you in the river. Ohjesusgod, Alice, why
why why? Oh, don't, don't answer me, Alice, I can't stand that: I
know it's me, I did it, but you got to know: I'm trying, I'll make up
for it, I will too, Alice. You won't be ashamed your Field's just
gone and forgot with no shame for what he done. Listen here,
Alice, I ain't never gonna stop till it's done, and I reckoned with it,
and it's right by you, if it takes twenty years—hear? You hear me,
Alice? Why don't you answer me? Alice! I been waiting all day for
your voice, just one sound since last night, cause I seen your face,
Alice, and now I'm waiting for you to say it so I'll know I'm getting
there cause I can hear it in my head, I been hearing it day and day
and day, like never stopping, only I want to hear it out, I'll know
I'm with you, in the same place, I done it, and you forgive me and
we'll be together. I work like a dog, Alice, yes—you believe it?
ole Field the farmer's son working like a dog in the city! Ain't it a
joke? But I got to, I stop one minute and you're there and then I'd
of had to leave work and start looking for you, there ain't no way to
stop if you get in my head. It's all I can do to keep you back—*Till
five* I'd tell me, *Till five*. That's all I could do, even when you was
there, say *Till five*, don't think about—I'd not even say your
name, but I heard it and I'd work harder, *Till five*, and come five
o'clock I'd be in my room and washed and changed, only now I'm
not even doing that, I just come straight here to the club and get
me that cool beer and a double shot to begin and another cool beer
and, oh man, I can say it *Alice*, like free—and you're right there.
You come floating up, far—I see you, just like you was, only
you're now, in your white dress, all of you so small, and all your
legs showing, that little mini, and all your shoulders, I'm smelling
your long black hair on me. I want to put my hand right in the
mirror and tell you Alice, come dance with me, honey. And you
know: I'm already dancing, my heart's dancing thinking about you
and you coming with that white dress, and my feet's starting. That
ball of light—you see it, Alice—it hits them colors round and
round, it goes and goes, and band time it beats with the band,
they send the old rhythm right into them lights and pretty soon
they're going right into you, like they're touching and warm, and
getting warmer, and your blood goes, it begins, it starts abeating,
abeating, and your blood beats, abeating; and it's your legs beating, and your toes, and your arms; and it's all of you pretty soon

abeating. I got to get up. I got to go get Alice. She's sitting there in the dark. She's at one of them tables. She's all alone waiting for me. She knows I'm coming. I see her eyes, all the light in her eyes, in the dark and holding it for me, yes she is. And I go right to her close, and I feel her hand and take her . . . and quick as anything it's you, Alice, you're right there against me so good it hurts, I'm about to bust, and a minute I shiver like, standing there and swaying, swaying, and I can feel it already going right into you, my hot and my blood like my skin's yours, and you come back into me, and me into you, and you can't tell which, and then moving and swaying like we're all alone, moving round in a circle, standing still and moving; and dipping, dipping, moving and moving; and the lights going round and round till it's like carrying, the music's lifting us and carrying. And I ain't letting you go, Alice, never a time: nothing going to stop us even with you klack-klack-klacking to a fast one and your arms legs and whole body and hair swinging and throwing and flying high and your bubs shaking and hips wiggling and legs leaping, and when I close my eyes feeling you I see you just the same through my eyelids, yes I *do*, that light comes right through, I can feel it—you believe that?—and you, I see you in it, waiting for you to come down, your face, and kiss me, only it don't. I keep thinking it will, I feel me getting longer and longer, I try, I keep reaching only it's like I ain't long enough, but if I got up enough steam and danced harder, I could move, I'd get so light I'd float up on the music, right smack up to you, and I'd feel your face against mine; and I get afraid, Alice: comes a minute—I know it's coming—and it's going to make me want to cry and yell, but I can't he'p it—I think if I open my eyes, I won't see it, but if I do it'll be gone, don't go, Alice! And it's water, everything's water, I'm looking, and there's your face, and all your hair, and the willow branch almost touching it, and a leaf floating by, and you still, looking at me out of the water, and I got to touch your face, Alice, I got to put my hand in the water and touch your face, both of my hands, I can't stand it, I'm reaching and quick my voice's saying *AliceAliceAliceAliceAliceAlice*, my blood's crying it, and all of me beating, and I open my eyes and a minute it's me under, and hands reaching down, but they're mine, going like *mad* like *mad* like *mad* like *mad* and you're there and you going like *mad mad mad mad mad*, your hips and arms and legs and hair and hair and hair hair hair hair hair drum drum drum drum drum woweeeee, we going and leaping leaping and pretty soon close rubbing and sliding, sliding and rubbing, oh baby Alice you going to make me come right here on the floor, slow slow grinding slow slow grinding grinding, and I'm getting there, getting on high, I feel it riding that music, that rhythm coming with a long slow heave, long long long now, and pulling pulling, and I'm getting there slow, slow moving up, up, oh Alice I'm going to, I'm going to, going to touch, right out and reach your face that's coming down to me. And then I'm waking up it's bright light I can't stand, sun, morning sun, and the walls all dirty wallpaper, them flowers like dead and dried in a winter field gone to seed, and dark ribbons straight down the walls, and that light, and them blinds making dark bars on the floor, my eyes're wet from the sun and the night before and I got to get up quick, I wish I was dead, my head's bustin, Jake'll pick me up in a minute. Good thing I'd moved close to the club or I'd be up the creek, only Alice I couldn't stand it, thinking it's the only place I'd get to you, and here I am dancing with you again, I'll never stop, no never till I'm with you 'one minute past eternity,' yes our song: and there I go, it's your face coming up close to the water, only like if I look long I'm under and looking up and you looking down at me, it gets all twisted and I wanted to get out from under the water and to you. Sometimes I want to move my arms only I can't, like the water's holding them down, I want to scream then, only the water's filling my mouth and then quick the water moves and you gone, gone, Alice, and I can't see or yell or touch, thinking I'll never see you again, about to go crazy thinking that, and thinking you're getting even for all them girls I'm dancing with and kissing and screwing, but Alice, you know something: I get dancing and get me going and feel them warm and begin to go, up, high, up up up, and—I don't know how come—but I ain't *here*, I'm floating, oh baby I'm going fast so fast sucked up in a thing so strong I know I'm going to hit, I know it—going to hit and pow explode and go everywhere, smithereens, and then all of a sudden it's you: pow and it breaks like fireworks and then honey it's so quiet and you come so clear, clearest light I even seen, like you're close as that ball turning round in the ceiling and if I reach up I'll touch your long hair and face I love: only somebody's crying, it's my momma—yes, momma—and I say Momma, what's making you cry? like I know only don't, and Poppa's standing there with his hand on her shoulder and looking at me like when my dog Wilbur got runned over, and I know: you said to me It'd get dark forever if I couldn't see you no more, Field; you said There's no man in this here world for me but you, Field, you know that, Field; you said I'd not live a day without you if I thought you believed Andrew Phelps ever come near me cept that one kiss he snuck and me not knowing he was there, it didn't mean a thing, I'd of run, I did slap him too; you said Nobody touched me the month I was at my cousin Willa Mae's, nobody ever would but you, Field, and the letters are from a boy likes me but you know I won't look at, I swear it, I'll swear on the Bible, I'll swear before Reverend Bullard and the whole church, Field; you said What's in my belly's yours, Field, gonna look like you, you wait, then you'll be ashamed you ever said a word, you'll take it all back and love me all your life, you will, just you wait and see. And oh, Alice, I do, I love you now like never before; never knew I'd love you so much I couldn't stand even to live without you. I got to go where you are. I had to find the way, Alice. I come one night and danced and there you was. You was in my arms, apressing and agliding, like a miracle come in me, and I knew I couldn't let you go: when I woke up it wasn't you, but I knew I'd had you for a minute, maybe a hour, maybe all night, and I'd get you back: so I come here, I danced, I danced, I kept dancing, I can't now: I'm getting to you, Alice, I know I am, and I won't stop, never, till I'm with you—you hear me? And maybe you'll tell me it's not doing any good, but you just wait till you see this time I mean it, I do, I'll never stop dancing till I'm in your arms forever and you can't let me go, I won't let you, only sometimes I can't make it, Alice, you know I get to falling, I get so weak—me—go ahead, *laugh!*—me, ole Field, getting so weak he almost can't stand up, but something pushes me, keeps me going till the last song and then go on like I'm dancing out the door and in the car and in bed even and sleeping too, it never stops, the room's still athumping when I wake up and all day that music's pounding in me when I'm banging nails and lugging boards. Come five o'clock it gets strong, stronger every minute, till I'm back in the dark and that light going round and the band comes *one minute past eternity*; it's like you, I'm near you, that place; like I lay my head right down in the dark against your skin, the dark's all warm, and you say Come on, honey, come onnnnn, Field, we'll dance, honey, and me getting up feeling you all soft and warm and cool too agin me, and fore I know it I'm dancing, I'm swinging and swaying and leaping bouncing and jerking, keeping time, keeping the beat with you and that music and that hot air touching like it's water and your face under water, it comes, it's looking at me, oh-jesus it's looking at me, and if just one time you'd say Field, it's your fault; but you never did, nobody ever accused me but me, and Momma and Poppa looking at me so soft and pitying like looking at my own dog, and Reverend Bullard's soft voice and all them people and nobody not one accusing, saying a word to me but me me me me *me*

The neon sign CLUB WANDERER burns around the clock. In the sun it fades a sickly blue and red, but with nightfall it beckons, stark and beautiful in the empty sky. With each opening of the door, some soul loosed from the SOUNDS spills onto the freeway. From outside, in the night traffic, you would not suspect the seething rhythm, the collective beat like a heart throbbing deep in the night; only the parking lot, filled to overflowing, tells you something is happening close by. During the week it is the lone pool player, seeking, who comes, and the isolated couple, the vagrant drinker, the so-called perpetuals; weekends it is the lovers, mates—couple time, rest and desire, escape and search—commingled with the usuals. The regulars know that if you go away for days, weeks, months, even years, and come back, some of them will be there; it is the place to find them; sit long enough and the missing will walk in, no longer phantoms from the past, for sooner or later nearly all return. "How's eveything on the West Coast?" "Hey, man, ain't seen you since Vegas." "Lauderdale! Too empty. Nothing doing!" The truckdrivers make the Wanderer known all over the country. "Wilson struck a hydrant on US 1, off Elizabethtown." "Heard about Field?" "Heard about Bess Wickham's shooting all the way up to Dayton." "What's Larry doing now?" "She's making it in New Orleans, got guts that girl." Inside, they wait—for dates, loan, two-timer, wife-stealer, thief, friend. Nobody is forgotton. Away long enough, he comes up in the conversation. "Can't stay away too long, it's in the blood." They have every confidence. When the moment comes, the light is burning outside, a stark, beckoning sign.

(*Walt Everst*: I got there too late. His landlady said Field just got took away—to Greenville. Had to turn me around directly and go back home.

Sue: Why was he dancin' that way, for what? I wanted him— yes, I did, me and I went through all that with him, drinking and dancing. My God, I'm sick of dancing; I never want to see a floor in my life, after him. Near killed me with dancing. What for? He'd not answer, he'd look through me, he'd look like I wasn't even there. It'd make me madder'n hell. Sometimes I even hit him and then he'd smile or laugh and grab me, and what could I do then, I wanted him so? I don't go near the Wanderer now. I hate that place, hate it.

Mrs. Wingfield: His daddy stops and stands in the fields. I see him from the kitchen. He stops work and looks, like he's waiting. Only he ain't waiting. He al'ays did. But he cain't now. He keeps lookin' into the ground, and sometimes up. Then he gits mad and works like you never seem him go. But I know he'll sell it. He's waitin' for me to put my foot down and say no. He knows I will too: he cain't stop workin' and sit. He knows that'd kill him sure. Used to be he'd look out there like it'd just go on, somebody else'd come, and somebody else, somebody he knew, and he'd die comf'table knowin' it was one-a his, like he had somethin' to do with it even after he was gone. But seems like to me now he just stops and looks up like he got no place to go.)

Sunday night

FIELD: Alice, you're talking to me, baby, I know you are—there's a sound I never did hear before in that music, like somebody touched the guitars in a way not before, and the piano and the drums and all together they got a extra sound never come before, makes my blood tingle and hum, me all humming, Alice, never hummed like this before; a sound come. What you think of that? A sound—it's taking me to you, I'm riding it, I sure am, Alice, taking me to you like it's your voice in my blood trying to tell me and if I open my mouth it'll come out—I will too, I'll open it—and you'll say it, me talking and you talking like one sound; then I'll know I got you, I'm touching you like that ball of light come to my hand at last, and I'll kiss your face happy out of my mind, blow it, and never leave you, whole hog. Only, Alice sometimes my hand don't do what I tell it, or my legs, I'm dancing in my head, only legs slow or dragging and arms flopping—how come?—I can't fall off now, honey; it's time, been too long; and Momma come last night right in the middle of the night and said Field? You hear me, Field? and I was saying Yes, Momma, only seemed like she'd not hear, saying Field? and my eyes wide open's could be in the pitch black cept for the light over the city. I come to a city, Alice, and Momma's in the city atalking, Field, son, we want you home, you got to come home or there'll be nothing left-a you, Field honey, and then what'll your poppa do, going along with you the way he done so you could try yourself out and then hopefully come home and take over the way he says you're supposed to, ain't no life this city life for a boy's got so much country in him, pure country your daddy says, says How come he's wasting pure country in the city, I'd like to know. Field, honey? And Momma's right there, only my eyes filled with that big dark and I can't touch her; and it's morning and Daddy he's standing there but real, says You going to a hospital, Field, or you ain't living long, and it's the first time I ever seen like a shadow of water in my daddy's eyes, and you know, Daddy he ain't never showing it, but this time ups and shouts at me A hospital, a hospital, you hear me, Lawton Wingfield? And you know, Alice, I had to out and laugh loud's I could to hear my daddy talk thataway, for a minute it was like you caring; and me getting up and putting on my clothes; Alice, I had to hang onto the bureau—you believe that?—and fell, I couldn't he'p it, but had to get out fore they called somebody, I ain't going to no hospital, and it's Sunday and the sun out and burning; everything's so green I think I never seen things before, a tad of grass around the house, but them trees swinging over the houses with wind, like you in it, Alice, it's that good: and Daddy's shouting at me, and me back at him, I couldn't he'p it, Alice, he don't understand, I'll go back home, Daddy, but you let me do it, I'll decide and then pop I'll be there one day on the stoop—okay, Daddy? and him standing there, but I know he's going to do something, I know it. So I got me away, I got to Bill Wamp's place by the church and sat in the fi'ty-six Ford up on blocks, up there on Ninth Street, cause I got this thing to do, my legs are abeat

with it even when they ain't moving, Alice, like dancing in my
head when I ain't dancing, it never stops, I ain't never stopping
cause long's I'm dancing I'm with you, honey, no matter what,
come hell or high water: and your face in the river, the water's
over it, only I feel water, air's all water, touching, only how can I
see your face and it's mine too, I feel the water, only why don't you
let me have it?—you ain't never accused me, only your eyes
looking out of the river at me are worse than anything, Alice; if
only one time you'd say Field, I done forgive you, one time Alice,
I'd maybe sleep a minute and rest and think She's beside me, I
don't worry none; but everywhere I go I'm seeing your face and
eyes in the sky and trees green and the sidewalk and through that
there Ford windshield and working in the cement and on bricks
and in the dark worse, the only thing, like your eyes are that big
white light over the city come down and holding me and never
letting me out, Alice honey, only please please Say it one time:
You done it, Lawton Wingfield, you killed me, so it'll be like I got
down on my knees before Momma and Poppa the first time and
said I did it, I can tell it all now, I did it, I didn't mean to, and to all
my buddies don't know and all the church and all the town and
God even, like as if He didn't know too, Alice; like it's this here
Sunday and I made it to the Sunday afternoon jazz session and
they're all here—like it is, Alice—they are here, every one of
them—and you give me the word, just say it, the word, Alice, and
I can throw me down right in the middle of all that music and
rhythm and pumping and tell it like it was: I killed Alice Falls, my
wife even if we didn't tie the knot yet, and I was wrong playing
around like she wasn't even mine to make her jealous and love me
more and not be able to stand one minute away from me, and
thinking she'll come round when I want her, and she did, she did
it like I told it, and carrying mine and me not knowing a while and
then when she says it, thinking she been cheating the way I'm
doing and wanting to kill her and did—just by walking off and
telling her I'll never see you again, I don't want to see your face,
never want to look at you, hope it's born dead and you gone with
it; and packing my things and telling them I'm going on construction in Huntsville, I'm going there and beginning; beginning, yes,
Alice, and it was the ending; Lonnie he come telling me first thing
I's in a room and making money and thinking Maybe I'll die and
never have to think about her again cause, honest, Alice, I never

thought of anything but you on the walls and in the mirror and in the bed till I'm thinking I can't never sleep in no small box like this room, no box of no kind, without I'm tight in with her and going crazy out of my mind with her. Momma said She's the sweetest thing this world knows, why'd she do a thing like that? and Daddy and Momma and everybody I know at the church and then Field, How come you stayed away? old Bickley says, and me *blind* with you, Alice, ready to die, and couldn't stay away from the Church one day after and that night—you know what, Alice?—I went there—sure you remember—and slept all night right beside you, me near dead too, wishing I was beside both of you, and not knowing, never knowing now, who it'd be, like me or you, a boy or a girl, or what'd it bring with it, maybe it'd have kids and its kids like forever, and it cut off with you in the river and I'm me wanting to know where you done it, how—you jumped off that Runkley bridge way up where we'd go night? or just slip and let yourself not move or fall? maybe you did fall? Jesus, Alice, God help me, it'll drive me crazy you don't tell me or just come down, come down from that light going and no don't tell me, just yell it out It's your fault, Lawton Wingfield, just yell it out, yelllllllll, it's in my blood, I can hear it all beating, oh Alice baby, you feel that rhythm, man there never was a band like the SOUNDS, and you dancing like you never danced before tonight, like we never was together thisaway, so close your're ole Field hisself, and that light it's getting so bright almost to blind me but I ain't taking my eyes off it one time, noooooo, Alice, you ain't leaving me tonight, you coming down, you coming close, you going to touch down with that white face and smiling and say Field honey, I love you, Field honey, don't never leave me; and I'm going to touch your face with both my hands, Alice, you so close you'll never get far from Field again, you feeling it now, Alice? that beat like it's your heart, feel it? It's abeat and abeat, uuuuuuuuhhhhhhhhh, man, Alice, it's bout to swell right out of me, it's moving and moving, it's leaping like it's going to bust out and go into this here room, like water, your face, come down, Alice, and kiss me and tell me it's all right, just one time, please, Alice, my heart's to bust if you don't, oh man, listen to that, that sound, that sound like them SOUNDS never made before, never, no, they going to carry me, oh that sound, Alice, it's going to carry me; look at that light, look, I'm looking: it never been so bright; Alice, if I reach I'm going to touch it, and I'll do it too, Alice, make my arms stretch out I don't care how long if you'll just one time come closer, say it; I been trying so hard, Alice, I never in my life tried so hard to do anything like dancing till I can't no more and every bit of me's going to you, I can't stop cause if I do, you won't be there; I'm afraid, Alice, yes I am, I got to tell you that, without you I'd die and I don't know how, this here's the only way to get to you, Alice, and be near you and never stop without your're in my arms, oh Alice you hear that beat, it's going, it's getting there, it's moving up up up, mannnnnnn, feel it a beat beat beat, my heart's going, it's so fast, it's making—listen to that, that sound, Alice it's coming, it's coming yes from down in me, it's in my blood, it's coming from my heart going to you, Alice; you hear it? yes you do, you do, I see it, I see your face, it's coming, Alice, jesusgod you do hear, you coming down, that light's getting there, I getting to it, I *am*, Alice, ohjesusgod it's beating beating abeat like never, abeat-abeat-abeat woweeeeeeeeeee going, I'm going to make I'm going to come right in my britches, Alice, if you, if you . . . yessss, bust out into the air, it's going to go right through my skin and into air and sweat and water and smoke and that light, it's so bright, and you, Alice, I see you, *Alice!* yes ohmygodjesus, Alice, thank you, baby, come on, come onnnnnn, we going to make it, we going to make it together, going to be there, I feel it coming, it's burning up up up, oh my blood and that heart's beating beating and this whole room growing and all light and you coming down, and now, Alice honey, your face, it's so close I can touch if I reach out with my hands, yes I will, I will, my heart's beating and my head and all this room, my heart busting out into this whole room, Alice, Now, now, tell them, *tell* them I done it and I made up for it, Alice, in the only way I know how, dancing, dancing, and to get to you, tell them. I'm burning, Alice, and yes I can now I will touch you; see, honey, my hands, they're moving, my arms, they're going right up to that light, reaching to touch, I'm going to touch you, I'm going to touch, I'm going to

SWEET TALK

STEPHANIE VAUGHN

SOMETIMES SAM AND I loved each other more when we were angry. "Day," I called him, using the surname instead of Sam. "Day, Day, Day!" It drummed against the walls of the apartment like a distress signal.

"Ah, my beautiful lovebird," he said. "My sugar sweet bride."

For weeks I had been going through the trash trying to find out whether he had other women. Once I found half a ham sandwich with red marks that could have been lipstick. Or maybe catsup. This time I found five slender cigarette butts.

"Who smokes floral-embossed cigarettes?" I said. He had just come out of the shower, and droplets of water gleamed among the black hairs of his chest like tiny knife points. "Who's the heart-attack candidate you invite over when I'm out?" I held the butts beneath his nose like a small bouquet. He slapped them to the floor and we stopped speaking for three days. We moved through the apartment without touching, lay stiffly in separate furrows of the bed, desire blooming and withering between us like the invisible petals of a night-blooming cereus.

We finally made up while watching a chess tournament on television. Even though we wouldn't speak or make eye contact, we were sitting in front of the sofa moving pieces around a chess board as an announcer explained World Championship strategy to the viewing audience. Our shoulders touched but we pretended not to notice. Our knees touched, and our elbows. Then we both reached for the black bishop and our hands touched. We made love on the carpet and kept our eyes open so that we could look at each other defiantly.

We were living in California and had six university degrees between us and no employment. We lived on food stamps, job interviews and games.

"How many children did George Washington, the father of our country, have?"

"No white ones but lots of black ones."

"How much did he make when he was Commander of the Revolutionary Army?"

"He made a big to-do about refusing a salary but later presented the first Congress with a bill for a half million dollars."

"Who was the last slave-owning president?"

"Ulysses S. Grant."

We had always been good students.

It was a smoggy summer. I spent long hours in air-conditioned supermarkets, touching the cool cans, feeling the cold plastic stretched across packages of meat. Sam left the apartment for whole afternoons and evenings. He was in his car somewhere, opening it up on the freeway, or maybe just spending time with someone I didn't know. We were mysterious with each other about our absences. In August we decided to move east, where a friend said he could get us both jobs at an unaccredited community college. In the meantime, I had invented a lover. He was rich and wanted to take me to an Alpine hotel, where mauve flowers cascaded over the stone walls of a terrace. Sometimes we drank white wine and watched the icy peaks of mountains shimmer gold in the sunset. Sometimes we returned to our room carrying tiny ceramic mugs of schnapps which had been given to us, in the German fashion, as we paid for an expensive meal.

In the second week of August, I found a pair of red lace panties at the bottom of the kitchen trash.

I decided to tell Sam I had a lover. I made my lover into a tall, blue-eyed blond, a tennis player on the circuit, a Phi Beta Kappa from Stanford who had offers from the movies. It was the tall blond part that needled Sam, who was dark and stocky.

"Did you pick him up at the beach?" Sam said.

"Stop it," I said, knowing that it was a sure way to get him to ask more questions.

"Did you have your diaphragm in your purse?"

We were wrapping cups and saucers in newspaper and nesting them in the slots of packing boxes. "He was taller than you," I said, "but not as handsome."

Sam held a blue and white Dresden cup, my favorite wedding present, in front of my eyes. "You slut," he said, and let the cup drop to the floor.

"Very articulate," I said. "Some professor. The man of reason gets into an argument and he talks with broken cups. Thank you Alexander Dope."

That afternoon I failed the California drivers' test again. I made four right turns and drove over three of the four curbs. The highway patrolman pointed out that if I made one more mistake I was finished. I drove through a red light.

On the way back to the apartment complex, Sam squinted into the flatness of the expressway and would not talk to me. I put my blue-eyed lover behind the wheel. He rested a hand on my knee and smiled as he drove. He was driving me west, away from the Vista View Apartments, across the thin spine of mountains which separated our suburb from the sea. At the shore there would be seals frolicking among the rocks and starfish resting in tidal pools.

"How come you never take me to the ocean?" I said. "How come every time I want to go to the beach I have to call up a woman friend?"

"If you think you're going to Virginia with me," he said, "you're dreaming." He eased the car into our numbered space and put his head against the wheel. "Why did you have to do it?"

"I do not like cars," I said. "You know I have always been afraid of cars."

"Why did you have to sleep with that fag tennis player?" His head was still against the wheel. I moved closer and put my arm around his shoulders.

"Sam, I didn't. I made it up."

"Don't try to get out of it."

"I didn't, Sam. I made it up." I tried to kiss him. He let me put my mouth against his, but his lips were unyielding. They felt like the skin of an orange. "I didn't, Sam. I made it up to hurt you." I kissed him again and his mouth warmed against mine. "I love you, Sam. Please let me go to Virginia."

"George Donner," I read from the guidebook, "was sixty-one years old and rich when he packed up his family and left Illinois to cross the Great Plains, the desert, and the mountains into California." We were driving through the Sierras, past steep slopes and the deep shade of an evergreen forest, toward the Donner Pass, where in 1846 the Donner family had been trapped by an early snowfall. Some of them died and the rest ate the corpses of their relatives and their Indian guides to survive.

"Where are the bones?" Sam said, as we strolled past glass cases at the Donner Pass Museum. The cases were full of wagon wheels and harnesses. Above us a recorded voice described the courageous and enterprising spirit of American pioneers. A man standing nearby with a young boy turned to scowl at Sam. Sam looked at him and said loudly, "Where are the bones of the people they ate?" The man took the boy by the hand and started for the door. Sam said, "You call this American history?" and the man turned and said, "Listen, mister, I can get your license number." We laughed about that as we descended into the plain of the Great Basin desert in Nevada. Every few miles one of us would say the line and the other one would chuckle, and I felt as if we had been married fifty years instead of five, and that everything had turned out okay.

Ten miles east of Reno I began to sneeze. My nose ran and my eyes watered, and I had to stop reading the guidebook.

"I can't do this anymore. I think I've got an allergy."

"You never had an allergy in your life." Sam's tone implied that I had purposefully got the allergy so that I could not read the guidebook. We were riding in a second-hand van, a lusterless, black shoebox of a vehicle, which Sam had bought for the trip with the money he got from the stereo, the TV, and his own beautifully overhauled and rebuilt little sports car.

"Turn on the radio," I said.

"The radio is broken."

It was a hot day, dry and gritty. On either side of the freeway, a sagebrush desert stretched toward the hunched profiles of brown mountains. The mountains were so far away—the only landmarks within three hundred miles—that they did not whap by the windows like signposts, they floated above the plain of dusty sage and gave us the sense that we were not going anywhere.

"Are you trying to kill us?" I said when the speedometer slid past ninety.

"Sam looked at the dash surprised and, I think, a little pleased that the van could do that much. "I'm getting hypnotized," he said. He thought about it for another mile and said, "If you had managed to get your license, you could do something on this trip besides blow snot into your hand."

"Don't you think we should call ahead to Elko for a motel room?"

"I might not want to stop at Elko."

"Sam, look at the map. You'll be tired when we get to Elko."

"I'll let you know when I'm tired."

We reached Elko at sundown, and Sam was tired. In the office of the Shangrila Motor Lodge we watched another couple get the last room. "I suppose you're going to be mad because I was right," I said.

"Just get in the van." We bought a sack of hamburgers and set out for Utah. Ahead of us a full moon rose, flat and yellow like a fifty-dollar gold piece, then lost its color as it rose higher. We entered the Utah salt flats, the dead floor of a dead ocean. The salt crystals glittered like snow under the white moon. My nose stopped running, and I felt suddenly lucid and calm.

"Has he been in any movies?" Sam said.

"Has who been in any movies?"

"The fag tennis player."

I had to think a moment before I recalled my phantom lover.

"He's not a fag."

"I thought you made him up."

"I did make him up but I didn't make up any fag."

A few minutes later he said, "You might at least sing something. You might at least try to keep me awake." I sang a few Beatles tunes, then Simon and Garfunkel, the Everly Brothers, and Elvis Presley. I worked my way back through my youth to a Girl Scout song I remembered as "Eye, Eye, Eye, Icky, Eye, Kai, A-nah." It was supposed to be sung around a campfire to remind the girls of their Indian heritage and the pleasures of surviving in the wilderness. "Ah woo, ah woo. Ah woo knee key chee," I sang. "I am now five years old," I said, and then I sang, "Home, Home on the Range," the song I remembered singing when I was a child going cross-country with my parents to visit some relatives. The only thing I remembered about that trip besides a lot of going to the bathroom in gas stations was that there were rules which made the traveling life simple. One was: do not hang over the edge of the front seat to talk to your mother or father. The other was: if you have to throw up, do it in the blue coffee can, the red one is full of cookies.

"It's just the jobs and money," I said. "It isn't us, is it?"

"I don't know," he said.

A day and a half later we crossed from Wyoming into Nebraska, the western edge of the Louisiana Purchase, which Thomas Jefferson had made so that we could all live in white, classical houses, and be farmers. Fifty miles later the corn began, hundreds of miles of it, singing green from horizon to horizon. We began to relax and I had the feeling that we had survived the test of American geography. I put away our guidebooks and took out the dictionary. Matachin, mastigophobia, matutolypea. I tried to find words Sam didn't know. He guessed all the definitions and was smug and happy behind the wheel. I reached over and put a hand on his knee. He looked at me and smiled. "Ah, my little buttercup," he said. "My sweet cream pie." I thought of my Alpine lover for the first time in a long while, and he was nothing more than mist over a distant mountain.

In a motel lobby near Omaha, we had to wait in line for twenty minutes behind three families. Sam put his arm around me and pulled a tennis ball out of his jacket. He bounced it on the thin carpet, tentatively, and when he saw it had enough spring, he dropped into an exaggerated basketball player's crouch and ran across the lobby. He whirled in front of the cigarette machine and passed the ball to me. I laughed and threw it back. Several people had turned to stare at us. Sam winked at them and dunked the ball through an imaginary net by the wall clock, then passed the ball back to me. I dribbled around a stack of suitcases and went for a lay-up by a hanging fern. I misjudged and knocked the plant to the floor. What surprised me was that the fronds were plastic but the dirt was real. There was a huge mound of it on the carpet. At the registration desk, the clerk told us the motel was already full and that he could not find our name on the advance reservation list.

"Nebraska sucks eggs," Sam said loudly as we carried our luggage to the door. We spent the night curled up on the hard front seat of the van like boulders. The bony parts of our bodies kept bumping as we turned and rolled to avoid the steering wheel and dash. In the morning, my knees and elbows felt worn away, like the peaks of old mountains. We hadn't touched each other sexually since California.

"So she had big ta-ta's," I said. "She had huge ta-ta's and a bad-breath problem." We had pushed on through the corn, across Iowa, Illinois and Indiana, and the old arguments rattled along with us, like the pots and pans in the back of the van.

"She was a model," he said. He was describing the proprietress of the slender cigarettes and red panties.

"In a couple of years she'll have gum disease," I said.

"She was a model and she had a degree in literature from Oxford."

I didn't believe him, of course, but I felt the sting of his intention to hurt. "By the time she's forty she'll have emphysema."

"What would this trip be like without the melody of your voice," he said. It was dark, and taillights glowed on the road ahead of us like flecks of burning iron. I remembered how, when we were undergraduates attending different colleges, he used to write me letters which said keep your skirts down and your knees together, don't let anyone get near your crunch. We always amused each other with our language.

"I want a divorce," I said in a motel room in Columbus, Ohio. We were propped against pillows on separate double beds watching a local program on Woody Hayes, the Ohio State football coach. The announcer was saying, "And here in front of the locker room is the blue and gold mat that every player must step on as he goes to and from the field. Those numbers are the score of last year's loss to Michigan." And I was saying, "Are you listening? I said I want a divorce when we get to Virginia."

"I'm listening."

"Don't you want to know why I want a divorce?"

"No."

"Well, do you think it's a good idea or a bad idea?"

"I think it's a good idea."

"You do?"

"Yes."

The announcer said, "And that is why the night before the big game Woody will be showing his boys reruns of the films *Patton* and *Bullitt*."

That night someone broke into the van and stole everything we owned except the suitcases we had with us in the motel room. They even stole the broken radio. We stood in front of the empty van and looked up and down the row of parked cars as if we expected to see another black van parked there, one with two pairs of skis and two tennis rackets slipped into the spaces between the boxes and the windows.

"I suppose you're going to say I'm the one who left the door unlocked," I said.

Sam sat on the curb. He sat on the curb and put his head into hands. "No," he said. "It was probably me."

The policeman who filled out the report tried to write "Miscellaneous Household Goods" on the clipboarded form, but I made him list everything I could remember, as the three of us sat on the curb—the skis and rackets, the chess set, a baseball bat, twelve boxes of books, two rugs which I had braided, an oak bed frame Sam had refinished. I inventoried the kitchen items: two bread cans, two cake pans, three skillets. I mentioned every fork and every measuring cup and every piece of bric-a-brac I could recall—the trash of our life, suddenly made valuable by the theft. When the policeman had left without giving us any hope of ever recovering our things, I told Sam I was going to pack and shower. A half hour later when I came out with the suitcases, he was still on the curb, sitting in the full sun, his cotton shirt beginning to stain in wing shapes across his shoulder blades. I reached down to touch him and he flinched. It was a shock—feeling the tremble of his flesh, the vulnerability of it, and for the first time since California I tried to imagine what it was like driving with a woman who said she didn't want him, in a van he didn't like but had to buy in order to travel to a possible job on the other side of the continent, which might not be worth reaching.

On the last leg of the trip, Sam was agreeable and compliant. If I wanted to stop for coffee, he stopped immediately. If I wanted him to go slower in thick traffic, he eased his foot off the pedal without a look of regret or annoyance. I got out the dictionary. Operose, ophelimity, ophryitis. He said he'd never heard of any of those words. Which president died in a bathtub? He couldn't remember. I tried to sing to keep him company. He told me it wasn't necessary. I played a few tunes on a comb. He gazed pleasantly at the freeway, so pleasantly that I could have made him up. I could have invented him and put him on a mountainside terrace and set him going. "Sammy," I said, "that stuff wasn't much. I won't miss it."

"Good," he said.

About three a.m. green exit signs began to appear announcing the past and the future: Colonial Williamsburg, Jamestown, Yorktown, Patrick Henry Airport. "Let's go to the beach," I said. "Let's just go all the way to the edge of the continent." It was a ludicrous idea.

"Sure. Why not."

He drove on past Newport News and over an arching bridge towards Virginia Beach. We arrived there just at dawn and found our way into a residential neighborhood full of small pastel houses and sandy lawns. "Could we just stop right here?" I said. I had an idea. I had a plan. He shrugged as if to say what the heck, I don't care and if you want to drive into the ocean that will be fine, too.

We were parked on a street that ran due east towards the water—I could see just a glimmer of ocean between two hotels about a mile away. "All right," I said, with the forced, brusque cheerfulness of a high school coach. "Let's get out and do some stretching exercises." Sam sat behind the wheel and watched me touch my toes. "Come on, Sammy. Let's get loose. We haven't done anything with our bodies since California." He yawned, got out of the van, and did a few arm rolls and toe touches. "All right now," I said. "Do you think a two-block handicap is about right?" He had always given me a two-block advantage during our foot races in California. He yawned again. "How about a one-and-a-half-block lead, then?" He crossed his arms and leaned against the van, watching me. I couldn't tell whether he had nodded, but I said anyway, "I'll give you a wave when I'm ready." I walked down the middle of the street past houses which had towels hanging over porch rails and toys lying on front walks. Even a mile from the water, I smelled the salt and seaweed in the air. It made me feel light-headed and for a moment I tried to picture Sam and myself in one of those houses with tricycles and toilet trainers and small latched gates. We had never discussed having a child. When I turned to wave, he was still leaning against the van.

I started out in a jog, then picked up the pace, and hit what seemed to be about the quarter-mile mark doing a fast easy run. Ahead of me the square of water between the two hotels was undulating with gold. I listened for the sound of Sam's footsteps but heard only the soft taps of my own tennis shoes. The square spread into a rectangle and the sky above it fanned out in ribs of orange and purple silk. I was afraid to look back. I was afraid that if I turned to see him, Sam might recede irretrievably into the merciless gray of the western sky. I slowed down in case I had gone too fast and he wanted to catch up. I concentrated on the water and listened to the still, heavy air. By the time I reached the three-quarters mark, I realized that I was probably running alone.

I hadn't wanted to lose him.

I wondered whether he had waited by the van or was already headed for Newport News. I imagined him at a phone booth calling another woman collect in California, and then I realized that I didn't actually know whether there was another woman or not, but I hoped there was and that she was rich and would send him money. I had caught my second wind and was breathing easily. I looked towards the shore without seeing it and was sorry I hadn't measured the distance and thought to clock it, since now I was running against time and myself, and then I heard him—the unmistakable sound of a sprint and the heavy, whooping intake of his breath. He passed me just as we crossed the main street in front of the hotels, and he reached the water twenty feet ahead of me.

"Goddammit, Day," I said. "You were on the grass, weren't you?" We were walking along the hard, wet edge of the beach, breathing hard. "You were sneaking across those lawns. That's a form of cheating." I drummed his arm lightly with my fists pretending to beat him up. "I slowed down because I thought you weren't there." We leaned over from the waist, hands on our hips, breathing towards the sand. The water rolled up the berm near our feet and flickered like topaz.

"You were always a lousy loser," he said.

And I said, "You should talk."

ᛞ ᛞ ᛞ

A JEAN-MARIE
COOKBOOK

JEFF WEINSTEIN

I STOLE TWO COOKBOOKS and read them when I knew I should be doing other things. I wanted to make a casserole of thinly-sliced potatoes, the non-waxy and non-baking kind, although the dish would be baked in cream. I found out from reading that what I wanted to do was no good unless I rubbed a clove of garlic around the inside of the pot, not that I'm adding the garlic itself, but that the cream seems to imbibe the flavor and hold it until you are ready. It was these fine points I wanted to know, the right and the wrong way to slice, the effective use of spices, why an earthenware dish 'worked' (the way yeast 'works') while a glass one didn't: the secrets of cooking. Some people argue that something should be done a certain way so it will taste a certain way, but how do they know that when they taste a dish they are all tasting the same thing? Experience makes a difference. For example, once I threw up when I ate a noodles and cheese casserole, so I won't eat one again, no matter how good. Experience even tells me how to feel about cooking something like a fried egg sandwich. I make them in bacon fat now, but for a long time I thought only big households with dirty tin cans filled with drippings, or a great constant cook like my friend Kit, could save bacon fat and properly cook with it. For years I would throw the good clear fat down the drain, and I still don't know how or why I changed. It's like baking; I can't bake now, although I read baking recipes and work them through in my head, but only if I see that they apply to someone else, to someone *who can bake*. The most difficult transition I know is to move from one sort of state like that to another, from a person who doesn't bake to one who does. I would like to find out how it is done.

*

It seems that Jean-Marie took on the cloak of 'gay' life in San Diego. He was a graduate student of art, interested in frescoes and teaching French on the side. Then, a year after he whispered he was going to remain celibate, mouthing the word as if he wasn't sure of its pronunciation, he started to skip classes. And one night he walked into the local gay bar, the one where people danced, called the Sea Cruise. At first he walked into the bar with women he knew from school and danced, commandeering them around the floor. Then he came with his old friend Mary, a head taller than he was, and they jerked around, absolutely matched. All this progressed over months; I would see Jean-Marie and Mary every time I was there, which probably means they were at the bar more often than I was. I can be sure they were always there together. I never ate dinner with them but I assume they would try to 'taste' things the same way. Considering their need to think of themselves as alike, the idea of them kissing is interesting. They would want to think they were feeling the same thing, mutual tongues, mutual saliva. Their pleasure would not be mutual, and they would have to avoid thinking about that. Can you like kissing yourself? Can you like kissing someone you falsely imagine to be like yourself? It seems like deception to me, and I wonder why they do it.

*

Good cooking knives are indispensible to good cooking, which I learned by reading. I am told that carbon steel is better than stainless steel, that it wears away and gets more flexible with use, but such knives have to be dried after they are washed, their tips protected by corks, and you are supposed to yell at anyone who uses your knives for opening jars or other obviously damaging things. I don't mean to be facetious here, but apparently knives are important. I stole a set of Sabatier (lion?) knives that I thought were the best, stainless steel, but later I found out about the carbon versus stainless and got a sinking feeling in my stomach, though I also knew I would cherish them less and use them more.

*

Then Jean-Marie discovered men, or males rather, and started dancing with them, kissing them, and going out with them. The first was a sixteen year old boy whose personality was all Jean-Marie's idea, and every time they met his time was spent looking for it, the way Puritans scanned nature to find signs of God. He and Jean-Marie probably did not sleep together, or if they did share a bed sometimes they probably didn't have sex. When this ended, by the boy leaving for San Francisco, Jean-Marie used disappointment as the excuse to pick up guys at the Sea Cruise, first the ones who liked to be mooned at, the quiet regulars, then the drugged-out ones, and then the ones made of stainless steel. He made the transition from gown to town by moving away from school to a dark house in the city, full of wood and plants and no light to read by. He slowly withdrew from the University and backed into San Diego, dropping old associations and living with a different opinion of himself. He sold his car so he could ride the municipal buses, and considered getting food stamps and general relief.

*

Here is a recipe I invented, a variation on scrambled eggs:
    2 eggs at room temperature
    cream, or half-and-half, sour cream, yogurt, though cream is best
    freshly ground black pepper
    a little salt
    butter (not margarine) unsalted butter is best
You take the eggs, beat them well but not frothy, then add a good
lump (I call it a dollop) of cream or whatever, and *stir* it in. Grind in
some pepper, add a little salt. Heat a good frying pan very slowly
(this is important) and melt in it a dollop of butter. When the butter
starts to 'talk' add the egg mixture. Cook it slowly until it starts to
curdle; this takes time, as it should, in the gentle heat. In the
meanwhile get your toast ready and some tea. You can't rush this.
Move the eggs around with a wooden spoon or fork; metal is not
good. When they look done, creamy and solid, turn them into a
warm plate. You may want to throw on some fresh chopped herbs,
watercress, cilantro, parsley, but plain is wonderful. I don't know
why these are a 'variation' on scrambled eggs, but they do taste like
no others. They even come out different every time, although some
people can't tell the difference, and a few people I know won't even
touch them.

*

When I met Jean-Marie on the bus he told me he got a poem
published, and I suspected it was about love:
    His beating heart
    My moist lips, etc.
It *was* about love, in rondelle form, for he hadn't left school as much
as he thought. The next night I had a friend over for dinner. I heard
he was a gourmet so I was nervous to impress him, although I'm not
usually like that. Unfortunately I got home late and had to rush
around to get everything ready, muttering to myself, but all at once I
changed my mind about the matter and decided I was doing something which should be a pleasure, so I stopped worrying about it.
Everything went well, basically because John wasn't much of a
gourmet. We had: sherry, iced mushrooms with lemon juice and no
salt, gratin dauphinois—a simple (hah!) casserole of thinly sliced
washed dried new potatoes so thin that two pieces make the thick-
ness of a penny, baked in a covered earthenware bowl rubbed with

garlic, salted, peppered, and filled with cream. The cover is taken off
towards the end of the baking so a brown crust forms. Eaten right
away, and it was heaven. We were talking about Cretan art. It's
important that the bowl be earthenware, that it be rubbed with
garlic, and that the cream and potatoes come to within ¾ of an inch of
the top of the uncovered casserole. We went up to the roof to grill the
steaks and talked about the view and how odd it was to be in
California. These steaks are called biftecks a la mode du pays de
vaux, grilled and seasoned fillet steaks on a bed of chopped hard-
boiled eggs, fines herbes (I had only dried herbs but I reconstituted
them if you know what I mean), lemon juice, and salt and pepper. I
also added some chopped watercress. Then you heat it all. It was in
this French glass dish I bought when I was so bored I could have
killed myself. I stole the fillets. We drank wine and talked of sex.
Then we had a salad of deveined spinach. He was really impressed;
and I was surprised, both that he was so easily moved and that it all
turned out so nicely. *I* was impressed too.

John brought a dessert, which was a home-baked apple pie, really
a tart, and it was not as good as all that, but I was happy he brought it.
It tasted much better the second day. We made out on the sofa then,
but all of a sudden I got an urge to break away and go dancing, and
John readily agreed. At the bar he fell 'in love' with this beautiful
Spaniard name Paco, who was drunk. They danced a lot together,
badly, but John finally had to take me home. I wondered if he went
back to meet Paco, but I thought not. John said he would see me
when he got back from his trip to the East Coast. I had a dream that
night in which I felt completely perverted and inhuman, and I think
the meal had something to do with it.

*

Jean-Marie, after his year out in San Diego, wrote a long letter
about promiscuity to the San Diego Union, which of course didn't
get printed, although a month after he sent it in they lifted a small
part of it and passed it off as opinion about a case where a lot of men
got arrested in the bathroom of the San Diego May Company, 'for
indiscriminate reasons' the paper said.

Dear Sirs: I am a gay male in San Diego and I want to talk about
sex, or the problem of promiscuity so many of us face. Most of us, gay

or not gay, are looking for someone to love, for a day, a year, or forever, and admittedly this is hard to do. But we have to try. However I don't understand why the only way many of the gay guys in San Diego try is by tricking. For those of you who don't know what tricking means, it's meeting someone, at a gay bar, in the park or on the street, going home and having sexual contact. Sometimes you don't even talk, because it would ruin everything. But when you do start conversations, they all go like this: what's your name (and you give your first name only), where are you from, what do you do, did you see . . . . . (a movie), etc., completely anonymous conversations, which is sad. Why do we do this? I don't really understand why, or why people hang around bathrooms, or even worse. It could be lust, but lust is just a screen for loneliness. Why doesn't the city of San Diego (or all cities) provide a place for people, gay and non-gay, to talk, dance, like a coffeehouse? This has worked elsewhere. But I do think that we as people should honestly question what they are doing. Sometimes I get so sick of what I am doing, going to bars every night, drinking when I don't want to drink, flirting when I don't want to flirt, staying out until two in the A.M. sweating and waiting for the right person, or at that point any person, that I don't know what to do. I could go back to the University, but I know the University is worse. I wonder if I was roped into this. There are some people I meet at the gay bars that I really think should be put away because of the way they act, and treat others. But other times I don't think that at all, and I just feel sorry for them. I wish I understood my appetites better, and I wish the city would do something about it.

*

I have never made a real dessert before, one that requires more than chopping up some fruits and adding whatever liqueurs I have around, so I thought I'd try something out of a cookbook, something called a chocolate bombe. I stuck to that one partly because I liked the name and partly because I like chocolate and also because I had some Mexican vanilla extract which would go well in it. 'Chocolate Bombe' I realized later would make a good title for a screenplay, but it would have to be about food, and very few things are. Food is shown in some movies, like the gourmet concoctions in Hitchcock's *Frenzy* or the banquet in *The Scarlet Empress* or in any number of bakery scenes with pastry on one side of the window and little faces, of boys usually, on the other. But nothing masterful or mature, and I don't think it's because food is silly or insignificant, but because it's hard to visualize people at a meal where food stands for their relationships or essences in some way, like the beef dish in *To The Lighthouse*. How can I say I was 'in the mood' to make something with cream, to watch something gel, to fill the beautiful mold sitting in the cupboard.

After I made the bombe, enough for ten people, there was so much left over that I left the key to my apartment outside the door and asked the couple in the next apartment to go into the freezer and help themselves, which they did, but other people helped themselves to my typewriter and television.

Chocolate Bombe (about ten servings)

Soak 1½ teaspoons of gelatin in one cup of cold water. Stir and bring to the boiling point 1 cup of milk, 1½ cups of sugar, and two tablespoons of unsweetened cocoa. Dissolve the gelatin in the hot mixture. Cool. Add one teaspoon of vanilla extract. Chill until about to set. Whip 2 cups of cream until thickened but not stiff. Fold it lightly into the gelatin mixture. Still-freeze in a lightly-greased mold, and unmold ½ hour before serving.

It tasted rich, although there were too many ice crystals in it. The best part was sampling the gelatin mixture before the cream was added, because it was so sweet and cold, just gelling, redolent of chocolate and Mexican vanilla. By the way, it doesn't come out tasting like pudding or jello; it's full of weight, like home-churned ice cream. It wasn't perfect, but because it came out at all I imagined it was better than it was.

Sometimes I eat because I'm lonely or disappointed. In fact, as I drive away from the bar at night, I tell myself (or the others in the car) it was 'amusing' or 'boring' or 'kinda fun', but almost always at the same point in the turn to the main stretch home I feel a hollow feeling, which, when I recognize it, says I'm hungry, and I look forward to something to eat. It's almost absolutely predictable: the masking talk, the turn, and then the hunger, and often I overeat before I go to bed. The few times I've gone home with someone from the bar I've been hungry in the same way, so I assume these sexual episodes aren't really happy ones. Sometimes I've been nauseous, but that's a different feeling for different reasons. I've gone home with only one person who offered me a full breakfast in the morning or who lived as if he cooked himself full meals. That was in New York

City, with a very nice guy who just wanted to fuck me and get me to
sniff amyl. He did get up early, and seemed to be making a lot of
money, although the only thing I can remember about how he spent
it was a really hideous gilt and glass table in his living room, and the
fact that he bought towels at Bloomingdale's the afternoon before,
spending more than a hundred dollars. The towels were hanging in
the bathroom without even having been washed. We took a taxi
home to his place, I remember now, I wasn't hungry and only
slightly sick to my stomach. I ate underripe bananas with a guy I was
'in love' with, but he was angry because I couldn't fuck him. And
once, in Denver, the only thing I found in the refrigerator of this guy
who picked me up, fucked me, and fell asleep at eight in the evening
was one of those mealy chocolate flavored wafers you use to gain
weight if you eat them with things or lose weight if you eat them
alone. There was literally nothing else in there. I forgot about
David. David made me a poached egg which tasted slightly of the
vinegar in the water, on whole wheat toast, and fresh juice, and tea. I
had many more of those breakfasts, even though we didn't have sex,
but I loved to sleep with David, and still would if we hadn't had that
fight about a story I wrote concerning him.

*

Jean-Marie became more and more bitter about his life, although
he didn't realize to what extent he was excluding himself from his
old friends, and especially from women. The world looks cruel when
you concentrate only upon the males you know or want to know, and
women become generalized and ignored, somehow peripheral.
Jean-Marie got sick of this but he didn't know why, and none of his
new friends could tell him. Certainly he was less stiff after a year in
the Sea Cruise, and sloughed around the dance floor as if he had
done it before, but . . .

But, he said, I'm special. I am a feminine man, and that's good, even
better than being a woman. He would peer into mirrors, for mirrors
were all over the walls of the rooms he haunted, and play with
disconnecting 'Jean-Marie' from the little boy he grew up with. His
head would twist and arch, one shoulder would rise, his nostrils
flared as he imagined what could be possible. He never looked
further down than his neck, and avoided parts of himself like his
nose or the jut of his ears. Certainly he was bitter because he

couldn't store this mirror-feeling, when his blood rushed and he could do anything. It wasn't vanity, this play in front of mirrors, nothing was being judged or compared, except perhaps the old with the new.

Oh ugh hmm. Do you really think so? Really I couldn't how could I? It wouldn't work . . . do you think so? Hmmm well. In far Peru there lived a llama he had no papa he had no mama he had no wife he had no chillun he had no use for penicillin . . . Jesus . . . yes of course I can come when do you want me . . . the brie please . . . fine I'll leave anytime of course but will they understand my English yes I know how important it is . . . God you're cute and you've gained weight hummph why do I get so much pleasure out of this . . . it's true isn't it.

*

I have made some errors in cooking, but these aren't nearly as important as errors in menu, or rather in the meal. I just heard of someone who swallowed a handful of aspirin, which made her sick. People are constantly eating to make themselves sick, to poison themselves, poison others, to forget, or to die. Someone once said stupidity takes corporeal form. I seem to have an aptitude for planning a happy meal, the combination of people, appetites, and what I called the 'attitude' of the food: the amounts, the way a hot dish is followed by a cool one, the interplay or colors, the sequence of dishes and their values. I do this best when I am alone because people eating at my house sometimes make me nervous, and although I plan the food, I can never plan the run of old friendships at a dinner table. There's a whole history of ruining meals; in certain places, if you wanted to get even with a family you ground up the bones of their bird or some other possession into the food you served to them—it's a way of breaking up hospitality. One example of this was a stew which consisted of the guests' children. People no longer realize the potential power in the act of sharing food, but they do suffer from the consequences whether or not they're aware of it. The menu of the most awful meal I ate:

mulligatawny soup and saltines
three bean salad

'oven-fried' chicken, I had the drumstick
mashed potatoes
green beans with butter
white bread and butter
ice cream and sugar wafers

There was something wrong with the soup but I didn't know what;
it tasted bitter, not from any single ingredient but from the expression on the face of the person who stirred it. Really. It was bitter
exactly the way a person is, in its 'sweat'. After the soup I said
something nasty to a guest who was invited just to meet me, and
everyone was embarrassed and tried to cover up. Mel belched out
loud and George got annoyed but didn't say anything; he merely
stabbed at his chicken and pushed it away. Judy spilled her milk on
my pants, accidentally I'm sure, so I had to get up and change. When
I got back George wasn't speaking to Nancy, and Mel was winking
and nodding with no subtlety at all across the table. It could be that
there were too many of us in the room, but we all had the same bad
taste in our mouths.

I once had breakfast (brunch) in a gay bar, waiting an hour for a
plate of bacon, two vulcanized eggs, and the pre-hashed potatoes
that get scraped around a hot surface for a few minutes until their
fetid water evaporates and they take on some color. Someone I didn't
know was rubbing my knee and my only friend there kept drinking
those morning drinks that make you anticipate evening, while the
air smelled of the night before. How could I eat? I did eat, ravenously, but managed only by insisting to myself that except for my
appetite I wasn't at all like the others around me. How long would
that last? One more meal there could do the trick, so I swore I'd
never eat at that bar again. I went home alone and looked at myself in
the mirror to see if I had changed, for the grease from the potatoes
was already beginning to appear on my forehead.

*My God no. If you put a flower in a vacuum all its essence leaves.
The fog might just be getting tired and collapsing into puddles . . .
grease . . . damp . . . those little flakes of skin sticking in patches,
nothing to show for all that reading, nothing to wear that fits, too big
or too small and who can keep up with all that sewing even when I
sew it unravels around my stitches. I'll throw it all out.*

*

Two Mirror Snacks

1) bacon fat or a mixture of butter and oil, not too much, a few
   small potatoes, boiled in their skins (leftovers are best) one
   or two peeled and crushed cloves of garlic the pulp, fresh or
   canned, of one tomato plenty of basil
   optional: cut pitted black olives, about 6
             a few sliced mushrooms
             a few celery leaves

Heat the fat or oil and butter in a small frying pan until very hot, put
in the potatoes and mix them around, breaking them into chunks but
not mashed. Add the garlic and some coarse salt if you have it,
stirring constantly until they take on some color. Add the rest of the
ingredients in any order you like (I add the olives last). Don't stir
towards the end, so the bottom burns a little. Turn out onto a plate,
add salt and freshly ground black pepper to your taste, and eat with
white wine or beer. Be sure to scrape all the burnt particles and
grease out with a spoon and eat them.

2) (you need a blender for this one)an egg
   a few big spoonfuls of plain yogurt
   enough wheat germ to cover it, but not more than a Tbsp.
   a good ripe banana, broken into pieces
   one cup of any mixture of:milk, half & half, fruit juice
   ½ tsp. of real vanilla extract (try Mexican vanilla)
   some sweetner, honey, sugar, ice cream, just a bit
   optional: a few spoons of protein powder
             a spoon of soy lecithin
             a tsp. of polyunsaturated flavorless oil

Add to the blender in the order mentioned, but don't fill to more
than ²/₃ capacity. Most protein powder tastes awful, so add only as
much as you think you need. Non-instant dried milk is a good
substitute. Blend at low speed for a few seconds, uncover, make sure
the wheat germ isn't sticking in clumps to the yogurt, and scrape the
now agglutinated protein powder off the sides of the blender and
repulverize, all with a rubber spatula. Smell it, taste it, add more of
what you think it needs. Cover and blend at medium speed for half a
minute. Have right away or refrigerate, but it will settle. Sometimes

I add an envelope of chocolate flavored instant breakfast or some powdered chocolate because the chocolate and orange juice (if that's your juice) taste great together. Fruit jam is also good. Obviously this recipe can take a lot of things, but remember your purpose.

Note that each mirror snack is a different response to feeling bad.

*

In his response to the bar, or in his response to the person he was afraid of becoming, Jean-Marie resorted to interests connected neither to school nor to the bar life he was now trying to avoid. He taught himself to knit, but when he found himself mooning over pictures of models in scarves and sweaters, he realized he didn't want to. Then he thought he'd learn to cook, revolted by the cold stupid meals he fixed for himself and by his unquestioning dependence on others for anything hot. One evening he had dinner with some of his University friends, baked ham and guacamole salad, for old times' sake. After dinner Jean-Marie asked them to try and describe the worst meal each of them could remember. He was stunned by his boldness—he never started things—but he was comfortable after the food and sat back to listen.

As they talked, Jean-Marie thought this was the most interesting conversation he'd heard since he left the University. He hated school, hated the lab scientists and art professors and the pretty jock behind the locker room cage who demeaned every woman as soon as she walked away. Yet even though the gay people at the Sea Cruise were gentle, they were more miserable with their lives than any group of people he knew. It was 'they' now, but tomorrow it could be 'we'. What could he do? Could he straddle the two and possibly be happy? He was beginning to guess that happiness isn't the issue here, and survival is more crucial. 'In what way' he thought 'is survival related to being happy?'

*

The most difficult dishes in any cookbook are the 'everyday' recipes, luncheon, bruncheon, egg, family dishes, cooking for survival when you have more important things to do or don't have much

money. Let's assume you don't have a family to feed but haven't
much time and want to be happy with what you are eating. Here is a
list of staples for 'everyday' meals:

milk
eggs, bought fresh a few at a time if possible
onions
oil or bacon drippings (bacon)
a little butter, unsalted
tomatoes, fresh and canned
garlic
cheap greens, vegetables in season
some cheese
bread, or flour to bake it
fresh boiling potatoes
chicken, all parts of it
lemons, possibly oranges
salt, black pepper
beer or wine

Staples are defined here not as what you need, but as what holds
things together. I know this list assumes there is an 'everyday'. Some
people, I know, have to cadge their next meal, for a place to prepare
it, for a place to eat. These are people you should ask in for a meal, if
possible.

I asked Jean-Marie to dinner. We agreed, although I don't remember why, to have a cooking contest. The rules were to prepare a
menu. We would each cook our own menu and then each other's,
which would take four nights. We decided on a judge who needed
the meals but who also understands more about food than anyone we
knew without being disgusting.

Jean-Marie's menu, using the staple list, one good piece of flesh or
fowl, some extra money, and one day's work:

consomme, iced, with chervil
carrotes marinees
boned leg of lamb, mustard coating (gigot a la moutarde)
boiled new potatoes with parsley butter

    sliced iced tomatoes with basil and olive oil
    orange pieces flambe
    cafe espresso
    the meal is served with a good French red wine'

My menu, with the same 'limitations':

    cream of potato and watercress soup
    stuffed mushrooms
    cucumbers and lemon juice
    roast duck with tangerine stuffing, lemon glaze
    parsley garnish
    garlic mashed potatoes
    spinach and cilantro salad, lemon juice dressing
    strawberry lemon ices
    the meal is served with cold Grey Riesling (California)

See appendix for comments on the selections. These are expensive meals, requiring not only food but many utensils and a lot of heat and cold (energy).

Jean-Marie and I met our judge, J., at my house the first evening, where I cooked my menu. J. said very little as we ate, although at one point he asked me for my recipe for stuffed mushrooms and their history:

Edythe's Stuffed Mushrooms

'My mother invented these one night when she ran out of clams to stuff. My father was rather demanding about the food their party guests (or rather his party guests) were served, and although my mother prided herself on her stuffed clams, it was still sort of slave-work for her. This is not to say that my father didn't like to cook—he did—but he would not clean up after his filth, to use my mother's words. She liked these mushrooms, which were moist and tasty, and I took her recipe and adjusted it to my tastes:

    large open mushrooms, the bigger the better, 3 per person
    at least one bunch of parsley
    juice of one lemon
    6 or so cloves of garlic, peeled

one or two cans of minced clams, drained
seasoned bread crumbs, Italian style
basil, fresh or dried
coarse salt
freshly ground black pepper
olive oil
plenty of freshly grated parmesan and/or romano cheese

The reason the quantities are vague is because I never measured them; the frying pan, a good heavy one, should determine the amount of everything. It almost always works out, and any leftover stuffing is delicious, although it should be refrigerated so you don't get food poisoning. The tricky part of this dish is making sure the mushrooms don't dry out, and all the soaking is for this purpose. Carefully twist the stems out of the mushrooms, so you are left with the intact cap and gills. Reserve the stems. With a spoon scrape the gills and all excess stuff out of the caps, so you are left with little bowls. As you finish this process, eating any mushrooms you may have broken, place the caps in a large bowl of cool water into which you've squirted the lemon juice. The mushrooms will soak in this; the acid prevents them from turning too brown. Mince the parsley flowerettes. Mince the garlic. Now, take each mushroom stem, chop off and discard the woody half, the part which stuck in the ground, and dice the remaining halves. Grate your cheese. Heat the frying pan slowly, then add at least ¼ inch of olive oil. This may seem like a lot, but it's necessary. When the oil gets fragrant, add the garlic. Before the garlic browns, add the clams and saute. Add the minced mushrooms, stirring constantly, the parsley, and keep cooking. Make sure nothing burns. Add salt, pepper, and enough bread-crumbs to soak up the excess clam and mushroom liquid. The basil should have been crushed and thrown in some time before; do add quite a bit. The stuffing should now be loose and moist but not liquid, and very hot. Remove from heat, and add most of your grated cheese, reserving some. Stir it all, and put it aside. If you think the mushrooms have soaked long enough, take each one out, shake out the water, and with a spoon put the stuffing in. Do this with a light hand and keep the stuffing as particulate as possible. Stuff all the mushrooms. Now, if you must, you can leave them sit for a while (do not refrigerate), but it is best to immediately put them into a lightly greased broiling dish, having preheated your oven or broiler sometime before, arrange touching in some kind of pattern, salt the tops, sprinkle with grated cheese and maybe a little olive oil, and run them under a hot broiler or in a very hot oven until both the stuffing is completely heated and the tops of the caps are not too tough and brown; it is an exact point. By that time the water in the mushrooms should have just steamed them, so they are perfectly cooked, neither raw and brittle nor rubbery and slick. If you want to be fancy, place the mushrooms, before you broil them, on a bed of carefully washed and deveined leaves of spinach, and broil them together. Some of the mushroom juice will run out onto the perfectly cooked spinach, which can be used to sop it all up.'

On the first evening Jean-Marie paled a bit when he tasted my mushrooms, perhaps because he didn't know how easy they were to make. On the second night Jean-Marie cooked, and we both knew our food was good, so this time we talked nicely and forgot the pretense of competition.

'But I know Louis the 15th had a head shaped like a pear.'

I should note that I did not tell our judge who cooked what. J. ate well, asking us to save portions of everything, so by the fourth night there should be two versions each of two different meals, three in miniature. Of course we were sickened at the prospect of so much rich food, but the concept of a cooking contest was still strange enough to be interesting. On the fourth night we talked about writing cookbooks and tasted a little bit of everything. Jean-Marie managed to make the mushrooms but could not even fake the ices, and my version of his marinated carrots was pale and sticky.

I say this in retrospect because at some point in our meal I couldn't tell what food was mine, or where it came from. Jean-Marie looked contemplative and sick. Our judge was so quiet we didn't see him most of the time. The courses were served by ghosts. Critical faculties must have faded, and we thought only of parody and death.

The grotesque prudishness and archness with which garlic is treated in this country has led to the superstition that rubbing the bowl with it before putting the salad in gives it sufficient flavor. It rather depends whether you are going to eat the bowl or the salad.

Jean-Marie left, J. left, I was left sitting alone not knowing when they had gone. There was a note:

I cannot tell the difference among your dishes because each bite was a universe. Why do you insist so much on difference and comparison? I was so happy to be eating, and it was all good food, that my joy overran any pose of judgment. When you cook something, and put it aside, how do you know who cooked it? Who were you that day? Who could have doctored the food, soured it, stolen it away and left a note of gibberish in its place? Certainly you can write a cookbook, but could it possibly predict a meal? It's an odd mirror to stare into, with no certainty in it. There was a point when I almost swallowed a bone, and some sherbet dribbled down my chin and stained the tablecloth. Did you notice? Would you have cooked that meal, or any meal, if I hadn't been there to eat it? Will your tablecloth wash out? (No matter, I blotted up the spill.) I do think you expect too much, but I would be pleased if you arranged your life so you could continue to cook. However I don't see that a cookbook could be anything but a reflection of imagined life, which is not a bad thing. I'd be happy to visit you again.

APPENDIX

Jean-Marie comments on his menu:
My menu is mainly French, relying on the good fresh vegetables of Southern California. The cold soup whets your appetite, the marinated carrots, which is a French country specialty, excites your now raging hunger and prepares your palate for the mustard flavor of the lamb. After all that cold stuff, the lamb and hot simple potatoes are a happy change. The red wine supports and is not pushed over by the strong flavors of the main dish. People should be talking at this point, as soon as the initial gobbling has stopped. The iced tomatoes provide color, if the conversation doesn't, and the basil is yet another welcome flavor. After a pause (which I never think is long enough) the oranges cool your mouths, 'degrease them' so to speak, and the espresso should be strong and black.

Comments on the other menu:
These are things I like. If the duck doesn't smoke up the whole house it can be quite a surprise, because people don't expect duck the way they expect chicken or lamb. The spinach and cilantro salad is also a surprise (especially if you don't wash the spinach enough) but seri-

ously people see the blue-green leaves of the spinach and think it's lettuce but the light is funny, and then the cilantro, a lighter yellow-green, flashes like little bits of afterglow or whatever that visual phenomenon is called. And when they eat it, it's the same thing, because all the bland cuddy spinach juice is punctuated by the herb, utterly unexpected. Ices cool everyone after the duck. The menu works; I don't have to explain exactly why, do I? By the way, Jean-Marie shouldn't repeat the mustard of the carrots in his lamb.

NOW I AM MARRIED

MARY GORDON

I AM THE SECOND WIFE, which means that, for the most part, I am spoken *to*. This is the first visit of my marriage and I am introduced around, to everyone's slight embarrassment. There is an unspoken agreement among people not to mention *her*, except in some clear context where my advantage is obvious. It would be generous of me to say that I wish it were otherwise, but I appreciate the genteel silences, and, even more, the slurs upon her which I recognize to be just. I cannot attempt to be fair to her: justice is not the issue. I have married, and this is an act of irrational and unjust loyalty. I married for this: for the pleasure of one-sidedness, the thrill of the bias, the luxury of saying, "But he is my husband, you see," and thereby putting to an end whatever discussion involves us.

337

My husband is English and we are staying in the house of his family. We do not make love here as we do at my mother's. She thinks sex is wicked, which is, of course, highly aphrodisiac, but here it is considered merely in bad taste. And as I lie, looking at the slope of my husband's beautiful shoulder, I think perhaps they are right. They seem to need much less sleep than I do, to be able to move more quickly, to keep their commitments with less fuss. I wish I found the English more passionate; surely there is nothing so boring as the reinforcement of a stereotype. But it is helpful to be considered Southern here; I am not afraid to go out on the street as I am in Paris or Rome, because all the beautiful women make me want to stay under the sharp linen of my hotel. No, here I feel somehow to have a great deal of color, which has, after all, to do with sex. The young girls I can see already turning into lumpish women in raincoats with cigarettes drooping from their lips. This, of course, makes it much easier. Even my sister-in-law's beauty is so different that it cannot really hurt me; it is the ease of centuries of her race's history that gave it to her, and to this I cannot hope to aspire.

Yesterday we went to a charity bazaar. One of the games entailed scooping marbles up with a plastic spoon and putting them through the hole of an overturned flower pot. My sister-in-law went first. Her technique was to take each marble, one at a time, and put it through the hole. Each one went neatly in. When it was my turn, I perceived the vanity of her discretion and my strategy was to take as many marbles as I could on the spoon and shovel them into the hole as quickly as possible. A great number of the marbles scattered on the lawn; but quite a few went into the hole, and, because I had lifted so many, my score was twelve; my sister-in-law's five. But both of us were pleased with our own performance, and appreciative of the rival technique.

I am very happy here. Yesterday in the market I found an eggplant: a rare and definite miracle for this part of the world. Today for dinner I made *ratatouille*. This morning I took my sister-in-law's basket and went out, married, to the market. I don't think that marriage has changed me, but for the first time, the salespeople appreciated, rather than resented, the time I took in choosing only the most heartwarming tomatoes, the most earnest and forthright meat. I was no longer a fussy bachelorette who cooked only sometimes and at her whim. I was a young matron in stockings and high heels. My selections, to them, had something to do with the history

they were used to. They were important; they were not for myself. I
had wanted to write this morning, but I had the responsibility of
dinner, served at one. I do not say this in complaint. I was quite
purely happy in my basket and my ring, in the approval of the
shopkeepers and the pedestrians. I am never so happy writing. It is
not that the housewife's tasks are in themselves repugnant: many of
them involve good smells and colors, satisfying shapes, and the
achievement of dexterity. They kill because they are not final. They
must be redone although they have just been finished. And so I am
doing this rather than polishing the beautiful Jacobean furniture
with the sweet-smelling lavendar wax. I am doing this because I am
dying, so that I will not die.

Marjorie

"Bring her in for a cup of coffee," I said to him. I saw you on the
street and you were so happy looking. Not me and my husband.
Dead fifteen years and a bloodier hypocrite never walked. I pretended I was sorry when he died, but believe me I was delighted.
He was a real pervert, all those public school boys won't do anything
for you till they're beaten, don't let them tell you anything about the
French, my dear.

I was just in France. I was kind of like an *au pair* girl to this
Communist bloke, only he was a millionaire. Well, they had a great
house with a river behind it and every day I'd meet the mayor of the
town there, both of us throwing our bottles from the night before
into the river. They had men go round with nets to gather up the
bottles and sell them. They know how to live there. The stores are all
empty here. Not that I'm much of a cook. We start our sherry here as
soon as we get up. Your coffee all right? Have a biscuit. I'll have one
too. I shouldn't . . . look at me around the middle. I'm getting to
look quite middle-aged, but there's some life in me yet, I think,
don't you?

Look at your husband sitting there with his blue eyes just as
handsome. Fancied him once myself, but he hadn't time for me.
Keep an eye on him, dear, he's got young girls in front of him all day.
Oh, I don't envy you that job. They must chase him all the time,
dear, don't they. Cheer up, a little jealousy puts spice in a marriage,
don't you think?

Well, there's a real witch hunt out for me in this building. I've taken in all the boys around town that've got nowhere to go. Just motherly. All of them on drugs, sleeping out every night. Well, my policy is not to chivvy and badger them. Tried marijuana myself once but I didn't get anything out of it because I didn't smoke it properly. But they all have a home here and I do them heaps more good than some virginal social worker with a poker you know where. Of course the old ladies around here don't like it. Mrs. Peters won't forgive me since I was so drunk that night and I broke into her house and started dancing with her. A poor gormless girl she's got for a daughter, afraid of her own shadow. Starts to shake if you as much as say good morning to her. Thirty-five, she is, if she's a day. Pious, that one. I've seen her chatting up the vicar every evening. You know what *she* needs. My husband was a parson. He was plagued with old maids. I'd 'uv been delighted if he'd rolled one down in my own bedroom just so's he'd leave me alone. Bloody great pervert, he was. And sanctimonious! My God. He looked like a stained glass window to the outsiders. And all the old biddies in the town following him around calling him father. Not me. I'd like to tell you what I called him.

Anyway, all the old bitches here think they can get me thrown out, but they're very much mistaken. This building happens to be owned by the Church of England, of which my husband happened to be a pillar. My pension comes from there, you know. Well, my dear, of course they can't throw one of the windows of the clergy out on her sanctified arse, so I'm really quite safe for the moment.

That's why I wouldn't get married again. I wouldn't give up that bloody pension for the life of me. I'll see they pay it to me till I die, the bloody hypocrites. "Yes, Mrs. Pierce, if you'd conduct your life in a manner suitable to a woman of your position." Bugger'em, I say. They're all dust, same as me.

No, I'm quitting Charlie. I've been with him five years but I must say the rigamarole is becoming trying. His wife sits home with their dachshunds, Wallace and Willoughby, their names are—did you ever hear anything so ridiculous—Wallace—and occasionally she'll ring up and say, "Is Charlie Waring there?" and I'll say, "Who? You must have the wrong number." Five years. It's getting ridiculous.

I think I'll take myself down to the marriage bureau. Thirty quid it costs for a year, and they supply you with names till you're satisfied. Of course, at my age what d'ye have left? And I'd want somebody respectable, you know, not just anybody. Of course you meet men in pubs, but never the right sort, are they? My dear, you wouldn't believe what I come home with some nights, I'm that hard up.

Anyway, Lucinda's sixteen and she's already on her second abortion. How she gets that way I don't know. She simply walked out of school. Told one of the teachers off when she told her to take off her makeup. She said to her, "My mother doesn't pay you to shout at me." Dried-up old bitches those teachers were. Of course, in point of fact, it's not me or her that's paying, it's the Church, but just the same, I see her point. They'll never want her more than they want her now, right. Isn't it true, they won't let us near a man till we're practically too old to enjoy one. Well, I've got her a Dutch cap now, though I don't suppose she'll use it. I never did. That's why I've got five offsprings. I'm sure I don't know what to do with them. Anyway, she's working part-time answering telephones for some lawyer and I'm sure he's got her flat on her back on his leather couch half the time. Smashing looking Indian chap. But it's pocket money for her. And we don't get along badly, the way some do. I give her her own way and if she gets into trouble we sort it out somehow. I suppose she'll get married in a year or so, only I hope it's not a fool or a hypocrite. Bloody little fool I was at her age. My dear, on my wedding night I didn't know what went where or why. Don't ask how I was so stupid. Of course my mother was a parson's wife too and I think she thought if she said the word sex the congregation would burn her house down. Dead right she *was*.

Well, you certainly are an improvement over the other one he was married to. My dear, she thought she could run everyone's life for them. Knew me a week and she came over one morning and said, uninvited, "Marjorie, you should get up earlier. Why don't you watch the educational programs on the telly." "Bugger off," I said and she never came near me again.

Well, I have to go off and see one of my old ladies. This one keeps me in clothes, so I've got to be attentive. Let me tell you, if you could see how respectable I am in front of her, my dear, you wouldn't believe. Well, I take her cashmere sweaters and hope the constable won't see me on the way out. One visit keeps Lucinda and me in clothes for a year. I don't care, it cheers her up, the poor old bugger. Hope someone'll be as good to me when I'm that age. But I'll probably be a cross old drunk, and I bloody well won't have any spare Dior gowns in my closet, that's sure.

You don't mind if I give your husband a kiss goodbye. Lovely. Oh, perhaps I'll just take another one. Fancied him myself at one time. Well, you're the lucky one, aren't you? Come over again, perhaps you could come for a meal, though what I could cook nowadays I'm sure I don't know. I don't suppose that would set well with the family. Can't say that I blame them, they have to live here. Well, slip in some time on the QT and I'll dig you out some tea. Make it afternoon, though, dears, I don't like mornings, though I'm ever so glad of your company.

Doris

I don't go anywhere by myself now. Three weeks ago I got a car but I took it back. I was so lonely driving. That was the worst. I think I'm afraid of everybody and everything now. I'm always afraid there's men walking behind me. I won't even go to post a letter in the evening. I was always afraid of the dark. My mother knew I was afraid of the dark so she made me sleep with the light off. She said if I kept on being afraid of the dark God wouldn't love me.

Of course, it's all so different now George is gone. People are like things, d'ye know what I mean? They're very nice, of course, and they do care for me and call, but it's all I don't know, shallow like. Of course, I do prefer the company of men. Not that I run down my own sex, but men are gentler, somehow, don't you think. The first month after George was gone all I could think about was who could I marry now. But now I look back on it I shudder, d'ye know what I mean. George bein' so sick and all that we didn't have a physical relationship for many years. And men like to be naughty. Sometimes, though, I do enjoy a man's companionship. After George lost his leg he said, "I can't give you much in the way of the physical, Mother." But we were terribly close, really. Talked about everything. He would insist on having his chair here by the door so's he could see everybody coming in. I used to kid him a lot about it. Winter and summer, never come close to the fire. He'd sit right there by the door, winter and summer. And Gwen would sit on the settee at night and never go out. I used to say to her, "Gwen, you must go out. Go to the cinema." But she was afraid, like, to leave her father. Even though I was here. She was afraid if she went out he'd be gone when she got back.

Of course, it was very hard on the children. It'll take them years to sort it out, I suppose. Perhaps they'll never sort it out. Gwen went down to eight stone. Bonnie she looked, but I was worried. Then she got these knots-like in her back and she stopped going to work altogether. Said she couldn't face the tubes anymore. She hated it; bein' smothered-like, she said, it was terrifying. But I think she wanted to be home with Daddy so we let her come home.

Colin has a lovely job now. Got a hundred blokes under him. But they're afraid he'll go back to university and quit so they don't pay him properly. He almost took a degree in logic but he broke down after two years. You should see his papers. Lovely marks on 'em. His professors said if he sat right down he'd come away with a first. But he got too involved, if you know what I mean. Forgot there was a world around him.

He's had a lot of lovely girls, and I guess he's had his fling, but I don't think he'll ever marry. After George died he said, "I don't know how to put it, Mum, but I'm just not that interested in sex." Once a few years ago he came out to the breakfast table. He was white as a ghost, I was worried. He said he felt a kind of calling. He was terrified, he said; he was sure God was calling him to his service. Well, George held his tongue and so did I. He asked Colin what it felt like and Colin said, "Don't ask me to describe it, Dad." He had a lot of sleepless nights and we called the vicar and he took him to the place where the young men go for the priesthood and Colin said that he liked it, but when the time came he never did go.

Him and his father were great pals. Colin of course was studying Western philosophy and he was very keen on it and George just as keen on the Eastern. Oh, they would argue and George would say, "Just read this chapter of the book I'm reading" and Colin would say, "I'm not interested, Dad." Then after George died he took all his books away with him to Bristol. I said, "I thought you weren't interested." He said, "I really always was, Mum."

Lynnie's going to be a mother in September. I'm not really keen on being a grandmother. I'm interested in my daughter; she's an adult. I'm not interested in babies. I've never seen anyone like her for being cheerful, though. That girl cannot be made miserable, not even for an hour. I'm sure it'll be a girl, the way she holds her back when she walks, straightlike. I suppose I'll be interested in it when it's born.

George had a kind of miraculous effect on people, though. One time our vicar asked him to address a group of young people. Four hundred of them there was, packed the house with chairs, they did.

And up on the stage one big armchair for George. One night I made them all mugs of tea, there must have been fifteen of them here on the floor. Half of them admitted they were on drugs. Purple hearts, goofballs, whatever they call them nowadays. And when they left here they said they were all right off them now.

Of course, he had this good friend, the bachelor vicar, Arthur. Like a father to him George was. A very intelligent man, but a terrible lot of problems. Spent all his time here, he did. He'd stay here till two o'clock on Sunday morning and then go home and write his sermons. Said George all but wrote his sermons for him. Once he told me he was jealous of George having me and me having George. Said it was the one thing he could never have. And him a wealthy man. His father had a big engineering firm in Dorset and a great house. Three degrees he has, too. But I think he's really like they say, neurotic. He *cannot* express his feelings. Me and George we told each other everything. We kept no secrets. Not Arthur, though. He's taken me out to dinner twice since George died, but I like plain food, d'ye know what I mean, and he took me out to this Japanese restaurant with Geisha girls and God knows what. Well, they gave me so much I sent half of it back and they said was there something Madame didn't like and I about died of shame. I think old Arthur's knocking but I'm not at home to him. Of course he's a wonderful priest, the kids in the youth group love him. He cried during the whole funeral service. I was so mortified. And he will not mention George's name. He says he can't forgive God for taking George.

I used to feel that way but I don't any more. When George was in so much pain-like, I'd go to the Communion rail and shake my fist at Christ on the Cross and say, "What d'ye know about suffering? You only suffered one day. My George has suffered years." I don't feel that way now. I think there's a reason for it, all that pain, even. George died without one drug in his body, he had that much courage.

Well, I guess I'll be getting you a bath. It's good you've come. You'll never regret the man you've married. George thought the world of him. We've only water enough for one bath. So one takes it tonight and one tomorrow. George and I used to bathe in the same water, but I think we were different from most.

I feel like I've known you all my life. I knew you'd be like this from the letters. Old friends they were, my man and yours. You're not like the first wife. She was a hard one, that one. Ice in her veins.

Perhaps I'll come and visit you in America. I have a job now at the hospital and three weeks holiday in July. Perhaps I'll come out to visit you. But what would I do the two of you out working. I hate to impose, you know. We used to have friends, widows they were and we'd invite them over and they'd say, "Oh, no thanks, we'd be odd man out." I never knew what they meant but now I know. Look at me talking. I can't even go to Epping by myself, and Lynnie made the trip when she was eight. Perhaps if you found out all the details for me. Wouldn't it be something!

It's good having someone in the house at night. I usually sleep with all the lights on, I'm that frightened on my own. I think I'm getting better with the job and all. But sometimes I'm very empty-like, and cold.

Elizabeth

I like living here on my own. Dear lord, who else could I live with? Like old Miss Bates, she lived with another teacher, for, oh, twenty years it must have been. They bought a dear little house in the Cotswolds to live in for their retirement. Lived there a year and up pops some cousin who'd been wooing Miss Campbell for forty years and off they go and get married. Well, Amelia Bates was furious and she wouldn't speak to Miss Campbell and they'd been like sisters for twenty years. Well, poor Miss Campbell died six months later and there's Amelia Bates on her own in that vast house full of regrets and sorrow.

Here's a picture of me in Algeria in 1923. Oh, I had a beautiful ride over on the ship, it took three days. Some people took a trip just to drink all the way, people are foolish. The first night I lay in my cabin and the ship was creaking so badly I was sure it was the end of me. I went up top and the waves were crashing around the deck and they said, "You'd better go down below, Miss," and that's where I met Mr. Saunders. Don't let the others in the family act so proud to you. When I found out that Ethel had cut you, ooh, I was angry. I wrote her a very cross letter. Her mum and dad were separated for years and he was living with a half-caste woman in India and afraid to even write his wife a letter. Of course, he should have left her and stayed with that other woman but he didn't have that much courage. He's been miserable ever since. Poor old Lawrence, he's a decent

old boy but terrified to death of Millie. You know she was just a
governess for his family when he fell in love with her. She was
good-looking, though, the best looking of all of us. Well, poor old
Lawrence when he came to Mt. Olympus (that was the name of my
father's house, dear. It fulfilled the ambitions of a lifetime for him)
well, when he came to Mt. Olympus to meet the family he came
down with malaria and was sick in bed for a month. Had to have his
meals brought up to him and his sheets changed three times a day.
Well, after that there was no getting out of it, he was quite bound.
Not that he thought of getting out of it then. People simply didn't in
those days, and that's why so many of them were so unhappy. I'm
sure things are much better now, in some ways, but nobody seems
much happier anyway, do they?

Here is a picture of the family I worked for in India. Now even I
had my mild scandal I suppose. It wasn't so mild to father. Millie
came home from India and told dear father a great tale. Father wrote
to Mr. Saunders and demanded that I be sent home. Then he wrote
to me and said I must come back upon my honour as his daughter
and an Englishwoman. We simply didn't answer the letters. Mr.
Saunders hid them in a parcel in his desk drawer and I simply threw
mine in the fire. Then Mr. Saunders took the family back to England
and I went back to Mt. Olympus. Father told me I must take a new
name and tell everyone I was married, that I was the widow of an
officer. I refused; I told him no one knew but him and Millie. Then
we never spoke of it.

I started a kindergarten then for the children in the town. Here is
the picture of the first class and here's one of your husband as a baby.
Wasn't he golden? Then mother got sick and I had to give it up.
Nobody took it on after that, it was a pity, really. I regretted that.

Here's a picture of cousin Norman. Doesn't he look a bounder?
Wrote bad checks and settled in Canada. He's a millionaire today.

I'm giving you these spoons as a wedding gift. They belonged to
my grandmother's grandmother. I think it's nice to have a few old
things. It makes you feel connected, somehow, don't you think?

I only hope my mind holds out on me. I love to read and I wouldn't
care if I were bedridden as long as my mind was all right. Mother
was all right for some time and then when she was in her seventies
she just snapped. She didn't recognize anybody in the family and
one night she came at Father with a knife and said he was trying to
kill her. We had to put her in the hospital then. It was supposed to

be the best one in England but it was awful. There were twenty women in a room not this size and in the evenings you could hear them all weeping and talking to themselves. It would have driven me quite mad and I was sane. Then she said the nurses were all disguising themselves to confuse her, and they were tyring to poison her. And then she said they wouldn't let her wash, and she was dirty and smelt ill. Well, we finally took her back home and father wouldn't let anyone see her. I gave up my position (I was working for that woman who writes those trashy novels that sell so well. And her daughter was an absolute hellcat) and came home. She'd call me every few minutes and say, "Elizabeth, what will we do if anyone comes? There isn't a speck of food in the house." And I would tell her no one would be coming. Then she'd say, "Elizabeth, what will we do if anyone comes, the house is so dirty." And it would go on like that. Sometimes she wouldn't eat for days, and sometimes she would stuff herself till she was quite ill. She died of a stomach obstruction in the end, but that was years later. Every night father would go in to her and say goodnight and kiss her and she was hurting us all. But sometimes she would just be her old self and joke with us after supper and play the piano and sing or read—she loved the Brontës—and we'd think she was getting better, perhaps. But the next morning she'd be looking out the window again, not talking to anyone.

I can't go near anyone who has any kind of mental trouble. When my friend Miss Edwards was so ill in that way she wrote and begged me to come and the family wrote and I simply couldn't. I get very frightened of those sorts of things. I suppose I shouldn't.

Here is a caricature my brother drew of the warden, and here is one of the bald curate and the fat parson who rode a bicycle. He was talented, our Dick, but of course he had a family to support and that awful wife of his put everything on her back that he earned. And here is one of our father turning his nose up at some Indian chap who was trying to sell him a rug he didn't fancy.

Here I am in Malta and here's one of me in Paris. Wasn't I gay then? When the Germans took over Paris, I wept and wept. I didn't want to go on. Have you been to Paris, dear? Beautiful city, isn't it? You feel anything could happen there. It wouldn't matter where you'd been or what you'd done, you could begin all over, no regrets or sorrows.

Here is a picture of your husband's mother, wasn't she beautiful.

Turn your head like that, you look rather like her when you put your face that way. She would have loved you, dear, and she was a beautiful soul. She used to laugh and laugh, even during the war when we'd have to stay in the shelter over night and we were terrified we wouldn't see the sunlight ever again. She'd tell us gay stories and make us laugh. She had a little bird, she used to call it Albert as a joke. She let him fly out all about the house on his own. And she taught the creature to say funny things; it was so amusing. She would be very happy for you, dear; she loved to see people happy.

I don't suppose I'll do any more traveling. I remember when I went to France last summer I said "Elizabeth, this is your last voyage," and I felt so queer. But I have this house and my garden and Leonard's wife Rosemary and I go out every week and do meals-on-wheels—we take food around to the shut-ins, dear. I suppose they'll be doing that for me some day, but not for a while, I don't think. I like to be active and work in the garden. These awful pillow roses have taken over everything and I haven't the heart to prune them. And then, when people come, it's so lovely, isn't it, I wish they could stay forever.

Susan

It's good to have company. Sometimes I feel as though I haven't had a day off in three years since Maria was born. Geoffrey doesn't seem to want to be weaned; he's seven months. I suppose he will when he's ready. It's the only thing that quietens him. I'm beginning to feel very tired. And now Maria wants everything from a bottle, she wants to be a baby too. I suppose they'll stop when they're ready.

My days are very ordered, though. I remember when I was single and I lived in London I'd think what will I do with myself now? And then I'd just go out and walk down the street and I'd look in the windows at the china and the materials and then I'd stop somewhere and have a cup of tea and go home and read something. It's so difficult, isn't it, to remember what that kind of loneliness was like when you're with people constantly. It's like hunger or cold. But now my time is all mapped out for me. I give everyone breakfast and then I do the washing up and we go for a walk and it's time for lunch. It goes on like that. It's better now. When we lived in the high-rise building I felt terribly alone. There would be other push-chairs in front of other doors and occasionally I'd hear a baby crying in the hall but I wouldn't know whose it was and when I opened the door there was never anybody in the corridor, only the queer yellow light. And I hated the air in that building. It tasted so false in my mouth and we couldn't open up any of the windows. It was beautiful at nights and I would hold the baby by the window and say, "moon," and "star," and sometimes when they were both asleep Frederick and I would stand by the window and look out over the city at all the lights. The car horns were muted like voices at the ocean; it was very nice. I liked it then. But I did feel terribly lonely.

Sometimes I go up to the attic and I look at the piles of my research in egg cartons but I don't even take it out. I suppose I should want to someday. I suppose I should get back to my Russian. But it all hangs around me like a cloud and I feel Maria tugging at me, pulling at my dress like a wave and I think how much more real it all is now, feeding and clothing, and nurturing and warming and I think of words like "research" and "report" and even "learning" and "understanding" next to those words and they seem so high, so far away, it's a struggle to remember what they mean.

I love marriage, though, the idea of it. I believe in it in a very traditional way. My friends from graduate school come over and they say I'm worn out and tired and I'm making a martyr of myself. I should make Frederick do some of the work. But it's the form of it I love and the repetition: certain tasks are his, some are mine. That's what these young people are all looking for, form, but it's a dirty word to them. I suppose I'm not that old, I'm thirty-two, that's young, I suppose, but I like feeling older. I wish I were fifty. I like not having a moment to myself, it's soothing and my life is warm and sweet like porridge. Before Geoffrey was born sometimes I'd spend the whole day and Maria was the only one I would talk to. She was two then and Frederick would come home and he was so terribly tired and I was too. We scarcely said a word to each other except "how's the baby today" or "your shirt got lost at the cleaner's." It was the happiest time of my life. She wanted to know everything, and sometimes we'd spend whole mornings doing things like taking the vacuum cleaner apart or boiling water or walking up and down stairs. Then Frederick would come home and he'd want to talk about Talleyrand or something and I couldn't possibly explain to him how perfectly happy I was all day, taking everything out of my sewing basket and showing it to Maria, he would have thought I was stark, staring mad.

But I love that: sleeping next to someone you haven't spoken to all day and then making love in the dark with our pajamas on and even then going to sleep not having spoken. It soothes me, like wet sand. We couldn't have that without marriage, I mean marriage in the old way, with the woman doing everything.

Here's something for your lunch. I cook such odd things now, sausages for the children, tins of soup, sandwiches. But I always make this stew for us. I just boil up a hambone with lentils and carrots. I suppose you're a very good cook. I used to be but now I don't like that kind of thing.

The babies have broken nearly all the china, so we use everything plastic now. Do you think it's terribly ugly? I do miss that, nice thin china and glassware, I miss it more than books and the cinema. And the furniture's terribly shabby now. We'll wait until they're grown to replace it.

Don't worry about what people say. When I married Frederick even his mum wouldn't come and people would run down his first wife, thinking they were doing me a favor, and all the time they were making it worse because I'd think if she was so bloody awful why did he marry her and then I thought if he loved her and she's so dreadful and he loves me I must be dreadful too. And I kept going around in circles and hating Frederick and myself and some poor woman whom I used to think of as a perfectly harmless remote monster. I could scarcely get out of bed in the morning, and people thought they were being kind. You must simply shore up all your courage to be silent. That's what I have done and sometimes I am so silent I like myself a great deal, no, more than that, I admire myself and that's what I've always longed for.

You shouldn't listen to me either, I'm probably half mad talking to babies all day. Only there's something sort of enormous and grey and cold about marriage. It's wonderful isn't it, being part of it? Or don't you feel that way.

Gillian

My mother had this thing about beauty, it was really very Edwardian the way she approached it. She had this absolutely tiny private income and my father took off the absolute second I was born and we hardly ever had any money and my mother kept moving around saying these incredible things like "it'll be better in the next town" and "when our ship comes in" and things like that you expect to read in some awful trashy novel.

But she was a beautiful woman and she taught me these oddly valuable things, about scent and clothes and makeup. I'm trying to be kinder to her now I'm forty. I suppose one gets some kind of perspective on things, but what I really remember is being terribly, terribly insecure all the time and frightened about money and resentful of other girls who wore smart clothes and went off to university when they weren't as smart as I was. My mother used to dress me in the most outlandish outfits as a child, velvet and lace, and what not. I hated it in school. I was forever leaving schools and starting in new ones and I was perpetually embarrassed.

Well, when I married for the first time I was determined to marry someone terribly stable and serviceable. As soon as I could I bought these incredibly severe clothes, they just about had buttons on them and I married Richard. I was eighteen. I suppose it is all too predictable to be really interesting—and we lived in this fanatically utilitarian apartment, everything was white and silver and I couldn't imagine why I felt cold all the time. Suddenly I found myself using words like beauty and truth, et cetera, and I went out and got a job so we could buy a really super house. I spent all my time looking at wallpaper and going to auctions and the house really was beautiful. Then I met Seymour and he was so funny and lugubrious—I just adored it. Here was this Jewish man taking me to little cabarets. The first time we went out he said to me, 'You know, Gillian, girl singers are very important,' and I hadn't the faintest idea what he was talking about. Here was this quite famous psychologist who bought a copy of Variety—that American show-people's paper—every day, but it was very odd, the first time I met him I thought how marvelous he'd be to live with.

And then, of course I did a terribly unstable thing, I suppose. Shades of my mother only more so I divorced Richard and married Seymour. He gave all his money to his wife and I let Richard keep everything of mine and we started out without a penny. We slept in the car in our clothes, but we were terribly happy. So I got a job and we got another lovely house, only this was a really cheerful one, a very motherly home. Then I went back to school. I suppose it's hard for you to understand how important it would be for me: doing something on my own with my mind and speaking up and having people listen. I'd had too much sitting on the sidelines pushing the silver pheasant down the damask cloth and cradling the salt cellar while the men spoke to each other. So I told Seymour I simply had to go back to college and he agreed with me for a while in theory but when the time came he said to me "what about the house." But I was very firm and I simply told him, "the house will simply be a bit less beautiful for a while." Then he understood how important it was to me, and he stood right behind me. We didn't do much entertaining for a while, but I did very well, really, everyone was surprised. I guess everyone else was much less smart than I expected.

Then I took a job teaching high school and it was a disaster, really. There were all these perfectly nice people who wanted to grow up and repair bicycles and I was supposed to talk about Julius Caesar and the subjunctive. It was all too absurd, really. I simply cared about the books too much to do it. I suppose to be a really good high school teacher you have not to care about the books so. Well, one day I simply didn't go back. I suppose it was awful, but there were plenty of people who wanted the job. I didn't feel too badly about it. Going in like that every day was making me so ill.

Now I've gone back to writing. I don't know if I'm any good. I don't suppose it matters, really. It's a serious thing, and that's important. I see everyone off in the morning and I go up to my study—the window looks out on a locust tree—and I write the whole day. The hardest thing is closing the door on Seymour and the children—but I do. I close the door on being a wife. I close the door on my house and all the demands. I suppose art demands selfishness and perhaps I'm not a great artist so perhaps it's all ridiculous and pitiable, but in the end it isn't even important whether I'm great or not—I'm after something, myself, I suppose, isn't that terribly commonplace. Only the soul, whatever that is, whatever we call it now—gets so flung about one is always in danger of losing it, of letting it slip away unless one is really terribly careful and jealous. And so it is important really and the only answer is, whatever the outside connections, that one must simply do it.

* * *

Who is right, and who is wrong? For years, I have waited for a sign, a sentence, periodic and complete. Now I begin to know there is a loneliness even in this love. I begin to think of death, of solids. My friend, who is my age, is already a widow. She says that no one will talk to her about it. Everyone thinks she is tainted. They are frightened by her contact with dead flesh, as if it clung to her visibly. I should prepare for a staunch widowhood. I begin to wish for my own death, because I am happy now and vulnerable to contagion. A friend of mine who has three children tells a story about a colleague of his, a New England spinster. She noted that he had been out sick four times that winter; she had been healthy throughout. "But that is because I have a wife and three children," he said, "and I am open to contagion."

There is something satisfying about marriage at this time. It is the satisfaction of a dying civilization: one perfects the form, knowing it has the thrill of doom upon it. There is a craftsmanship here; I am conscious of a kind of labor. It is harder than art and more dangerous. Last night was very hot. I didn't want to wake my husband so I moved into the spare bedroom where I could thrash, guiltlessly. I fell asleep and then heard him wake, stir, and feel for me. I ran to the door of our bedroom. "You gave me a fright. I reached for you and the bed was empty," he said. Now I know I am not invisible. Things matter. My feet impress a solid earth now. I am full of power.

The most difficult thing is my tremendous pride. To admit that there are some things I do not know is like a degrading illness. My husband tries to teach me how to use a hoe, a machete. I do not learn easily. I throw the tools at his feet and in anger I weep and kick. He knows something I do not; can I forgive him? He is tearing down a wall; he is building a fireplace. I am upstairs in the bedroom, reading, dizzy with resentment. I come down and say, "I'm going away for a few days. Until you finish this." Then I cry and confess: I do not want to go away, but I hate it that he is demolishing and building and that I am reading. It is not enough that I have made a custard and a beautiful parsley sauce for the fish. He hands me a hammer, a chisel, a saw. I am clumsy and ill with my own incapacity. When he tries to show me how to hold the saw correctly, I hit him, hard, between the shoulder blades. I have never hit another person like this; I am an only child. So he becomes the brother I was meant to hit. I make him angry. He says I should have married someone with no skills, no achievements. What I want, he says, is unlimited power. He is right. I love him because he is powerful, because he will let me have only my fair share. Stop, he says, for I ask too much of everything. Take more, there is more here for you, I tell him, for he is used to deprivation. We are learning to be kind to one another, like milky siblings.

Two people in a house, what else is it? I love his shoes, his shirts. I want to embrace his knees and tell him "You are the most splendid person I have ever known." Yet I miss my friends, the solitude of my own apartment with its plangent neuroses, the coffee cups where mold grew familiarly, the little grocery store on the corner with the charge account in my name only.

But I feel my muscles flex, grow harder, grow supple with intimacy. We are very close; I know every curve of his body; he can call to mind in a moment the pattern of my veins. He is my husband, I say, slowly, swallowing a new, exotic food. Does this mean everything or nothing? I stand with him in an ancient relationship, in a ruined age, listening beyond my understanding to the warning voices, to the promise of my own substantial heart.

CORDIALS

DAVID KRANES

It WASN'T UNTIL THE WAITRESS brought her Benedictine and she felt her first contraction that Lynn even thought of herself as being pregnant. She was anatomically thin and had managed to conceal the fact for well over seven months, with a regimen of boiled turnips and cold consommé—and the reminder was badly timed to say the least. She had wanted to sleep with David Marker from the moment she and Jack had spent a Saturday with the Markers sailfishing three months ago out at Wildwood, but there'd been interferences at just about every point. She had called him; he had called her; they had tried one afternoon at her apartment only to find her son Adam home from Hotchkiss as a surprise. Fall in New York is a difficult time to have an affair: everything starting up, schedules over-crowded again; and so this evening was to have been an island for both of them.

"Something the matter?" David asked her.

She smiled. "No."

"You winced."

"Just anxious, I guess."

"As am I."

She rubbed the knuckles of his hand, climbing each ridge, kneading the loose skin in the depressions with her forefinger and thumb.

"Do you want to leave now?" he asked.

"Let's finish our drinks," she said, her eyes partly on her watch, wondering when the next contraction would come. It came seven minutes later. She drained her glass: "All through," she said.

David smiled, breathed in his Drambuie and drained it. "Let's go," he said.

He helped her on with her coat. "Where are we . . . ?"

"A friend lent me his studio."

"Where?"

"Rowayton."

"That's an hour."

"Fifty minutes. And it's a nice Indian summer. We'll drive with the windows down. Sea smell's an aphrodisiac."

"I don't need an aphrodisiac." Her voice was surprisingly soft and quiet.

David nodded to the maitre de, and pushed the door open; she went out. "It's a great place—this place—this studio."

Lynn breathed the late September West 52nd Street smells, and felt another contraction coming on.

When they cloverleafed onto the Merritt Parkway, the tugs were coming regularly, just under five minutes. Both the front windows were down. David had the heater on, her coat off. She had her face against his neck, her jaw pressed there. She'd worn no bra—she didn't really need to—and he was moving the tips of his right middle fingers over the nipple, under her burgundy knit.

"You're perspiring," he said, trying to make it sound playful.

"Yes." She bit at him. "It's the heater. The blower's going right up my dress." She knew, in fact, it was probably lactating.

"Rowayton?" There was a hum in her voice.

"There are fourteen-foot ceilings," David traced her neck. "And a fireplace."

"Had you planned on using the fireplace?"

"For a fire, sure; not for us."

"I don't know if I can wait." Lynn felt her body tightening again, watched the speedometer climb from 70 to 85.

"You'll love it," David said to her; "it's on the shore. You can hear the ocean. Waves. It's a great rhythm. Great keeping time to. Natural. Nothing rushed." He let his hand slide slowly down to her leg. She picked it up, kissed it. She looked at her watch: three minutes and twenty seconds; she picked up and kissed his hand when she felt the next contraction again; three minutes and fifteen.

"How long until we get there?" she asked him.

"Twenty—twenty-five minutes." He played with her nipple again. She held her breath. "You're really remarkable," he told her. "I've been clawing half New York's concrete for three months."

"Me too," she said. "I've been having the most amazing fantasies."

"I'm not very good at waiting," David told her, then smiled.

"Nor am I." She thought about it; it was true. "I wait for very few things."

"Waiting fantasies are strange." He began to slide his hand down to her abdomen. "They make you feel almost adolescent." She picked his hand up again, kissed it, checked her watch. "Your heart's jumping."

"There's a motel in Mamaroneck," she said.

"One quarter hour, *max*," he told her. The pains were coming every two minutes plus.

When they pulled in beside the studio and cut their lights, Lynn's spasms were only a minute, or slightly more, apart. Like a schoolboy, David started to undress her in the car; she put two hands against his chest: "Let's go inside."

He smiled; "O.K.," then kissed her eyes, let himself out, and walked around to her door. She could smell the sea, as he'd predicted, and it smelled as though her own body had become huge, grown unlit and infinite and moved outside to become anatomy in the night around her. She became her own child briefly— undelivered though dependent and scared. She thought of when she was fourteen, parking out near Coney Island with a boy named Arnold, the "Tennessee Waltz" on the car radio, how her whole mouth had trembled, how her thigh muscles had gone slack. She heard the door button click, felt the sea wind against her hair, smelled the blown redolence of herself.

Lynn didn't like being aggressive. She had always hated that role, it ruined everything; but she pulled David inside and when he wanted to get a fire going, she said *no*.

"Why?"

"Please."

"Lynn, that's the whole . . ."

"Afterward!"

"I may want to sleep."

"Please!"

"O.K."

She pulled him to the bed.

She had continually fantasized David's undressing her, three months lived it in her mind: its being gentle, slow; kisses, where he placed them, breast, belly, hip; when they came. And so against her better judgment she let him, let it work out, let the mind come true. True: she stood there, in the dark, arching, moving, turning slightly for him on the balls of her heels. And David carried it off: it was worth the concealment, worth the pain. The hands played, the kisses came on time, in form. She felt the zipper on her dress move down, slipped her arms out, felt the dress fall around her hips. She felt her water break. "David," she said, and pulled him in.

She dug at him, made his shoulder bleed, bit his face. It helped to get the pain out. He was trembling, "Jesus! Jesus-God! Jesus, Lynn," he said. "God, come on! Off our feet! Off our feet! Talk about adolescents! God!"

"Then get undressed," she told him.

"You!"

"David . . . "

"Do it. You—"

His jacket was already off. His neck was moving on its base; his breath, heavy, wet. "Christ, you're incredible! You're incredible!" he said.

She couldn't help it. They were somewhere between twenty and thirty seconds apart now, and the pain and pressure was too much. She grabbed the collar of his shirt and tore, ripped it down, spread it, snapping all the buttons in a line. They landed, light as crickets, on the rug. "Fantastic!" David was moaning. "Oh, fantastic! Wow!"

She yanked his belt. "Oh, God!" She felt it uncinch. She broke the button above the fly and heard the zipper whine. The pants fell past his knees.

"O.K." she managed, her voice strained and tight, "You do the rest."

"No. Please." He was rocking. "You. The shoes!"

"David . . . "

"O.K. I'm sorry," He stepped out of things. "I'm sorry." He let other things drop. She saw his shape sit on the bed's edge, pull his shoes off. She didn't know how she was going to make it as she removed her panties and came close.

He pulled the bedspread down. She found a wastebasket and slid it beside the bed. She moved against him, kept his hands on her back, pressing her whole anatomy hard, violently down, against, trying to create hard enough pressure to displace some of the pain. She screamed. She dug in. She fought against him with her fists and knees. He kept bellowing sounds to match hers, saying things like: *God*—he thought his fantasies were pretty advanced, but— *Jesus*—he realized now that they were—*Christ*—naive. But as they tore and fought against each other, Lynn felt herself giving way and knew that what she'd hoped for was impossible. She could not last. She could not hold out.

She slid down his body slowly, marking it with her teeth, clearing herself as where she could. When the baby came, it came easily and she was able crudely to slice the cord, get everything in the waste-basket and cover it with the bedspread without really losing much of the rhythm of the foreplay. She submitted to David pulling at her, at her shoulders, slid back up along him, joining, both of them, three minutes later, coming almost together under the bloodsoak of sheets.

David lay with his head off the far edge of the bed, making sounds. Lynn played one hand over his ribs, blew breath gently against his sweat. She could smell herself—herself, the ocean and her own birth, but could not keep them apart. She thought she heard a steamer, way out in Long Island Sound. Shortly afterward, when David showered, she took the basket out to the small pier of the studio front and emptied it into the sea. Standing there briefly, she tasted herself again, her own fetality, felt the darkness—warm, salty, moist, in membranes layered out and out around her. The moon, real and untelevised above, seemed a strange opening in space, a place she might ultimately move to, go. She ached, but could not feel her body. It was an abstract ache, one in air.

Inside, they came together one more time: much quicker, less violent, more studied, more synchronized. David did not shower. Instead, he dressed himself hurriedly and lit a long cigar.

"Did I hurt you?" he asked. "I'm always afraid . . . "

"No," Lynn reassured him from the bathroom. She stopped herself with toilet paper, pulled on her panties, and dropped her dress over her head. "No." Somehow it was true.

"Hey—you start?"

"What?"

"Your period start?"

" . . . Yes."

In the car, on the way back to Manhattan, they talked enthusiastically about St. Croix.

Her husband, Jack, was sitting on the long couch going through briefs in his blue bathrobe when she came in. There was a small snifter of crème de cacao on the coffee table to his right. They said hello. She kissed him on his forehead and hung up her coat.

"Where you been?"

"Theater."

"What'd you see?"

"*Long Day's Journey*."

"How was it?"

"Fantastic.' ' She straightened her hair.

"Great play." Jack wrote a sentence in the margin of his brief. "There's some triple sec there, if you want."

"Thanks."

"Picked it up on the way home."

She poured a cordial glass half full. The smell of orange reminded her somehow of Christmas, kumquats from Florida fruit packages she had bitten into in lost distant Decembers as a child. She crossed the room. She stood in front of their window wall, looking out. The lights beyond, below, all the bunched thousands of them, looked like perforations. She stared at the reflected milk stains on her dress, her reflection seeming to spread out across the perforations to surround her until, searching the distance, she was gone.

"Did you find it?"

"Hmmm?"

"Find the triple sec."

"Yes. Fine. Thanks."

"See the letter from Ad?"

"No. What's he say?"

"They beat Taft 21 to 20. He pulled a ligament in his knee. He's been having whirlpools. Nothing serious. They took X rays at the Sharon Hospital. He's seeing Cynthia Kaufmann this weekend. Listen—do you want to?"

"Hmmm?"

"You at all horny?"

She pressed the cordial glass against her lips. The fruity taste rose up, viscous, wet; it made orange seeds of her eyes. "Maybe later," she said.

"Can't hear you."

She took the glass away, wet her lips. "Maybe later."

"Sure, O.K."

Her eyes watered. She experienced the only moment akin to incest she had ever felt. She thought of her son, Adam, in the whirlpool. Her knee hurt.

HOME

JAYNE ANNE PHILLIPS

I'M AFRAID Walter Cronkite has had it, says Mom. Roger Mudd always does the news now. How would you like to have a name like that? Walter used to do the conventions and a football game now and then. I mean he would sort of appear, on the sidelines. Didn't he? But you never see him anymore. Lord. Something is going on.

Mom, I say. Maybe he's just resting. He must have made a lot of money by now. Maybe he's tired of talking about elections and mine disasters and the collapse of the franc. Maybe he's in love with a young girl.

He's not the type, says my mother. You can tell *that* much. No, she says, I'm afraid it's cancer.

My mother has her suspicions. She ponders. I have been home with her for two months. I ran out of money and I wasn't in love, so I have come home to my mother. She is an educational administrator. All winter long after work she watches television and knits afghans.

Come home, she said. Save money.

I can't possibly do it, I said. Jesus, I'm twenty-three years old.

Don't be silly, she said. And don't use profanity.

She arranged a job for me in the school system. All day I tutor children in remedial reading. Sometimes I am so discouraged that I lie on the couch all evening and watch television with her. The shows are all alike. Their laugh tracks are conspicuously similar; I think I recognize a repetition of certain professional laughters. This laughter marks off the half hours.

Finally I make a rule: I won't watch television at night. I will watch only the news, which ends at 7:30. Then I will go to my room and do God knows what. But I feel sad that she sits there alone, knitting by the lamp. She seldom looks up.

Why don't you ever read anything? I ask.

I do, she says. I read books in my field. I read all day at work, writing those damn proposals. When I come home I want to relax.

Then let's go to the movies.

I don't want to go to the movies. Why should I pay money to be upset or frightened?

But feeling something can teach you. Don't you want to learn anything?

I'm learning all the time, she says.

She keeps knitting. She folds yarn the color of cream, the color of snow. She works it with her long blue needles, piercing, returning, winding. Yarn cascades from her hands in long panels. A pattern appears and disappears. She stops and counts; so many stitches across, so many down. Yes, she is on the right track.

Occasionally I offer to buy my mother a subscription to something mildly informative: *Ms, Rolling Stone, Scientific American*.

I don't want to read that stuff, she says. Just save your money. Did you hear Cronkite last night? Everyone's going to need all they can get.

Often I need to look at my mother's old photographs. I see her sitting in knee-high grass with a white gardenia in her hair. I see her dressed up as the groom in a mock wedding at a sorority party, her black hair pulled back tight. I see her formally posed in her cadet nurse's uniform. The photographer has painted her lashes too lushly, too long; but her deep red mouth is correct.

The war ended too soon. She didn't finish her training. She came home to nurse only her mother and to meet my father at a dance. She married him in two weeks. It took twenty years to divorce him.

When we traveled to a neighboring town to buy my high school clothes, my mother and I would pass a certain road that turned off the highway and wound to a place I never saw.

There it is, my mother would say. The road to Wonder Bar. That's where I met my Waterloo. I walked in and he said, 'There she is. I'm going to marry that girl.' Ha. He sure saw me coming.

Well, I asked, why did you marry him?

He was older, she said. He had a job and a car. And mother was so sick.

My mother doesn't forget her mother.

Never one bedsore, she says. I turned her every fifteen minutes. I kept her skin soft and kept her clean, even to the end.

I imagine my mother at twenty-three; her black hair, her dark eyes, her olive skin and that red lipstick. She is growing lines of tension in her mouth. Her teeth press into her lower lip as she lifts the woman in the bed. The woman weighs no more than a child. She has a smell. My mother fights it continually; bathing her, changing her sheets, carrying her to the bathroom so the smell can be contained and flushed away. My mother will try to protect them both. At night she sleeps in the room on a cot. She struggles awake feeling something press down on her and suck her breath: the smell. When my grandmother can no longer move, my mother fights it alone.

I did all I could, she sighs. And I was glad to do it. I'm glad I don't have to feel guilty.

No one has to feel guilty, I tell her.

And why not? says my mother. There's nothing wrong with guilt. If you are guilty, you should feel guilty.

My mother has often told me that I will be sorry when she is gone.

I think. And read alone at night in my room. I read those books I never read, the old classics, and detective stories. I can get them in the library here. There is only one bookstore; it sells mostly newspapers and *True Confessions* oracles. At Kroger's by the checkout counter I buy a few paperbacks, best sellers, but they are usually bad.

The television drones on downstairs.

I wonder about Walter Cronkite.

When was the last time I saw him? It's true his face was pouchy, his hair thinning. Perhaps he is only cutting it shorter. But he had that look about the eyes. . . .

He was there when they stepped on the moon. He forgot he was on the air and he shouted, 'There . . . there . . . now. . . . We have contact!' Contact. For those who tuned in late, for the periodic watchers, he repeated: 'One small step. . . .'

I was in high school and he was there with the body count. But he said it in such a way that you knew he wanted the war to end. He looked directly at you and said the numbers quietly. Shame, yes, but sorrowful patience, as if all things had passed before his eyes. And he understood that here at home, as well as in starving India, we would pass our next lives as meager cows.

My mother gets *Reader's Digest*. I come home from work, have a cup of coffee, and read it. I keep it beside my bed. I read it when I am too tired to read anything else. I read about Joe's kidney and Humor in Uniform. Always, there are human interest stories in which someone survives an ordeal of primal terror. Tonight it is Grizzly! Two teenagers camping in the mountains are attacked by a bear. Sharon is dragged over a mile, unconscious. She is a good student loved by her parents, an honest girl loved by her boyfriend. Perhaps she is not a virgin; but in her heart, she is virginal. And she lies now in the furred arms of a beast. The grizzly drags her quietly, quietly. He will care for her all the days of his life. . . . Sharon, his rose.

But alas. Already, rescuers have organized. Mercifully her boyfriend is not among them. He is sleeping en route to the nearest hospital; his broken legs have excused him. In a few days, Sharon will bring him his food on a tray. She is spared. She is not demure. He gazes on her face, untouched but for a long thin scar near her mouth. He thinks of the monster and wonders at its delicate mark. Sharon says she remembers nothing of the bear. She only knows the tent was ripped open, that its heavy canvas fell across her face.

I turn out my light when I know my mother is sleeping. By then my eyes hurt and the streets of the town are deserted.

My father comes to me in a dream. He kneels beside me, touches my mouth. He turns my face gently toward him.

Let me see, he says. Let me see it.

He is looking for a scar, a sign. He wears only a towel around his waist. He presses himself against my thigh, pretending solicitude. But I know what he is doing; I turn my head in repulsion and stiffen. He smells of a sour musk and his forearms are black with hair. I think, it's been years since he's had an erection. . . .

Finally he stands. Cover yourself, I tell him.

I can't, he says. I'm hard.

On Saturdays I go to the Veterans of Foreign Wars rummage sales. They are held in the drafty basement of a church, rows of collapsible tables piled with objects. Sometimes I think I recognize the possessions of old friends: a class ring, yearbooks, football sweaters with our high school insignia. Would this one have fit Jason?

He used to spread it on the seat of the car on winter nights when we parked by country churches and graveyards. There seemed to be no ground, just water, a rolling, turning, building to a dull pain between my legs.

What's wrong? What is it?

Jason, I can't. . . . This pain. . . .

It's only because you're afraid. If you'd let me go ahead. . . .

I'm not afraid of you, I'd do anything for you. But Jason, why does it hurt like this?

We would try. But I couldn't. We made love with our hands. Our bodies were white. Out the window of the car, snow rose up in mounds across the fields. Afterward, he looked at me peacefully, sadly.

I held him and whispered, soon, soon. . . . we'll go away to school.

His sweater. He wore it that night we drove back from the football awards banquet. Jason made All State but he hated football.

I hate it, he said. So what? he said. That I'm out there puking in the heat? Screaming 'kill' at a sandbag?

I held his award in my lap, a gold man frozen in mid-leap. Don't play in college, I said. Refuse the money.

He was driving very slowly.

I can't see, he said. I can't see the edges of the road. . . . Tell me if I start to fall off.

Jason, what do you mean?

He insisted I roll down the window and watch the edge. The banks of the road were gradual, sloping off in brush and trees on either side. White lines at the edge glowed in dips and turns.

We're going to crash, he said.

No, Jason. You've driven this road before. We won't crash.

We're crashing, I know it, he said. Tell me, tell me I'm OK. . . .

Here on the rummage sale table, there are three football sweaters. I see they are all too small to have belonged to Jason. So I buy an old soundtrack, "The Sound of Music." Air, Austrian mountains. And an old robe to wear in the mornings. It upsets my mother to see me naked; she looks at me so curiously, as though she didn't recognize my body.

I pay for my purchases at the cash register. Behind the desk I glimpse stacks of *Reader's Digests*. The Ladies' Auxiliary turns them inside out, stiffens and shellacs them. They make wastebaskets out of them.

I give my mother the record. She is pleased. She hugs me.

Oh, she says, I used to love the musicals. They made me happy. Then she stops and looks at me.

Didn't you do this? she says. Didn't you do this in high school?

Do what?

Your class, she says. You did "The Sound of Music."

Yes, I guess we did.

What a joke. I was the beautiful countess meant to marry Captain Von Trapp before innocent Maria stole his heart. Jason was a threatening Nazi colonel with a bit part. He should have sung the lead but sports practices interfered with rehearsals. Tall, blond, aged in make-up under the lights, he encouraged sympathy for the bad guys and overshadowed the star. He appeared just often enough to make the play ridiculous.

My mother sits in the blue chair my father used for years.

Come quick, she says. Look. . . .

She points to the television. Flickerings of Senate chambers, men in conservative suits. A commentator drones on about tax rebates.

There, says my mother. Hubert Humphrey. Look at him .

It's true. Humphrey is different, changed from his former toady self to a desiccated old man, not unlike the discarded shell of a locust. Now he rasps into the microphone about the people of these great states.

Old Hubert's had it, says my mother. He's a death mask.

That's what he gets for sucking blood for thirty years.

No, she says. No, he's got it too. Look at him! Cancer. Oh.

For God's sake, will you think of something else for once?

I don't know what you mean, she says. She goes on knitting.

All Hubert needs, I tell her, is a good roll in the hay.

You think that's what everyone needs.

Everyone does need it.

They do not. People aren't dogs. I seem to manage perfectly well without it, don't I?

No, I wouldn't say that you do.

Well, I do. I know your mumbo-jumbo about sexuality. Sex is for those who are married, and I wouldn't marry again if it was the Lord himself.

Now she is silent. I know what's coming.

Your attitude will make you miserable, she says. One man after another. I just want you to be happy.

I do my best.

That's right, she says, be sarcastic.

I refuse to answer. I think about my growing bank account. Graduate school, maybe in California. Hawaii. Somewhere beautiful and warm. I will wear few clothes and my skin will feel the air.

What about Jason, says my mother. I was thinking of him the other day.

Our telepathy always frightens me. Telepathy and beyond. Before her hysterectomy, our periods often came on the same day.

If he hadn't had that nervous breakdown, she says softly, do you suppose. . . .

No, I don't suppose.

I wasn't surprised that it happened. When his brother was killed, that was hard. But Jason was so self-centered. He thought everyone was out to get him. You were lucky to be rid of him. Still, poor thing. . . .

Silence. Then she refers in low tones to the few months Jason and I lived together before he was hospitalized.

You shouldn't have done what you did when you went off to college. He lost respect for you.

It wasn't respect for me he lost—He lost his fucking mind, if you remember—

I realize I'm shouting. And shaking. What is happening to me? My mother stares.

We'll not discuss it, she says.

She gets up. I hear her in the bathroom. Water running into the tub. Hydrotherapy. I close my eyes and listen. Soon, this weekend. I'll get a ride to the university a few hours away and look up an old lover. I'm lucky. They always want to sleep with me. For old time's sake.

I turn down the sound of the television and watch its silent pictures. Jason's brother was a musician; he taught Jason to play the pedal steel. A sergeant in uniform delivered the message two weeks before the state playoff games. Jason appeared at my mother's kitchen door with the telegram. He looked at me, opened his mouth, backed off wordless in the dark. I pretend I hear his pedal steel; its sweet country whine might make me cry. And I recognize this silent movie. . . . I've seen it four times. Gregory Peck and his submarine crew escape fallout in Australia, but not for long. The cloud is coming. And so they run rampant in auto races and love affairs. But in the end, they close the hatch and put out to sea. They want to go home to die.

Sweetheart? My mother calls from the bathroom. Could you bring me a towel?

Her voice is quavering slightly. She is sorry. But I never know which part of it she is sorry about. I get a towel from the linen closet and open the door of the steamy bathroom. My mother stands in the tub, dripping, shivering a little. She is so small and thin; she is smaller than I. She has two long scars on her belly, operations of the womb, and one breast is misshapen, sunken, indented near the nipple.

I put the towel around her shoulders and my eyes smart. She looks at her breast.

Not too pretty is it, she says. He took out too much when he removed that lump.

Mom, it doesn't look so bad.

I dry her back, her beautiful back which is firm and unblemished. Beautiful, her skin. Again, I feel the pain in my eyes.

But you should have sued the bastard, I tell her. He didn't give a shit about your body.

We have an awkward moment with the towel when I realize I can't touch her any longer. The towel slips down and she catches it as one ends dips into the water.

Sweetheart, she says. I know your beliefs are different from mine. But have patience with me. You'll just be here a few more months. And I'll always stand behind you. We'll get along.

She has clutched the towel to her chest. She is so fragile, standing there, naked, with her small shoulders. Suddenly I am horribly frightened.

Sure, I say, I know we will.

I let myself out of the room.

Sunday my mother goes to church alone. Daniel calls me from D.C. He's been living with a lover in Oregon. Now he is back east; she will join him in a few weeks. He is happy, he says. I tell him I'm glad he's found someone who appreciates him.

Come on now, he says. You weren't that bad.

I love Daniel, his white and feminine hands, his thick chestnut hair, his intelligence. And he loves me, though I don't know why. The last few weeks we were together I lay beside him like a piece of wood. I couldn't bear his touch; the moisture his penis left on my hips as he rolled against me. I was cold, cold. I huddled in blankets away from him.

I'm sorry, I said. Daniel, I'm sorry please . . . what's wrong with me? Tell me you love me anyway. . . .

Yes, he said. Of course I do. I always will. I do.

Daniel says he has no car, but he will come by bus. Is there a place for him to stay?

Oh yes, I say. There's a guest room. Bring some Trojans. I'm a hermit with no use for birth control. Daniel, you don't know what it's like here.

I don't care what it's like. I want to see you.

Yes, I say. Daniel, hurry.

When he arrives the next weekend, we sit around the table with my mother and discuss medicine. Daniel was a medic in Vietnam. He smiles at my mother. She is charmed though she has reservations; I see them in her face. But she enjoys having someone else in the house, a presence: a male. Daniel's laughter is low and modulated. He talks softly, smoothly: a dignified radio announcer, an accomplished anchor man.

But when I lived with him, he threw dishes against the wall. And jerked in his sleep, mumbling. And ran out of the house with his hands across his eyes.

After we first made love, he smiled and pulled gently away from me. He put on his shirt and went to the bathroom. I followed and stepped into the shower with him. He faced me, composed, friendly, and frozen. He stood as though guarding something behind him.

Daniel, turn around. I'll soap you back.

I already did.

Then move, I'll stand in the water with you.

He stepped carefully around me.

Daniel, what's wrong? Why won't you turn around?

Why should I?

I'd never seen him with his shirt off. He'd never gone swimming with us, only wading, alone, disappearing down Point Reyes Beach. He wore longsleeved shirts all summer in the California heat.

Daniel, I said, you've been my best friend for months. We could have talked about it.

He stepped backwards, awkwardly, out of the tub and put his shirt on.

I was loading them on copters, he told me. The last one was dead anyway; he was already dead. But I went after him, dragged him in the wind of the blades. Shrapnel and napalm caught my arms, my back. Until I fell, I thought it was the other man's blood in my hands.

They removed most of the shrapnel, did skin grafts for the burns. In three years since, Daniel made love five times; always in the dark. In San Francisco he must take off his shirt for a doctor; tumors have grown in his scars. They bleed through his shirt, round rust-colored spots.

Face-to-face in bed, I tell him I can feel the scars with my fingers. They are small knots on his skin. Not large, not ugly. But he can't let me, he can't let anyone, look: he says he feels wild, like raging, and then he vomits. But maybe, after they removed the tumors. . . . Each time they operate, they reduce the scars.

We spend hours at the Veterans's Hospital waiting for appointments. Finally they schedule the operation. I watch the black-ringed wall clock, the amputees gliding by in chairs that tick on the linoleum floor. Daniel's doctors run out of local anesthetic during the procedure and curse about lack of supplies; they bandage him with gauze and layers of Band-Aids. But it is all right. I buy some real bandages. Every night I cleanse his back with a sponge and change them.

In my mother's house, Daniel seems different. He has shaved his beard and his face is too young for him. I can grip his hands.

I show him the house, the antiques, the photographs on the walls. I tell him none of the objects move; they are all cemented in place. Now the bedrooms, my room.

This is it, I say. This is where I kept my Villager sweaters when I was seventeen, and my dried corsages. My cups from the Tastee Freez labeled with dates and boys' names.

The room is large, blue. Baseboards and wood trim are painted a spotless white. Ruffled curtains, ruffled bedspread. The bed itself is so high one must climb into it. Daniel looks at the walls, their perfect blue and white.

It's a piece of candy, he says.

Yes, I say, hugging him, wanting him.

What about your mother?

She's gone to meet friends for dinner. I don't think she believes what she says, she's only being my mother. It's all right.

We take off our clothes and press close together. But something is wrong. We keep trying. Daniel stays soft in my hands. His mouth is nervous; he seems to gasp at my lips.

He says his lover's name. He says they aren't seeing other people.

But I'm not other people. And I want you to be happy with her.

I know. She knew . . . I'd want to see you.

Then what?

This room, he says. This house. I can't breathe in here.

I tell him we have tomorrow. He'll relax. And it is so good just to see him, a person from my life.

So we only hold each other, rocking.

Later, Daniel asks about my father.

I don't see him, I say. He told me to choose.

Choose what?

Between them.

My father. When he lived in this house, he stayed in the dark with his cigarette. He sat in his blue chair with the lights and television off, smoking. He made little money; he said he was self-employed. He was sick. He grew dizzy when he looked up suddenly. He slept in the basement. All night he sat reading in the bathroom. I'd hear him walking up and down the dark steps at night. I lay in the dark and listened. I believed he would strangle my mother, then walk upstairs and strangle me. I believed we were guilty; we had done something terrible to him.

Daniel wants me to talk.

How could she live with him, I ask. She came home from work and got supper. He ate it, got up and left to sit in his chair. He watched the news. We were always sitting there, looking at his dirty plates. And I wouldn't help her. She should wash them, not me. She should make the money we lived on. I didn't want her house and his ghost with its cigarette burning in the dark like a sore. I didn't want to be guilty. So she did it. She did it all herself. She sent me to college; she paid for my safe escape.

Daniel and I go to the Rainbow, a bar and grill on Main Street. We hold hands, play country songs on the juke box, drink a lot of salted beer. We talk to the barmaid and kiss in the overstuffed booth. Twinkle lights blink on and off above us. I wore my burgundy stretch pants in here when I was twelve. A senior pinched me, then moved his hand slowly across my thigh, mystified, as though erasing the pain.

What about tonight? Daniel asks. Would your mother go out with us? A movie, a bar? He sees me in her, he likes her. He wants to know her.

Then we will have to watch television.

We pop popcorn and watch the late movies. My mother stays up with us, mixing whiskey sours and laughing. She gets a high color in her cheeks and the light in her eyes glimmers up; she is slipping, slipping back and she is beautiful, oh, in her ankle socks, her red mouth and her armour of young girl's common sense. She has a beautiful laughter. She and Daniel end by mock armwrestling; he pretends defeat and goes upstairs to bed.

My mother hears his door close. He's nice, she says. You've known some nice people, haven't you?

I want to make her back down.

Yes, he's nice, I say. And don't you think he respects me? Don't you think he truly cares for me, even though we've slept together?

He seems to, I don't know. But if you give them that, it costs them nothing to be friends with you.

Why should it cost? The only cost is what you give, and you can tell if someone is giving it back.

How? How can you tell? By going to bed with every man you take a fancy to?

I wish I took a fancy oftener, I tell her. I wish I wanted more, I can be good to a man, but I'm afraid . . . I can't be physical, not really. . . .

You shouldn't.

I should. I want to, for myself as well. I don't think . . . I've ever had an orgasm.

What? she says. Never? Haven't you felt a sort of building up, and then a dropping off . . . a conclusion? Like something's over?

No, I don't think so.

You probably have, she assures me. It's not necessarily an explosion. You were just thinking too hard, you think too much.

But she pauses.

Maybe I don't remember right, she says. It's been years, fifteen years, and in the last years of the marriage I would have died if your father had touched me. But before, I know I felt something. That's partly why I haven't . . . since . . . what if I started wanting it again? Then it would be hell.

But you have to try to get what you want. . . .

No, she says. Not if what you want would ruin everything. And now, anyway. Who would want me.

I stand at Daniel's door. The fear is back; it has followed me upstairs from the dead dark bottom of the house. My hands are shaking. I'm whispering . . . Daniel, don't leave me here.

I go to my room to wait. I must wait all night, or something will come in my sleep. I feel its hands on me now, dragging, pulling. I watch the lit face of the clock: three, four, five. At seven I go to Daniel. He sleeps with his pillow in his arms. The high bed creaks as I get in. Please now, yes . . . he is hard. He always woke with erections . . . inside me he feels good, real, and I tell him no, stop, wait . . . I hold the rubber, stretch its rim away from skin so it smooths on without hurting and fills with him . . . now again, here, yes but quiet, be quiet . . . oh Daniel . . . the bed is making noise . . . yes, no, but be careful, she . . . We move and turn and I forget about the sounds. We push against each other hard, he is almost there and I am almost with him and just when it is over I think I hear my mother in the room directly under us. . . . But I am half dreaming. I move to get out of bed and Daniel holds me. No, he says. Stay. . . .

We sleep and wake to hear the front door slam.

Daniel looks at me.

There's nothing to be done, I say. She's gone to church.

He looks at the clock. I'm going to miss that bus, he says. We put our clothes on fast and Daniel moves to dispose of the rubber . . . how? The toilet, no, the wastebasket. . . . He drops it in, bends over, retrieves it. Finally he wraps it in a Kleenex and puts it in his pocket. Jesus, he swears. He looks at me and grins. When I start laughing, my eyes are wet.

I take Daniel to the bus station and watch him out of sight. I come back and strip the bed, bundle the sheets in my arms. This pressure in my chest . . . I have to clutch the sheets tight, tighter. . . .

A door clicks shut. I go downstairs to my mother. She refuses to speak or let me near her. She stands by the sink and holds her small square purse with both hands. The fear comes. I hug myself, press my hands against my arms to stop shaking. My mother runs hot water, soap, takes dishes from the drainer. She immerses them, pushes them down, rubbing with a rag in a circular motion.

Those dishes are clean, I tell her. I washed them last night.

She keeps washing, rubbing. Hot water clouds her glasses, the window in front of us, our faces. We all disappear in steam. I watch the dishes bob and sink. My mother begins to sob. I move close to her and hold her. She smells as she used to smell when I was a child and slept with her.

I heard you, I heard it, she says. Here, in my own house. Please . . . how much can you expect me to take? I don't know what to do about anything. . . .

She looks into the water, keeps looking. And we stand here just like this.

THE CIGARETTE BOAT

BARBARA MILTON

It was St. Patrick's Day in Miami. Bryn Corley was looking in the mirror, deciding whether or not to curl her hair. When she curled it, it came out tight and blonde and emphatic like Jean Harlow's; when she sleeked it off her face the Grace Kelly came forward.

How she looked tonight was very important. She and Frank Kiernan had been invited to dine at the home of Maggie Bickle, a rich and very well-connected old woman. It was not inconceivable that Robert Mitchum would be there. Bryn thought she would curl her hair.

This could be her big break. She had an idea that if she walked into an office—any office, even in Hollywood—with a good tan they would offer her a job. And she very much wanted to be offered a job. For three years she had been out of the market and out of the country. But even in Europe the women she knew had interesting jobs and were making good salaries.

"I wonder if it's too late to get in as a starlet?" she asked herself. "I may be thirty-one but I've never been prettier. I'm thin and I'm tan and I speak French fluently."

She knocked over a warm bottle of Sasson Hair Oil and turned quickly to see if Frank had stirred. He was napping after a day of department stores. He was sixty-five years old and liked to buy her things.

Out of the room she tiptoed with her tape recorder and quietly shut the door to the bedroom. Slipping across the living room and into the kitchen she picked up a bottle of vitamin B-15. Bryn had been told it would keep you young forever but only if you pop about eight at a time. She tossed twelve into her mouth and washed them down with six M&M's. Then she opened the refrigerator for a swig of Lite beer.

Beside the beer, in an almost empty refrigerator, stood a bottle of tonic water and an ancient alarm clock. Frank had six new-fangled clocks around the apartment but this was the only one that kept perfect time. Frank liked it because he knew how to set it. You turned the big knob in back and big hands moved; you turned the little knob and the little hand moved. Frank was obsessed with time but Bryn couldn't stand the ticking. It was her idea to keep the clock in the refrigerator.

"Really," she thought. "I have no concept of time at all." When her brother came down she asked him what month it was. "Oh, come on," he said condescendingly.

"It's St. Patrick's Day." She snapped her fingers. "I wish I had something green to wear."

Her fingers tapped the buttons on the recorder. One pushed the play button, another rolled back the volume. Wherever she went (except out to dinner) the tape recorder was with her. Her fingers governed it like an accountant's, a calculator.

Uh Uh Uh Uh Staying Alive

Bryn played disco music when she was free to dance and country and western when stillness was called for. But now the disco and vitamins filled her with boogie. Her teeth pressed in over her lower lip and her chin and shoulders harmonized in a series of small jerks. She had seen the movie *Saturday Night Fever* three times and John Travolta was her latest unrequited ethnic love.

Out on the terrace she leaned over the railing, smiling at the sun and her own good fortune. Seven stories below million dollar yachts sat motionless while cigarette boats rolled with the motion of the water.

"I want to be a star!" thought Bryn with the enthusiasm of a first thought. She had already told Frank that she wanted a career and preferably one that took place in L.A. He said he would ask Maggie Bickle. Maggie knew everyone, especially in Hollywood.

"Is she really very rich?" Bryn asked when Frank woke up.

"Yes, she's very rich."

Bryn decided on the Grace Kelly look and brushed and brushed and brushed back her hair.

Out into the pink and gray twilight that hung heavily over the concrete strips of Miami, Bryn drove Frank's Cadillac. Frank was sitting on her right in his blue and white seersucker, pressing an invisible brake with his loafer.

"Right here. Slow down to 50. Better get into the outer lane. Take this exit."

Though Bryn hated taking directions, she needed him tonight and would humour him with obedience. She glanced at herself in the rearview mirror just as the car passed under a street lamp. It was horrible what fluorescent lighting could do. You were driving along feeling your Grace Kelly bone structure and you checked into the mirror to be sure it was true but what the mirror gave back to you was the yellowing criss-cross of age by your eyes. Bryn looked at Frank. Except for his eyes, he was in pretty good shape.

A tall, thin, angular man, Frank was caught in the vortex between elegant and grotesque. The way that he dressed—the jacket, the polo shirt, the gray straight-legged trousers—was elegant. How he signalled waiters, turned his ear only when spoken to, said nothing when he had nothing to say—all this was elegant. But his disease: they called it moon-eyes in horses. Moon-eyes meant horses would eventually go blind. Frank had a year and half of sight to go. After that, the white half-moons that were invading his irises would rise up completely and block out the light. Even now Frank couldn't see at night. There was something terrifying in his look. Bryn had seen children refuse to approach him, but Frank was no martyr; he stayed away from children. He kept company instead with horses and women and preferred horses because they didn't pity him. That's why he liked Bryn because she didn't either. He often told her that she reminded him of his favorite mare who happened to be barren yet full of herself. He said she was feisty and quirky and lusty. No good for breeding but excellent for display.

Bryn parked the Cadillac at the dead end of one of the more delapidated streets, across from a high stucco wall covered with kudzu and broken glass. As she and Frank approached the gate, three fierce white dogs hurled themselves against the bars. The dry black skin around their teeth wrinkled up into the shiny wetness of their pink and freckled gums.

"Hoopla!" shouted a man who was standing in the doorway. One of the dogs bounded up to him and a uniformed houseboy rushed from the Spanish mansion to restrain the other two.

"Don't worry," said the Colonel. "They only bite delivery boys."

Colonel Bickle, known as Bic, looked like a Kentucky Colonel. His hair was white-yellow, his large face was bright red, his nose looked swollen and he had no beard.

"Shake the hand of the owner of the winner of today's race." He was friendly and gracious and held a large trophy.

"Who won it?" asked Frank.

"Big Duke."

Bryn shook his hand and entered the high, beamed living room. From the mantel up, the room looked like a church. Below, it was more like a storeroom for different periods of antique junk. In the Victorian cluster, plopped against the gold velvet of a Queen Anne's chair, sat Maggie Bickle. She didn't notice Bryn at first. She seemed far away, in her own meditation. Her face was still handsome; her profile was noble; one gray strand fell loose from her rider's knot. Bound up inside the sheen of a green and purple pantsuit, her large body was rigid. She could barely move her neck. At the nape of her neck the zipper was half-open. And she seemed angry. Glancing back at Bic who was getting credit for her race horse, she raised her eyes to Bryn.

"Who are you?"

"Oh, I'm Bryn Corley. What a marvelous room this is. I've heard so much about you."

Maggie didn't answer. Frank hurried toward her and stooped to embrace her while Bryn made herself comfortable and spread her skirt on the settee.

On the coffee table stood an unopened box of corn chips.

"May I have one?" Bryn asked.

"Help yourself," said Maggie dryly.

Dinner was to be served aboard a mahogany yacht. Mr. Mitchum would not be there. Bic led the way across the back lawn through the azaleas and the gardenias and the aloe plants, past the grand old cedars dripping globs of Spanish moss, along the cockled sea wall to the mahogany yacht. It gleamed like Bryn's mother's dining room table.

Frank stayed behind with Maggie. Both of them were horse-breeders. They had begun discussing an epidemic of gonorrhea among the horses in Maryland where both maintained their large farms.

Bryn crossed the gangplank ahead of Bic. She was startled at the expanse and dryness of the deck. She always assumed that in spite of massive exteriors, yachts were just boats, damp and claustrophobic inside.

Bic told her that this yacht was a Trumpie. The Trumpie was the Rolls Royce of yachts. This was no fragile floating thing subject to the wind or the current in the water. This yacht was a vault with its own handsome young Captain and a young Irish cook who had been educated by the best chefs in France. The cook did everything: cook, serve and keep the boat clean.

The yacht was immaculate. Every room was carpeted and curtained. The furniture was ample; the living room was wide. There was an organ, a television, a desk and an easy chair. Over the dining room table was a crystal chandelier.

And built into the wall along the staircase leading down to the sleeping quarters below were bookshelves filled with first-editions and leather bound books. In the master bedroom a color T.V. set sat on a shelf over the foot of the double bed. Smaller T.V. sets were placed between twin beds in two of the three other guest rooms. Even the bathroom was a normal-sized bathroom, but with luxurious trimmings. When Bryn sat down on the mahogany toilet seat she pulled out and read twelve astrological messages written on consecutive squares of the toilet paper. She reached for a handle that was not there and then noticed a brass pedal on the floor at her feet. A gentle swish of fragrant blue water circled and cleaned and refilled the bowl.

"The best thing about it," said Bic who had been waiting for Bryn by the staircase, "is that if you don't like your neighbors you can pick up and leave."

"It's better than fences!" joked Bryn. She liked her line and would store it for her memoirs. "To pick up and leave can be better than fences."

While they waited on the deck for their more businesslike partners, Allan, the cook, came to take orders for drinks. After he left there was a moment of silence while Bic looked out over the water. "It was the most terrible thing I ever saw," he said, "and it happened right out there in the harbor." His voice trembled, like a child telling a ghost story. "Out of the clear blue came this sharp, skinny speedboat—they're called cigarettes. This one buzzed right in front of us. It splashed us on purpose right up on the deck here then turned and headed straight for a small yellow yacht. A big, gray-haired woman was sitting on the deck fishing and —we couldn't believe it—the cigarette jumped over her and landed on the other side. It might have hit a wave or something but it looked so deliberate.

"We sped over to check on the woman thinking she must have been terrified—well, it was much worse than that. Her legs had been cut off just above the knees. We gave her our blankets. And all the ice we had with us. We phoned for the Coast Guard. What else could we do?"

"How old was she?" Bryn asked.

"Around sixty-five."

"Did she go into shock?"

"Of course she went into shock!"

"Is she alive?"

"Last I heard."

"I can't imagine a person of that age surviving a thing like that," said Bryn looking down at her own knees. She would rather lose one of her lungs than have either of her legs harmed. She had always admired her beautiful legs.

Bryn turned from the sea back to the gangplank where Maggie was crossing with the support of Frank's arm. As the two of them descended into the yacht, Bryn stood up to join them but Frank signalled her down.

"Dinner is ready," announced Allan politely.

"Get in here," yelled Maggie from below. "We want to eat."

Maggie was plunked sourly at the head of the table on a red leather bench that was built in the wall.

The first course was pompano. Bryn was very fond of pompano and her appetite was not curbed by Maggie's talk of gonorrhea.

"It all happened in the Queen's stables."

"Did the Queen know?"

"No, but her manager did."

"Why didn't he tell her?"

"He was too polite," said Frank.

"How did it get to America?"

"A French stallion brought it."

"Those French stallions!" said Bryn who had spent two years in Paris.

After the pompano Allan brought out the artichokes: four whole artichokes and two different sauces.

"I can't eat all that!" snapped Maggie.

Allan removed the plate and brought it back with half an artichoke. He then refilled the wine glasses and returned to the kitchen.

"Wonderful little fellow," said Bic. "We could never replace him."

"Remember Sonny?" asked Maggie. "That little pony we found in our front yard?"

"Sonny?" asked Bic.

"We found this pony in our front yard and nobody ever claimed him. We kept him around—he made a great little teaser."

"What's a teaser?" asked Bryn.

"A teaser," said Frank putting his elbows on the table. He coughed and cleared his throat and wiped his mouth with a napkin. His cloudy blue eyes, which were generally half-closed, were wide open. "It's like this. You don't want to get your stallion's balls kicked off by some bitch mare who's not in heat. So you get another, smaller horse—or maybe a pony—to tease her. You tie her down by all but one leg then you mount the tease on her. If she's in heat, she'll take him. Just as he's about to come you have a couple of men ready to yank his penis out and twist it to the side."

"The poor teaser!" said Bryn.

"Oh well. We give them a whore a couple times a year."

"The best teaser I ever saw had a crooked penis," said Maggie.

"What's a whore ?"

"A whore is a mare who is always in heat but never gets pregnant."

"Why call her a whore?"

"Because she loves it, that's why."

"Why not call her a teaser too?"

"No, the mares are called testers. When a stallion has just come down from the racetracks, he's either a virgin or hasn't screwed in six months. His first load of sperm is going to be stale. You don't want to put it into a good mare, so you bring the test mare in and the stallion unloads into her. Otherwise, it's just a waste." He turned his palms up, then returned them to his lap where he picked up his napkin and wiped off his hands.

The roast beef with mushroom sauce arrived in very thin slices on individual plates. A wedge of tomato sat like a rose to the side.

"Iggy?" called Maggie to an ugly yellow dog who was asleep on a chair in the corner. "Come over here, Iggy."

The dog jumped to the floor and crawled under the table where Maggie delivered several slices of beef.

"You should have seen him in the hospital," said Maggie.

"They smuggled him in in a blanket. I thought I was going to die and I wanted to say goodbye to him. I was kissing him one last time when Duke Wayne called. I was crying so hard I couldn't talk to him. He said, 'That's okay, Maggie. I understand. I'll call you tomorrow.' I love that man. He's got cancer. I think maybe I'll call him later tonight."

"Shall I bring you the phone?" asked Bryn enthusiastically.

"After dinner," said Maggie, looking a little taken back.

As Allan came out with a fresh bottle of wine, Bryn asked Maggie if she was going to eat her mushrooms.

"No," said Maggie. "I don't like mushrooms."

"Do you think I could have them? Unless, of course, Iggy wants them. Perhaps I could share them with Iggy."

"Iggy doesn't like mushrooms either," said Maggie coldly.

After Bryn had finished Maggie's mushrooms and the roast beef left on Frank's plate, she glanced at the beef still lying on Bic's, but Allan removed it before she could ask.

"Do you have coffee?" said Frank.

"Yes, sir. There's a fruit salad for dessert."

Maggie pointed to a large basket of fancy fruit. "Robert Mitchum sent us that. He was here last night."

"He was?" moaned Bryn, aching with disappointment. She asked Allan, "Do you have any ice cream?"

"I have chocolate ice cream."

"Ummmmm, my favorite."

"You *do* like to eat," observed Maggie. "How do you stay so slim?"

"I play a lot of tennis," said Bryn quickly. "I'm getting pretty good at it, wouldn't you say, Frank?"

Frank held his hand out and tipped it back and forth.

When Allan came back with dessert, Frank cleared his throat again. He was a three-pack-a-day man and had to do this often. His head gave an involuntary shake and he leaned back in his seat. "I want to ask you something," he announced to no one in particular.

"What is it, sweetheart?" said Maggie.

"Bryn wants to go to Hollywood. She wants to get a job there."

"What kind of job?"

"Something to do with the movies."

"You want to be an *actress?*" asked Maggie.

"No, no, I don't want to be an actress. I want to work in the production end of things. Maybe with an agent or something."

"An agent! What do you want to work with an agent for?"

"I know it's the armpit of the industry," Bryn said. "But you've got to start somewhere."

Maggie turned to Frank.

"She knows what I think of the idea," said Frank. "She knows that I think that it's futile and foolish. But she wants to go anyway. Is there anything you can do for her?"

"You want my advice, honey?" Maggie said to Bryn. "Stay away from it. There is no worse place in the world than Hollywood and I've known some lousy places. Look at the horse business! But let me tell you, the horse business is nothing compared to Hollywood. I ought to know. I was up for Scarlett."

"You were up for Scarlett!" Bryn's eyes opened wide and she lost her sophistication.

"And they damn near took me, too. But they put me on this train with David Selznick and he tried to get me to do something all the way from New York to Los Angeles. Can you imagine that? Listen, honey, you know what you have to do in order to make it in Hollywood? You have to sleep with Jews. You wouldn't want to do that."

"I'd like to enjoy my own mistakes."

Maggie shook her head. "Where's Liza?" she asked Bic. "Liza would take her around."

Bryn lifted the bowl and scooped out the last spoonful of ice cream, all the while keeping her eyes on Maggie. Then she put the bowl down, wiped off her chin, and became serious. Her voice lost its girlish impressionability.

"Look. I love the movies. It's been the one thing I've been

interested in all my life. When I lived in New York, I saw ten, sometimes twenty movies a week. A couple double features in an afternoon were nothing to me. I stood in line for two hours in the pouring rain to see the seven A.M. showing of *The Godfather* and I had already seen it the night before.

"And I've been in several movies. One in Switzerland with Al Pacino and a couple of others. And I write too. I've been writing my memoirs every day for a year. That's what I really want to be. I want to be a writer."

"Oh, pooh," said Frank. "She can't write."

Bryn put her chin in one hand and without looking at Frank flicked her lighter at his unlit cigarette. He took her hand and brought the flame forward.

"Well," said Maggie appraising Bryn like a race horse. "It shouldn't be too hard to find a job for a girl as smart and attractive as you are. Bic, let's call Sam Spiegel. He can get her a job. Maybe a small one at first."

"Oh, I don't mind," said Bryn, full of hope.

"When are you ready to start?"

"Well, I have to go to Paris. And, ummm, sublet my apartment. And I sort of thought I might go to Greece. God," she mused out loud, "I hate to work in the summer. Maybe at the end of August? Or the beginning of September?"

"Forget it, baby," said Maggie.

Bryn lowered her eyes and Frank leaned back in his chair.

"We'll see what we can do for you," the Colonel said sweetly.

Maggie turned all her attention to Frank and asked about an old girlfriend of his and how she was doing in the business he helped start. Frank said she was doing very well and had already paid back his initial investment. Bryn all of a sudden felt overwhelmingly tired and restless and bored and she wanted to go home.

"Maybe we ought to go," she said. "You've been ill. We shouldn't keep you awake."

"Oh, hell, I don't sleep anyway. I slept four hours after the operation and that was it. Haven't slept since," said Maggie.

"Take pills," said Bryn.

"Don't take pills," said Frank.

"I never take pills," said Maggie. "I'd rather not sleep than take pills."

"So would I," said Frank.

"At least I'm *doing* something. I know I'm alive."

Bryn took a cigarette from Frank's pack. He lit it for her as Maggie looked on disapprovingly. Maggie turned to Bic. "Let's call the Duke now."

"We could do that."

"Better yet, let's send him the trophy. We'll have it engraved: To the Duke from Big Duke. He'll love that. He's not going to last long. One lung and he's still smoking. Now it's his heart."

"How old is he?" asked Bryn inhaling.

"Seventy-one."

"How old are you?"

"Seventy-one." Maggie looked at Bryn and then turned to Frank. "He's got one of those breathers."

"He probably has pneumonia," said Bryn. "When you get old, pneumonia gets you."

Maggie winced and reached for Frank's hand. He looked at her with sad affection and nodded for Bryn to pass the cigarettes.

"They're all gone," Bryn said. "I guess we'll have to go."

"Don't go," said Maggie. "Just stop smoking cigarettes."

"It's just a habit."

"Get another habit. One that's good for you."

"But I like smoking. I just took it up."

From the galley they heard footsteps.

"Is that you, Captain?" she called out.

A young male voice said that it was. He came into the living room. The Captain was tall, blond and movie-star handsome.

"Oh," said Bryn brightening. "I bet you smoke Marlboros."

"He doesn't smoke," said Maggie coldly.

The Captain smiled. "Well, I just happen to have some cigarettes with me." He tossed a pack of Marlboros into Bryn's lap.

"Thanks," smiled Bryn.

Frank reached into her lap and took out the cigarettes, put two in his mouth, lit both, and gave one back to Bryn.

"We couldn't keep him if we didn't let him bring his beautiful playmates on board," said Maggie. "They stay a few days, then he starts flirting with the other girls. The first ones get mad and before you know it they're gone."

"Test mares," laughed Bryn flashing her blue eyes at the Captain.

"We'll need you to help Maggie back to the house," said Bic.

"Certainly," said the Captain who stood back with his arms folded.

Bryn went up to him and said, "Kiss me, I'm Irish."

He backed away and said, "Sorry, I'm not."

"May I have a light then?" she said holding a cigarette.

"Sure," he said lighting it and then, "keep the matches."

"You were talking to him for a half an hour!" said Frank as Bryn drove home.

"I was talking to him for *three* minutes," said Bryn.

"You have no sense of propriety."

"I'm not a piece of property."

"What are you then?"

Bryn turned to look at him. She looked at him until the car began to swerve off the road.

"I might have been something if you hadn't interfered."

"How did I interfere?"

"By telling Maggie you thought it was foolish for me to go to Hollywood. The whole point of tonight's dinner was to get me a job and I'm as unemployed now as I ever was. Frank, I think you could have tried harder."

Frank remained silent until they got back to his condominium. He sat down on the sofa and put his head in his hands. Bryn walked past him and into the kitchen. She stood at the counter clutching the alarm clock, waiting for him to go to bed so she could sleep on the couch. Finally, she got tired of waiting and went into the living room. He was sitting on the sofa in the same position she had left him. After a moment he looked up and narrowed his eyes as if he'd been thinking.

"You'll never find a job because you've never stayed with one thing long enough to pick up any skills. And if you think you'll find a husband, you can forget that too. You've no interest in house-keeping and you don't know how to cook. No man wants a wife who doesn't know how to cook. The only thing you're good at is being some man's mistress. And if you want my opinion you're not very good at that."

She threw the alarm clock at him. It ricocheted off his forehead into a picture of his favorite stallion. The glass cracked, the stand collapsed, and the picture slapped flat onto the surface of the table. There was a scratch above Frank's eye.

"I'm sorry!" Bryn cried, afraid he was going to hit her. "I'm really sorry, Frank. Let's not fight anymore."

"If only you'd touch me—show some sign of affection." It was hard for Frank to say this. The words got caught in his throat and he looked down at his hands. Bryn moved forward and set the picture straight up again and offered to have the glass replaced the next day.

That night, for the first time in their three months together, Bryn fell asleep in Frank's arms. He held her very gently and was careful not to apply the least bit of pressure. She felt so safe that when she fell asleep she dreamed that he was holding her. Then he nodded off and rolled over onto her shoulder. She woke from the pressure of the iron weight of his arm.

"Frank," she repeated in a low speaking voice until he turned over and away from her, leaving her once more alone. She couldn't sleep. She took a couple of sleeping pills out of the drawer and turned on the Merle Haggard tape just below Frank's hearing level. He began to snore. She took a pen light and shone it on the back of his neck. A thousand lines cracked the skin like a parched Mojave desert. The white hairs, sparse as cacti, stood up straight and short and stubbly. When she turned the light off, she could shut her eyes and see his neck.

Miami between four and five in the morning was jet grey. The pollution from the planes and the cars on the highway gelled with the light from the forthcoming dawn. Bryn drove Frank's Cadillac off an exit ramp toward the ocean.

The thick, black ocean rolled in like sleep. Bryn lay on her side, her head on her arm. "Think," she commanded, but thought didn't come easily. All she knew was that if she left Frank she would have to get a job.

She *should* have had a job by now. All of that travelling and all those celebrities. All of those people who were going to do something for her. She had been in *one movie:* one. Playing a girl with a broken arm. Every morning they spent forty-five minutes putting the cast on. Before lunch, they took it off; after lunch, they put it on again. Not once was it ever seen in the movie. All that was seen was the back of her head. She got the part by doing a tap-dance. Imagine that. Doing a tap-dance to play the part of a cripple.

Bryn fell asleep on the edge of the shoreline. When she woke up her knees were floating in water. The tide deposited a small shell beside her and quickly drew back leaving a long wrinkled wake in the soft wet sand.

Then something happened. Something Bryn had never seen before. There was a catch in the water, a hesitation. And then, in a moment, she saw a definite shift. The next wave didn't quite reach the foam left over from the last one and the one after that lapped to a lower mark still.

"I just saw the exact moment the tide changed! It must mean something," she sighed.

All around her the waves rushed up hopefully and even more quickly were sucked back to sea.

When Frank got up Bryn was sitting on the terrace drinking tea with three tablespoons of honey and reading the *National Enquirer*.

"Oh," she grabbed her stomach. "Jackie Wilson died. That really saddens me."

"Who's Jackie Wilson?" asked Frank.

"He sang 'Tears on My Pillow'."

Frank sat down and took her hand and looked at her tenderly. She could tell he was thinking of how she fell asleep in his arms.

"Do you remember?" he asked.

"Remember what?" She didn't want to hurt him but she couldn't stand it when he mooned this way. Besides, she had decided to be a stewardess and she had to get away.

"You know, Frank, I was thinking. I really have to earn some money."

"I'll give you money."

"No, I mean I have to earn my own."

"Well?"

"What do you think about my becoming a stewardess?"

"A stewardess! That's just a waitress in the sky. Why not be a pilot?"

"I hate responsibility."

"Well then travel around with me. I have to go to Europe at the end of May."

"Frank, really, I have to get out on my own. I have no identity· here. I'm tired of being a 'Frank Kiernan' girl."

"You think you're going to find your identity serving coffee, tea and milk?"

"I love travelling and I love serving people. My very favorite job involved serving people."

"What was that?"

"I sold ice cream from a truck when I was sixteen."

"Look. I was thinking about going to Alaska."

"Alaska! I've always wanted to go to Alaska."

"I want to go this summer."

"But it's just March!" groaned Bryn.

"It's too damn cold to go up there in March."

"Alaska," Bryn sighed. It was becoming a mantra.

"Well, think about it and let me know what you're thinking."

Bryn thought about it all through her tennis lesson. After the lesson she stopped at the bar.

"Iced tea," she said to the bartender. "Have you ever been to Alaska?"

"No," he said serving up the iced tea.

Bryn took out her cigarettes and matches the Captain had given her. Inside of the matchbook which was white on the outside was a note that read "You can reach me at" and then gave the number.

"He likes me!" cried Bryn. "I knew that he liked me."

She slid off the barstool and crossed the dance floor, languidly placing one foot in front of the other. She pressed a white cube and a red one on the jukebox, thinking, "Maybe the Captain would like to go to Alaska." She had a burning desire to go to Alaska. "Or maybe I'll take a Greyhound and go all by myself."

PRETEND DINNERS

W. P. KINSELLA

For Barbara Kostynyk

It was Oscar Stick she married. The thing that surprise me most about Oscar and Bonnie getting together is that Oscar be a man who don't really like women, and Bonnie seem to me a woman who need more love than anybody I ever knowed.

She was Bonnie Brightfeathers to start with and a girl who always been into this here Women's Lib stuff. She been three years older than me for as long as I can remember. That age make quite a difference at times. When she was eighteen she don't even talk to a kid like me, but now that she's 23 and I'm 20, it don't seem to make any difference at all.

401

Bonnie Brightfeathers graduate the grade twelve class at the Residential School with really good report cards. She hold her head up, walk with long steps like she going someplace, and she don't chase around with guys or drink a lot. Her and Bedelia Coyote is friends and they always say they don't need men for nothing.

"A woman without a man be like a fish without a bicycle," Bedelia say all the time. She read that in one of these MS Magazines that she subscribe to, and she like to say it to my girlfriend Sadie One-wound when she see us walk along the road have our arms around each other.

After high school Bonnie get a job with one of these night patrol and security companies in Wetaskiwin. Northwest Security and Investigations is the right name. She wear a light brown uniform and carry on her hip in a holster what everybody say is a real gun. She move away from her parents who got more kids than anything else except maybe beer bottles what been throwed through the broke front window of their cabin and lay in the yard like cow chips. She move from the reserve to Wetaskiwin after her first pay cheque. Pretty soon she got her own little yellow car and an apartment in a new building at the end of 51st avenue.

All this before she was even nineteen. It was almost a year later that I got to know her good. A Government looking letter come to the reserve for her and her father ask me to take it up to Wetaskiwin the next time I go. That same night I went in Blind Louis Coyote's pickup truck and Bonnie invite me up to her apartment after I buzzed the talk-back machine in the lobby.

It be an apartment where the living room/bed room be all one. The kitchen is about as big as most closets but she got the whole place fixed up cheerful: soft cushions all over the place, lamps with colored bulbs, and pretty dishes. She got too a record player and a glass coffee table with chrome legs. The kitchen table be so new that it still smell like the inside of a new car. There are plants too, hang on a wool rope from the ceiling and brush my shoulder when I cross the room to sit on her sofa. Whole apartment ain't big enough to swing a cat in, but it is a soft, warm place to be, like the inside of a sleeping bag.

Bonnie is a real pretty person remind me some of my sister Illianna. She got long hair tied in kind of a pony-tail on each side of her head and dark eyes just a little too big for her face. Her skin is a browny-yellow color like furniture I seen in an antique store window. She is a lot taller than most Indian girls and real slim. She wear cut off jeans and a scarlet blouse the night I come to see her.

She give me a beer in a tall glass. I don't even get to see the bottle except when she take it out of the fridge. She put out for us some peanuts in a sky-blue colored dish the shape of a heart while she talk to me about how happy she is.

This is about the time that I write down my first stories for Mr. Nichols. Being able to do something that I want to do sit way off in the future like a bird so high in the sky that it be just a speck, but I can understand how proud Bonnie feel to see her life turning out good.

"Someday, Silas, I'm going to have me a whole big house. I babysit one time for people in Wetaskiwin who got a living room bigger than this whole apartment." She pour herself a beer and come sit down beside me.

"You know what they teached us at the Home Economics class in high school? About something called gracious living. Old Miss Lupus, she show us how to set a table for a dinner party of eight. She show us what forks to put where and learned us what kind of wine to serve with what dish."

Bonnie got at the end of her room the top half of a cupboard with doors that are like mirrored sunglasses, all moonlight colored and you can sort of see yourself in them. When she tell me the cupboard is called a hutch I make jokes about how many rabbits she could keep in there.

"I remember Bedelia Coyote saying, 'Hell, we have a dinner party for fifteen every night, but we only got eleven plates so the late ones get to wait for a second setting, if the food don't run out first.'"

After a while Bonnie show me the inside of the cupboard. She got two dinner plates be real white and heavy, two sets of silver knives, spoon, and fat and thin forks, two wine glasses with stems must be six inches long, and four or five bottles of wine and liquor. The bottles be all different colors and shapes.

"Most everybody make fun of that stuff Miss Lupus teach us, but I remember it all good and I'm gonna use it someday. One time Sharon Fence-post asked, 'What kind of wine do you serve with Kraft Dinner?' and Miss Lupus try to give her a straight answer, but everybody laugh so hard we can't hear what she say."

Bonnie take down the bottles from the cabinet to show me. "I buy them because they look pretty. See, I never even crack the seals," and she take out a tall bottle of what could be lemon pop except the label say, *Galliano*. She got too a bottle of dark green with a neck over a foot long and it have a funny name that I have to write down on the back of a match book, *Valpolicella*.

"We put on pretend dinners up there at the school. They got real fancy wine glasses, look like a frosted window, and real wine bottles except they got in them only water and food coloring. We joke about how Miss Lupus and Mr. Gortner, the principal, drink up all the real wine before they fill up the bottles for us to pretend with. Vicki Crowchild took a slug out of one of them bottles, then spit it clean across the room and say, 'This wine tastes like shit.' Miss Lupus suspended her for two weeks for that.

"See this one," Bonnie say, and show me a bottle that be both a bottle and a basket, all made of glass and filled with white wine. "Rich people do that," she say, "put out wine bottles in little wood baskets. They sit it up on the table just like a baby lay in a crib."

There is a stone crock of blue and white got funny birds fly around on it, and one that be stocky and square like a bottle of Brute Shaving Lotion, and be full of a bright green drink called *Sciarda*. I'd sure like to taste me that one sometime.

It is like we been friends, Bonnie and me, for a long time, or better than friends, maybe a brother and sister. Bonnie got in her lamp soft colored light bulbs that make the room kind of golden. She put Merle Haggard on the record player and we talk for a long time. Later on, my friends Frank and Rufus give me a bad time 'cause I stay there maybe three hours and leave them wait in the truck. They tease me about what we maybe done up there, but I know we are just friends and what anybody else think don't matter.

"Sit up to the table here, Silas, and I make for you a pretend dinner," Bonnie say. She put that heavy plate, white as new snow, in front of me, and she arrange the knife and other tools in the special way she been taught.

"Put your beer way off to the side there. Beer got no place at pretend dinners," and she set out the tall wine glasses and take the glass bottle and basket and make believe she fill up our glasses. "Know what we having for dinner?"

"Roast moose," I say.

Bonnie laugh pretty at that, but tell me we having chicken or maybe fish 'cause when you having white wine you got to serve only certain things like that with it.

"I remember that, the next time we have a bottle in the bushes outside Blue Quills Hall on Saturday night," I tell her.

Bonnie make me a whole pretend dinner, right from things she say is appetizers to the roast chicken stuffed with rice. "What do you want for dessert?" she ask me. When I say chocolate pudding, she say I should have a fancy one like strawberry shortcake or peaches with brandy. "Might as well have the best when you making believe."

I stick with chocolate pudding. I like the kind that come in a can what is painted white inside.

"Some of this here stuff is meant to be drunk after dinner," Bonnie say, waving the tall yellow bottle that got the picture of an old fashioned soldier on the label. "I ain't got the right glasses for this yet. Supposed to use tiny ones no bigger than the cap off a whiskey bottle. This time you got to pretend both the bottle and glass. Miss Lupus tell us that people take their after dinner drinks to the living room, have their cigarette there and relax their stomach after a big meal."

I light up Bonnie's cigarette for her and we pretend to relax our stomachs.

"I'm gonna really do all this oneday, Silas. I'm gonna get me a man who likes to share real things with me, but one who can make believe too."

"Thought you and Bedelia don't like men?"

"Bedelia's different from me. She really believe what she say, and she's strong enough to follow it through. I believe women should have a choice of what they do, but that other stuff, about hating men, and liking to live all alone, for me at least that just be a front that is all pretend like these here dinners."

She say something awful nice to me then. We talking in Cree and it be a hard language to say beautiful things in. What Bonnie say to me come up because we carried on talking about love. I say I figure most everybody find someone to love at least once or twice.

"How many people you know who is happy in their marriage?" Bonnie say.

"Maybe only one or two," I tell her.

"I don't want no marriage like I seen around here. For me it got to be more. I want somebody to twine my nights and days around, the way roses grow up a wire fence."

When I tell her how pretty I figure that is her face break open in a great smile and the dimples on each side of her mouth wink at me. I wish her luck and tell her how much I enjoy that pretend dinner of hers. Bonnie got a good heart. I hope she find the kind of man she looking for.

That's why it be such a surprise when she marry Oscar Stick.

Oscar is about 25. He is short and stocky with bowed legs. He walk rough, drink hard, and fist-fight anybody who happen to meet his eye. He like to stand on the step of the Hobbema General Store with his thumbs in his belt loops. Oscar can roll a cigarette with only one hand and he always wear a black felt hat that make him look most a foot taller than he really is. He rodeo all summer and do not much in the winter.

Oscar be one of these mean, rough dudes who like to see how many women he can get and then he brag to everybody and tell all about what he done with each one.

"A woman is just a fuck. The quicker you let her know that the better off everybody is." Oscar say that to us guys one night at the pool hall. He is giving me and my friend Frank Fence-post a bad time 'cause we try to be mostly nice to our girlfriends.

"Always let a woman know all you want to do is screw her and get to hell away from her. It turns them on to think you're like that. And everyone thinks they is the one gonna change your mind. You should see how hard they try, and the only way a woman know to change you is to fuck you better. . ." and he laugh, wink at us guys, and light up a cigarette by crack a blue-headed match with his thumbnail.

Guess Bonnie must of thought she could change him.

"Bedelia's never once said 'I told you so' to me. She been a good friend." It is last week already and it is Bonnie Stick talking to me.

Not long after that time three years ago when her and Oscar married, her folks got one of them new houses that the Indian Affairs Department build up on the ridge. After things start going bad for Oscar and Bonnie they move into Brightfeathers' old cabin on the reserve.

"It was Bedelia who got the Welfare for me when Oscar went off to rodeo last summer and never sent home no money."

I met Bonnie just about dusk walking back to her cabin from

Hobbema. She carrying a package of tea bags, couple of Kraft Dinner, and a red package of DuMaurier cigarettes. She invite me to her place for tea.

We've seen each other to say hello to once in a while but we never have another good visit like we did in Wetaskiwin. I am just a little bit shy to talk to her 'cause I know about her dreams and I only have to look at her to tell that things turned out pretty bad so far.

She still wear the tan colored pants from her uniform but by now they is faded, got spots all over them, and one back pocket been ripped off. Bonnie got a tooth gone on her right side top and it make her smile kind of crooked. She got three babies and look like maybe she all set for a fourth by the way her belly bulge. I remember Oscar standing on the steps of the store saying, "A woman's like a rifle: should be kept loaded up and in a corner."

She boil up the tea in a tin pan on the stove. We load it up with canned milk and sugar. Bonnie look over at the babies spread out like dolls been tossed on the bed. The biggest one lay on her stomach with her bum way up in the air. "We got caught the first time we ever done it, Oscar and me," and she make a little laugh as she light up a cigarette. "This here coal-oil lamp ain't as fancy as what I had in the apartment, eh?"

We talk for a while about that apartment.

"I really thought it would be alright with Oscar. I could of stayed working if it weren't for the babies. They took back the car and all my furniture 'cause I couldn't pay for it. At first Oscar loved me so good, again and again, so's I didn't mind living in here like this," and she wave her hand around the dark cabin with the black woodstove and a few pieces of broke furniture. "Then he stopped. He go off to the rodeo for all summer, and when he is around he only hold me when he's drunk and then only long enough to make himself happy.

"I shouldn't be talking to you like this, Silas. Seems like every time I see you I tell you my secrets."

I remind her about those pretty words she said to me about twining around someone. She make a sad laugh. "You can only pretend about things like that. . .they don't really happen," and she make that sad laugh again. "Sometimes I turn away from him first just to show I don't give a care for him either. And sometimes I feel like I'm as empty inside as a meadow all blue with moonlight, and that I'm gonna die if I don't get held. . ."

Bonnie come up to me and put her arms around me then. She fit herself up close and put her head on my chest. She hang on to me so tight, like she was going to fall a long way if she was to let go. I feel my body get interested in her and I guess she can too 'cause we be so close together. I wonder if she is going to raise her face up to me and maybe fit her mouth inside mine the ways girls like to do.

But she don't raise her face up. "It ain't like you think," she say into my chest. "I know you got a woman and I got my old man, wherever he is. It's just that sometimes. . ." and her voice trail off.

I kind of rub my lips against the top of her head. Her arms been holding me so long that they started to tremble. "I charge up my batteries with you, Silas. Then I can go along for another while and pretend that everything is going to be okay. Hey, remember the time that I made up the pretend dinner for you? I still got the stuff," she say, and take her arms from around me. From under the bed she bring out a cardboard box say Hoover Vacuum Cleaner on the side, and take out that tall wine bottle, and the heavy white plates, only one been broke and glued back together so it got a scar clean across it.

She clear off a space on the table and set out the plates and wine glasses. One glass got a part broken out of it, a V shape, like the beak of a bird. The wine bottles is dusty and been empty for a long time.

"Oscar drink them up when he first moved in with me, go to sleep with his head on the fancy table of mine," Bonnie say as she tip up the tall bottle. She laugh a little and the dimples show on each side of her mouth.

"I'll take the broke glass," she say, "though I guess it not make much difference if we don't have no wine. If you're hungry, Silas, I make some more tea and there's buscuits and syrup on the counter."

"No thanks," I say. "We don't want to spoil these here pretend dinners by having no food."

HARMONY OF THE WORLD

CHARLES BAXTER

I

IN THE SMALL OHIO TOWN where I grew up, many homes had parlors that contained pianos, sideboards, and sofas, heavy objects signifying gentility. These pianos were rarely tuned. They went flat in summer around the fourth of July and sharp in winter at Christmas. Ours was a Story and Clark. On its music stand were copies of Stephen Foster and Ethelbert Nevin favorites, along with one Chopin prelude that my mother would practice for twenty minutes every three years. She had no patience, but since she thought Ohio — all of it, every scrap — made sense, she was happy and did not need to practice anything. Happiness is not infectious, but somehow her happiness infected my father, a pharmacist, and then spread through the rest of the household. My whole family was obstinately cheerful. I think of my two sisters, my brother, and my parents as having artificial pasted-on smiles, like circus clowns. They apparently thought cheer and good Christian words were universals, respected everywhere. The pianos were part of this cheer. They played for celebrations and moments of pleasant pain. Or rather: someone played them, but not too well, since excellent playing would have been faintly antisocial. "Chopin," my mother said, shaking her head as she stumbled through the prelude. "Why is he famous?"

When I was six, I received my first standing ovation. On the stage of the community auditorium, where the temperature was about 94°, sweat fell from my forehead onto the piano keys, making their ivory surfaces slippery. At the conclusion of the piece, when everyone stood up to applaud, I thought they were just being nice. My playing had been mediocre; only my sweating had been extraordinary. Two years later, they stood up again. When I was eleven, they cheered. By that time I was astonishing these small-town audiences with Chopin and Rachmaninoff recital chestnuts. I thought I was a genius and read biographies of Einstein. Already the townspeople were saying that I was the best thing Parkersville had ever seen, *that I would put the place on the map*. Mothers would send their children by to watch me practice. The kids sat with their mouths open while I polished off another classic.

Like many musicians, I cannot remember ever playing badly, in the sense of not knowing what I was doing. In high school, my identity was being sealed shut: my classmates called me "el señor longhair," even though I wore a crewcut, this being the 1950s. Whenever the town needed a demonstration of local genius, it called upon me. There were newspaper articles detailing my accomplishments, and I must have heard the phrase "future concert career" at least two hundred times. My parents smiled and smiled as I collected applause. My senior year, I gave a solo recital and was hired for umpteen weddings and funerals. I was good luck. On the fourth of July the townspeople brought out a piano to the city square so that I could improvise music between explosions at the fireworks display. Just before I left for college, I noticed that our neighbors wanted to come up to me ostensibly for small talk, but actually to touch me.

In college I made a shocking discovery: other people existed in the world who were as talented as I was. If I sat down to play a Debussy etude, they would sit down and play Beethoven, only louder and faster than I had. I felt their breath on my neck. Apparently there were other small towns. In each one of these small towns there was a genius. Perhaps some geniuses were not actually geniuses. I practiced constantly and began to specialize in the non-Germanic piano repertoire. I kept my eye out for students younger than I was, who might have flashier technique. At my senior recital I played Mozart, Chopin, Ravel, and Debussy, with encore pieces by Scriabin and Thomson. I managed to get the audience to stand up for the last time.

I was accepted into a large midwestern music school, famous for its high standards. Once there, I discovered that genius, to say nothing of talent, was a common commodity. Since I was only a middling composer, with no interesting musical ideas as such, I would have to make my career as a performer or teacher. But I didn't want to teach, and as a performer I lacked pizzazz. For the first time, it occurred to me that my life might be evolving into something unpleasant, something with the taste of stale bread.

I was beginning to meet performers with more confidence than I had, young musicians to whom doubt was as alien as proper etiquette. Often these people dressed like tramps, smelled, smoked constantly, were gay or sadistic. Whatever their imbalances, they were not genteel. *They did not represent small towns*. I was struck by their eyes. Their eyes seemed to proclaim, "The universe believes in me. It always has."

My piano teacher was a man I will call Luther Stecker. Every year he taught at the music school for six months. For the following six months he toured. He turned me away from the repertoire with which I was familiar and demanded that I learn several pieces by composers whom I had not often played, including Bach, Brahms, and Liszt. Each one of these composers discovered a weak point in me: I had trouble keeping up the consistent frenzy required by Liszt, the mathematical precision required by Bach, the unpianistic fingerings of Brahms.

I saw Stecker every week. While I played, he would doze off. When he woke, he would mumble some inaudible comment. He also coached a trio I participated in, and he spoke no more audibly then than he did during my private lesson.

I couldn't understand why, apart from his reputation, the school had hired him. Then I learned that in every Stecker-student's life, the time came when the Master collected his thoughts, became blunt, and told the student exactly what his future would be. For me, the moment arrived on the third of November, 1966. I was playing sections of the Brahms Paganini Variations, a fiendish piece on which I had spent many hours. When I finished, I saw him sit up.

"Very good," he said, squinting at me. "You have talents."

There was a pause. I waited. "Thank you," I said.

"You have a nice house?" he asked.

"A nice house? No."

"You should get a nice house somewhere," he said, taking his handkerchief out of his pocket and waving it at me. "With windows. Windows with a view."

I didn't like the drift of his remarks. "I can't afford a house," I said.

"You will. A nice house. For you and your family."

I resolved to get to the heart of this. "Professor," I asked, "what did you think of my playing?"

"Excellent," he said. "That piece is very difficult."

"Thank you."

"Yes, technically excellent," he said, and my heart began to pound. "Intelligent phrasing. Not much for me to say. Yes. That piece has many notes," he added, enjoying the *non sequitur*.

I nodded. "Many notes."

"And you hit all of them accurately. Good pedal and good discipline. I like how you hit the notes."

I was dangling on his string, a little puppet.

"Thousands of notes, I suppose," he said, staring at my forehead, which was beginning to get damp, "and you hit all of them. You only forgot one thing."

"What?"

"The passion!" he roared. "You forgot the passion! You always forget it! Where is it? Did you leave it at home? You never bring it with you! Never! I listen to you and think of a robot playing! A smart robot, but a robot! No passion! Never ever ever!" He stopped shouting long enough to sneeze. "You *should* buy a house. You know why?"

"Why?"

"Because the only way you will ever praise God is with a family, that's why! Not with this piano! You are a fine student," he wound up, "but you make me sick! Why do you make me sick?"

He waited for me to answer.

"*Why do you make me sick?*" he shouted. "Answer me!"

"How can I possibly answer you?"

"By articulating words in English! Be courageous! Offer a suggestion! Why do you make me sick?"

I waited for a minute, the longest minute my life has seen or will ever see. "Passion," I said at last. "You said there wasn't enough passion. I thought there was. Perhaps not."

He nodded. "No. You are right. No passion. A corruption of music itself. Your playing is too gentle, too much good taste. To play the piano like a genius, you must have a bit of the fanatic. Just a bit. But it is essential. You have stubbornness and talent but no fanaticism. You don't have the salt on the rice. Without salt, the rice is inedible, no matter what its quality otherwise." He stood up. "I tell you this because sooner or later someone else will. You will have a life of disappointments if you stay in music. You may find a teacher who likes you. Good, good. *But you will never be taken up! Never!* You should buy a house, young man. With a beautiful view. Move to it. Don't stay here. You are close to success, but it is the difference between leaping the chasm and falling into it, one inch short. You are an inch short. You could come back for more lessons. You could graduate from here. But if you are truly intelligent, you will say goodbye. Goodbye." He looked down at the floor and did not offer me his hand.

I stood up and walked out of the room.

Becalmed, I drifted down and up the hallways of the building for half an hour. Then a friend of mine, a student of conducting from Bolivia, a Marxist named Juan Valparaiso, approached, and, ignoring my shallow breathing and cold sweat, started talking at once.

"Terrible, furious day!" he said.

"Yes."

"I am conducting *Benvenuto Cellini* overture this morning! All is going well until difficult flute entry. I instruct, with force, flutists. Soon all woodwinds are ignoring me." He raised his eyebrows and stroked his huge gaucho mustache. "Always! Always there are fascists in the woodwinds!"

"Fascists everywhere," I said.

"Horns bad, woodwinds worse. Demands of breath made for insanes. Pedro," he said, "you are appearing irresoluted. Sick?"

"Yes," I nodded. "Sick. I just came from Stecker. My playing makes *him* sick."

"He said that? That you are making him sick?"

"That's right. I play like a robot, he says."

"What will you do?" Juan asked me. "Kill him?"

"No." And then I knew. "I'm leaving the school."

"What? Is impossible!" Tears leaped instantly into Juan's eyes. "Cannot, Pedro. After one whipping? No! Disappointments everywhere here. Also outside in world. Must stick to it." He grabbed me by the shoulders. "Fascists put here on earth to break our hearts! Must live through. You cannot go." He looked around wildly. "Where could you go anyway?"

"I'm not sure," I said. "He said I would never amount to anything. I think he's right. But I could do something else." To prove that I could imagine options, I said, "I could work for a newspaper. You know, music criticism."

"Caterpillars!" Juan shouted, his tears falling onto my shirt. "Failures! Pathetic lives! Cannot, cannot! Who would hire you?"

I couldn't tell him for six months, until I was given a job in Knoxville on a part-time trial basis. But by then I was no longer writing letters to my musician friends. I had become anonymous. I worked in Knoxville for two years, then in Louisville — a great city for music — until I moved here, to this city I shall never name, in the middle of New York state, where I bought a house with a beautiful view.

In my home town, they still wonder what happened to me, but my smiling parents refuse to reveal my whereabouts.

II

Every newspaper has a command structure. Within that command structure, editors assign certain stories, but the writers must be given some freedom to snoop around and discover newsworthy material themselves. In this anonymous city, I was hired to review all the concerts of the symphony orchestra and to provide some hype articles during the week to boost the ticket sales for Friday's program. Since the owner of the paper was on the symphony board of trustees, writing about the orchestra and its programs was necessarily part of good journalistic citizenship. On my own, though, I initiated certain projects, wrote book reviews for the Sunday section, interviewed famous visiting musicians — some of them my ex-classmates — and during the summer I could fill in on all sorts of assignments, as long as I cleared what I did with the feature editor, Morris Cascadilla.

"You're the first serious musician we've ever had on the staff here," he announced to me when I arrived, suspicion and hope fighting for control on his face. "Just remember this: be clear and concise. Assume they've got intelligence but no information. After that, you're on your own, except you should clear dicey stuff with me. And never forget the Maple Street angle."

The Maple Street angle was Cascadilla's equivalent to the Nixon Administration's "How will it play in Peoria?" No matter what subject I wrote about, I was expected to make it relevant to Maple Street, the newspaper's mythical locus of middle-class values. I could write about electronic, aleatory, or post-Boulez music *if* I suggested that the city's daughters might be corrupted by it. Sometimes I found the Maple Street angle, and sometimes I couldn't. When I failed, Cascadilla would call me in, scowl at my copy and mutter, "All the Juilliard graduates in town will love this." Nevertheless, the Maple Street angle was a spiritual exercise in humility, and I did my best to find it week after week.

When I first learned that the orchestra was scheduled to play Paul Hindemith's *Harmony of the World* symphony, I didn't think of Hindemith, but of Maple Street.

III

Working on the paper left me some time for other activities. Unfortunately, there was nothing I knew how to do except play the piano and write reviews.

Certain musicians are very practical. Trumpet players (who love valves) tend to be good mechanics, and I have met a few composers who fly airplanes and can restore automobiles. Most performing violinists and pianists, however, are drained by the demands of their instruments and seldom learn how to do anything besides play. In daily life they are helpless and stricken. In midlife the smart ones force themselves to find hobbies. But the less fortunate come home to solitary apartments without pictures or other decorations, warm up their dinners in silence, read whatever books happen to be on the dinner table, and then go to bed.

I am speaking of myself here, of course. As time passed, and the vacuum of my life made it harder to breathe, I required more work. I fancied I was a tree, putting out additional leaves. I let it be known that I would play as an accompanist for voice students and other recitalists, if their schedules didn't interfere with my commitments for the paper.

One day I received a call at my desk. A quietly controlled female voice asked, "Is this Peter Jenkins?"

"Yes."

"Well," she said, pausing, as if she'd forgotten what she meant to tell me, "this is Karen Jensen. That's almost like Jenkins, isn't it?" I waited. "I'm a singer," she said, after a moment. "A soprano. I've just lost my accompanist and I'm planning on giving a recital in three months. They said you were available. Are you? What do you charge?"

I told her.

"Isn't that kind of steep? That's kind of steep. Well, I suppose . . . I can use somebody else until just before, and then I can use you. They say you're good. And I've read your reviews. I really admire the way you write!"

"Thank you."

"You get so much information into your reviews! Sometimes, when I read you, I imagine what you look like. Sometimes a person can make a mental picture. I just wish the paper would publish a photo or something of you."

"They want to," I said, "but I asked them to please don't."

"Even your voice sounds like your writing!" she said excitedly. "I can see you in front of me now. Can you play Fauré and Schubert? I mean, is there any composer or style you don't like and won't play?"

"No," I said. "I play anything."

"That's *wonderful!*" she said, as if I had confessed to a remarkable tolerance. "Some accompanists are so picky. 'I won't do this, I won't do that.' Well, *one* I know is like that. Anyhow, could we meet soon? Do you sightread? Can we meet at the music school downtown? In a practice room? When are you free?"

I set up an appointment.

She was almost beautiful. Her deep eyes were accented by depressive bowls in quarter-moon shadow under them. Though she was only in her late twenties, she seemed slightly scorched by anxiety. She couldn't keep still. Her hands fluttered as they fixed her hair; she scratched nervously at her cheeks; and her eyes jumped every few seconds. Soon, however, she calmed down and began to look me in the eye, evaluating me. Then *I* turned away.

She wanted to test me out and had brought along her recital numbers, mostly standard fare: a Handel aria, Mozart, Schubert, and Fauré. The last set of songs, *Nine Epitaphs,* by an American composer I had never heard of, Theodore Chanler, was the only novelty.

"Who is this Chanler?" I asked, looking through the sheet music.

"I . . . I found it in the music library," she said. "I looked him up. He was born in Boston and died in 1961. There's a recording by Phyllis Curtin. Virgil Thomson says these are maybe the best American art songs ever written."

"Oh."

"They're kind of, you know, lugubrious. I mean they're all epitaphs written supposedly on tombstones, set to music. They're like portraits. I love them. Is it all right? Do you mind?"

"No, I don't mind."

We started through her program, beginning with Handel's "*Un sospiretto d'un labbro pallido*" from *Il Pastor fido*. I could immediately see why she was still in central New York state and why she would always be a student. She had a fine voice, clear and distinct, somewhat styled after Victoria de los Angeles (I thought), and her articulation was superb. If these achievements had been the whole story, she might have been a professional. But her pitch wobbled on sustained notes in a maddening way; the effect was not comic and would probably have gone unnoticed by most non-musicians, but to me the result was harrowing. She could sing perfectly for several measures and then she would miss a note by a semi-tone, which drove an invisible fingernail into my scalp. It was as though a gypsy's curse descended every five or six seconds, throwing her off pitch; then she was allowed to be a great singer until the curse descended again. Her loss of pitch was so regularized that I could see it coming and squirmed in anticipation. I felt as though I were in the presence of one of God's more complicated pranks.

Her choice of songs highlighted her failings. Their delicate textures were constantly broken by her lapses. When we arrived at the Chanler pieces, I thought I was accustomed to her, but I found I wasn't. The first song begins with the following verse, written by Walter de la Mare, who had crafted all the poems in archaic epitaph style:

> Here lyeth our infant, Alice Rodd;
> > She were so small,
> > Scarce aught at all,
> But a mere breath of Sweetness sent from God.

The vocal line for "She were so small" consists of four notes, the last two rising a half-step from the two before them. To work, the passage requires a dead-eye accuracy of pitch:

Singing this line, Karen Jensen hit the D-sharp but missed the E and skidded up uncontrollably to F-sharp, which would sound all right to anyone who didn't have the music in front of his nose, as I did. Only a fellow-musician could be offended.

Infuriated, I began to feel that I could *not* participate in a recital with this woman. It would be humiliating to perform such lovely songs in this excruciating manner. I stopped playing, turned to her to tell her that I could not continue after all, and then I saw her bracelet.

I am not, on the whole, especially observant, a failing that probably accounts for my having missed the bracelet when we first met. But I saw it now: five silver canaries dangled down quietly from it, and as it slipped back and forth, I saw her wrist and what I suddenly realized *would* be there: the parallel lines of her madness, etched in scar tissue.

The epitaphs finished, she asked me to work with her, and I agreed. When we shook hands, the canaries shook in tiny vibrations, as if pleased with my dutiful kindness, my charity, toward their mad mistress.

IV

Though Paul Hindemith's reputation once equalled Stravinsky's and Bartók's, it suffered after his death in 1963 an almost complete collapse. Only two of his orchestral works, the *Symphonic Metamorphoses on Themes of Weber* and the *Mathis der Maler* symphony, are played with any frequency, thanks in part to their use of borrowed tunes. One hears his woodwind quintets and choral pieces now and again, but the works of which he was most proud — the ballet *Nobilissima Visione, Das Marienleben* (a song cycle), and the opera *Harmonie die Welt* — have fallen into total obscurity.

The reason for Hindemith's sudden loss of reputation was a mystery to me; I had always considered his craftsmanship if not his inspiration to be first-rate. When I saw that the *Harmony of the World* symphony, almost never played, would be performed in our anonymous city, I told Cascadilla that I wanted to write a story for that week on how fame was gained and lost in the world of music. He thought that subject might be racy enough to interest the tone-deaf citizens of leafy and peaceful Maple Street, where no one is famous, if I made sure the story contained "the human element."

I read up on Hindemith, played his piano music, and listened to the recordings. I slowly found the music to be technically astute but emotionally arid, as if some problem of purely local interest kept the composer's gaze safely below the horizon. Technocratic and oddly timid, his work reminded me of a model train chugging through a tiny town where only models of people actually lived. In fact, Hindemith did have a lifelong obsession with train sets: in Berlin, his took up three rooms, and the composer wrote elaborate timetables so that the toys wouldn't collide.

But if Hindemith had a technocrat's intelligence, he also believed in the necessity of universal participation in musical activities. Listening was not enough. Even non-musical citizens could learn to sing and play, and he wrote music expressly for this purpose. He seems to have known that passive, drugged listening was a side-effect of totalitarian environments and that elitist composers such as Schoenberg were engaged in antisocial Faustian projects that would bewilder and infuriate most audiences, leaving them isolated and thus eager to be drugged by a musical superman.

As the foremost anti-Nietzschean German composer of his day, therefore, Hindemith left Germany when his works could not be performed, thanks to the Third Reich; wrote textbooks with simple exercises; composed a requiem in memory of Franklin Roosevelt, set to words by Walt Whitman; and taught students, not all of them talented, in Ankara, New Haven, and Buffalo ("this caricature of a town"). As he passed through late middle age, he turned to a project he had contemplated all his life, an opera based on the career of the German astronomer Johannes Kepler, author of *De Harmonice Mundi*. This opera, a summary of Hindemith's ideas, would be called *Harmony of the World*. Hindemith worked out the themes first in a symphony, which bore the same title as the opera, and completed it in 1951. The more I thought about this project, the more it seemed anachronistic. Who believed in world harmony in 1951? Or thereafter? Such a symphony would have to pass beyond technical sophistication into divine inspiration, which Hindemith had never shown any evidence of possessing.

It occurred to me that Hindemith's lifelong sanity had perhaps given way in this case, toppled not by despair (as is conventional) but by faith in harmony.

V

For the next rehearsal, I drove to Karen Jensen's apartment, where there was, she said, a piano. I'd become curious about the styles of her insanity; I imagined a hamster cage in the kitchen, a doll-head mobile in the living room, and mottos written with different colored inks on memo pads tacked up everywhere on the walls.

She greeted me at the door without her bracelet. When I looked at her wrist, she said, "Hmmm. I see that you noticed. A memento of adolescent despair." She sighed. "But it does frighten people off. Once you've tried to do something like that, people don't really trust you. I don't know why exactly. Don't want your blood on their hands or something. Well, come on in."

I was struck first by her forthrightness and secondly by her tiny apartment. Its style was much like the style in my house. She owned an attactive but worn-down sofa, a sideboard that supported an antique clock, one chair, a glass-top dinner table, and one nondescript poster on the wall. Trying to keep my advantage, I looked hard for tell-tale signs of insanity but found none. The piano was off in the corner, almost hidden, unlike those in the parlors back home.

"Very nice," I said.

"Well, thanks," she said. "It's not much. I'd like something bigger, but . . . where I work, I'm an administrative assistant, and they don't pay me very much. So that's why I live like a snail here. It's hardly big enough to move around in, right?" She wasn't looking at me. "I mean, I could almost pick it up and carry it away."

I nodded. "You just don't think like a rich person," I said, trying to be hearty. "They like to expand. They need room. Big houses, big cars, fat bodies."

"Oh, I know!" she said, laughing. "My uncle . . . would *you* like to stay for dinner? You look like you need a good meal. I mean, after the rehearsal. You're just skin and bones, Pet— . . . may I call you Peter?"

"Sure." I sat down on the sofa and tried to think up an excuse. "I really can't stay, Miss Jensen. I have another rehearsal to go to later tonight. I wish I could."

"That's not it, is it?" she asked suddenly, looking down at me. "I don't believe you. I bet it's something else. I bet you're afraid of me."

"Why should I be afraid of you?"

She smiled and shrugged. "That's all right. You don't have to say anything. I know how it goes." She laughed once more, faintly. "I never found a man who could handle it. They want to show you *their* scars, you know? They don't want to see any on you, and if they discover any, they just run." She slapped her right hand into her forehead and then ran her fingers through her hair. "Well, shit. I didn't mean to do this *at all!* I mean, I admire you so much and everything, and here I am, running on like this. I guess we should get down to business, right? Since I'm paying you by the hour."

I smiled professionally and went to her piano.

Beneath the high culture atmosphere that surrounds them, art songs have one subject: love. The permutations of love (lust, solitude, and loss) are present in abundance, of course, but for the most part they are simple vehicles for the expression of that one emotion. I was reminded of this as I played through the piano parts. As much as I concentrated on the music in front of me, I couldn't help but notice that my employer stood next to the piano, singing the words sometimes toward me, sometimes away. She was rather courageously forcing eye-contact on me. She kept this up for an hour and a half until we came to the Chanler settings, when at last she turned slightly, singing to the walls.

As before, her voice broke out of control every five seconds, giving isolated words all the wrong shadings. The only way to endure it, I discovered, was to think of her singing as a post-modern phenomenon with its own conventions and rules. As the victim of necessity rather than accident, Karen Jensen was tolerable.

> Here sleep I,
> Susannah Fry,
> No one near me,
> No one nigh:
> Alone, alone
> Under my stone,
> Dreaming on,
> Still dreaming on:
> Grass for my valance

And coverlid,
Dreaming on
As I always did.
'Weak in the head?'
Maybe. Who knows?
Susannah Fry
Under the rose.

There she was, facing away from me, burying Susannah Fry, and probably her own past and career into the bargain.

When we were done, she asked, "Sure you won't stay?"

"No, I don't think so."

"You really haven't another engagement, do you?"

"No," I admitted.

"I didn't think so. You were scared of me the moment you walked in the door. You thought I'd be crazy." She waited. "After all, only ugly girls live alone, right? And I'm not ugly."

"No, you aren't," I said. "You're quite attractive."

"Do you think so?" she asked, brightening. "It's so nice to hear that from you, even if you're just paying a compliment. I mean, it still means *something*." Then she surprised me. As I stood in the doorway, she got down on her knees in front of me and bowed her head in the style of one of her songs. "Please stay," she asked. Immediately she stood up and laughed. "But don't feel obliged to."

"Oh, no," I said, returning to her living room. "I've just changed my mind. Dinner sounds like a good idea."

After she had served and we had started to eat, she looked up at me and said, "You know, I'm not completely good." She paused. "At singing."

"What?" I stopped chewing. "Yes, you are. You're all right."

"Don't lie. I know I'm not. You know I'm not. Come on: let's at least be honest. I think I have certain qualities of musicality, but my pitch is . . . you know. Uneven. You probably think it's awfully vain of me to put on these recitals like this. With nobody but friends and family coming."

"No, I don't."

"Well, I don't care what you say. It's . . . hmm, I don't know. People encourage me. And it's a discipline. Music's finally a discipline that rewards you. Privately, though. Well, that's what my mother says."

Carefully, I said, "She may be right."

"Who cares if she is?" she laughed, her mouth full of food. "I enjoy doing it. Like I enjoy doing this. Listen, I don't want to seem forward or anything, but are you married?"

"No."

"I didn't think so." She picked up a string bean and eyed it suspiciously. "Why aren't you? You're not ugly. In fact you're all right looking. You obviously haven't been crazy. Are you gay or something?"

"No."

"No," she agreed, "you don't look gay. You don't even look very happy. You don't look very anything. Why is that?"

"I should be offended by this line of questioning."

"But you're not. You know why? Because I'm interested in you. I hardly know you, but I like you, what I can see. Don't you have any trust?"

"Yes," I said, finally.

"So answer my question. Why don't you look very anything?"

"Do you want to hear what my piano teacher once said?" I asked. "He said I wasn't enough of a fanatic. He said that to be one of the great ones you have to be a tiny bit crazy. Touched. And he said I wasn't. And when he said it, I knew all along he was right. I was waiting for someone to say what I already knew, and he was the one. I was too much a good citizen, he said. I wasn't possessed."

She rose, walked around the table to where I was sitting, and stood in front of me, looking down at my face. I knew that whatever she was going to do had been picked up, in attitude, from one of her songs. She touched the back of my arm with two fingers on her right hand. "Well," she said, "maybe you aren't possessed, but what would you think of me as another possession?"

VI

In 1618 at the age of seventy, Katherine Kepler, the mother of Johannes Kepler, was put on trial for witchcraft. The records indicate that her personality was so deranged, so deeply offensive to all, that if she were alive today she would *still* be called a witch.

One of Kepler's biographers, Angus Armitage, notes that she was "evil-tempered" and possessed an interest in unnamed "outlandish things." Her trial lasted, on and off, for three years; by 1621, when she was acquitted, her personality had disintegrated completely. She died the following year.

At the age of six, Kepler's son Frederick died of smallpox. A few months later, Kepler's wife, Barbara, died of typhus. Two other children, Henry and Susanna, had died in infancy.

Like many another of his age, Kepler spent much of his adult life cultivating favor from the nobility. He was habitually penniless and was often reduced, as his correspondence shows, to begging for handouts. He was the victim of religious persecution, though luckier in this regard than some.

After he married for a second time, three more children died in infancy, a statistic that in theory carries less emotional weight than one might think, given the accepted levels of infant mortality for that era.

In 1619, despite the facts cited above, Kepler published *De Harmonice Mundi*, a text in which he set out to establish the correspondence between the laws of harmony and the disposition of planets in motion. In brief, Kepler argued that certain intervals, such as the octave, major and minor sixths, and major and minor thirds, were pleasurable, while other intervals were not. History indicated that mankind had always regarded certain intervals as unpleasant. Feeling that this set of universal tastes pointed to immutable laws, Kepler sought to map out the pleasurable intervals geometrically, and then to transfer that geometrical pattern to the order of the planets. The velocity of the planets, rather than their strict placement, constituted the harmony of the spheres. This velocity provided each planet with a note, what Armitage calls a "term in a mathematically determined relation."

> In fact, each planet performed a short musical scale, set down by Kepler in staff notation. The length of the scale depended upon the eccentricity of the orbit; and its limiting notes could generally be shown to form a concord (except for Venus and the Earth with their nearly circular orbits, whose scales were of very constricted range). . . . at the Creation . . . complete concord prevailed and the morning stars sang together.

VII

We began to eat dinner together. Accustomed to solitude, we did not always engage in conversation. I would read the newspaper or ink in letters on my geometrically patterned crossword puzzles at my end of the table, while Karen would read detective novels or *Time* at hers. If she had cooked, I would clear and wash the dishes; if I had cooked, she did the cleaning. Experience and disappointments had made us methodical. She told me that she had once despised structured experiences governed by timetables, but that after several manic-depressive episodes, she had learned to love regularity. This regularity included taking lithium at the same time — to the minute — each day.

The season being summer, we would pack towels and swimming suits after dinner and drive out to one of several public beaches, where we would swim until darkness came on. On calm evenings, Karen would drop her finger in the water and watch the waves lap outward. I favored immature splashing, or grabbing her by the arm and whirling her around me until I released her and she would spin back and fall into the water, laughing as she sank. One evening, we found a private beach, two hundred feet of sand all to ourselves, on a lake thirty miles out of town. Framed on both sides by woods and well-hidden from the highway, this beach had the additional advantage of being unpatrolled. We had no bathhouse in which to change, however, so Karen instructed me not to look as she walked about fifty feet away to a spot where she undressed and put on her suit.

Though we had been intimate for at least a week, I had still not seen her naked: like a good Victorian, she demanded the shades be drawn, the lights out, and the covers pulled discreetly over us. But now, with the same methodical thoroughness, she wanted me to see her, so I looked, despite her warnings. She was bent over, under the tree boughs, the evening light breaking through the leaves and casting broken gold bands on her body. Her arms were delicate, the arms of a schoolgirl, I thought, an impression heightened by the paleness of her skin, but her breasts were full, at first making me think of Rubens' women, then of Renoir's, then of nothing at all. Slowly, knowing I was watching her, she pinned her hair up. Not her breasts or arms, but that expression of vague contentment as she looked out toward the water away from me: *that* made me feel a tingling below my heart, somewhere in an emotional center near my stomach. I wanted to pick her up and carry her somewhere, but with my knees wobbly it was all I could do to make my way over to where she stood and take her in my arms before she cried out. "Jesus," she said, shivering, "you gave me a surprise." I kissed her, waiting for inspiration to direct me on what to do next: pick her up? Carry her? Make love to her on the sand? Wade into the water with her and swim out to the center of the bay, where we would drown together in a Lawrentian love-grip? But then we broke the kiss; she put on her swimsuit like a good citizen, and we swam for our usual fifteen minutes in silence. Afterwards, we changed back into our clothes and drove home, muttering smalltalk. Behavior inspired by and demonstrating love embarrassed both of us. When I told her that she was beautiful and that I loved her, she patted me on the cheek and said, "Aw, how nice. You always try to say the right thing."

VIII

The Maple Street angle for *Harmony of the World* ran as follows: SYMPHONY OF FAITH IN A FAITHLESS AGE. Hindemith, I said, wished to confound the skeptics by composing a monument of faith. In an age of organized disharmony, of political chaos, he stood at the barricades defending tonality and traditional musical form. I carefully avoided any specific discussion of the musical materials of the symphony, which in the Schott orchestral score looked over-complex and melodically ugly. From what I could tell without hearing the piece, Hindemith had employed stunning technique in order to disguise his lack of inspiration, though I did not say so in print. Instead, I wrote that the symphony's failure to win public support was probably the result of Hindemith's refusal to use musical gimmicks on the one hand and sticky sweet melodies on the other. I wrote that he had not been dismayed by the bad reviews *Harmony of the World* had received, which was untrue. I said he was a man of integrity. I did not say that men of integrity are often unable to express joy when the occasion demands. Cascadilla liked my article. "This guy sounds like me," he said, reading my copy. "I respect him." The article ran five days before the concert and was two pages away from the religion-and-faith section. Not long after, the symphony ticket office called me to say that my piece had caused a rush of ticket orders from ordinary folk, non-concert types, who wanted to hear this "religious symphony." The woman from the business office thanked me for my trouble. "Let's hope they like it," I said.

"Of course they will," she assured me. "You've told them to."

But they didn't. Despite all the oratory in the symphony, it was spiritually as dead as a lampshade. I could see why Hindemith had been shocked by the public reaction. Our audience applauded politely in discouragement, and then I heard an unusual sound for this anonymous city: one man, full of fun and conviction, booing loudly from the balcony. Booing the harmony of the world! He must be a Satanist! Don't intentions mean anything? So what if the harmony and joy were all counterfeit? The conductor came out for a bow, smiled at the booing man, and very soon the applause died away. I left the hall, feeling responsible. Arriving at the paper, I wrote a review of crushing dullness that reeked of bad faith. Goddamn Hindemith! Here he was, claiming to have seen God's workings, and they sounded like the workings of a steam engine or a trolley car. A fake symphony, with optimism the composer did not feel! I decided (but did not write) that *Harmony of the World* was just possibly the largest, most misconceived fiasco in modern music's history. It was a symphony that historically could not be written by a man who was constitutionally not equipped to write it. In my review, I kept a civil pen: I said that the performance lacked "luster," "a certain necessary glow."

IX

"I'm worried about the recital tomorrow."

"Aw, don't worry. Here, kiss me. Right here."

"Aren't you listening? I'm worried."

"I'm singing. You're just accompanying me. Nobody's going to notice you. Move over a little, would you? Yeah, there. That pillow was forcing my head against the wall."

"Why aren't you worried?"

"Why should I be worried? I don't want to worry. I want to make love. Isn't that better than worrying?"

"Not if I'm worried."

"People won't notice *you*. By the way, have you noticed that when I kiss you on the stomach, you get goosebumps?"

"Yes. I think you're taking this pretty lightly. I mean, it's almost unprofessional."

"That's because I'm an amateur. A 100% amateur. Always and totally. Even at this. But that doesn't mean I don't have my moments. Mmmmmm. That's better."

"I thought it would maybe help. But listen. I'm still worried."

"Uhhhn. Oh, wait a minute. Wait a minute. Oh, I get it."

"What?"

"I get it. You aren't worried about yourself. You're worried about me."

X

Forty people attended her recital, which was sponsored by the city university's music school, in which Karen was a sometime student. Somehow we made our way through the program, but when we came to the Chanler settings, I suddenly wanted Karen to sing them perfectly. I wanted an angel to descend and to take away the gypsy's curse. But she sang as she always had — off pitch — and when she came to "Ann Poverty," I found myself in that odd region between rage and pity.

> Stranger, here lies
> Ann Poverty;
> Such was her name
> And such was she.
> May Jesu pity
> Poverty.

But I was losing my capacity for pity.

In the green room, her forty friends came back to congratulate her. I met them. They were all very nice. She smiled and laughed:

there would be a party in an hour. Would I go? I declined. When we were alone, I said I was going back to my place.

"Why?" she asked. "Shouldn't you come to my party? You're my lover after all. That *is* the word."

"Yes. But I don't want to go with you."

"Why?"

"Because of tonight's concert, that's why."

"What about it?"

"It wasn't very good, was it? I mean, it just wasn't."

"I thought it was all right. A few slips. It was pretty much what I was capable of. All those people said they liked it."

"Those people don't matter!" I said, my eyes watering with anger. "Only the music matters. Only the music is betrayed, they aren't. They don't know about pitch, most of them. I mean, Jesus, they aren't genuine musicians, so how would they know? Do you really think what we did tonight was good? It wasn't! It was a travesty! We ruined those songs! How can you stand to do that?"

"I don't ruin them. I sing them adequately. I project feeling. People get pleasure from them. That's enough."

"It's awful," I said, feeling the ecstatic lift-off into rage. "You're so close to being good, but you *aren't* good. Who cares what those ignoramuses think? They don't know what notes you're *supposed* to hit. It's that goddamn slippery pitch of yours. You're killing those songs. You just *drop* them like watermelons on the stage! It makes me sick! I couldn't have gone on for another day listening to you and your warbling! I'd die first."

She looked at me and nodded, her mouth set in a half-moue, half-smile of non-surprise. There may have been tears in her eyes, but I didn't see them. She looked at me as if she were listening hard to a long-distance call. "You're tired of me," she said.

"I'm not tired of you. I'm tired of hearing you sing! Your voice makes my flesh crawl! Do you know why? Can you tell me why you make me sick? Why do you make me sick? Never mind. I'm just glad this is over."

"You don't look glad. You look angry."

"And you look smug. Listen, why don't you go off to your party? Maybe there'll be a talent scout there. Or roses flung riotously at you. But don't give a recital like this again, please, okay? It's a public disgrace. It offends music. It offends *me*."

I turned my back on her and walked out to my car.

XI

After the failure of *Harmony of the World,* Hindemith went on a strenuous tour that included Scandinavia. In Oslo, he was rehearsing the Philharmonic when he blinked his bright blue eyes twice, turned to the concertmaster, and said, "I don't know where I am." They took him away to a hospital; he had suffered a nervous breakdown.

XII

I slept until noon, having nothing to do at the paper and no reason to get up. At last, unable to sleep longer, I rose and walked to the kitchen to make coffee. I then took my cup to the picture window and looked down the hill to the trees of the conservation area, the view Stecker had once told me I should have.

The figure of a woman was hanging from one of the trees, a noose around her neck. I dropped my coffee cup and the hot coffee spilled out over my feet.

I ran out the back door in my pajamas and sprinted painfully down the hill's tall grass toward the tree. I was fifty feet away when I saw that it wasn't Karen, wasn't in fact a woman at all, but an effigy of sorts, with one of Karen's hats, a pillow head, and a dress hanging over a broomstick skeleton. Attached to the effigy was a note:

> In the old days, this might have been me. Not anymore. Still, I thought it'd make you think. And I'm not giving up singing, either. By the way, what your playing lacks is not fanaticism, but concentration. You can't seem to keep your mind on one thing for more than a minute at a time. *I* notice things, too. You aren't the only reviewer around here. Take good care of this doll, okay?
>
> XXXXX,
> Karen

I took the doll up and dropped it in the clothes closet, where it stands to this hour.

Hindemith's biographer, Geoffrey Skelton, writes, "[On the stage] the episodic scenes from Kepler's life fail to achieve immediate dramatic coherence, and the basic theme remains obscure. . . ."

She won't of course see me again. She won't talk to me on the phone, and she doesn't answer my letters. I am quite lucidly aware of what I have done. And I go on seeing doubles and reflections and wave motion everywhere. There is symmetry, harmony, after all. I suppose I should have been nice to her. That, too, is a discipline. I always tried to be nice to everyone else.

On his deathbed, Hindemith has Kepler sing:

> *Und muss sehn am End:*
> *Die grosse Harmonie, das is der Tod.*
> *Absterben ist, sie zu bewirken, not.*
> *Im Leben hat sie keine Statte.*
>
> Now, at the end, I see it:
> the great harmony: it is death.
> To find it, we must die.
> In life it has no place.

XIII

Hindemith's words may be correct. But Dante says that the residents of limbo, having never been baptised, will not see the face of God. This despite their having committed no sin, no active fault. In their fated locale, they sigh, which keeps the air "forever trembling." No harmony for them, these guiltless souls. Through eternity, the residents of limbo — where one can imagine oneself if one cannot stand to imagine any part of hell — experience one of the most shocking of all the emotions that Dante names: "duol senza martíri," grief without torment. These sighs are rather like the sounds one hears drifting from front porches in small towns on soft summer nights.

SARAH COLE: A TYPE OF LOVE STORY

RUSSELL BANKS

To begin, then, here is a scene in which I am the man and my friend Sarah Cole is the woman. I don't mind describing it now, because I'm a decade older and don't look the same now as I did then, and Sarah is dead. That is to say, on hearing this story you might think me vain if I looked the same now as I did then, because I must tell you that I was extremely handsome then. And if Sarah were not dead, you'd think I were cruel, for I must tell you that Sarah was very homely. In fact, she was the homeliest woman I have ever known. Personally, I mean. I've *seen* a few women who were more unattractive than Sarah, but they were clearly freaks of nature or had been badly injured or had been victimized by some grotesque, disfiguring disease. Sarah, however, was quite normal, and I knew her well, because for three and a half months we were lovers.

Here is the scene. You can put it in the present, even though it took place ten years ago, because nothing that matters to the story depends on when it took place, and you can put it in Concord, New Hampshire, even though that is indeed where it took place, because it doesn't matter where it took place, so it might as well be Concord, New Hampshire, a place I happen to know well and can therefore describe with sufficient detail to make the story believable. Around six o'clock on a Wednesday evening in late May a man enters a bar. The place, a cocktail lounge at street level with a

437

restaurant upstairs, is decorated with hanging plants and unfinished wood paneling, butcherblock tables and captain's chairs, with a half dozen darkened, thickly upholstered booths along one wall. Three or four men between the ages of twenty-five and thirty-five are drinking at the bar, and they, like the man who has just entered, wear three piece suits and loosened neckties. They are probably lawyers, young, unmarried lawyers gossiping with their brethren over martinis so as to postpone arriving home alone at their whitewashed townhouse apartments, where they will fix their evening meals in radar ranges and, afterwards, while their tv's chuckle quietly in front of them, sit on their couches and do a little extra work for tomorrow. They are, for the most part, honorable, educated, hard-working, shallow, and moderately unhappy young men. Our man, call him Ronald, Ron, in most ways is like these men, except that he is unusually good-looking, and that makes him a little less unhappy than they. Ron is effortlessly attractive, a genetic wonder, tall, slender, symmetrical, and clean. His flaws, a small mole on the left corner of his square but not-too-prominent chin, a slight excess of blond hair on the tops of his tanned hands, and somewhat underdeveloped buttocks, insofar as they keep him from resembling too closely a men's store mannequin, only contribute to his beauty, for he is beautiful, the way we usually think of a woman as being beautiful. And he is nice, too, the consequence, perhaps, of his seeming not to know how beautiful he is, to men as well as women, to young people, even children, as well as old, to attractive people, who realize immediately that he is so much more attractive than they as not to be competitive with them, as well as unattractive people, who see him and gain thereby a comforting perspective on those they have heretofore envied for their good looks.

Ron takes a seat at the bar, unfolds the evening paper in front of him, and before he can start reading, the bartender asks to help him, calling him "Sir," even though Ron has come into this bar numerous times at this time of day, especially since his divorce last fall. Ron got divorced because, after three years of marriage, his wife had chosen to pursue the career that his had interrupted, that of a fashion designer, which meant that she had to live in New York City while he had to continue to live in New Hampshire, where his career had got its start. They agreed to live apart until he could continue his career near New York City, but after a few months, between conjugal visits, he started sleeping with other women, and she started sleeping with other men, and that was that. "No big deal," he explained to friends, who liked both Ron and his wife, even though he was slightly more beautiful than she. "We really were too young when we got married, college sweethearts. But we're still best friends," he assured them. They understood. Most of Ron's friends were divorced by then too.

Ron orders a scotch and soda, with a twist, and goes back to reading his paper. When his drink comes, before he takes a sip of it, he first carefully finishes reading an article about the recent re-appearance of coyotes in northern New Hampshire and Vermont. He lights a cigarette. He goes on reading. He takes a second sip of his drink. Everyone in the room, the three or four men scattered along the bar, the tall, thin bartender, and several people in the booths at the back, watches him do these ordinary things.

He has got to the classified section, is perhaps searching for someone willing to come in once a week and clean his apartment, when the woman who will turn out to be Sarah Cole leaves a booth in the back and approaches him. She comes up from the side and sits next to him. She's wearing heavy, tan cowboy boots and a dark brown, suede cowboy hat, lumpy jeans and a yellow tee shirt that clings to her arms, breasts, and round belly like the skin of a sausage. Though he will later learn that she is thirty-eight years old, she looks older by about ten years, which makes her look about twenty years older than he actually is. (It's difficult to guess accurately how old Ron is, he looks anywhere from a mature twenty-five to a youthful forty, so his actual age doesn't seem to matter.)

"It's not bad here at the bar," she says, looking around. "More light, anyhow. Whatcha readin'?" she asks brightly, planting both elbows on the bar.

Ron looks up from his paper with a slight smile on his lips, sees the face of a woman homelier than any he has ever seen or imagined before, and goes on smiling lightly. He feels himself falling into her tiny, slightly crossed, dark brown eyes, pulls himself back, and studies for a few seconds her mottled, pocked complexion, bulbous nose, loose mouth, twisted and gapped teeth, and heavy but receding chin. He casts a glance over her thatch of dun-colored hair and along her neck and throat, where acne burns

against gray skin, and returns to her eyes, and again feels himsel
falling into her.

"What did you say?" he asks.

She knocks a mentholated cigarette from her pack, and Roɪ
swiftly lights it. Blowing smoke from her large, wing-shapeɑ
nostrils, she speaks again. Her voice is thick and nasal, a chocolate
colored voice. "I asked you whatcha readin', but I can see now.'
She belts out a single, loud laugh. "The paper!"

Ron laughs, too. "The paper! *The Concord Monitor!*" He is noɪ
hallucinating, he clearly sees what is before him and admits—no,
he asserts—to himself that he is speaking to the most unattractive
woman he has ever seen, a fact which fascinates him, as if instead
he were speaking to the most beautiful woman he has ever seen or
perhaps ever will see, so he treasures the moment, attempts to
hold it as if it were a golden ball, a disproportionately heavy object
which—if he doesn't hold it lightly and with precision and firm-
ness—will slip from his hand and roll across the lawn to the lip of
the well and down, down to the bottom of the well, lost to him
forever. It will be merely a memory, something to speak of
wistfully and with wonder as over the years the image fades and
comes in the end to exist only in the telling. His mind and body
waken from their sleepy self-absorption, and all his attention
focuses on the woman, Sarah Cole, her ugly face, like a wart hog's,
her thick, rapid voice, her dumpy, off-center wreck of a body, and
to keep this moment here before him, he begins to ask questions of
her, he buys her a drink, he smiles, until soon it seems, even to
him, that he is taking her and her life, its vicissitudes and woe,
quite seriously.

He learns her name, of course, and she volunteers the information that she spoke to him on a dare from one of the two women
still sitting in the booth behind her. She turns on her stool and
smiles brazenly, triumphantly, at her friends, two women, also
homely (though nowhere as homely as she) and dressed, like her,
in cowboy boots, hats and jeans. One of the women, a blond with
an underslung jaw and wearing heavy eye makeup, flips a little
wave at her, and as if embarrassed, she and the other woman at the
booth turn back to their drinks and sip fiercely at straws.

Sarah returns to Ron and goes on telling him what he wants to
know, about her job at the Rumford Press, about her divorced

husband who was a bastard and stupid and "sick," she says, as if filling suddenly with sympathy for the man. She tells Ron about her three children, the youngest, a girl, in junior high school and boy-crazy, the other two, boys, in high school and almost never at home anymore. She speaks of her children with genuine tenderness and concern, and Ron is touched. He can see with what pleasure and pain she speaks of her children; he watches her tiny eyes light up and water over when he asks their names.

"You're a nice woman," he informs her.

She smiles, looks at her empty glass. "No. No, I'm not. But you're a nice man, to tell me that."

Ron, with a gesture, asks the bartender to refill Sarah's glass. She is drinking white Russians. Perhaps she has been drinking them for an hour or two, for she seems very relaxed, more relaxed than women usually do when they come up and without introduction or invitation speak to him.

She asks him about himself, his job, his divorce, how long he has lived in Concord, but he finds that he is not at all interested in telling her about himself. He wants to know about her, even though what she has to tell him about herself is predictable and ordinary and the way she tells it unadorned and clichéd. He wonders about her husband. What kind of man would fall in love with Sarah Cole?

2

That scene, at Osgood's Lounge in Concord, ended with Ron's departure, alone, after having bought Sarah's second drink, and Sarah's return to her friends in the booth. I don't know what she told them, but it's not hard to imagine. The three women were not close friends, merely fellow workers at Rumford Press, where they stood at the end of a long conveyor belt day after day packing *TV Guides* into cartons. They all hated their jobs, and frequently after work, when they worked the day shift, they would put on their cowboy hats and boots, which they kept all day in their lockers, and stop for a drink or two on their way home. This had been their first visit to Osgood's, a place that, prior to this, they had avoided out of a sneering belief that no one went there but lawyers and insurance men. It had been Sarah who had asked the others why that should keep them away, and when they had no answer for her, the three had decided to stop at Osgood's. Ron was right, they had been there over.an hour when he came in, and Sarah was a little drunk. "We'll hafta come in here again," she said to her friends, her voice rising slightly.

Which they did, that Friday, and once again Ron appeared with his evening newspaper. He put his briefcase down next to his stool and ordered a drink and proceeded to read the front page, slowly deliberately, clearly a weary, unhurried, solitary man. He did not notice the three women in cowboy hats and boots in the booth in back, but they saw him, and after a few minutes Sarah was once again at his side.

"Hi."

He turned, saw her, and instantly regained the moment he had lost when, the previous night, once outside the bar, he had forgotten about the ugliest woman he had ever seen. She seemed even more grotesque to him now than before, which made the moment all the more precious to him, and so once again he held the moment as if in his hands and began to speak with her, to ask questions, to offer his opinions and solicit hers.

I said earlier that I am the man in this story and my friend Sarah Cole, now dead, is the woman. I think back to that night, the second time I had seen Sarah, and I tremble, not with fear but in shame. My concern then, when I was first becoming involved with Sarah, was merely with the moment, holding onto it, grasping it wholly as if its beginning did not grow out of some other prior moment in her life and my life separately and at the same time did not lead into future moments in our separate lives. She talked more easily than she had the night before, and I listened as eagerly and carefully as I had before, again, with the same motives, to keep her in front of me, to draw her forward from the context of her life and place her, as if she were an object, into the context of mine. I did not know how cruel this was. When you have never done a thing before and that thing is not simply and clearly right or wrong, you frequently do not know if it is a cruel thing, you just go ahead and do it, and maybe later you'll be able to determine whether you acted cruelly. That way you'll know if it was right or wrong of you to have done it in the first place.

While we drank, Sarah told me that she hated her ex-husband because of the way he treated the children. "It's not so much the money," she said, nervously wagging her booted feet from her perch on the high barstool. "I mean, I get by, barely, but I get them fed and clothed on my own okay. It's because he won't even write them a letter or anything. He won't call them on the phone, all he calls for is to bitch at me because I'm trying to get the state to take him to court so I can get some of the money he's s'posed to be paying for child support. And he won't even think to talk to the kids when he calls. Won't even ask about them."

"He sounds like a bastard," I said.

"He is, he is," she said. "I don't know why I married him. Or stayed married. Fourteen years, for Christ's sake. He put a spell over me or something. I don't know," she said with a note of wistfulness in her voice. "He wasn't what you'd call good-looking."

After her second drink, she decided she had to leave. Her children were at home, it was Friday night and she liked to make sure she ate supper with them and knew where they were going and who they were with when they went out on their dates. "No dates on schoolnights," she said to me. "I mean, you gotta have rules, you know."

I agreed, and we left together, everyone in the place following us with his or her gaze. I was aware of that, I knew what they were thinking, and I didn't care, because I was simply walking her to her car.

It was a cool evening, dusk settling onto the lot like a gray blanket. Her car, a huge, dark green Buick sedan at least ten years old, was battered, scratched, and almost beyond use. She reached for the door handle on the driver's side and yanked. Nothing. The door wouldn't open. She tried again. Then I tried. Still nothing.

Then I saw it, a V-shaped dent in the left front fender creasing the fender where the door joined it, binding the metal of the door against the metal of the fender in a large crimp that held the door fast. "Someone must've backed into you while you were inside," I said to her.

She came forward and studied the crimp for a few seconds, and when she looked back at me, she was weeping. "Jesus, Jesus, Jesus!" she wailed, her large, frog-like mouth wide open and wet with spit, her red tongue flopping loosely over gapped teeth. "I can't pay for this! I *can't!*" Her face was red, and even in the dusky light I could see it puff out with weeping, her tiny eyes seeming almost to disappear behind wet cheeks. Her shoulders slumped, and her hands fell limply to her sides.

Placing my briefcase on the ground, I reached out to her and put my arms around her body and held her close to me, while she cried wetly into my shoulder. After a few seconds, she started pulling herself back together and her weeping got reduced to sniffling. Her cowboy hat had been pushed back and now clung to her head at a precarious, absurdly jaunty angle. She took a step away from me and said, "I'll get in the other side."

"Okay," I said almost in a whisper. "That's fine."

Slowly, she walked around the front of the huge, ugly vehicle and opened the door on the passenger's side and slid awkwardly across the seat until she had positioned herself behind the steering wheel. Then she started the motor, which came to life with a roar. The muffler was shot. Without saying another word to me, or even waving, she dropped the car into reverse gear and backed it loudly out of the parking space and headed out the lot to the street.

I turned and started for my car, when I happened to glance toward the door of the bar, and there, staring after me, were the bartender, the two women who had come in with Sarah, and two of the men who had been sitting at the bar. They were lawyers, and I knew them slightly. They were grinning at me. I grinned back and got into my car, and then, without looking at them again, I left the place and drove straight to my apartment.

3

One night several weeks later, Ron meets Sarah at Osgood's, and after buying her three white Russians and drinking three scotches himself, he takes her back to his apartment in his car—a Datsun fastback coupe that she says she admires—for the sole purpose of making love to her.

I'm still the man in this story, and Sarah is still the woman, but I'm telling it this way because what I have to tell you now confuses me, embarrasses me, and makes me sad, and consequently, I'm likely to tell it falsely. I'm likely to cover the truth by making Sarah a better woman than she actually was, while making myself appear worse than I actually was or am; or else I'll do the opposite, make Sarah worse than she was and me better. The truth is, I was pretty, extremely so, and she was not, extremely so, and I knew it and she knew it. She walked out the door of Osgood's determined to make love to a man much prettier than any she had seen up close before, and I walked out determined to make love to a woman much homelier than any I had made love to before. We were, in a sense, equals.

No, that's not exactly true. (You see? This is why I have to tell the story the way I'm telling it.) I'm not at all sure she feels as Ron does. That is to say, perhaps she genuinely likes the man, in spite of his being the most physically attractive man she has ever known. Perhaps she is more aware of her homeliness than of his beauty, just as he is more aware of her homeliness than of his beauty, for Ron, despite what I may have implied, does not think of himself as especially beautiful. He merely knows that other people think of him that way. As I said before, he is a nice man.

Ron unlocks the door to his apartment, walks in ahead of her, and flicks on the lamp beside the couch. It's a small, single bedroom, modern apartment, one of thirty identical apartments in a large brick building on the heights just east of downtown Concord. Sarah stands nervously at the door, peering in.

"Come in, come in," he says.

She steps timidly in and closes the door behind her. She removes her cowboy hat, then quickly puts it back on, crosses the livingroom, and plops down in a blond easychair, seeming to shrink in its hug out of sight to safety. Ron, behind her, at the entry to the kitchen, places one hand on her shoulder, and she stiffens. He removes his hand.

"Would you like a drink?"

"No . . . I guess not," she says, staring straight ahead at the wall opposite where a large framed photograph of a bicyclist advertises in French the Tour de France. Around a corner, in an alcove off the living room, a silver-gray ten-speed bicycle leans casually against the wall, glistening and poised, slender as a thoroughbred racehorse.

"I don't know," she says. Ron is in the kitchen now, making himself a drink. "I don't know . . . I don't know."

"What? Change your mind? I can make a white Russian for you. Vodka, cream, kahlua, and ice, right?"

Sarah tries to cross her legs, but she is sitting too low in the chair and her legs are too thick at the thigh, so she ends, after a struggle, with one leg in the air and the other twisted on its side. She looks as if she has fallen from a great height.

Ron steps out from the kitchen, peers over the back of the chair, and watches her untangle herself, then ducks back into the kitchen. After a few seconds, he returns. "Seriously. Want me to fix you a white Russian?"

"No."

Ron, again from behind, places one hand onto Sarah's shoulder, and this time she does not stiffen, though she does not exactly relax, either. She sits there, a block of wood, staring straight ahead.

"Are you scared?" he asks gently. Then he adds, "*I* am."

"Well, no, I'm not scared." She remains silent for a moment. "You're scared? Of what?" She turns to face him but avoid his eyes.

"Well . . . I don't do this all the time, you know. Bring home a woman I . . .," he trails off.

"Picked up in a bar."

"No. I mean, I like you, Sarah, I really do. And I didn't just pick you up in a bar, you know that. We've gotten to be friends, you and me."

"You want to sleep with me?" she asks, still not meeting his steady gaze.

"Yes." He seems to mean it. He does not take a gulp or even a sip from his drink. He just says, "Yes," straight out, and cleanly, not too quickly, either, and not after a hesitant delay. A simple statement of a simple fact. The man wants to make love to the woman. She asked him, and he told her. What could be simpler?

"Do you want to sleep with *me*?" he asks.

She turns around in the chair, faces the wall again, and says in a low voice, "Sure I do, but . . . it's hard to explain."

"What? But what?" Placing his glass down on the table between the chair and the sofa, he puts both hands on her shoulders and lightly kneads them. He knows he can be discouraged from pursuing this, but he is not sure how easily. Having got this far without bumping against obstacles (except the ones he has placed in his way himself), he is not sure what it will take to turn him back. He does not know, therefore, how assertive or how seductive he should be with her. He suspects that he can be stopped very easily, so he is reluctant to give her a chance to try. He goes on kneading her doughy shoulders.

"You and me . . . we're real different." She glances at the bicycle in the corner.

"A man . . . and a woman," he says.

"No, not that. I mean, different. That's all. Real different. More than you . . . you're nice, but you don't know what I mean, and that's one of the things that makes you so nice. But we're different. Listen," she says, "I gotta go. I gotta leave now."

The man removes his hands and retrieves his glass, takes a sip, and watches her over the rim of the glass, as, not without difficulty, she rises from the chair and moves swiftly toward the door. She stops at the door, squares her hat on her head, and glances back at him.

"We can be friends. Okay?"

"Okay. Friends."

"I'll see you again down at Osgood's, right?"

"Oh, yeah, sure."

"Good. See you," she says, opening the door.

The door closes. The man walks around the sofa, snaps on the television set, and sits down in front of it. He picks up a *TV Guide* from the coffee table and flips through it, stops, runs a finger down the listings, stops, puts down the magazine and changes the channel. He does not once connect the magazine in his hand to the woman who has just left his apartment, even though he knows she spends her days packing *TV Guides* into cartons that get shipped to warehouses in distant parts of New England. He'll think of the connection some other night, but by then the connection will be merely sentimental. It'll be too late for him to understand what she meant by "different."

4

But that's not the point of my story. Certainly it's an aspect of the story, the political aspect, if you want, but it's not the reason I'm trying to tell the story in the first place. I'm trying to tell the story so that I can understand what happened between me and Sarah Cole that summer and early autumn ten years ago. To say we were lovers says very little about what happened; to say we were friends says even less. No, if I'm to understand the whole thing, I have to say the whole thing, for, in the end, what I need to know is whether what happened between me and Sarah Cole was right or wrong. Character is fate, which suggests that if a man can know and then to some degree control his character, he can know and to that same degree control his fate.

But let me go on with my story. The next time Sarah and I were together we were at her apartment in the south end of Concord, a second floor flat in a tenement building on Perley Street. I had stayed away from Osgood's for several weeks, deliberately trying to avoid running into Sarah there, though I never quite put it that way to myself. I found excuses and generated interests in and reasons for going elsewhere after work. Yet I was obsessed with Sarah by then, obsessed with the idea of making love to her, which, because it was not an actual *desire* to make love to her, was an unusually complex obsession. Passion without desire, if it gets expressed, may in fact be a kind of rape, and perhaps I sensed the danger that lay behind my obsession and for that reason went out of my way to avoid meeting Sarah again.

Yet I did meet her, inadvertently, of course. After picking up shirts at the cleaner's on South Main and Perley Streets, I'd gone down Perley on my way to South State and the post office. It was a Saturday morning, and this trip on my bicycle was part of my regular Saturday routine. I did not remember that Sarah lived on Perley Street, although she had told me several times in a complaining way—it's a rough neighborhood, packed dirt yards, shabby apartment buildings, the carcasses of old, half-stripped cars on cinderblocks in the driveways, broken red and yellow plastic tricycles on the cracked sidewalks—but as soon as I saw her, I remembered. It was too late to avoid meeting her. I was riding my bike, wearing shorts and tee shirt, the package containing my folded and starched shirts hooked to the carrier behind me, and she was walking toward me along the sidewalk, lugging two large bags of groceries. She saw me, and I stopped. We talked, and I offered to carry her groceries for her. I took the bags while she led the bike, handling it carefully, as if she were afraid she might break it.

At the stoop we came to a halt. The wooden steps were cluttered with half-opened garbage bags spilling egg shells, coffee grounds, and old food wrappers to the walkway. "I can't get the people downstairs to take care of their garbage," she explained. She leaned the bike against the bannister and reached for her groceries.

"I'll carry them up for you," I said. I directed her to loop the chain lock from the bike to the bannister rail and snap it shut and told her to bring my shirts up with her.

"Maybe you'd like a beer?" she said as she opened the door to the darkened hallway. Narrow stairs disappeared in front of me into heavy, damp darkness, and the air smelled like old newspapers.

"Sure," I said and followed her up.

"Sorry there's no light. I can't get them to fix it."

"No matter. I can see you and follow along," I said, and even in the dim light of the hall I could see the large, dark blue veins that cascaded thickly down the backs of her legs. She wore tight, white-duck bermuda shorts, rubber shower sandals, and a pink sleeveless sweater. I pictured her in the cashier's line at the supermarket. I would have been behind her, a stranger, and on seeing her, I would have turned away and studied the covers of the magazines, *TV Guide, People, The National Enquirer,* for there was nothing of interest in her appearance that in the hard light of day would not have slightly embarrassed me. Yet here I was inviting myself into her home, eagerly staring at the backs of her ravaged legs, her sad, tasteless clothing, her poverty. I was not detached, however, was not staring at her with scientific curiosity, and because of my passion, did not feel or believe that what I was doing was perverse. I felt warmed by her presence and was flirtatious and bold, a little pushy, even.

Picture this. The man, tanned, limber, wearing red jogging shorts, Italian leather sandals, a clinging net tee shirt of Scandinavian design and manufacture, enters the apartment behind the woman, whose dough colored skin, thick, short body, and homely, uncomfortable face all try, but fail, to hide themselves. She waves him toward the table in the kitchen, where he sets down the bags and looks good-naturedly around the room. "What about the beer you bribed me with?" he asks. The apartment is dark and cluttered with old, oversized furniture, yard sale and second-hand stuff bought originally for a large house in the country or a spacious apartment on a boulevard forty or fifty years ago, passed down from antique dealer to used furniture store to yard sale to thrift shop, where it finally gets purchased by Sarah Cole and gets lugged over to Perley Street and shoved up the narrow stairs, she and her children grunting and sweating in the darkness of the hallway—overstuffed armchairs and couch, huge, ungainly dressers, upholstered rocking chairs, and in the kitchen, an old maple desk for a table, a half dozen heavy oak diningroom chairs, a high, glass-fronted cabinet, all peeling, stained, chipped and squatting heavily on a dark green linoleum floor.

The place is neat and arranged in a more or less orderly way, however, and the man seems comfortable there. He strolls from the kitchen to the livingroom and peeks into the three small bedrooms that branch off a hallway behind the livingroom. "Nice place!" he calls to the woman. He is studying the framed pictures of her three children arranged like an altar atop the buffet. "Nice looking kids!" he calls out. They are. Blond, round-faced, clean, and utterly ordinary-looking, their pleasant faces glance, as instructed, slightly off camera and down to the right, as if they are trying to remember the name of the capital of Montana.

When he returns to the kitchen, the woman is putting away her groceries, her back to him. "Where's that beer you bribed me with?" he asks again. He takes a position against the doorframe, his weight on one hip, like a dancer resting. "You sure are quiet today, Sarah," he says in a low voice. "Everything okay?"

Silently, she turns away from the grocery bags, crosses the room to the man, reaches up to him, and holding him by the head, kisses his mouth, rolls her torso against his, drops her hands to his hips and yanks him tightly to her, and goes on kissing him, eyes closed, working her face furiously against his. The man places his hands on her shoulders and pulls away, and they face each other, wide-eyed, as if amazed and frightened. The man drops his hands, and the woman lets go of his hips. Then, after a few seconds, the man silently turns, goes to the door, and leaves. The last thing he sees as he closes the door behind him is the woman standing in the kitchen doorframe, her face looking down and slightly to one side, wearing the same pleasant expression on her face as her children in their photographs, trying to remember the capital of Montana.

5

Sarah appeared at my apartment door the following morning, a Sunday, cool and rainy. She had brought me the package of freshly laundered shirts I'd left in her kitchen, and when I opened the door to her, she simply held the package out to me as if it were a penitent's gift. She wore a yellow rain slicker and cap and looked more like a disconsolate schoolgirl facing an angry teacher than a grown woman dropping a package off at a friend's apartment. After all, she had nothing to be ashamed of.

I invited her inside, and she accepted my invitation. I had been reading the Sunday *New York Times* on the couch and drinking coffee, lounging through the gray morning in bathrobe and pajamas. I told her to take off her wet raincoat and hat and hang them in the closet by the door and started for the kitchen to get her a cup of coffee, when I stopped, turned, and looked at her. She closed the closet door on her yellow raincoat and hat, turned around, and faced me.

What else can I do? I must describe it. I remember that moment of ten years ago as if it occurred ten minutes ago, the package of shirts on the table behind her, the newspapers scattered over the couch and floor, the sound of windblown rain washing the sides of the building outside, and the silence of the room, as we stood across from one another and watched, while we each simultaneously removed our own clothing, my robe, her blouse and skirt, my pajama top, her slip and bra, my pajama bottom, her underpants, until we were both standing naked in the harsh, gray light, two naked members of the same species, a male and a female, the male somewhat younger and less scarred than the female, the female somewhat less delicately constructed than the male, both individuals pale-skinned with dark thatches of hair in the area of their genitals, both individuals standing slackly, as if a great, protracted tension between them had at last been released.

We made love that morning in my bed for long hours that drifted easily into afternoon. And we talked, as people usually do when they spend half a day or half a night in bed together. I told her of my past, named and described the people I had loved and had loved me, my ex-wife in New York, my brother in the Air Force, my father and mother in their condominium in Florida, and I told her of my ambitions and dreams and even confessed some of my fears. She listened patiently and intelligently throughout and talked much less than I. She had already told me many of these things about herself, and perhaps whatever she had to say to me now lay on the next inner circle of intimacy or else could not be spoken of at all.

During the next few weeks we met and made love often and

always at my apartment. On arriving home from work, I would phone her, or if not, she would phone me, and after a few feints and dodges, one would suggest to the other that we get together tonight, and a half hour later she'd be at my door. Our love-making was passionate, skillful, kindly, and deeply satisfying. We didn't often speak of it to one another or brag about it, the way some couples do when they are surprised by the ease with which they have become contented lovers. We did occasionally joke and tease each other, however, playfully acknowledging that the only thing we did together was make love but that we did it so frequently there was no time for anything else.

Then one hot night, a Saturday in August, we were lying in bed atop the tangled sheets, smoking cigarettes and chatting idly, and Sarah suggested that we go out for a drink.

"Now?"

"Sure. It's early. What time is it?"

I scanned the digital clock next to the bed. "Nine-forty-nine."

"There. See?"

"That's not so early. You usually go home by eleven, you know. It's almost ten."

"No, it's only a little after nine. Depends on how you look at things. Besides, Ron, it's Saturday night. Don't you want to go out and dance or something? Or is this the only thing you know how to do?" she teased and poked me in the ribs. "You know how to dance? You like to dance?"

"Yeah, sure . . . sure, but not tonight. It's too hot. And I'm tired."

But she persisted, happily pointing out that an air-conditioned bar would be cooler than my apartment, and we didn't have to go to a dance bar, we could go to Osgood's. "As a compromise," she said.

I suggested a place called the El Rancho, a restaurant with a large, dark cocktail lounge and dance bar located several miles from town on the old Portsmouth highway. Around nine the restaurant closed and the bar became something of a roadhouse, with a small country-western houseband and a clientel drawn from the four or five villages that adjoined Concord on the north and east. I had eaten at the restaurant once but had never gone to the bar, and I didn't know anyone who had.

Sarah was silent for a moment. Then she lit a cigarette and drew the sheet over her naked body. "You don't want anybody to know about us, do you? Do you?"

"That's not it . . . I just don't like gossip, and I work with a lot of people who show up sometimes at Osgood's. On a Saturday night especially."

"No," she said firmly. "You're ashamed of being seen with me. You'll sleep with me, but you won't go out in public with me."

"That's not true, Sarah."

She was silent again. Relieved, I reached across her to the bedtable and got my cigarettes and lighter.

"You owe me, Ron," she said suddenly, as I passed over her. "You owe me."

"What?" I lay back, lit a cigarette, and covered my body with the sheet.

"I said, 'You owe me.' "

"I don't know what you're talking about, Sarah. I just don't like a lot of gossip going around, that's all. I like keeping my private life private, that's all. I don't *owe* you anything."

"Friendship you owe me. And respect. Friendship and respect. A person can't do what you've done with me without owing them friendship and respect."

"Sarah, I really don't know what you're talking about," I said. "I am your friend, you know that. And I respect you. I really do."

"You really think so, don't you?"

"Yes."

She said nothing for several long moments. Then she sighed and in a low, almost inaudible voice said, "Then you'll have to go out in public with me. I don't care about Osgood's or the people you work with, we don't have to go there or see any of them," she said. "But you're gonna have to go to places like the El Rancho with me, and a few other places I know, too, where there's people *I* work with, people *I* know, and maybe we'll even go to a couple of parties, because *I* get invited to parties sometimes, you know. I have friends, and I have some family, too, and you're gonna have to meet my family. My kids think I'm just going around bar-hopping when I'm over here with you, and I don't like that, so you're gonna have to meet them so I can tell them where I am when I'm not at home nights. And sometimes you're gonna come over and spend the evening at my place!" Her voice had risen as she heard her

454

demands and felt their rightness until now she was almost shouting at me. "You *owe* that to me. Or else you're a bad man. It's that simple."

It was.

7

The handsome man is over-dressed. He is wearing a navy blue blazer, taupe shirt open at the throat, white slacks, white loafers. Everyone else, including the homely woman with the handsome man, is dressed appropriately, dressed, that is, like everyone else—jeans and cowboy boots, blouses or cowboy shirts or tee shirts with catchy sayings printed across the front, and many of the women are wearing cowboy hats pushed back and tied under their chins. The man doesn't know anyone at the bar or, if they're at a party, in the room, but the woman knows most of the people there, and she gladly introduces him. The men grin and shake his hand, slap him on his jacketed shoulder, ask him where he works, what's his line, after which they lapse into silence. The women flirt briefly with their faces, but they lapse into silence even before the men do. The woman with the man in the blazer does most of the talking for everyone. She talks for the man in the blazer, for the men standing around the refrigerator, or if they're at a bar, for the other men at the table, and for the other women, too. She chats and rambles aimlessly through loud monologues, laughs uproariously at trivial jokes, and drinks too much, until soon she is drunk, thick-tongued, clumsy, and the man has to say her goodbyes and ease her out the door to his car and drive her home to her apartment on Perley Street.

This happens twice in one week, and then three times the next—at the El Rancho, at the Ox Bow in Northwood, at Rita's and Jimmy's apartment on Thorndike Street, out in Warner at Betsy Beeler's new house, and, the last time, at a cottage on Lake Sunapee rented by some kids in shipping at Rumford Press. Ron no longer calls Sarah when he gets home from work; he waits for her call, and sometimes, when he knows it's she, he doesn't answer the phone. Usually, he lets it ring five or six times, and then he reaches down and picks up the receiver. He has taken his jacket and vest off and loosened his tie and is about to put supper, frozen manicotti, into the radar range.

"Hello?"

"*Hi.*"

"How're you doing?"

"*Okay, I guess. A little tired.*"

"Still hung-over?"

"*No. Not really. Just tired. I hate Mondays.*"

"You have fun last night?"

"*Well, yeah, sorta. It's nice out there, at the lake. Listen,*" she says, brightening. "*Whyn't you come over here tonight? The kids're all going out later, but if you come over before eight, you can meet them. They really want to meet you.*"

"You told them about me?"

"*Sure. Long time ago. I'm not supposed to tell my own kids?*"

Ron is silent.

"*You don't want to come over here tonight. You don't want to meet my kids. No, you don't want my kids to meet you, that's it.*"

"No, no, it's just . . . I've got a lot of work to do . . ."

"*We should talk,*" she announces in a flat voice.

"Yes," he says, "we should talk."

They agree that she will meet him at his apartment, and they'll talk, and they say goodbye and hang up.

While Ron is heating his supper and then eating alone at his kitchen table and Sarah is feeding her children, perhaps I should admit, since we are nearing the end of my story, that I don't actually know that Sarah Cole is dead. A few years ago I happened to run into one of her friends from the press, a blond woman with an underslung jaw. Her name, she reminded me, was Glenda, she had seen me at Osgood's a couple of times and we had met at the El Rancho once when I had gone there with Sarah. I was amazed that she could remember me and a little embarrassed that I did not recognize her at all, and she laughed at that and said, "You haven't changed much, mister!" I pretended to recognize her, but I think she knew she was a stranger to me. We were standing outside the Sears store on South Main Street, where I had gone to buy paint. I had recently remarried, and my wife and I were redecorating my apartment.

"Whatever happened to Sarah?" I asked Glenda. "Is she still down at the press?"

"Jeez, no! She left a long time ago. Way back. I heard she went back with her ex-husband. I can't remember his name. Something Cole."

I asked her if she was sure of that, and she said no, she had only heard it around the bars and down at the press, but she had assumed it was true. People said Sarah had moved back with her ex-husband and was living in a trailer in a park near Hooksett, and the whole family had moved down to Florida that winter because he was out of work. He was a carpenter, she said.

"I thought he was mean to her. I thought he beat her up and everything. I thought she hated him," I said.

"Oh, well, yeah, he was a bastard, all right. I met him a couple of times, and I didn't like him. Short, ugly, and mean when he got drunk. But you know what they say."

"What do they say?"

"Oh, you know, about water seeking its own level."

"Sarah wasn't mean when she was drunk."

The woman laughed. "Naw, but she sure was short and ugly!"

I said nothing.

"Hey, don't get me wrong, I liked Sarah. But you and her . . . well, you sure made a funny-looking couple. She probably didn't feel so self-conscious and all with her husband," the woman said seriously. "I mean, with you . . . all tall and blond, and poor old Sarah . . . I mean, the way them kids in the press room used to kid her about her looks, it was embarrassing just to hear it."

"Well . . . I loved her," I said.

The woman raised her plucked eyebrows in disbelief. She smiled. "Sure, you did, honey," she said, and she patted me on the arm. "Sure, you did." Then she let the smile drift off her face, turned and walked away.

When someone you have loved dies, you accept the fact of his or her death, but then the person goes on living in your memory, dreams and reveries. You have imaginary conversations with him or her, you see something striking and remind yourself to tell your loved one about it and then get brought up short by the knowledge of the fact of his or her death, and at night, in your sleep, the dead person visits you. With Sarah, none of that happened. When she was gone from my life, she was gone absolutely, as if she had never existed in the first place. It was only later, when I could think of her as dead and could come out and say it, my friend Sarah Cole is dead, that I was able to tell this story, for that is when she began to enter my memories, my dreams, and my reveries. In that way I learned that I truly did love her, and now I have begun to grieve over her death, to wish her alive again, so that I can say to her the things I could not know or say when she was alive, when I did not know that I loved her.

8

The woman arrives at Ron's apartment around eight. He hears her car, because of the broken muffler, blat and rumble into the parking lot below, and he crosses quickly from the kitchen and peers out the livingroom window and, as if through a telescope, watches her shove herself across the seat to the passenger's side to get out of the car, then walk slowly in the dusky light toward the apartment building. It's a warm evening, and she's wearing her white bermuda shorts, pink sleeveless sweater, and shower sandals. Ron hates those clothes. He hates the way the shorts cut into her flesh at the crotch and thigh, hates the large, dark caves below her arms that get exposed by the sweater, hates the flapping noise made by the sandals.

Shortly, there is a soft knock at his door. He opens it, turns away and crosses to the kitchen, where he turns back, lights a cigarette, and watches her. She closes the door. He offers her a drink, which she declines, and somewhat formally, he invites her to sit down. She sits carefully on the sofa, in the middle, with her feet close together on the floor, as if she were being interviewed for a job. Then he comes around and sits in the easy chair, relaxed, one leg slung over the other at the knee, as if he were interviewing her for the job.

"Well," he says, "you wanted to talk."

"Yes. But now you're mad at me. I can see that. I didn't do anything, Ron."

"I'm not mad at you."

They are silent for a moment. Ron goes on smoking his cigarette.

Finally, she sighs and says, "You don't want to see me anymore, do you?"

He waits a few seconds and answers, "Yes. That's right." Getting up from the chair, he walks to the silver-gray bicycle and stands before it, running a fingertip along the slender cross-bar from the saddle to the chrome plated handlebars.

"You're a son of a bitch," she says in a low voice. "You're worse than my ex-husband." Then she smiles meanly, almost sneers, and soon he realizes that she is telling him that she won't leave. He's stuck with her, she informs him with cold precision. "You think I'm just so much meat, and all you got to do is call up the butcher shop and cancel your order. Well, now you're going to find out different. You *can't* cancel your order. I'm not meat, I'm not one of your pretty little girlfriends who come running when you want them and go away when you get tired of them. I'm *different*. I got nothing to lose, Ron. Nothing. You're stuck with me, Ron."

He continues stroking his bicycle. "No, I'm not."

She sits back in the couch and crosses her legs at the ankles. "I think I *will* have that drink you offered."

"Look, Sarah, it would be better if you go now."

"No," she says flatly. "You offered me a drink when I came in. Nothing's changed since I've been here. Not for me, and not for you. I'd like that drink you offered," she says haughtily.

Ron turns away from the bicycle and takes a step toward her. His face has stiffened into a mask. "Enough is enough," he says through clenched teeth. "I've given you enough."

"Fix me a drink, will you, honey?" she says with a phony smile.

Ron orders her to leave.

She refuses.

He grabs her by the arm and yanks her to her feet.

She starts crying lightly. She stands there and looks up into his face and weeps, but she does not move toward the door, so he pushes her. She regains her balance and goes on weeping.

He stands back and places his fists on his hips and looks at her. "Go on and leave, you ugly bitch," he says to her, and as he says the words, as one by one they leave his mouth, she's transformed into the most beautiful woman he has ever seen. He says the words again, almost tenderly. "Leave, you ugly bitch." Her hair is golden, her brown eyes deep and sad, her mouth full and affectionate, her tears the tears of love and loss, and her pleading, outstretched arms, her entire body, the arms and body of a devoted woman's cruelly rejected love. A third time he says the words. "Leave me, you disgusting, ugly bitch." She is wrapped in an envelope of golden light, a warm, dense haze that she seems to have stepped into, as into a carriage. And then she is gone, and he is alone again.

He looks around the room, as if searching for her. Sitting down in the easy chair, he places his face in his hands. It's not as if she has died; it's as if he has killed her.